JAMES ROY DALEY'S
TERROR TOWN

BOOKS of the DEAD

TERROR TOWN

Copyright 2010 by James Roy Daley

Cover Art by Steven Gilberts
Book Design by James Roy Daley
Cover Design by Cynthia Gould

FIRST EDITION

10 9 8 7 6 5 4 3 2 1

For more information subscribe to: booksofthedead.blogspot.com

For direct sales and inquiries contact:
besthorror@gmail.com

BOOKS of the DEAD

More great titles from
<u>BOOKS OF THE DEAD</u>

BEST NEW ZOMBIE TALES (Vol. 1)
BEST NEW ZOMBIE TALES (Vol. 2)
BEST NEW ZOMBIE TALES (Vol. 3)
JAMES ROY DALEY'S - INTO HELL
JAMES ROY DALEY'S - 13 DROPS OF BLOOD
MATT HULTS - ANYTHING CAN BE DANGEROUS
BEST NEW VAMPIRE TALES (Vol. 1)
MATT HULTS - HUSK
CLASSIC VAMPIRE TALES

From ghosties and ghoulies,
Long leggitie beasties,
And all things that go bump in the night,
Good Lord, deliver us!

~16th Century Prayer

TERROR
TOWN

PROLOGUE:
CLOVEN ROCK

The people that lived in Cloven Rock considered the town's final Monday a beautiful one, like most of the days in the recent weeks. The sun was shining; the air was clean and warm. Flowers bloomed and birds sat among the branches singing songs only birds could understand. Dogs chased master's Frisbees and people said hello to strangers, not to suggest that thousands of tourists roamed the beachfront or the area that passed as the downtown core. That wasn't the case; there were only a few. If you asked one of the locals why things were this way, the answer would be simple: Cloven Rock was an inclusive town, an uncomplicated town, a town that didn't encourage a vacationer crowd even though sightseers would have flocked to it religiously. Many residents thought the town was special and they were right. It *was* special. It wasn't a small place trying to be a big place. It was a town without civic uncertainty.

The Yacht Club Swimming Pool, a Cloven Rock favorite, had a full house the day before the town was lost. They also had an open door policy; if you were respectful, courteous, and didn't pee in the pool, you were welcome anytime. Also on that day, friends sailed the calm waters of Cloven Lake and children built sandcastles on Holbrook Beach. Kids played in Easton Park while the people on the large wooden deck at the Waterfront Café enjoyed the spectacular view. The post office closed early. An ice cream store called Tabby's Goodies was doing good business and a mile and a half up the road the men and woman working at the Cloven Rock Docks fought for, and won, a fifty-cent raise. Spirits were high at the Docks, and the personnel were getting along just fine. It wasn't surprising. Nearly half the workforce was related and the other half was considered family.

The Cloven Rock Police Department was not at full strength

when things turned ugly. One officer was on vacation, one had gone home due to an illness in the family, and two had the day off. Of the nine remaining officials, only Tony Costantino, Joel Kirkwood, and Mary O'Neill, were on duty when the reports came in. The other four were either at home or on call. Normally this wouldn't be deemed a problem. Most locals figured a thirteen-person police force was nothing short of overkill anyhow. The Rock hadn't had a stitch of recorded violence in six years.

The community as a whole didn't know horror, as most tight-knit communities can understand. It knew long days, family activities, and simple living. It knew Thanksgiving, Christmas, and Easter. It knew family.

But sadly, like all communities, Cloven Rock had its share of tragedy.

2007 was a bad year.

It was the year a local artist named George Gramme had his hands caught in his motorcycle chain while he was working on it. He suffered two broken wrists and lost four of his fingers. He also lost his artistic spirit and the means to keep that spirit alive. In the weeks following he put his motorcycle up for sale and fell into a state of depression that changed him into a different man.

Two weeks later the town's senior librarian, Angela Lore, died from cancer on the same day that 'odd-job' Martin West fell off a ladder and broke both of his legs while shingling his neighbor's roof.

2007 was also the year a car accident claimed the lives of three teenagers.

As the story goes, a half dozen youngsters were drinking on the unnamed road surrounding Holbrook's pond. After several hours of alcohol consumption, the six youths plunked their butts inside two vehicles. In one car, Andrew Cowles and Dean Lee, a pair of borderline delinquents, drove home without incident and arrived safely. The second car, loaded with four of the sweetest kids you'd ever meet, weren't so lucky. Two brothers, Guy and Henri Lemont, along with May Lewis and Lizzy Backstrom, the youngest of the crew, decided it would be a good idea to take a quick jaunt to Hoppers Gas on the 9th line. But on the way to Hoppers *something* stepped onto the road causing Guy to swerve left and lose control of the vehicle.

As luck would have it, Stanley Rosenstein, a foreman at the

Docks and an all-around good guy, pulled his truck from his driveway the same moment Guy changed lanes.

Guy didn't see the truck in time. The car clipped Stanley's front bumper, veered off the road, rolled three times, and slammed into a large maple tree, roof first. The two brothers, Guy and Henri, were killed instantly. May Lewis spent nine days in critical condition before she passed away while her parents and grandparents watched. Lizzy Backstrom escaped with a broken back, three broken ribs, a punctured lung, two broken legs, and wide assortment of cuts, scrapes and bruises. Most figured she was lucky to be alive. A few figured she was *unlucky* to be alive. Once she was able to speak she said a bear stepped in front of the car and Guy swerved to miss it. There weren't many bears in Cloven Rock so the statement generated a cluster of questions she wasn't prepared to answer. She pushed the inquisition aside, saying, "It might not have been a bear but wasn't a deer either. I don't know what it was."

Two months later, Lizzy broke down in tears, telling her friend Julie Stapleton that a monster *the size of a tank* stepped in front of Guy's car and she got a real good look at it. She said the beast seemed like something from another planet and if Guy were alive he'd be the first to confirm.

Julie, sworn to secrecy, became worried about Lizzy's mental wellbeing. She thought her friend had brain damage. Of course, Julie's knowledge on matters concerning the brain could have been written on the on tip of her thumb, but that hardly mattered. She also didn't know that Stanley Rosenstein—the man driving the pickup that fateful night—had a similar story. If she had known this little noodle of information she may have kept her big mouth shut. Or talked to Lizzy. Either way, that's not what happened. Instead, Julie betrayed her oath, feeling it was necessary to tell Lizzy's parents what their daughter was thinking. This forced a confrontation between Mr. and Mrs. Backstrom and Lizzy, who denied everything and never spoke to Julie again. Not ever. And a year later Stanley Rosenstein found himself separated from his wife, in rehab, and in need of psychiatric evaluation.

He thought there were monsters in Cloven Rock.

∞∞∞Θ∞∞∞

There were other tragedies.

Four summers before the heartbreaking car accident Simon Wakefield, the town's only dentist, drowned in his backyard swimming pool while his wife Leanne talked to her sister not forty feet away. The year before that, faulty wiring caused a fire that burned Stephen Pebbles' house to the ground. To make matters worse, his insurance expired the week before. Ironically, two weeks later the town was hit with a rainstorm that caused over two million dollars in damages. Stephen was quoted as saying that the rain should have come two weeks sooner; it would have saved his life's investments.

The tales go on: tales of love gone astray, broken homes, poor health, and financial ruin. But these stories shouldn't be focused on, even if they're commonly considered the most interesting. Tales of sorrow don't express the true face of Cloven Rock's two hundred and nine years of existence. They pepper it in a negative light that was seldom felt or witnessed.

Cloven Rock was a peaceful community, a pleasant community. It was a place where folks could retire from work and enjoy a simple life. The town was good to grow up in, good to live life in, and good to grow old in. The problems were minimal and living was easy. People were friendly and the air tasted sweet with the spice of nature.

On the eve of its extinction, nobody knew what was coming. The locals never expected terror to reveal its vile and horrid face. Not in Cloven Rock. Not in a town of 1,690. The concept seemed out of the question.

But they didn't know the heart of Nicolas Nehalem.

And only Stanley Rosenstein and Lizzy Backstrom had seen the monsters that dwelled in the dark shadows beneath the streets.

Something from another planet, Lizzy had said. *If Guy were alive he'd be the first to confirm.*

Stanley Rosenstein would have agreed.

It was the first Monday of June when Cloven Rock began showing the world a different face. And for many of the people that lived in the undersized and joyful town, it would be the last Monday they would ever know.

This is what happened:

CHAPTER ONE:
NICOLAS NEHALEM

1

Nicolas Nehalem woke up from a happy dream and shifted his near-dead weight into a new position. His eyes opened and closed, opened and closed. He licked the dryness from his lips and ran his tongue across his teeth while forcing himself awake. The dream faded; he was some form of insect, if he remembered correctly, and upon awaking he noticed that his left hand felt funny. He could feel pins and needles pricking his fingers and a lack of sensation in his thumb and wrist. He must have been sleeping wrong, cutting off the circulation.

No biggie; it would pass.

The room was dark. A cool breeze blew through the open window, causing the thin off-white drapes to flutter. The clock on the nightstand said it was 4:08 am and while Nicolas was looking at it time moved ahead by one minute.

The babies were crying again. And they were crying *loudly*.

It was the crying that woke him. The babies seemed to cry more and more these days. He wondered if the girls missed their mothers. It was only logical if they did.

Nicolas sat up. He clicked on a lamp, grabbed his librarian-issue spectacles from the nightstand, and slid them on his face. He put his feet on the cold hardwood floor one after another. CLUMP. CLUMP. For no real reason he looked over his shoulder, lifted his feet, and dropped them down again. CLUMP. CLUMP.

The other side of the bed was empty. It was always empty.

He put a hand into the vacant space and squeezed the sheets with his fingers.

Taking care of the girls would be easier if he wasn't alone with the job. Being a father was hard, and being an only parent was harder still. Some days he wasn't sure if he could take the pressure of fatherhood. It was tougher than it seemed.

He pulled his hand away from the sheets and stumbled across the room. He entered the bathroom, washed his hands very thoroughly and poured himself a cup of water. The cup had a picture of a clown on it. The clown had a big red nose and was holding a balloon. The water inside the mug was warm but he didn't mind. His throat felt parched and the liquid quenched his thirst nicely. He poured himself a second helping, re-entered the bedroom, and sat the cup on the nightstand, next to the clock and the lamp.

A brown-checkered housecoat hung from a shiny brass hook on the bedroom door. A pair of furry blue slippers sat near the dresser. He put the housecoat on and tied the cotton belt in a cute little bow. He slid his feet into the slippers and stumbled down the hall, rubbing the sleep-cooties from his eyes.

With a yawn and a burp he glanced into a spare bedroom.

The room was loaded with boxes. Not empty boxes. Full boxes. Boxes filled with goodies that go BANG.

Beside this room was a second spare bedroom. He stopped at the door and looked inside. There was no bed in the room. No dressers either. Nicolas had converted the room into his own private laboratory.

He was making stuff, just in case.

He had boxes of diatomaceous earth, sodium carbonate, ballistite, ethanol, ether, guncotton, sulfuric acid, oleum, azeotropic, nitric acid, and about ten other things that were hard to find at the local convenience store. He also had a large maple desk that housed a laboratory distillation setup. This setup included a heating tray, a still pot, a boiling thermometer, condenser, distillate/receiving flask, a vacuum/gas inlet, a still receiver, a heating bath, and a cooling bath.

Looking at his toys, Nicolas nodded and smiled.

They were fine; he was just making sure.

He entered the kitchen, flicked on the overhead light and opened the refrigerator door. The inside of the fridge needed to be cleaned; it had adopted a funny smell. There were a few items that had really gone bad, including an old turkey sandwich that was sitting behind an empty carton of orange juice on the bottom shelf. The sandwich was nearly four weeks old and had turned green and black with mold. The spores inside the sandwich bag looked like moon craters.

Nicolas didn't notice. Or maybe he didn't care.

A bottle of baby formula sat on the top shelf, ready to go. In Nicolas' current state of semi-awareness his fatherly duties just became ten times easier. It was a small victory but a good one.

The babies kept crying. Or was it just one?

Yes—one voice, not two. He wondered whose throat the wailing had spawned from.

Someone was being bad. Someone was being good.

He warmed the bottle in the microwave for two minutes and forty-five seconds while looking at his warped reflection in the kitchen window. His light brown hair was sticking straight up on one side, his eyes were puffy and his five o'clock shadow had become a three-day-old beard. He wasn't extremely overweight, but the way his fat bunched around his waistline was far from attractive. He was thirty-eight years old but looked fifty or more.

Probably not getting enough sleep, he assumed.

A bell rang. He opened the microwave door and retrieved the formula. The bottle was too hot, way too hot. Crazy hot. He tested it on his arm and felt the milky fluid burn like liquid fire.

Good enough.

He opened the door to the basement, walked down a rickety staircase, and clicked on a florescent light, spooking a cockroach from its resting place. The roach scurried across the wall in an arched line and Nicolas tried to catch it between his finger and his thumb. He missed. The cockroach fell to the floor. Its tiny legs hustled towards a crack in the wall and in it went. The bug was gone.

Oh well, he thought. *Better luck next time.*

The basement smelled bad, much worse than the inside of the fridge. It smelled like piss, shit, sweat, blood, and rot.

The crying was louder now, much louder. If he had neighbors they'd complain for sure. This was a nugget of information that didn't sit well with Nicolas, not in the slightest. Neighbors shouldn't have to put up with such nonsense. *It just wasn't right.* If *he* lived next to a noisy house he'd be seething in anger and out of his mind with rage.

Nicolas walked through a room that housed hundreds of shoes, countless jeans, shirts, socks, underwear, hats, wallets, belts, watches, and coats. He opened a cellar door and turned on another light.

The crying stopped immediately.

He walked down a second staircase. It only had nine stairs and none of them were very big. The unfinished room at the base of the staircase had a very low ceiling. Walking inside the room meant that you had to crouch down and tuck your head into your shoulders like a turtle. The room was cold; it was always cold. In the wintertime it was freezing. The walls were made of rock and seemed permanently moist.

The smell of shit and piss was strong now, strong enough to make a healthy man sick and a sick man pass out.

And there she was: Cathy Eldritch.

Cathy was thirty-one years old; her birthday fell on New Years Eve. She was right where Nicolas had left her, fourteen years ago—

Inside a cage.

2

Cathy Eldritch was naked and covered in scars. Her ribcage stuck out from her skin and her muscles had wilted to noodles. Her large and unsightly nipples were dry and cracked, centering breasts that were non-existent. Her arms and legs were nothing more then sticks, elbows, and knees. Her few remaining teeth were black and rotting; her hair was long and crawling with bugs. Below the pits that housed her bright and sunken eyes—eyes that seemed far too alive and knowing, like Sun Gods buried in an apocalyptic badland—her nose had become as thin as a wafer and crusted with dehydrated wounds. Lips that were so tragically withered and cracked made her look like a mummy, or a living corpse, or like a horror-story monster that needed to be buried in the earth and forgotten, a ghoul that lurked in the darkest corners of the most twisted and perverted minds. All of her toes and three of her fingers had been amputated, proof she had been a *bad girl* thirteen times.

Nicolas named Cathy Eldritch: Kathy the Kitten.

She was a trooper and he knew it; nobody lasted fourteen years. It seemed damn near impossible.

Nicolas Nehalem approached the wire cage, which was nothing more than a modified, three-foot by three-foot square. He smiled a strange and outlandish smile, laced in twisted logic and perverted reason.

After opening a small door on the right side of the pen, he dropped the bottle of formula inside. The bottle rolled between two walls of wire and landed on the caged floor.

Cathy couldn't reach the bottle. Not yet. Not until Nicolas released a lever that would unlock a small door inside the coop.

"What do you say, Kathy?" He adjusted his glasses and slid a hand beneath his housecoat. He began stroking himself calmly.

Cathy's eyes were filled with starvation and madness.

At one time she wanted to kill this man, make him pay, make him bleed. She had despised him more than anything else in the world. Now she only wanted her nightmare to be over. She wanted to die. Not in theory, and not in some exaggerated way that people say it but don't really mean it. She wanted to die for real. She wanted this life to end and whatever was waiting for her on the other side to begin. And she was close, *so* close. She had been clinging to death's front door for as long as she could remember. All she had to do was stop drinking the formula and she would cross over. All she had to do was die. But she couldn't. She just couldn't. She was famished—and her hunger wouldn't allow her mind to say no to the bottle. She needed the bottle, the formula. And for this reason she didn't hate Nicolas. Not now. She hated herself for needing him.

She said, "Thank you daddy. I love you."

"Very well done," Nicolas replied, knowing she hated expressing her love. His voice sounded calm, yet agitated; it always sounded agitated. "You're a good baby today, yes you are; yes you are."

Nicolas wrinkled his nose playfully, raised his shoulders and opened his housecoat so Cathy could see his semi-erect penis. He released the lever on the top of the cage.

The bottle rolled another two inches.

Cathy rammed a hand through the small cage door and grabbed the formula; flies buzzed around her. She put the bottle to her mouth and drank greedily, burning her mouth and tongue. She hardly even noticed.

On the other side of the room were two more cages. One was empty. It had been empty for three weeks. The other cage had a young girl in it. The girl's name was Olive Thrift. She was fourteen years old, might have been Asian. At this stage, it was hard to tell.

Nicolas named her Pumpkin.

Olive said, "Daddy, may I have a bottle too? I've been very good lately. I didn't cry tonight or anything. Honest I didn't."

"I'm sorry dear," Nicolas said, stepping away from Kathy the Kitten. "I only brought one bottle with me. I guess I wasn't thinking."

"Oh." Olive's eyes slipped down to the stumps on her hands. She only had three fingers left; she didn't want to lose them. A multi-legged insect walked across her face and she swatted it away thoughtlessly. "Okay daddy. I understand. I love you."

"I love you too, Pumpkin. Have a nice night. I'll see you tomorrow, or maybe the next day."

"Daddy?"

"Yes dear?"

"Can I please have some water? Both of my containers are empty."

"Mine are too," Cathy quickly announced. "Can you fill mine too?"

Nicolas approached Olive's cage with his housecoat wide open and his genitals exposed. He put his knuckles to the wire.

Olive suspected that he would. He had been doing that a lot lately. She figured it made him feel like royalty.

She crawled toward Nicolas on her mangled digits and knobby knees, closed her dark and cheerless eyes and put her lips to the wire. Flies flew in circles around her. She kissed his hand as gently as she could manage.

"You're a good little Pumpkin," Nicolas said. "Yes you are. And if you keep being a good little girl I'll never have to smash your face in with a sledgehammer. Or set your cage on fire. Because you don't want that, do you? No. Of course not."

Nicolas walked across the room, smiling insanely. He lifted a hose from a hook on the wall, turned a faucet, and approached Olive spewing hose-water where it fell. As he stood over Olive's cage, she held out two water jugs and he filled them. He made his way to Cathy's cage and poured water inside her coop for a little more than twenty seconds. She was able to fill one container and wet her hair before he dropped the hose and turned the faucet off, deciding enough was enough.

At the top of the stairs he clicked the light switch on and off, several times. He was tired. He hadn't been sleeping well plus he had to get up early. He had things to do, although he couldn't quite remember what those things were.

"Oh yeah," he whispered. A grin that could have given a slaughterhouse butcher nightmares crept across his face like a spider on a corpse. "Now I remember."

Closing the cellar door, he thought he heard a whimper.

Sounded like Pumpkin.

Pumpkin was a good girl; she was trying. And that's what counted most in his books: trying. He hadn't been forced to punish her lately, which was a nice change. Not since the incident with Pauline Stupid-Head had he been forced to perform one of his little operations. Not since he emptied the third cage.

Thinking about Pauline's empty cage made him sad and lonely.

Empty cages need to be filled. Sure they did. An empty cage was wrong; everybody with a lick of sense knows *that*. But Nicolas was a busy man, he had things on his mind and his work was never done. The cage would have to wait.

Nicolas crawled into bed wearing his housecoat. He lifted his cup from the nightstand, smiled at the clown holding the balloon, and slowly emptied the cup's contents on the floor. Water splashed, creating a miniature lake where no lake had once been. He named this lake, Lake Empty Cage. He wondered how long the lake would last, and when he would be forced to make a new one.

The clock beside him read 4:19 am.

It was late, too late for feeding babies and making lakes. Maybe tomorrow he would punish Kathy the Kitten for waking him—maybe, but maybe not. He wasn't sure yet. He would see how he felt in the morning.

∞∞∞⊖∞∞∞

Nicolas woke up early, went to the kitchen and mixed another bottle of formula. He warmed it perfectly, added a little chocolate and brought it to Olive; he apologized for not giving her a bottle the night before. Afterwards, he cleaned the basement and found each of his babies something to read. He gave them fresh blankets, a rice-crispy square, and a nice cup of coffee. Shortly after, he stepped inside a closet, stripped naked, and screamed for twenty minutes while pushing his fingers into his eyes.

CHAPTER TWO:
JUNE 1ST, MONDAY AFTERNOON

1

His hands were bleeding. Not much, but some—right around his knuckles and the tips of his fingers. The wounds were starting to feel bad, and as the day wore on he figured the irritation would grow increasingly worse. He had a scrape on his knee that hurt when he touched it and a bruise on his shin that ached constantly. His hair had become wild, soiled with dirt, dust and sweat. He was shirtless; his shoulders and chest glistened. His slim waistline and impressive abdominal muscles were swollen from his efforts. The blue jeans that clung to his body were beyond dirty, and even when the pants were 'fresh from the drawer' clean they *looked* dirty. They *always* looked dirty. The jeans were a special pair that were set aside for times like this: grubby times, labor times, times when getting filth up to your eyeballs and annoying cuts in your hands were an expected part of the program.

Dan McGee was his name.

Daniel; named after a wise and honorable prophet whose faith in God had protected him in the Lion's Den. This fact was not kept in the forefront of Dan's thinking, but it was ironic. At least now it was, now that he was standing at the mouth of precarious exploration.

He was at the cottage.

Cottage.

Truth be told, the place looked more like a house built next to a lake. It was a summer home really, but Dan considered it a cottage.

He wasn't sure why. The building, located just outside Cloven Rock, had two floors, not including the basement. It had a full kitchen, two bathrooms, four bedrooms, a laundry room, and a deck that was large enough to accommodate seventy-five people or more. It also had a garage and an attic. The building was secluded, but not completely secluded. It was one of three cottages built together on a small, fat peninsula. There were no others for a quarter-mile in either direction. And now, as Daniel McGee discovered, his summer home had something else. Something he never knew about until just this minute, something interesting and almost certainly hazardous.

Dan cleared his throat and walked across the dusty room.

The floor was littered with tools: hammers and saws, drills and screwdrivers, crowbars and wrenches and everything else he needed. Some of it was piled around an open toolbox; some was scattered about.

He stepped past three rolls of thirty-year-old carpet and lifted a bottle of water from where he left it, next to the rotting pickets on the warped and rickety staircase. He drank two swallows quickly, poured water into his free hand, and slapped it onto his face, cleaning himself slightly. Still feeling dirty, he poured a splash of water over his head. The water wasn't cold but it *was* refreshing, which was exactly what he wanted. After returning the bottle to its home on the stairs he ran his fingers through his sopping hair and took a deep breath.

He was excited. That was the truth of it.

He felt energized.

Six hours earlier the basement was loaded with junk: Boxes of clothing from years gone by, old furniture, unloved artwork, boring books, unwanted appliances, out of date electronics, rusted tools, VHS tapes, pointless sporting equipment, photographs that meant nothing, corroded machinery, unfashionable clothing; the list went on and on.

He cleared it all out.

The photographs and tools were put away. The rest of the stuff went into garbage bags and charity bins. The bags were thrown next to the garage. The bins were placed in the hallway, close to the exit. Once the basement had been cleared, he unhinged a door, knocked down a pair of walls, removed some baseboards, and pulled out the carpet. The sub-floor beneath the carpet was moldy and rotten. He lifted half of it, exposing the concrete floor beneath.

That's when he made his discovery.

Dan licked his lips.

He was alone, and had gotten a fair amount finished so far. If his wife had been with him his accomplishments would have been cut in half. He would have been subjected to a twenty-minute debate regarding every worn-out pair of shoes. Dan hated that. Working was hard enough without dealing with a committee, and that's what Sandra seemed to be at times like this. A committee. She was a good woman, no question. The girl was an intelligent sweetheart. She had the face of a model and a body that could make a Playboy photographer hot under the collar and hard under the zipper. But at times like this, *look out*. Everything was a discussion. Everything was questioned. That's why Dan took the week off work; he wanted to get to the cottage a few days sooner than Sandra and get things done.

If he had known that he would never see her again—never even *talk* to her again—he would have done things differently. But he didn't know. He figured he'd enjoy a few days on his own and life would continue on, just like before.

He was wrong.

Dan approached this *thing* he had uncovered beneath the carpet, still rubbing his chin.

It was a door, a trapdoor in the floor.

Its size: two and a half feet by two and a half feet, give or take a few inches. Looked like that famous cellar door in the Evil Dead movies, without the medieval chains strapping it down. It had a small hole you could slide fingers into, which seemed to be the handle. The hinges were rusted brown and the unstained wood was faded, knotted, and looked almost grey in color.

Dan put his fingers into the slot and pulled.

The door was heavier than it looked so Dan repositioned himself into a sturdier pose and tried his luck again, putting more muscle into it this time. The door unlatched. He opened it slowly. Hinges screeched and squeaked. A dull metal casing was exposed and a nasty, stale odor crept into the room. Once the door was at a ninety-degree angle, a dark hole in the floor came into Dan's line of vision; it looked like an open throat in the earth.

Muscles straining, Dan grunted, but the hard part was over. He let go of the handle and stepped back. Gravity pulled the door the other way and the trapdoor stopped in the air with a *CLINK*.

He wondered why.

Walking around the opening he found his answer: there *was* a chain. It connected the door to the floor. The chain was old, rusted and thick—not quite medieval, but still fifty years past its prime. It had big one-inch loops and seemed perfectly suited to chain Cujo to his doghouse.

Daniel looked down the dark hole, somewhat amazed. There was a ladder attached to one of the four walls. A dusty light switch sat next to it.

Pit, he thought. *Is that what this is? A pit? Why is there a pit in my basement? And what's down there? Anything good? Anything valuable?*

Dan smiled.

Valuable. He liked the sound of that.

Crouching down, he flicked the light switch on.

Nothing happened.

He tried again.

Still, nothing happened.

After walking around the opening several times, Dan thought about the cottage. He figured it to be a hundred and some odd years old. What if the previous owners were hiding treasures? Or what if the previous owners didn't even know the pit was there, and the items in the cellar (assuming there *were* items in the cellar) were not worth a few hundred bucks, or few thousand, but a few million? Was it possible? Could he be standing at the brink of incredible fortune?

Dan's eyes narrowed.

Sure it was possible. *Anything* was possible. Building a dream house with Popsicle sticks was possible, but was it likely? Was the cellar loaded with gold and silver artifacts from Kings and Queens a hundred years dead? No, of course not. Not here. Not in Cloven Rock. The basement was probably filled with rats, dirt, spiders, and dust… and a large bucket filled to the brim with sweet fuck all.

Still, the pit was an interesting find.

An interesting find indeed.

2

Dan headed upstairs with his mind racing. He entered the kitchen and snagged a beer from the fridge. The ice-cold Corona was delicious, even without the taste of lime. He drank half the bottle and washed his hands and face in the kitchen sink. Being so dirty, he needed to do more. He needed a long shower and a wardrobe change but technically he wasn't finished working. The sub-floor was only half pulled up, rolls of carpet were leaning in the corner near the staircase, and he hadn't even begun yanking the ceiling down. All said, he was only half finished today's job. Still, the work portion of the day seemed to have ended, or if nothing else, put on hold.

He kept thinking about the pit.

What was down there?

Dan threw on an old and faded t-shirt, one of his favorites. He thought it was cool looking and it fit like a glove. The shirt had a drawing of a demon with its wings spread wide and it said BLACK SABBATH in long gothic letters. In a smaller font near the bottom of the shirt, below the demon's evil grin, it said 666 - HEAVEN & HELL. It was a throwback item, a reminder of a time in his life when he didn't care about insurance policies, the stock exchange, real estate, investment funds, and all the other things that helped him turn his quarters into dollars, his assets into prosperity, and his wealth into his own personally restricted freedom.

He stepped outside with his Corona in hand, gazing into the sky. The heat from the sun was beginning to ease and the wind was blowing mildly. Looking at his watch, he contemplated his next move.

It was a little after four-thirty. He was hungry and would soon need food. But that wasn't a concern, not yet anyhow. Up until this point the plan was this: finish gutting the basement and go into town for dinner. But was that still the plan, or had things changed? His predicament was simple yet he didn't know what to do.

Dan walked across the gravel driveway and opened the garage door. Sunlight entered the space. He spotted a flashlight sitting on his workbench and couldn't help thinking it was just what he needed.

As he picked it off the bench, something else caught his attention: a kerosene lantern. It was old, red, and slightly rusty. He wondered if it would come in handy.

Sure, he thought. *Might as well grab it, just in case.*

He lifted the lantern from a hook on the wall and shook it back and forth. Kerosene swished inside; the lantern seemed about half full.

"Good enough," he whispered.

He finished his beer and sat the bottle on a bench. He left the garage with the flashlight in one hand and the lantern in the other. Once he was in the kitchen he clicked the flashlight on and off, insuring that it worked. He opened the fridge, snagged another beer, cracked it, and drank. A moment later he lit the lantern with a wooden match. At first the lantern didn't work; the wick was dry and stubborn. But after a bit of fiddling and manual persuasion the lantern worked just fine.

Dan entered the basement, walked past the rolls of carpet, the planks of baseboards and the scattered tools. He approached his new discovery with a smile. He felt like a kid again, a kid at Christmas. Oddly enough, he recognized it too. There was no wondering why; he knew. This was the first time in twenty years he had received a gift that could be *anything*. Sure, it might be nothing, but that was part of the reason he felt so giddy.

It might be nothing; might be anything.

Way better than a birthday present, no doubt.

For Dan, the yearly gift exchange had lost its magic long ago. No matter what he received, he always had an idea what the gift would be—a book, a shirt, a pair of shoes, a coffee mug. After a while it didn't matter; it was all the same crap. Year after year he received things purchased at the mall, or online, or wherever. Yawn. And year after year he knew the price range by considering the person that offered the gift. Double yawn.

Yeah, this was different all right. This was invigorating.

He sat at the edge of the pit with his beer at his side. Drops of water rolled off the bottle. He put a foot on the ladder. The ladder creaked, sounding like a loose floorboard. He wondered if it was stable. The more weight he put on the ladder the more it creaked, but not in a bad way. It seemed secure enough; it seemed okay.

Dan turned the flashlight on and pointed the light down the hole. He couldn't see the bottom. Slowly, carefully, he stood on the ladder. The rung cried out more now than before but it didn't waver, didn't budge. He turned the flashlight off, slid it into his front pocket, lifted the lantern, and began his descent. Immediately he noticed the change in the air: the space was colder, the unpleasant odor was strong. The pit smelled like mold, like earth, and like something else, something he couldn't put his finger on.

The lantern wobbled and bounced off the ladder a few times. The flames danced and flickered but they didn't go out. Climbing wasn't easy, he discovered, but it wasn't impossible either. The fingers in his right hand—already sore and bleeding from tearing the basement apart—felt tight and strained as they wrapped around the rungs. The fingers in his left hand felt even worse as they juggled between the rungs and the thin metal handle of the lantern.

The walls seemed to glow; the shadows were strong and sharp.

He descended more—eleven, twelve, thirteen rungs into the pit. Now fourteen. Now fifteen. Surely the bottom couldn't be much further away.

Sixteen.

Seventeen.

Eighteen.

He stopped climbing and looked down.

Nothing.

He pulled the flashlight from his pocket and turned it on. As he pointed it beneath his feet he illuminated a large spider's web, the biggest he had ever seen. After a slight pause, Dan returned the flashlight to his pocket and continued his descent. Rung after rung he traveled. His fingers burned. Spider's webbing clung to his clothing. His patience wavered, but only for a moment. And in that moment he considered returning to the surface, but he had to wonder what would happen next. Would he think about the pit until he tried his luck again? Probably, so what was the point of giving up so soon? He couldn't leave this mystery unsolved—no way, no chance. He had to keep going, keep climbing, for every rung he passed increased his curiosity and amazement. He was getting hooked on exploration, and so far he loved the adventure.

He kept climbing.

And climbing.

What is this, he thought, *a bottomless pit?*

The consideration seemed less absurd with every passing breath. But it *was* absurd. It was. The pit *couldn't* be bottomless. It just *couldn't be*. Bottomless pits didn't exist.

Who would build something like this, he wondered, *and why? Was the pit a part of the cottage originally, or had the cottage been built on top of this vault for some reason?*

And how deep is it?

Thirty-eight.

Thirty-nine.

Forty.

It wasn't a cellar, Daniel decided. It was a shaft, a coalmine. But that didn't seem right either. Mines were thick and rough, opened by explosives. This was more like a secret tunnel or something, made with concrete.

It's getting cold down here, he thought. *Really cold!*

Crawling through another large spider-web, he thought about returning to the surface to get a long sleeve shirt.

He decided against it, for now.

Fifty-two.

Fifty-three.

Fifty-four.

Daniel stopped climbing a second time. Again he retrieved his flashlight and pointed it towards the bottom… if there was one.

Nothing.

If there was one? What kind of thinking was that? *Of course* there was a bottom. There *had* to be a bottom. There was *always* a bottom!

Climbing.

And climbing.

Sixty-eight.

Sixty-nine.

This was crazy! How much deeper could he go?

He rested the lantern on a rung and leaned it against the wall. He was tired of hauling the bloody thing around; his fingers were killing him.

He descended a few more steps and stopped again. He was in the shadows now. It was dark... really dark; he didn't like it.

"Hello," Dan yelled loudly. His voice echoed off the walls; the repeated word became quieter and deeper in tone.

He heard something foreign and unfamiliar, like a high-pitched voice, like whispering or squeaking; he wasn't sure which. Not surprisingly, his childlike wonder slipped away and was replaced with boyhood fear. His arms sprouted a thousand tiny bumps. His chest muscles tightened and an arctic shiver rolled down his spine in a rippling wave.

"Hello," he said again. And this time his voice was quieter, more timid. He heard something else, the pitter-patter of feet, lots of feet. Sounded like an insect... maybe, a really *large* insect—one big enough to wear a leash. *Clickety, clickety, click.*

Or create those webs.

Or maybe—

His mind drew a blank.

He didn't know what he was hearing, but he was afraid now, very afraid; of this there was no denying. Like a child, he was afraid of the dark, afraid of his own shadow. Or was this fear more logically grounded? Was there something inside the pit with him that was deserving of these emotions? Something dangerous?

He heard that strange sound again, like rainfall tapping against a glass table.

And a shadow in the darkness moved.

He was sure of it.

And for no reason at all, he wondered if he would ever see his wife again, never thinking for a moment that the answer might actually be no.

3

There was a moment, brief as it was, when Daniel thought he would faint. His fingers loosened, his knees became weak and his head started to sway. He imaged his feet being yanked away from the ladder by large muscular hands.

If he fainted, how far would he fall exactly? Ten feet? A thousand feet?

He didn't know. More than that, he didn't *want to know*.

He remembered once, when he was eleven, he had fallen from a tree and landed flat on his back. His lungs felt like they had been stomped; the wind was knocked out of him. The whole world seemed to stop and he wasn't sure if he'd be able to stand. Looking back, he got off lucky. But how lucky would he be this time? How lucky would he be if he fell ten stories and his ribs exploded as his legs shot through his shoulders?

This adventure was *over*. Daniel was gettin' the hell out of dodge while the gettin' was good.

Moving up two rungs, he grabbed the lantern.

He heard the sound again: *Clickety, clickety, click.*

That did it. He was racing up the ladder now; his muscles were straining and his knees were pumping. Suddenly the air seemed warmer, fresher. It tasted cleaner. Within no time at all he was nearing the top, the exit. A terrible image came to his mind: the door slamming shut, trapping him in the pit with... with...

With what?

Just what the hell was he so worried about?

Didn't matter. He wanted out. And he wanted out *now*.

He reached the top and scrambled free of the hole, plunking the lantern down in the first spot he found. He looked around the room. Nothing was altered; nothing had changed. His beer was sitting by the hole untouched, drops of water clung to the glass. The room was destroyed; tools were everywhere, rolls of carpet sat near the staircase.

Everything was exactly the same.

He pulled the flashlight from his pocket, turned it on, and pointed it into the pit. There was nothing to see, nothing at all.

Dan stood up and walked in a circle with his heart racing, his blood pumping, and his face gone flush. He felt like laughing, or crying, or maybe even screaming half-heartedly with his hands waving in the air like a contestant on *The Price is Right*. He wasn't sure what to think. His emotions were hypersensitive and illogical. He felt like a child again, afraid of the monster hiding beneath the bed with dagger teeth and a hunger for killing that couldn't be quenched. And that wasn't him. That wasn't Daniel McGee, friend of the environment, lover of classic rock, cousin of James McGee—*the Terror of Martinsville,* killer of the innocent.

Dan closed his eyes.

Why am I thinking about James again, he wondered. *Am I not freaked out enough without recalling the shame of my family tree?*

He opened his eyes and looked down the hole.

Nothing.

Daniel let out a deep breath and laughed.

Scared of my own shadow, he assumed. *And why? There's nothing down there but a bunch of rats.*

No, not rats, he thought. *Bats! Of course! That's what I heard; that's what I saw. Bats!*

Dan put a hand on his forehead and smiled. How could he be so foolish? How could he be such a baby?

Now he understood what had happened: he yelled, a couple bats squeaked and took flight and that was all, nothing more, nothing less. And another thing: the pit's floor had to be close. It just *had* to be. Ladders don't go on forever. Only a fool would think otherwise.

He looked down the hole one last time before turning away, shaking his head back and forth.

Bats.

"Of course," he mumbled. Sometimes he could be so stupid.

He turned the lantern off and closed the trap door, slamming it shut with a TWHACK.

Dust clouded the room.

He felt better, however, bats or no bats, he wasn't going down there again. Not alone anyhow. Nobody even knew where he was. What if he fell? What if he got hurt? What if the ladder broke? He'd lie on the pit floor with his legs smashed into a thousand pieces as rodents drank the blood that poured from his wounds. In short: he'd die. And even if he didn't die, even if his wife Sandra figured out where he was hiding (with his legs smashed apart and the blood draining from his body) that wouldn't be until Friday night at the earliest. This was *Monday*. He didn't want to be in a cold dark tomb with rats and bats (and God only knows what else) for the next five days. No friggin' way.

Dan left the basement, satisfied with his decision: he was done for the day.

He considered calling his wife but couldn't. He had forgotten his cell phone at home and the house line inside the cottage wasn't connected.

Oh well. No worries. He'd give Sandra a ring later somehow.

He showered, and *my-oh-my* did it feel good. Good for the body; good for the soul. Afterwards he threw the same faded t-shirt on again, figuring it wasn't that dirty.

He jumped into his car, headed for Cloven Rock.

On his way into town, he drove past a long row of homes, an empty field, and St. Peter's church. The church had a tall steeple and a pair of gargoyles above the front door. On one side of St Peter's was a cemetery. The trees near the back of the necropolis seemed as old as the hills. A windmill sat near a wooden bridge that had been designed for horses, not cars. Beneath the bridge, water stumbled over rocks that crayfish and minnows called home.

The other side of the church didn't have a graveyard, but a house. It was built with large, multi-colored rocks, rather than brick. And inside the humble abode, which looked clean, pleasant, and not the least bit disorderly, lived Father Mort Galloway. *(And Galloway sat alone, always alone, forever alone, drinking his favorite gin and killing time by the glass. That's what he did most days: killed time. The priest had lost his faith, which had become so common among priests his age that it almost seemed fashionable. But he wasn't the first to lose faith in the church, nor would he be the last. His faith was lost years earlier, after his parents died in a boating accident that claimed the lives of more than two hundred men, women, and children. It was hard to speak of God after a slap in the face like that; nevertheless he tried. Some days Galloway wondered if he ever really had faith. And some days— —not many, but some—he figured the bulk of his faith would return. It was a nice thought, even if it seemed like a lie. But lying was nothing new for a priest like Galloway; he did it every Sunday in front of many, and every day in front of few. His entire life was a lie at this point, a lie he didn't know how to escape. What kind of life could he have after so many years of priesthood? Exactly, what kind of job could he possibly hold down?)*

Dan drove on, passing another row of houses.

Walking next to a ditch was a boy with a fishing rod in one hand and a box of tackle in the other. He might have been ten years old. Might have been younger. Looking at the child was like seeing a living postcard.

If Dan was to summarize the reasons he liked Cloven Rock in a single image, a simple portrait of the boy with the rod might be it. Cloven Rock was a link to another time, a time before technology became king and the communication age turned the entire planet into a global village.

Being in the Rock was like having a life transfusion: out with the city, in with the town. He wondered why he shouldn't stay in the Rock 'til the end of his days, which oddly enough, had already arrived.

4

Dan drove along King Street, parked against a curb, walked past the Laundromat and the Post Office and entered Cloven Rock's weekend bar of choice: *The Big Four O.* It was owned and operated by two brothers: William and Roger McMaster. The McMaster boys were Cloven Rock's answer to Ernie and Bert, being that both men were pushing fifty and lived together in the same house.

Dan entered the tavern and sat on a stool by the counter, next to a man he had never seen before: Nicolas Nehalem.

Nicolas shifted in his chair and stirred his coffee with a spoon, making the spoon rattle inside the mug.

Dan made brief eye contact and nodded.

Nicolas returned the gesture, hiding his distaste.

There was a pretty girl standing behind the counter that Daniel didn't recognize. Looked about twenty-one. She had dark hair and nice features. She wore tight, charcoal colored jeans, a thick black belt, and a black dress shirt. There were two buttons attached to the breast pocket on her shirt. One button had a picture of Nostferatu with his fangs pointing out and his hands in the air like animal claws. The other button said THE SEX PISTOLS in scary pink letters.

She approached Dan with a dimpled smile, saying, "What can I get you?"

Now that the girl was facing him he could see her makeup was understated and pale, accented with black eyeliner. Combining that with her wardrobe gave her a minimalist Gothic look.

Maybe it's a new style, Dan thought. *Punk light.*

"You new here?" Dan asked politely.

"No, not really," the girl said, tapping a glossy fingernail on the counter top. "I'm a Cloven Rock girl, born and raised. I lived here until I went to university, just outside of Martinsville. I'm back now. You a seasonal regular?"

"Suppose you could say that. I've been spending my summer weekends here for about ten years. I'm Daniel, last name's McGee."

"Hello, Daniel. My name is Cameron."

"Like Cameron Diaz."

"Spelled the same and everything. But for the record, with 'Cameron' being one of the oldest clans in Scotland, the name was making the rounds before her time. Know what I mean?"

Dan smiled and said, "Never met a Cameron before."

"There's a first time for everything, I guess. Roger and Will, they're my cousins."

"Oh yeah?"

Cameron nodded. "My folks have a place right around the corner."

"You're a McMaster?"

"No sir. English. The McMaster's are on the other side of the family tree. Coffee?"

"Beer."

"Bud?

"Corona."

"Ah... you're one of the Corona guys. Roger picked up a case last week, said the summer folk drink it like water."

Dan's smile became a grin. "Tastes good to me."

"Me... I'm not picky. Beer is beer." Cameron opened a bar fridge and lifted a Corona from the rack. She cracked the bottle with an opener she kept in her back pocket and placed the drink on the bar. "You need a lime?"

"Have you got one?"

"Nope."

"Didn't think so. You guys never have limes."

Cameron smiled.

She looked wholesome when she smiled, like a girl you could introduce to your mother. Dan figured if she downsized the Gothic look she'd be perfect, if such a thing existed. Not that he hated the way she looked. He didn't. But still, the dark and mysterious facade didn't quite fit Cameron's personality. She seemed more conventional somehow.

"Tell you what," Cameron said. "I'll pick up a few limes the next time I go shopping."

"Yeah, right."

"Honest, I will. I'm always shopping for the bar. One more thing on the grocery list is no big deal."

Dan took a drink. Switching the bottle from one hand to the other, he said, "Menu?"

Cameron reached beneath the counter, snagged a menu, and handed it over. The menu was old and nasty and needed to be thrown away.

Dan opened it saying, "Some things never change."

"Same old menu."

"Same old menu." Dan agreed, wondering how many times he looked at that very one.

Cameron's eyes drifted. "Back in a minute."

She approached a man and a woman sitting in a booth on the far side of the restaurant. They were in their seventies; the only other customers in the pub. The man was Jay Hopper of Hopper's Gas. He wore a tweed jacket and smelled like after-shave. The woman was his half-sister Emily. Her hair looked like a white ball of yarn. They were having a bite to eat before Jay worked the evening shift.

Nicolas Nehalem, still sitting beside Daniel, watched Cameron from the corner of his eye while pursing his lips tight and curling a hand into a fist.

Impulsively, Dan reached for his pocket. He wanted to check the time on his cell, but remembered that he had no phone. The clock on the wall said it was a quarter to seven. He scanned the restaurant's menu, knowing what was on it, what was good, and what wasn't worth eating. Most of the food was greasier that a machine-shop mechanic, which he feared was the reason he liked it.

Cameron returned from Jay's table.

Dan said, "I'll have a steak sandwich, medium rare."

"Fries?"

"Mashed."

"Coming right up."

She slid the menu beneath the counter and entered the kitchen.

Dan watched her hips moving back and forth until she was gone. She was a sexy *Goth* girl, a rarity for sure. Most Goth girls he knew of looked depressed, irritated, and in need of vitamin D.

The front door opened and Roger McMaster, owner of *The Big*

Four O, came waltzing in, dressed in jeans and a t-shirt. He had short curly hair and a carefree smile.

"Mister McGee," Roger said, extending his hand. "You're back!"

Dan turned towards the man and lifted his bottle. "I'm back."

As the two men shook hands, Nicolas Nehalem squeezed his teeth together and knocked his fist against the table. He wanted to smash Roger in the face with his coffee cup and slash Daniel's throat open with a corkscrew. Those two fuckers were ruining everything. Why the hell did they have to be here now? Why not later? Why not tomorrow? Couldn't they tell they were *not* wanted?

After slapping some money on the counter, Nicolas pushed his glasses high upon his nose and marched out the front door, cursing under his breath.

Roger, ignoring Nicolas, said, "Great to see you, Dan."

"You too, brother. Where's Will?"

"Ah, he's around. Said he might pop by later. Can I buy you a beer?"

"You sure can. You can buy me two beers if you want."

"Yeah well... just 'cause I own the place doesn't mean you can't buy me a drink now and again."

Dan smiled. "Want me to buy *you* a beer?"

"Sure."

Both men laughed and Cameron stepped out from the kitchen. "Hey Roger," she said. "How ya doing?"

Roger slapped his hands together; his eyes were wide and cheerful. "Cameron, you met Daniel yet?"

Cameron adjusted her belt and lifted Nicolas' money from the table. "Why yes I did. He was telling me all kinds of terrible things about you."

"Yeah, I'm sure."

"No it's true. He was telling me how cheap you are and how you're a stud with the ladies..."

Roger rolled his eyes. "Pfft. Now I know you're lying. Hey Cam, set us up, will ya?"

"Bud?"

Roger nodded. "Bud."

"Another Corona, Dan?"

Daniel took a good-sized drink from the bottle. "Another Corona would be just great."

The two men sat down and started in on a long conversation about nothing, making good-natured jokes along the way.

Stanley Rosenstein entered the restaurant looking twenty years older than he did on the day he was in the car accident, the day the teenagers died, the day he saw the *thing* on the road and his life was damaged beyond repair. He ordered take-out without making eye contact with anybody, speaking with a soft and nervous tone. Life had become hard for the man; it was easy to see. He appeared to be hanging on to his sanity with his fingernails.

The steak sandwich came and Roger ordered another round.

Stanley Rosenstein received his take-out and left without saying a word, keeping his head low.

Jay Hopper and Emily paid their bill and left the restaurant, leaving a three fifty tip. And as strange as it may seem, Jay Hopper leaving the restaurant is somewhat of a turning point in this tale. Fact is, if Jay knew about Daniel's discovery he may of said something worth considering, and the hours ahead might have played out differently. He didn't say anything though, and the hours ahead played out worse than most people could possibly imagine.

∞∞∞⊖∞∞∞

When Jay Hopper was just an orange haired kid with a face full of freckles, he worked construction for a man named Lester Long. It was Lester's company that built Daniel's house and the monstrosity that was beneath it. In fact, it was the last job Lester ever worked on. Once the job was completed he moved as far away from Cloven Rock that his wife would allow, and died a few years later in his sleep.

Long story short: Lizzy Backstrom and Stanley Rosenstein weren't the only ones that believed there were monsters living in Cloven Rock. Some of the old-timers did too. They just didn't talk about it.

∞∞∞⊖∞∞∞

When Dan finished eating, Roger closed the kitchen for the night and sent the cook home. The cook was a man named Azul Bunta;

he'd been working there for five years.

After Azul left the building, Cameron cracked a Corona for herself, counted her cash, finished her paperwork, and closed the restaurant. Sitting on a bar stool between Roger and Dan, she joined the conversation.

Dan said, "So listen guys, I found something today that's a little bit peculiar. I can't stop thinking about it."

Roger lifted an eyebrow. "Really? That sounds interesting. Tell us more."

"Yeah Daniel. Let's hear it."

Dan adjusted the stool beneath him, took a sip from his bottle, and wiped a drop of beer from his chin. He said, "I came into town last night, alone. Sandra stayed home."

"Sandra?" Cameron asked.

"That Dan's wife," Roger said. "She's a cutie."

Cameron smiled. "Oh yeah?"

Dan almost blushed. "You wanna hear this story or not?"

"Of course," Roger said.

"Just buggin' ya," Cameron said. "We'll behave, promise."

"Yeah, Dan. We're listening."

"Okay. Well, I got in to town last night, like I said. I opened my place for the summer... you know, got the water running and stuff. This week I plan on renovating the basement."

"Oh wow."

"That's a big job," Cameron said, tilting her bottle outwards.

"I know it is," Dan replied. "I took two weeks off work and I might need to take a third. I want to put a bar down there, hardwood floors. I want to make it nice, you know? I want to be able to bring friends down there."

Roger said, "Sounds great."

"Hopefully it will be. So, today I got up early and cleaned out the garbage, took down a couple of walls, tore out the carpet..."

"Damn," Roger said. "I'm impressed."

"Me too," Cameron agreed.

"Thanks. Anyways... after I removed the carpet I pulled out the sub-floor, and I found a door in the *floor*, in the *concrete!*"

Roger wrinkled his nose and squinted his eyes. "What kind of door?"

"A trap door; a secret cellar or something."

Cameron leaned in. "What was inside?"

Dan smiled. "Well, this is where things get weird. There was a hole in the floor. It was like a manmade mineshaft or something, a tunnel going straight into the earth."

"Oh wow," Roger said, his eyes widening. "We should go down there somehow."

"Going down isn't a problem."

"No?"

"There's a metal ladder attached to a wall. It reminded me of a sewer ladder, know what I mean?"

Roger said, "I've haven't been inside many sewers, but I can imagine. Did you go down?"

"Yes."

"Really!" Cameron almost jumped off her stood. The excitement she felt was obvious, an open book, she was easy to read. Suddenly she seemed very young. "What was down there? Did you see anything good?"

"Yeah, Dan. Tell us. What did you find?"

Dan lifted his bottle, swallowing the last of his beer. "I went down with a flashlight and a lantern. The ladder was longer than I expected it to be. I never reached the bottom."

Cameron said, "How far did you travel?"

"You know what? It seemed really far when I was climbing. I was alone and I didn't expect to go down so far. It was dark and cold. I thought the floor was right there, like it was a normal cellar. After a while I got worried. Nobody knew where I was or what I was doing; nobody knew I was down there. I started thinking I might get hurt or something, and nobody would find me. Then I heard a rat squeak, or maybe it was a bat. I don't know. I just…" Feeling embarrassed, Dan stopped talking.

"Don't worry, man," Roger said. "Nobody should go into a place like that alone, especially if nobody knows you're down there. You were right to get out."

"I guess."

Cameron said, "But tell me, how far down did you travel?"

Dan tallied the rungs in his mind. "Maybe sixty, sixty-five feet. But it felt like more. Sixty feet might not sound like much inside an open space with the lights on. But inside that shaft, I don't know. It felt…"

"That's pretty far," Roger said. "I would've gotten out of there too."

"Yeah," Cameron said. "I can't believe you found a secret tunnel in your basement. That's so cool! Can I see it?"

"You want to?" Dan asked.

"Yes! Of course! This is amazing! It's like something from a movie! *Journey to the Center of the Earth*, something like that."

Dan looked at Roger, hunting his opinion.

Roger said, "I'd love to check it out."

"Really?"

"Absolutely. One condition though, if we find anything valuable, we split it."

"Three ways!" Cameron added. Now she did jump off of her stool. She looked almost ecstatic. "Can we split it three ways?"

Dan said, "If we find anything good we'll split it."

Cameron said, "You promise?"

Dan nodded. "Yes. I promise."

Not half as excited as Cameron, Roger finished his drink. "Want another beer, Dan?"

"You buying?"

"Wait!" Cameron said, with her eyes suddenly bulging. "We should do it right now, don't you think?"

"I don't know," Roger said. "What do you say, Dan?"

Truthfully, Dan wanted to get back to his basement ASAP. His entire project was now in 'handyman limbo' and that made him feel both anxious and concerned. Until he knew what was down there it was hard to keep working. He *could* keep working, he supposed. And he would if need be, but he didn't want to. He wanted to figure out what was going on. The very fact that the pit existed was affecting his design plans. Originally, he wanted the bar sitting where the trap door was located. Now it seemed like the area should be left open.

Playing it cool, he said, "Going to my place now is fine with me. But we need more flashlights."

"Awesome!" Cameron finished her beer quickly and slammed the bottle down. "Let's do it!"

Dan grinned. "Are you always this hyper?"

"Duh," Cameron said, making a silly face. "What do you want from me? I've got energy. I've got drive. I've got nothing better to do, so… yeah. I'm kind of hyper about this one. Excuse me for living."

"Don't you have a boyfriend or something to calm you down?"

Roger made an exaggerated GULP in his throat. "Uh-oh," he said. "Shouldn't talk about the boyfriend, Dan."

"Why not?"

Cameron tore into the conversation like a hungry lion. "That no-good, two-timing, cheating, asshole! Don't get me started on him! That liar! I want to tear his balls off and feed them to his mother. He's such a jerk! Such a stupid *JERK!*"

"Yikes," Dan said. "Sorry I asked. Let's find a better topic, okay?"

"Yes, please." Roger said with a groan. He had heard it all, *several* times. The last thing he wanted was to have Cameron bitch about her ex again.

"His name," Cameron said, "is Paul LaFalce, in case you run into him. He works at Hopper's Gas over on the 9th Line."

"Jay Hopper was just here," Roger interjected. "Sitting in the corner. He's a nice guy; big football fan."

"I know who Jay Hopper is," Daniel said.

"Yeah, whatever," Cameron spat, taking back her story. "Paul pumps gas for Jay. And he's a prick. He screwed Missy and Bridget and he's dating an ugly whore named Julie Stapleton."

"Okay, Dan said. "I understand. He's an asshole and he cheated on you. Got it."

"More than once! Way more than once! He didn't just cheat on me. Apparently he was doing every girl in Cloven Rock, again and again… the bastard! OH! He makes me so mad!"

Roger said, "Cam. Please, honey, no more. Okay?"

Cameron didn't listen. "I kept thinking it was me, you know? He wouldn't touch me; he wouldn't talk on the phone. I couldn't understand!"

"Cam, honey. Please. Calm down."

Daniel put his hand on Cameron's arm, and with the kindest voice he could muster, he said, "If you don't shut up about your boyfriend you won't be invited to my place. You'll have to sit here alone, crying by yourself until your eyes dry up and fall from your head. Is that what you want?"

Cameron was stunned. As her jaw unhinged, she said, "What?"

"You heard me. You're more fun when you don't think about old ghosts. Go back to being hyper and crazy, would you? This side of you grosses me out. It makes me feel bad."

"It's like that, is it?" Cameron asked, smiling.

"Yes," Daniel said, mocking her with his voice. "It's like that. This conversation is..." Dan paused, trying to find clever words. He settled with, "Is not the droids I'm looking for."

Cameron chuckled. "Pfft. Not the droids you're looking for?"

"That's right."

"Who are you, Ben Kenobi?"

Dan nodded. "I've got two Wookies, a Jawa, and a big bag of light-sabers, hiding in my basement. Do you want to help me find them or cry about the gasman? It's your choice."

"I don't like you," Cameron said playfully.

"I don't like you, either," Dan said, flaunting his used car sales-man smile. "But it's nice to see you know about *Star Wars*."

"I've got two older brothers. I know about a lot of things."

"Like The Sex Pistols."

"Yes, like The Sex Pistols."

Dan's salesman smile became a schoolyard bully's grin. "The Sex Pistols suck. You're a loser."

Cameron's smile widened.

This man, she decided, was hilarious... and completely full of crap. He probably liked The Sex Pistols more than she did. And not only that, he had drained her anger away almost magically. He was a Jedi, that's what he was. He was a shit-disturbing, mind-altering, Jedi.

Acknowledging this, Cameron realized something: she liked Dan-iel. Yes, he was too old for her, ten years off the mark from her point of view. But he was funny and cute, maybe even hot. He looked cool in his Black Sabbath t-shirt; his hair was dark and his muscles were strong and lean. He was city, not country. He had character, and baby, that shit mattered. From what she had seen, Dan was sensitive, smart, and able to read people perfectly. He was fun to be around, too.

She liked him all right, liked him a lot. And she was single now, looking for love, a little remuneration to help ease the pain of a terri-ble break-up. Maybe she needed a *man* in her life, not another boy. Maybe she needed someone like Dan. Was it possible the attraction was a two way street? She thought that perhaps it was.

Silence claimed the room.

Roger disrupted it: "Should we get going?"

Cameron heard the words, but their meaning did not register. She was thinking about Daniel now, wondering if she could find a way to get him alone.

5

Nicolas Nehalem sat in his car across from the Laundromat, eying *The Big Four O*. He had a squirrel lying on the seat beside him. He had driven past the rodent, then decided to go back and scoop him up. The poor little guy was still alive, gasping for air, and squealing in pain. The squirrel had been run over by a truck. Its back legs were crushed. Intestines were sticking through a long grisly tear in its stomach. Its tail was twisted awkwardly. A little pink piece of meat hung from its mouth, surrounded by fur that was sticky with blood.

Nicolas felt a connection with the rodent, and named him Fuzzy.

But it wasn't Fuzzy that brought Nicolas to *The Big Four O*. It was the girl behind the counter: Cameron.

She captured his interest a week earlier.

Rewind: Last Wednesday Nicolas had lunch at *The Big Four O* and Cameron served him. He ordered a hamburger without the bun, three hardboiled eggs, and a glass of chocolate milk. She said it was a strange order. He said she was beautiful. She smiled politely and walked away. When she returned, Nicolas said, "What's your name?" She told him. Nicolas smiled and said nothing more. And as the day wore on, Nicolas repeated her name over and over inside his mind. It was rattling around his thoughts for hours. *Cameron, Cameron, Cameron...* All at once, it was decided: he would fill his empty cage with Cameron.

Fast forward: Nicolas was excited.

Inside the car, he pressed a button. The automatic window rolled up. He hit another button. The window rolled down. This went on for over ten minutes, and all the while the squirrel wheezed and cried and felt more pain then most people can imagine.

Then something happened, something that made Nicolas smile with delight: a fly landed on the steering wheel and when Nicolas slapped it, the fly fell onto his lap. The insect was stunned, but alive.

Delicately, carefully, Nicolas lifted the fly by its wings. This was so good it was making him dizzy. He had a fly, a squirrel, and soon he'd have Cameron too.

How lucky can one man be?

He kissed the fly and petted it and held it by its legs; and when nobody was looking he opened his zipper, pulled his pants to his knees and pressed the insect against his manhood.

"That feels *good*," he groaned psychotically.

After a moment he looked out the window. The coast was still clear. He pressed his shoulders deep into the seat, tightened his muscles and licked his lips. And when he grew tired of his strange little affair he placed the fly onto his tongue and sucked it down his throat.

Fuzzy gasped and Nicolas picked his nose. When his nose began bleeding he licked the blood from his finger. He liked the taste of blood. Sometimes he would bite his fingers just to taste the juice inside. Sometimes he'd cut his babies fingers off for similar reasons.

Inside the restaurant, lights dimmed.

It seemed as though Cameron was getting ready to leave.

Nicolas pulled his pants up and started the car. He put a hand on Fuzzy and Fuzzy bit his finger. The bite didn't bother him. It didn't make him upset. He imaged himself as a God and the rodent was one of his many creations, and he was a merciful God, powerful and tolerant, compassionate beyond comprehension.

Today he'd fill his empty cage.

6

Roger scribbled a note on a napkin and left it in a place that was easy to see. The note said:

Hey William, guess who's back in town? Dan McGee!
Cam and I have to gone to his place for a while.
You should come. We'll be in the basement (don't ask).
~Roger.

Dan watched him write. "Is your brother going to see that?"

Roger nodded. "His time is divided between home and work. He usually pops by after we close. Sometimes he cooks. Sometimes he checks inventory and makes sure things are turned off. It's his routine."

"You think he'll come to my place?"

Roger shrugged. "He might. Want me to grab a six pack?"

Dan smiled. Apparently Roger knew how to read minds. "Sure. You guys want to ride with me?"

Roger said, "Can you drive me home later?"

"Yeah, no problem. Or you can stay at my place the night... if you want."

"Maybe. Let's play it by ear."

"I'm dropping my car off at home," Cameron said. "Can you pick me up? If I'm drinking I'd rather not have my car."

"No problem," Roger said. "Right Dan?"

"Right."

Roger went behind the bar, pulled beers from the fridge and placed them in a bag. Dan and Cameron stepped outside. Roger turned off the lights, stepped outside, and locked the door. Dan and Roger jumped into Dan's car and drove, making a pit stop at Roger's place for more supplies. Cameron followed.

Inside Roger's garage they found two more flashlights, one 25-foot extension cord, one 20-foot extension cord and one 15-foot extension cord. They also found two 500-watt work-lights in Roger's basement; each of them had a yellow casing and was designed to blast a serious amount of light into dark places.

"Perfect," Daniel said. He looked at Cameron and quickly looked away. "This stuff will help for sure."

Roger made a joke about sending him the bill as Cameron toyed with her hair. They returned to their cars and drove to Cameron's place.

Cameron changed vehicles.

They drove on.

Dan noticed a car in the rearview mirror, following along like it was heading to the same destination. It seemed unusual but not extraordinary; he wondered if the car was following on purpose. A moment later the car pulled off the road and disappeared from view, which seemed to answer his question.

Once they arrived at Dan's cottage they went straight to the basement.

Roger carried the extension cords and the flashlights. Dan carried the work lights. Cameron carried the bag of alcohol in one hand and a radio in the other. When Roger asked what's the radio was for, she replied, "So we can listen to music, stupid." Dan laughed and Roger said, "Very funny." Dan opened the trapdoor with a grunt as Cameron plugged the radio into an outlet. A song by *Joy Division* came on, making Dan wonder if Cameron enjoyed anything from her own era. Cameron turned the volume low and approached the pit with a smile. All three of them looked down the hole. And when they saw the darkness that seemed to have no end, nobody said a word.

7

Nicolas followed Cameron's car, humming along with a song on the radio. When Cameron made a pit stop at Roger's place, he turned the radio off and drove around the corner. He parked, waited, and followed them once they were driving. When they stopped at Cameron's place he slowed but kept moving. Through the rearview mirror, he watched Cameron change from one car to the next. This wasn't good. He wanted her to be alone at some point soon. Following them undetected could only become harder now that they made two pit stops.

He turned the car around, waited a few seconds, and followed Dan's car to Stone Path Road. He knew Stone Path very well. He lived on a small, nearly uninhabited loop called Stone Crescent, and the two streets were attached. Stone Path Road and Stone Crescent were shaped like a lollipop on a stick. Stone Crescent was the lollipop. Stone Path was the stick. This meant both streets were a dead end, and there was no way for Cameron to escape without him knowing. No way at all.

Cameron was trapped.

Nicolas pulled next to the ditch, turned his engine off and let Dan drive away. He waited a few minutes, giving Cameron time to settle down, get comfortable, and kick off her shoes. During this time he lifted Fuzzy by his broken legs and squeezed the rodent as hard as he was able.

A smile crept across his face.

Claws scratched frantically. Eyes bulged. Teeth snapped together in a mix of pain, fury, and desperation.

Nicolas said, "Oh Fuzzy, what's wrong, buddy?"

Still clamping his fingers like a vice, he changed gears inside his mind. Nicolas smashed the rodent against the dashboard three times, causing animal innards to explode against the window and floor. Guts splashed everywhere. Now Nicolas' feet were kicking, his mouth was wide open and his glasses fell to his lap. He slapped the animal's mangled body against the passenger's seat repeatedly, bouncing it against the padded fabric.

Suddenly he was furious.

His face turned red and his eyeballs quivered like he was having an epileptic fit. Screaming, he crushed the rodent's body against his chin and inhaled the wild scent with a loud and noisy snort. Blood dripped from his fingers. It ran down his face and neck. After a few seconds he blasted the tiny creature's body against the steering wheel like a slave driver cracking a whip. Fuzzy snapped in half. The rodent's head, chest, and his two front legs flew through the air, smacked against the windshield, and fell onto the dash. Gore hung from the exposed ribcage like pasta.

Nicolas looked at the mangled legs squished between his fingers. Anger, frustration, and excitement, became diluted with feelings he didn't understand: loss, despair, misery, confusion. The emotional overload was too much. He began crying. His face turned red and his bottom lip launched into the foxtrot.

"It's not fair," he exclaimed, loudly. "It's just not fair!"

When he was done with his brief, yet psychotically expressive bout of mourning, he rolled down the window and tossed Fuzzy's legs outside. They hit the ground with a *SPLOTCH* and rolled in the dirt. He lifted his glasses from his lap, wiped the dribbles of gore from the lenses, and placed them on his teary-eyed face. He started the car and drove, ignoring the string of intestines that was clinging to his hair and the blood dripping from his chin. He didn't care how he looked—driving down Stone Path Road with his fingers strangling the steering wheel and guts rolling off his stubble, but he did consider shooting himself. He also considered setting the town on fire, and wondered what it would be like to go on a nice, big, killing spree.

The upper half of Fuzzy sat on the dashboard near the steering wheel, lying in a small pond of blood. Black bubble eyes stared lifelessly out the window, still looking very much alive. Drops of purple and red waste blemished the glass, framing the animal's body with macabre style. And as the animal's mouth slid open one final time, and the car's wheels rolled towards their destination, Nicolas wondered if there was such a thing as rodent heaven. If so, the squirrel was surely there.

8

It was Roger that spoke first. "Wow," he said. "Just... wow."

Dan couldn't help but agree. Looking down such an unusual hole was astonishing. "See the light switch attached to the wall? It doesn't work."

Roger eyed the switch quickly before looking down the hole again. "No?"

"Nope."

Cameron picked a hammer off the floor, stepped close to the edge, and dropped it.

As the hammer disappeared from view, Dan looked at Cameron flabbergasted. "Hey! I need that!"

"So what?" Cameron replied. "We're going down there, aren't we?"

"Yeah but... " Dan trailed off, reflecting on the fact that he didn't reach the bottom earlier. He considered the value of the hammer. It wasn't worth much, ten bucks maybe. Still, he couldn't help thinking he'd soon buy a new one.

"I didn't hear it hit," Roger said. "Did you?"

"No," Cameron said.

"I wasn't listening," Dan admitted. A moment later he grabbed a crowbar off the floor. His intention was obvious.

"Don't you *need that* Dan?" Cameron mocked. "It looks *important.*"

Dan smiled. "We're going down there, *remember?*"

"Oh," Cameron said with a grin. "That's right! *I forgot!* You're so smart!"

Roger rolled his eyes.

Daniel dropped the tool. All three of them listened. Seconds slipped past and nobody heard a thing. In time, Roger stepped away from the edge saying, "That is one deep hole."

"Seems that way, doesn't it?" Dan replied. "Know what? You guys should chill out a minute. I'm going to the garage to grab another extension cord."

As Daniel went upstairs, Cameron lifted the bag of alcohol and pulled out a beer. "I'm assuming you want one?"

"Sure do."

She tossed Roger a Bud and took one for herself.

Roger opened the bottle. Beer foamed. He put his mouth to the opening, drank like a second year college student, and sat the bottle on the floor next to a screwdriver. Afterwards, he unraveled an extension cord and plugged it into an outlet. He tied the female end of one cable to the male end of another, holding them together with a knot. He tied the second cord to the third. Now three extension cables were connected and the knots he created insured they wouldn't become unplugged.

Cameron said, "Maybe you should wrap the cable around the pickets."

"Huh?"

"The pickets," she repeated, pointing towards the staircase. "The pickets in the stairs. Knot the extension cable around a few of them so it doesn't get pulled from the outlet in wall. It will, you know."

Roger looked at the cable, the outlet, and the pickets. "Oh yeah," he said. "Now I get it. Good idea."

He followed her instructions.

Daniel returned. "I've got two more cables. One isn't very long, eight feet maybe. But the other one is a thirty footer."

"Nice."

"Hand 'em over," Roger said. "I'll knot 'em together."

Daniel passed the cables to Roger. "I'm going to put the beers in the fridge."

"Cool."

Daniel went upstairs with the bag of booze and returned with an open beer in his hand.

Roger tied the last of the cables together. "Now, the moment of truth."

He tied the work light to the extension cables and plugged the light in. 500 watts of white light blasted the room.

"So far, so good," Cameron said, putting a hand on her hip.

Daniel agreed. "Yep. So far so good."

Roger hung the light over the hole and when he lowered it, he kept his arms steady. As the light descended the weight in his hands increased. Soon, the light became quite heavy and he asked Daniel for assistance. Dan took the cable in his hands, relieving Roger of the full burden. The two men released more and more cable. The knots tightened. The light fell farther into the pit, slowly spinning in a circle, knocking out webs and lighting the area around it. Looking down, there wasn't much to see: just a ladder and four walls, really. Nothing more.

"I can't believe how far the light is dropping," Cameron said with her eyes wide. "It's like a bottomless pit."

"That's what I thought," Daniel laughed, still releasing cable.

Soon, the cable was unraveled, all ninety-something feet of it. When the men released their grip, the strain the cable put on the pickets was more than they anticipated. The pickets bowed in the middle, threatening to snap. There was no way the cable's male end would have stayed in the outlet without the pickets help—no chance, not in one hundred million years.

"What now?" Cameron asked.

Dan lifted an eyebrow. "Still want to go down?"

"I do," Cameron said, sounding slightly unsure.

"I do too." Roger confirmed, offering happy a smirk. "I'm just wondering what the smart thing to do might be."

"Meaning?"

"Meaning, what should we do? Drop a flashlight? I'd like to know where the bottom is, don't you?"

After a moment of silence, Daniel said, "I've got an idea."

"Yeah?"

"Yeah. Hold on. I'll be right back."

Daniel ran to the kitchen and opened the cupboard doors beneath the sink. There was a bag of sponges sitting in a milk crate, along with some cleaning materials and rags. He grabbed the sponges and closed the doors. After riffling through a couple of drawers he found a half-roll of duct tape. He took the tape and the sponges downstairs, unrolled a long piece of tape and dropped the roll on the floor. After opening the bag of sponges he pulled one out and dropped the bag onto the floor by his feet. With the line of tape against the sponge, he picked up a flashlight.

"Wait," Cameron said.

"Why?"

"I know what you're doing."

"And?" Dan pressed the flashlight against the sponge and began taping them together.

"And it's a great idea: wrapping sponges around the flashlight. You're going to sponge it and drop it, right? You want to drop the flashlight without breaking it."

"Yeah."

"Well, you know what we should do?"

"No, what?"

"Do you have a *Nerf* football, or better yet a beach ball? If we could deflate a beach ball halfway we could put the light inside the ball a bit, you know... giving it more protection. Or we could wrap the light inside a couple of plastic balls I guess. What do you think?"

"Not bad," Dan said.

"We could do both," Roger said. "We could wrap the flashlight inside the sponges *and* between a couple of balls. How about that Dan, do you have any balls?"

"I think so. Want me to look?"

"Yes," Roger said, taking the sponge/flashlight/tape combination from Dan's hand. "You look and I'll tape the sponges to the flashlight."

"This is exciting!" Cameron said. "I feel like I'm starting an adventure!"

Dan nodded. "It'll be interesting to see what's down there."

"Absolutely," Roger agreed. "I never expected to be on a quest today."

Dan slapped his hands together. "You want to come to the garage with me, Cam? Help me look?"

"Sure."

"Okay then, let's go!"

9

Nicolas Nehalem drove along Stone Path Road slowly, inspecting every car parked in every driveway. If the driveway was long and he needed a closer look, he parked and approached the building on foot. He was systematic and methodical. Cameron was located in a perfectly terrible position, and the only way she'd escape would be due to negligence on his part. And that wasn't going to happen.

Nicolas found three driveways together that led onto a short, fat peninsula; he had himself a winner.

Dan's car was located beneath the shade of a large elm tree, two hundred feet from the road, in the driveway of a summer home that looked like it cost a Hollywood fortune. The house was big and beautiful and stylishly elegant.

Nicolas walked around the house slowly and cautiously, making note of the surrounding area. He peeked through the building's windows with care, which were strong and thick and designed to give intruders a hard time.

He didn't see anyone inside the house, figured Cameron and her friends were either upstairs or in the basement. Either way, it didn't matter. He wanted to wait until the evening turned to night and the sky became black.

Nicolas returned to his car, which wasn't far from Dan's driveway. He opened the trunk and let out a small gasp, surprised at what he discovered.

Pauline Anderson, a.k.a., Pauline Stupid-Head, was in the trunk. She looked five years dead.

She wasn't.

The corpse was only twenty-six days old, but her body told a different story.

Pauline's muscles had shriveled; her skin had deteriorated. She was exceedingly dehydrated on the day she died—the day Nicolas emptied his cage, dragging her from her shit-filled pen, screaming and crying, pleading and begging, only to have her throat slit while Olive and Cathy watched in terror.

Now she looked truly monstrous, horrific.

Her lips had curled into tight stringy worms. Her eyes had fallen into her head. Chipped arrowhead teeth pointed in all directions, encased inside her purple, rotting maw. Her hands had no fingers; her feet had few toes. Her arms and legs looked like they had been embalmed, salted, and cured. The only place on her body that seemed recently deceased was her stomach, which was a soup bowl of maggots and flies.

It was hard to believe she just turned sixteen.

Nicolas scratched his ear and sighed. "I forgot about you," he said. "I forgot you were back there. You should have told me."

He laughed. He made a joke.

"Now where am I going to put Cameron, huh? Do you think I should let her ride up front? I don't. My God, girl... you've been nothing but trouble since you were thirteen years old."

Nicolas considered throwing the corpse in the bushes but decided against it. Uncalculated moves could only bring unwanted trouble. He was better off leaving her in the trunk. Cameron might not like being back there with a corpse but *tough-tit said the shit*, she'd get over it. And besides, home was only three minutes away.

He lifted a shotgun and a box of shells from beside Pauline's corpse. He placed them on the gravel and pushed the carcass to the back of the trunk, making room for Cameron. He closed the trunk with a grunt, lifted the shotgun and the shells from the road, and walked up the driveway grinning.

Halfway to the house he stopped, listening to the sound of a door opening. He could hear people stepping outside. A man and a woman were talking.

Nicolas scratched his head.

Maybe Cameron had a husband. If so, that was bad. He didn't like breaking up married couples, but he'd do it if he had to.

"Okay baby," he whispered. "Daddy's coming." With his shotgun close to his chest he looked at the bloated moon, which was peeking up from behind a line of trees that looked healthy and green.

Soon it would be time for adoption.

10

Cameron and Daniel entered the garage. Dan clicked on the overhead light, walked past a small fishing boat, and approached a workbench.

Cameron said, "So, Daniel. Where's the wife?"

"Home."

"And where's home?"

"About an hour south of here, in little town called Martinsville. You know it?"

"Everyone knows Martinsville. I went to school near there, remember? The place is famous. You didn't know James McGee, did you? The guy that killed those people?"

"Actually," Daniel said with shoulders slumping, "I knew him very well. James was my cousin."

Cameron was shocked. "Really?"

"Yep. Sad to say, but it's true."

"I can't believe it!"

"Well, believe it. We have the same last name and everything."

"That's right! You said that your last name was McGee. That's amazing!"

"Oh, real amazing. Too bad my uncle wasn't Adolph Hitler."

"No, I don't mean it like that. It's just that… you seem so normal."

"I *am* normal."

"That's not what I mean. I just… it's weird to think you're related to a psychopath."

Daniel glanced at the floor. "I guess."

The conversation wasn't going the way Cameron anticipated. She wanted to get to know Daniel in a *good* way, not like this. She was hoping he'd say he had a troubled marriage and it was ending. She wanted him to be looking for someone different, someone young and energetic, like her. Instead they were talking about the *Terror of*

Martinsville, who—as it turned out—was a close relative. *Yikes*. How did *that* happen? Somehow the conversation made a wrong turn and ended up in Horror City.

Needing to mend the verbal exchange, Cameron steered the discussion into neutral ground. "See any beach balls?"

Dan looked inside an old trunk. "If I have *balls*," he said with a grin and a smirk, "they're in here."

He pulled out a football and a basketball. They looked heavy. "This is it, and I don't think they're going to be very helpful."

"Maybe we should stick with the sponges?"

"Yeah, maybe."

Dan tossed the balls into the trunk.

Something moved on the other side of the garage window. It might have been the shadow from a tree, but Dan didn't think so. He thought someone was out there.

Cameron took Daniel's hand and gave it a squeeze.

"Sorry," she said. "I didn't mean to make you feel uncomfortable. I had no idea you were related to James McGee." She moved closer and her eyes widened. She squeezed his hand tighter, tilting her head to the side.

"That's okay," Dan said, stepping back. A line appeared in his forehead. "I'm not uncomfortable."

"That's good. I don't want you to feel bad."

"I know."

"I want to make you feel good."

Dan may or may not have felt awkward before, but here and now... he was standing with a beautiful young girl holding hands. They were alone. And she was looking at him in a way that made him feel guilty, like he was supposed to wrap his arms around her and give her a kiss. But he couldn't do that. He was happily married; he was in love.

But still...

Cameron's dark hair was cut just below the shoulder. Her eyes were big and beautifully, perfectly stunning above the thin arc of her nose. Her lips were full; her breasts were neither large nor small, but just the size Daniel liked breasts to be.

These things added up.

Dan was uncomfortable, all right. Worse than that, Cameron was blocking the exit. Was she blocking it on purpose? He hoped not, but that seemed to be the situation.

He said, "Wanna get going?"

Cameron could hear the nervousness in his voice. Reluctantly, she released his hand and stepped back, saying, "Okay."

Daniel slipped past her and walked a straight line, forgetting about the shadow in the window.

What just happened? he wondered. *Did Cameron hit on me? She knows I'm married. And she's too young for me. Doesn't she realize the age difference is ten years or more? Shouldn't she be with guys her own age? What the hell is that crazy girl thinking?*

As they entered the house, Cameron said, "Hey Daniel, want to give me a tour of your place? I'd love to see it."

She's on the rebound, Dan thought. *She's pissed off at what's-his-name and now she looking for action, trying to create a moment.*

"Uh… sure, Cam," he said, playing nonchalant. But it was so strange. He remembered these moves from high school. Being older, he could see right through this stuff. Didn't she know that? Dan cleared his throat. "I'll give you the tour later. Right now I want to do the basement thing."

He went straight for the basement door and made his way down the stairs, not giving her a chance to debate the matter. He was fast; quickness was his polite defense.

Cameron followed.

Smiling, Roger said, "Any luck?" He was sitting at the edge of the hole, eager to descend.

Dan shook his head. "Not really. We found a couple balls in the garage but they wouldn't be helpful. Too heavy. Things wouldn't be better, just different."

"Oh."

"You know," Cameron said, looking at Roger inquisitively. "I have an umbrella in my car. Maybe we could use it like a parachute."

"Naw," Roger said. "I just wanna go down there. Screw the umbrella." He held the flashlight, now wrapped inside nine strategically placed sponges. "I'll carry this bad-boy as far as I can, then I'll drop it."

Dan picked a flashlight off the floor and slid it between his belt and his jeans.

The doorbell rang.

Roger laughed. "Who could that be?"

Daniel laughed too. "Damned if I know. I didn't tell anyone I was here, and Sandra's working 'til Friday... so, who knows?" He shrugged. "Whatever. I'll be back in a second."

"Don't be long," Cameron said with a naughty smile.

Dan returned the smile with the naughtiness removed. *Wow*, he thought, turning away. *She never quits.*

11

Nicolas had watched Cameron and Daniel interacting in the garage. He was standing near the window, listening to their conversation through the glass. He caught some of what they were saying, and he didn't like what he was hearing. They seemed friendly, *too* friendly, in his opinion. He whispered, "What am I going to do about this?"

This was a tough situation, one he didn't care for at all. But what could he do?

He considered shooting the man and taking Cameron to his home immediately. Problem was, he knew there was somebody else inside the house, maybe even two or three somebodies.

What would happen when the shotgun blasted?

Those somebodies will come out, that's what! They'll come running, wanting to know what the fuss is about. What then? Do I shoot 'em? Do I shoot 'em all? Is that my plan... or is that PLAN B?

A tough spot all right. Very tough.

He allowed Cameron and the man to finish their conversation and return indoors without incident, which seemed smart.

Play it cool, he told himself. *If I play it cool, the visitors will go home and I'll be able to deal with Cameron, alone. That way, things will run smoothly.*

A new idea came: *maybe Cameron will want to come to my place.*

That was a possibility.

She'll want to...

But what if more people arrive? What if the house becomes a party house? What then? Do I join the party? Go home? Wait for Cameron to step outside and smash her head open with a rock?

Waiting seemed dangerous.

Nicolas considered walking in, blasting everyone in sight and taking the girl. It was a reasonable thing to do. It was practical and rational, fast and fun... but was it right?

He let the idea swish around awhile.

He had never done anything so bold before, so dangerous— walking inside and killing everyone. *Wow.* That was risky.

But it *would* be fun.

There will be trouble afterwards, guaranteed. The cops will be snooping. Might as well face the facts and figure the angles before inviting the weight of world to drop by for a visit.

Nicolas spat on the wall and watched the liquid roll down the wood. He put a finger in the wet spot, drew a happy face, crept into the shadows, and lifted the shotgun.

Somebody new was approaching.

Nicolas released a twisted grin. And as he squeezed the shotgun tight, his eyes turned to slits.

12

Standing on the step with a hand on each hip was Dan's good friend, Patrick Love. Pat was a good kid, twenty-three years old, friendly. His parents had a cottage next door.

"Well look who it is," Dan said, answering the door with a smile. "Patrick! What's shakin' buddy?

The two men slapped hands and embraced with a hug.

Pat said, "Hey man, I saw the lights on and came over to say hi!"

"Good to see you!"

"Yeah, you too! I'm doing the cottage thing all week long. Couple pals are coming up on Wednesday, a couple more on Thursday, and a whole gang of them are coming on Friday night."

"Where are your parents in all of this? Do they know you're having a weeklong party?"

Pat smirked. "First of all, it's not a weeklong party. It's a week*end* party, and yes—they know. They gave me the cottage for the week, said I could do what I wanted."

Daniel laughed. "Why did they do that?"

"Because I finished college and I am a respectable adult now… *duh*. What do you think?"

"Daniel laughed again, saying, "A respectable adult? You wish, man."

"It's true. Believe it or not I'm done school, and this is my week to celebrate. My parents have been *very cool* lately. They took me out to diner, gave me a thousand bucks. They even helped me finance a car."

Dan embellished a look of astonishment, but in truth he didn't need to embellish much. He was impressed. Patrick was constantly impressing Dan in one way or another. "You have a car now?"

"How else could I get here, fly?"

"I don't know. You alone?"

"Yeah. How about you? Where's Sandra?"

"Sandra's home. She's coming on Friday."

"Hey! That's just in time for my party!"

"I guess it is."

"Sweet. So you're alone too?"

"Actually—" Daniel stepped back and held the door open. "Come on in. I've got people in the basement."

Pat stepped inside and closed the door. "In the basement? Why? I've seen your basement, Dan... it's awful. Looks like *Mordor* down there. All you need is *the Great Eye* and a bunch of hairy *Orcs*."

"Not any more."

"No?"

Dan walked to the kitchen, opened the fridge, and handed Pat a beer. "I'm renovating," he said. "And I found a... shit. I don't know what to call it. A pit?"

"A pit? You found a pit in your basement? What are you, high?"

Dan smiled. "Come look."

13

They entered in the basement, Dan first, then Pat.

Patrick smiled at Roger, who was sitting at the base of the trap-door. They knew each other from the restaurant.

Roger nodded.

Pat said, "Hey."

"Who's this?" Cameron asked, trying to look cute.

"This is Patrick Love, a good friend of mine. He's got a cottage a couple doors down. Patrick, meet Cameron."

"Hi."

"Hi."

As an afterthought, Daniel said, "Patrick's single."

Cameron shot Daniel a dirty look as she clamped her flashlight to a belt loop.

Patrick said, "I'm not single."

Daniel looked at Cameron and shrugged, playing the fool. Turning to Pat, he said, "No?"

"No."

"But you're always single."

"No I'm not."

"Every summer, you're single. True or false?"

"I don't know… but I'm not single now and I haven't been single for six or seven months."

Daniel shook his head in mock disgust. "Oh yeah, what's her name?"

Pat took a swing of beer. "Her name is 'shut up.' You'll meet her on Friday."

"Yeah Dan," Roger said, growing impatient. "Are we investigating or what?"

Pat made his way across the room and looked down the hole. "Holy shit… you weren't kidding. You have a pit in your basement."

Dan nodded. "It's deep alright. We're about to explore, wanna come?"

"Hell ya."

"Then let's do it."

"Finally." Roger made his way down several rungs. "You sure the ladder will hold?"

Dan sat his bottle down, pulled a book of matches from his pocket, and lit one. With the match, he lit the lantern. "As sure as I can be. I went down a couple hours ago. I think it'll hold."

"Good enough for me," Roger said. He descended.

Cameron looked down the hole with a troubled expression before positioning herself on the ladder. Her first few steps were slow and careful.

Dan said, "You okay?"

"Yeah, it's just... I'm worried about the ladder."

"I think the ladder's fine."

"Alright." Cameron said into her chest, swallowing back her fears. "If you say so." She began her descent.

Pat and Dan followed.

∞∞∞ ⊖ ∞∞∞

Halfway between the 500-watt work-light and the doorway, Roger stopped climbing, changed the sponged-flashlight from one hand to the other and adjusted his footing. Looking up, he could see an odd shaped silhouette inside a square box of light, climbing very slowly. With the assumption that things were going as planned, he continued his descent. But he was cold now, and wished he'd brought a jacket. After climbing another half-dozen feet he stopped again, shouting, "Hey Daniel! It's freezing down here! You should have warned me!"

Still near the top of the ladder, Daniel stopped climbing. "That's right," he said to himself. "I totally forgot." Louder: "I'll grab us sweaters!"

Now Cameron stopped. "You're leaving us?"

"Only for a second." Daniel moved up two rungs.

"But... " she huffed.

"Cameron, it's cold down there. Can't you feel it yet? I'm grabbing us something to wear because we'll need it. Trust me. So just keep climbing, please. No offence, but you're slower than shit."

Cameron's eyes shifted left and right as her lips pursed together. Reluctantly she said, "Alright." But Roger seemed to be *way* down there now, and she had a bad feeling growing inside the hollows of her stomach, a *very* bad feeling.

She looked up, seeing that Patrick had also stopped climbing. He had no choice; he was caught between the two of them.

Higher than Pat, Daniel scrambled up the ladder. He plunked the lantern on the floor, pulled his body from the hole, and moved across the basement promptly. He didn't run but he moved fast, careful not to step on any tools that were lying about. Within a few seconds he was upstairs, looking through the front closet.

A jean jacket, a sweater, a blue hoodie, and a black hoodie, were bundled together in a ball.

The front door was open.

That's odd, he thought, looking outside. *Why is the door open?*

Seeing nothing out of the ordinary he closed the door and made his way to the basement, figuring Pat had left the door open. But was Pat in charge of closing the door, or was *he* in charge?

Standing at the mouth of the hole, Daniel yelled, "Hey Roger, I'm going to drop a jacket. Catch it?"

Roger had just descended past the work light. He said, "Wait a second, 'kay? Don't drop the jacket 'til I say."

Daniel said, "Hey Cameron, Pat… watch your head a minute and I'll try not to hit you with this thing."

Patrick leaned against the ladder.

Cameron looked up. She wanted out. That was the truth of the matter. She didn't care about the temperature or the clothing that was being dropped. She wanted out of the hole. It was all she could think about. It was beginning to nag at her, but she didn't want to say anything because being a team player was important. Besides, she'd be kicking herself if she didn't go down there and the guys found something valuable and *didn't* split it with her.

"Cameron," Daniel repeated. "Did you hear me?"

"I hear you. I'm just thinking, is all. Don't worry about it."

"You okay?"

"I'm fine."

Beneath them, Roger yelled, "I'm going to drop the flashlight!

Here it goes!"

He let the flashlight fall from his hand and watched it drop. For a moment he thought it would fall forever, but of course, it didn't. It hit the ground, bouncing a couple times before settling. Best of all, the light didn't break. It kept on shinning; the sponges worked beautifully.

"Bingo!" Roger shouted. "I can see the ground! It's not too much farther. Maybe another sixty feet."

"Hey Pat," Dan said, talking loudly. "Change of plan. I'm going to drop this stuff down to you first. The sweater is for Cameron."

"Yeah, okay."

"Be careful. If you catch it, great, but if not, let it fall. You can put it on at the bottom. Ready?"

"Ready."

Dan dropped the sweater and the blue hoodie together. They floated and tumbled and slid along a wall. Patrick caught them with ease.

"Nicely done," Dan said. "Hey Roger! Are you ready for the jacket?"

"Drop it!"

"Okay! Here it comes!"

Daniel dropped the jacket, making sure it wouldn't hit Pat or Cameron. It didn't. The jacket hugged the wall on the far side and went right past, looking like an oversized broken balloon, plummeting and rolling. Roger put his hand out, hoping to catch it. The 500-watt light put a glare in his eye and as a result he couldn't see the jacket coming. It cuffed his elbow and kept moving, bouncing and tumbling off the wall again. It hit the ground next to the flashlight with an empty thump, darkening the area below.

"Damn," Roger mumbled. "Missed it."

Daniel yelled, "You okay?"

Stepping down two more rungs, Roger shouted, "It went past me! No worries… see you at the bottom!"

"Great! Be with you in a minute!" Daniel pulled the black hoodie over his head and stepped onto the ladder. He started climbing down fast. Knowing the bottom was reasonably close energized him.

Pat dropped a sweater to Cameron.

Cameron caught it and pulled it over her head. A moment later Pat and Cameron continued their descent to the sound of Daniel's excited voice saying, "I'm catching up!"

Feeling the ladder shake in her hands, Cameron climbed faster, ignoring the fact that small pieces of dirt were falling from the bottom of Patrick's shoes. Nervous tension tickled her senses. Her stomach started to feel funny. It wasn't the height bothering her, but she was never a fan of tight spaces and falling debris. Still, she felt some level of comfort knowing Daniel had joined them once again. Not wanting Patrick on top of her, she said, "Slow down, I'm moving as fast as I can."

Pat slowed, mindful of the situation.

Daniel slowed too. "Be careful Cameron. I didn't mean to rush you. The last thing we need is an accident."

"Don't worry. I'm being careful." Cameron reached the work light, which was bright to a point of blinding. Once she passed it the temperature seemed to plunge.

Roger reached the bottom and felt an unexpected rush of energy. The air was filled with a damp, musty smell that reminded him of being inside an old barn. He dismissed the foul scent, even though it was strong and unpleasant. The hammer and the crowbar were on the ground, along with the flashlight and the jacket. He pushed the tools towards the nearest wall with his feet and lifted the jacket off the concrete floor. As he slid an arm into the jacket sleeve, he looked left and right. He couldn't see much; the place was a darkened mystery. With the jacket on he lifted the flashlight off the ground, ripped the sponges and the duct tape free, and dropped the unwanted material next to the hammer. He moved the light in a sweeping motion, slowly stepping into the shadows. The area around him seemed big, though it was nearly impossible to tell for sure.

"Hey Roger?" It was Cameron.

"Yeah?"

"Point the light this way, would you? I can't see anything."

Roger directed the flashlight's beam up the shaft.

Cameron began climbing again, faster now than before. When she reached the bottom she was glad to be off the ladder. Her arms and legs were tired, her back was sore, her heart was thumping quickly and her fingers were beginning to ache. "Thanks."

"No problem." Roger pointed his flashlight up the shaft again, guiding Pat through his last few steps. He did the same for Daniel.

"Thanks man," Dan said as he jumped to the ground. "What's that smell?"

"Not sure."

"Almost smells like moss or something."

"Yeah. I was thinking the same thing. It's a swamp smell."

Cameron unhooked her flashlight, turned it over in her fingers, and switched it on. The beam of light hit Daniel in the chest before it found his empty hands. "Hey Dan, where's the lantern?"

Daniel huffed, looking semi-embarrassed. "Like an idiot, I forgot it. The stupid thing is sitting next to the trapdoor."

"Smooth move."

"I know."

"Guys." Roger walked a couple feet, stepping into a short hallway. "Look at this." The flashlight beam hit the wall, illuminating three light switches. The switches were black; the wall was gray.

"Nice," Pat said with a smile.

Daniel flicked the switches on one at a time. Seconds passed. Something hummed. Overhead, fluorescent lights flickered, flashed, and eventually came on. Now they could see what was around them, and what they were standing in.

"Oh my God," Roger said, rubbing a hand against the side of his face.

Pat took a step forward. "This is amazing."

Cameron's eyes widened and her mouth slinked open. Taking Daniel by the hand, she whispered, "I know exactly what you mean."

14

William McMaster looked like his brother Roger, only he was taller and had a bigger frame. He was the type of guy that analyzed things frequently and figured he was getting ripped off constantly. For this reason, plus a few others, most of the locals liked Roger more than William. He knew it. Didn't like it. More often than not he was grumpy and frustrated. People figured he had unresolved issues, which he did. But deep down, when you got past his analyzing and his negativity, his issues and his rough exterior, Will was a nice man with a big heart.

He entered *The Big Four O* through the side door, which was ratty, weathered, and not worth a roll of quarters. It had rust on the knob and dried paint hanging from the wood. He thought about replacing the door often, along with the doormat, the hinges, and at least four of the windows on the backside of the building. Wasn't going to happen today, though. William wasn't alone. He was with Beth Dallier, a longtime friend.

Beth was a tough old girl, tougher than an army boot. She had strong hands, a thick neck, and a nest of hair looked like it had been cut it with a knife. Her lips were big and her nose was wide. Some assumed she was gay. Others figured she was bi-sexual. William didn't know or care. If he had to place a bet, he'd say she was asexual, which was a term he had only recently come across. It fit though, fit like a glove.

"Mind your step." William flicked the overhead lights on and made his way to the counter.

Beth followed, walking along like a lumberjack. Heavy footsteps rumbled through the building. "Beer?"

"You want one? I don't plan on being here long."

"I'd rather have a couple drinks here than pay for them all night at the Waterfront Café. Let's sink a couple and go, yes? I'll get the first round when we get there."

William nodded, stepped behind the bar and lifted a bottle of Jack Daniels from a shelf. He poured a pair of shots and put the bottle away.

"To your health," he said.

"Down the hatch."

Beth and William clinked glasses and swallowed the whiskey with eyes squeezed tight. Will snagged couple beers from the fridge and put the shot glasses in the sink. He opened the bottles and handed one to Beth as she plunked herself on a stool.

Wrapping her knuckles on the bar, she said, "What's this?"

"What's what?"

Beth lifted Roger's letter, glanced at the first line and handed it over.

William scanned the words quickly, mumbling while he read. His eyes seemed to expand while he was reading. "Huh. Looks like Cam and my brother are drinking over at Daniel's place. Wanna go there?"

"I don't know. Maybe. Do I know Daniel? Who's that?" Beth stroked her chin like she had a beard on it, which, thankfully, she didn't. Her skin was clear and smooth. Physically, it was her best feature.

"You might know 'em. He's a summer guy. Good looking, friendly, has that city vibe."

"City vibe? Most city guys tend to come into town acting like they own the place."

William raised an eyebrow. "Cameron's city folk."

"Yeah... but she's one of us too. A couple of years in university doesn't make you city, not completely. She's different now, though. Do you see it?"

"Cam's embarrassed is all. I can tell. That boyfriend stuck the knife in and twisted it a fair bit, and now she's... let's just say she's having a tough time. You don't need a PHD to recognize *that*."

"Huh."

Beth took a fair sized drink of beer followed by another. Will stepped into the kitchen. A few seconds later he stepped out again, satisfied that things were okay.

"What do you want to do, Will? Wanna hang with your brother?"

Although he wasn't ready for another beer, he pulled two more from the fridge and slid one towards Beth. "Yeah, let's say hello. You can meet Daniel, if you don't know him already. After a bit we'll hit the Waterfront; maybe they'll join us. If they do, well, the more the merrier. If they don't, that's good too. It'll give us somethin' to talk about while we drink."

Beth finished her beer with authority, slid the empty bottle across the bar and watched it move. "Sounds good to me," she said. Clearing her throat, she opened her next beer. "We'll go after this drink."

15

"What is it?" Cameron asked, squeezing Daniel's hand.

"Not sure," Daniel moved away from Cameron, uncoupling their fingers as he stepped out of the hall and into the giant room.

"I know what it is," Roger said with a nod. "Sure I do. It's a bomb shelter."

"Really?" Cameron squinted her eyes and furrowed her brow. She had her doubts. Bomb shelters on television were average in size, wall-to-wall computers, and loaded with supplies. This room was enormous—the size of two gymnasiums attached together. It had forty-foot ceilings. And not only that, it was empty. There was nothing in it, nothing at all. No food, no water—nothing. "A bomb shelter? You sure?"

"Just look around. The walls are made of concrete; the room is absolutely *buried* in the earth. What else could it be?"

"I don't know, but why would there be a bomb shelter here? This isn't New York City; it's Cloven Rock."

Roger chuckled. "Question for you Cam… during a nuclear holocaust, where would you rather be… New York City or Cloven Rock? Or here's another way to look at it: if you wanted to kill as many people as possible, where should you detonate a bomb? Here, or somewhere bigger? This is a bomb shelter, built by someone with lots of money. You can count on it." He turned away. "Hey Dan, you bought this place like, what, ten years ago?"

"About that, yeah."

"Who'd you buy it from?"

"Uh, I could check the records I guess, but off-hand I don't know. I only met the guy twice. I dealt with the real estate agent."

"This is so cool," Pat said. "We could play indoor soccer."

"Yeah," Dan said. "Too bad the balls are still in the garage."

Dan and Pat walked towards the center of the room. Footsteps echoed off the walls. Cameron turned in a circle before walking quickly to catch up. Roger just stood there. He was partly amazed, partly ready for a warmer climate. There was nothing to see here, nothing to do. The mystery had been solved and the prize was nothing more than the memory of the climb.

"Hey guys," he said. "Where're ya going?"

"To look around." Daniel clicked off his flashlight.

"Yeah," Pat agreed. "Let's take a walk."

Roger scrunched his face and lifted his shoulders in disagreement. "Look around... at what? There's nothin' to see in here. The place is empty!"

"Come on Rog," Dan said. "Don't be a stick in the mud. Live a little."

"But—" Roger rolled his eyes. They were going to investigate the big empty room no matter what he thought. He couldn't change their minds. The choice was clear. He could either A) climb up the ladder alone and be a *loser*, or B) join his friends. Not much selection from his point of view. "Shit guys... wait for me."

Roger dashed towards them.

Cameron walked backwards, looking at the ceiling. She thought she saw something move, but with the duct work and the shadows it was hard to tell.

Daniel stopped walking completely.

Once they were all together, Daniel said, "Let's circle the room once and head back up."

"Damn straight," Roger said. "It's cold down here. You sure you wanna circle the room? Maybe we should just go back."

Daniel frowned.

Pat said, "Let's look around."

Roger shook his head. "Again, I must ask: look at what? This place is empty! It's a big vacant box."

"You're a big vacant box," Cameron said, smirking.

Daniel giggled. He glanced into Cameron's eyes and smiled. Before he knew he would do it his line of vision rolled down her body, slowing at her breasts. Whoops. It was an honest mistake. Oh well, too late now.

Cameron grinned.

And Dan realized that he liked this girl. Not just physically, and not enough to have an affair with (he loved his wife too much for that), but Cameron was a fun girl to be around. She mixed her femininity and her 'just one of the guys' thing nicely.

Silence.

Pat said, "Hey, what's that?"

"What?"

"That!" He pointed to something embedded in the wall, and together, the four explorers walked across the room slowly, investigating the unknown. "It's a big door." Pointing at a handle. "See?"

It was a door, all right, a big wooden one. But it didn't look like a house door or a cupboard door; it didn't look like a car door or a set of patio doors. It was the size of a garage door, and it looked like part of the wall, with a handle.

Roger wondered if something good was hiding behind of it.

It's a secret room, Daniel thought, *a secret room inside a secret room.*

"Maybe we'll find treasures down here yet!" Roger said. "Should I open it?"

"Treasure?" Patrick mocked, releasing a condescending chuckle. "Do you idiots expect to find *treasure*? That's hilarious."

"You never know," Cameron contested.

"Yes you do. Treasures are only found in movies where pirates have a patch over one eye and a parrot strapped to a shoulder. Are you guys for real?"

With a soft, mocking voice, Roger said, "Treasure is the wrong word, old boy. The proper word is 'antiques'. We were hoping to find some antiques; know what I mean? We're hoping to find something that might have been worth a fair bit of change a hundred years ago, and has increased in value since… like pottery, or rare art. We're not expecting to find a trunk filled with gold or a shiny chalice."

"Oh," Pat said, scratching himself behind the ear. "Yeah, I guess that could happen. Well then, I stand mistaken. Let's open the door!"

Daniel wrapped his fingers around the handle. He pushed and pulled on the door. It moved both ways freely, and the nasty smell they noticed earlier became all the more noticeable.

Cameron stepped back. The smell reminded her of rotten fruit, spoiled milk, wet fur, and decaying meat. Needless to say, she didn't care much for the aroma. It gave her a bad feeling deep inside. Something was wrong here. The warning flares were blasting inside her mind the way they always did when something was off beam. Experience had taught her that ignoring her premonitions only led to grief and sorrow, and she had learned from her past to respond to her instincts. "I don't want to be here," she said flatly, keeping her voice in check.

Pat examined her face. "What?"

"You heard me. I want to get going. It smells bad down here and I don't like it. I want to go upstairs."

"But Cameron," Roger said, putting his hand on her arm. "Why?"

Cameron pulled her arm away vigorously. "I'm scared, is that okay with you? Something isn't right down here. Can't you feel it? There's something in that room. I can tell."

Roger's shoulders slumped. "Cameron—"

"I don't care if you believe me... I can *sense* it. It's like I'm standing inside a dream that's about to become a nightmare, you know? I feel like Carrie White at the bloody prom. I don't like being down here, not at all. Not one bit. Look where we are!" She took a step back, lifted her shoulders and extended her arms. "I don't like the smell down here. I don't like that big creepy door, and I don't want any part of what's behind it. I'm getting out."

"It does stink," Patrick quietly said, adding a shoulder shrug to his statement. "I wasn't going to say anything but I've got to admit, she's not wrong. Smells like monkey shit down here. In fact, it smells like monkey shit *covered* in monkey shit."

Cameron needed out. She turned away from the three men and she started walking towards the ladder. She wanted to run as fast as her legs would carry her, only pride didn't allow it. She forced herself to stay calm, forced herself to walk. Everything would be okay as long as she moved away from the door and out of the cellar. *(Bomb shelter, she reminded herself. This isn't a cellar; it's a bomb shelter. Who knows what's down here? It could be anything!)*

"Wait Cameron," Roger said. "You're being silly!"

She wasn't listening.

"Let her go," Daniel said.

"But—"

"Rog, how long do we plan on staying down here? You want to spend the night? Like you said, it's friggin' cold down here."

Roger grunted. "The amount of time we're down here will depend on what we find. How big is this next room, and what do you think is inside? Anything good?"

As the two men turned towards the door, it swung towards them. Cameron was right. Something *was* inside and it wasn't treasure. Something was alive and looking at them, pushing the door open, making the hinges squeak.

Pat didn't notice. He was looking at Cameron, and slowly walking towards her. He said, "Awe, don't go. Stay!"

Roger stepped back a foot. His mouth slid open and his eyes widened.

Daniel put a hand to his face. His flashlight slipped from his fingers, bounced off the floor, and rolled towards Pat.

Pat stopped eying Cameron when the light hit the floor. Instinctively, he looked down. Seeing the light roll towards his feet, he crouched to pick it up.

And the thing in the darkness, the thing with no name, shuffled its enormous legs, snapped three of its twelve sets of jaws, and began to hiss.

It sounded angry.

It sounded like a kettle.

16

William returned to his car much like his brother had, with a bag filled with beer bottles in one hand, and a set of keys in the other. The car was a 1979 firebird, rusted to the nines.

In the front seat was Hellboy, a pure brown Boxer that had big bulging eyes and feet the size of snowshoes. He was the type of dog that slobbered all over the place, never stopped shedding, had lots of gunk in its fur, and dropped turds the size of watermelons all over the yard. On a better note, the dog rarely barked and never went to the bathroom in places that caused trouble. But he did have a fair amount of energy and some days William wondered why he shelled out six hundred bucks for the stupid thing. Eat, sleep, and piss: that's what Hellboy did. When he wasn't begging for a walk, or getting walked, or begging for food, or unloading one of his watermelon sized turds, that's what he did: eat, sleep, and piss. It was quite a life.

As Beth and William opened the car doors, Will said, "Get in the back seat dog... now!"

Hellboy lowered his head, licked his snout, and wagged his stumpy tail, shaking his ass (and half his body) in the process. He jumped onto the backseat gracelessly, with his snowshoe feet thumping the fabric. He walked in small circles before his head found residence between the two front seats. He licked Beth's large arm as she plunked herself into the car.

Once they were on the road, William rolled down his window, pulled a smoke from his pack, and lit it. He offered one to Beth, even though he only had four left. He was good like that, a generous man.

"How far?" Beth asked, taking a cigarette from the pack.

"By the time your smoke is gone we'll be there."

"Yeah?" Beth raised an eyebrow. "We'll see." She lit the cigarette and rolled down her window.

Hellboy plodded around the backseat. He stuck his head out the window, opened his mouth, and allowed his tongue to unfurl. His tongue flapped and fluttered like a thick, wet flag. Drool hung from his jaw and drops of white spittle hit the side of the car every few seconds; he was a doggie rain-machine. Occasionally he tried to bite the air.

They drove past Nicolas Nehalem's car and pulled into Daniel's driveway a few seconds later. Beth crushed her cigarette in the dirt and followed Will to the front door, admiring the flowerbed in the yard. No flowers yet, she noticed, but the brickwork looked stunning.

William rang the bell twice then checked the door. It was unlocked. He stepped inside. Beth followed. Hellboy entered next with his stumpy tail tucked low. He didn't bark, but *did* consider it.

Something, the dog knew, was wrong.

17

Legs were everywhere, long and heavy, muscular and strong. They were covered in a thick brown fur, similar to that of a scavenging hyena. Limbs—eleven feet long, twelve feet long, sometimes *thirteen* feet long—were equipped with three, often four sets of fat, elbow-like joints. Below the ankle joint—if that's what it was—the limbs were endowed with a sharp, curved point. It was a stinger, shaped like a sickle. But not all limbs were created this way; some were different, ending with a hard, black claw, like those on a lobster or crab.

The body of the creature was fat and round. Its skin was dark leather, swimming in bugs, bubbles, and patches of thin hair. But these things didn't characterize the body. To be accurate, the body's husk was crowded with two basic elements: eyes and mouths. Yes, the back end of the creature had a large anus cavity, a *single* anus cavity, shaped like a volcano. But the rest of the body was nourished in eyes and mouths. The eyes were black and swollen, the size of a man's fist. They had no lids, lashes or brows. They were globular, shiny— terrifyingly empty. The mouths were nearly the size of a medicine ball, loaded with teeth. Some were eyeteeth, fangs, daggers; most were crushers, molars, used for cutting food and grinding. Many were squared like a brick. Some looked like small anvils; some were rounded, broken and cracked. In a few places, there were no teeth at all. Just holes. And from behind these daggers and anvils, these bricks and holes, the creature screamed its kettle sounds.

SQUUUUUUEEEE*EEEEEEEEEEEE.*

Daniel ran.

Cameron turned.

Roger huffed with his eyes pinned to the beast.

Patrick picked the flashlight off the ground. "You dropped this," he said.

Oblivious.

Not because he couldn't hear what was happening, but because everything happened at once: Patrick Love spoke, Daniel McGee ran, Cameron English turned away, and the monster shrieked, pouncing like a wolf-spider, knifing Roger McMaster while he gasped. It used three stingers concomitantly, stabbing ribs and lungs and breaking Roger's back before he had a chance to move. Then Pat was knocked over and a clawed foot landed on him, holding him against the ground.

Roger screamed a breathless scream, which the others felt more than heard. Blood filled his lungs. His body twitched violently, the creature's eyes crawled on him like venomous snakes and for a brief and horrific moment the monster's enormous teeth held their position in front of his face. It was the calm before the storm; the calm before the teeth came snapping together, chomping Roger's face in half.

Begging, Roger said, "Please."

That was all.

The teeth slammed into his skull. Blood and brains splashed in several directions. Body convulsing, Roger's arms slapped against fur. A piece of bone fell, banging off a trembling shoulder. Legs quivered like they were being electrocuted as the creature pulled its husk in a new position. It bit down a second time, using a new set of jaws, a fresh set, an empty set. Now Roger's head was gone. In its place was a fountain of blood, a jet stream of blood, a tornado of blood that didn't want to end. The man's neck was a nozzle spraying freely. Arms and legs turned limp.

The creature bit down again, devouring Roger's neck and the top part of his chest. A crescent appeared in the area between the shoulders, which was hemispherical now, shaped like a half moon, a grotesque smile, the reaper's sickle. Shoulders slumped low and lifeless on each side of the wound, deflating above the remains of a t-shirt, which slid into dripping red piles around the dead man's waist.

The creature changed position, pulling its body through the doorway.

Legs shifted and lifted. Roger was stabbed again. A fourth mouth tore a shoulder apart and a bright wash of blood poured from the wound. An arm fell to the floor. The monster repositioned its meal and tore a generous opening into Roger's ribcage. Intestines dropped in a coiled heap. The next bite took the other shoulder—the *left* shoulder. This time, the arm went with it. The bite after that created a cavity in Roger's abdominal area. The cavity made a horrific opening that ended near his pelvic bone. Entrails hung like noodles. Seven mouths were feeding; five waited in line. The eighth bite was a large one, taking ribs, spine, bowels and pelvis. Two legs remained. One landed beside Pat, splashing in the fresh red pond. Two mouths consumed the limb, dividing their food above the knee. Roger's final leg was snatched up with mouths devouring their food in near-equal portions. The beast shuffled its legs again. And all that remained of Roger was a rope of intestine, an arm, and a few hard to define pieces, sitting together in a puddle of gore.

18

Daniel ran, shouting, "Run! Get out of here!"

Cameron's shoulders shot upward as she spun herself around. Her eyes clamped onto the great creature and her mind seemed to lock up, frozen between thoughts. Inspirations vanished; questions became lost. She didn't run. Just watched. Mouth open, eyes wide, she watched the beast stab its limbs into Roger's body. She watched him convulse as the beast devoured his head.

Daniel ran past.

He stopped, turned around. He could see Cameron's feet glued to the ground and Roger's limbs dancing madly, doing the funky chicken.

"Run!" he said again; then he went back. Not that he wanted to go back; he didn't. He wanted to run fast and keep on running until everything seemed like some terribly impossible dream. But sometimes people don't do what they *want* to do. Sometimes they do what they *have* to do. And Daniel McGee had to go back.

He grabbed Cameron by the arm and pulled. Cameron tripped and fell. She landed on her elbows hard enough to break them. Pain shocked her senses. Dirt puffed into the air. Her flashlight rolled across the ground, circling a half loop before it stopped rolling. She let out a squeal and glanced at the monster again. It looked like a fourteen-foot wide bowling ball with legs and teeth.

She eyed Pat, still trapped beneath a limb.

His arms waved and his feet kicked. He was trying to scream, but with the air crushed out of him he was unable.

"Oh my God," she whispered, still sitting on the floor.

Daniel stepped in front of her, blocking her view of the beast and its prey. He looked half mad with fear, half mad with frustration. "CAMERON! GET UP NOW! LET'S GO!"

She said, "Oh shit! We've got to get out of here!"

"COME ON!"

"What?"

"GET UP! GET UP! FOR GOD'S SAKE, GET THE HELL UP OR I'M LEAVING YOU HERE!"

Daniel looked over his shoulder, away from Cameron. What he saw made him feel lightheaded. The creature—the thing, whatever it was—was eating Roger. Eating him quickly, without pause, without hindrance. One big bite at a time, Roger was disappearing. Being swallowed. Being chewed.

Like a fat kid on a cookie, he thought oddly.

Cameron twisted her body to the left, stealing another glimpse.

Both of them saw the same thing now: the creature was consuming Roger's chest. Blood poured on the floor, onto Patrick. Quite simply, buckets of blood were falling. Neither could believe their eyes. There was more blood rushing out of him than either thought possible. And while Daniel figured the beast would come charging at them within seconds, Cameron was sure the creature's eyes were not focused on Roger, but on her.

It was watching.

Cameron staggered to her feet, feeling a wave of nausea that made the room spin. Her eyes watered and fluid ran from her nose.

Daniel grabbed her by the hand and pulled.

They were running now, running towards the exit. Daniel was the fast one. Maybe under different circumstances Cameron would be faster. But here, now, it was Daniel. His legs moved quick and efficiently, with strong easy strides, like he was born to run, born to escape impossible situations.

Cameron's feet slapped against the ground awkwardly, her head was too low, her arms were swinging wildly and her balance was off. She was ready to fall to her knees, twist an ankle, crash.

For Cam's benefit, Daniel slowed his pace. It was against his better judgment but he didn't want her to fall a second time. If she did it would be the end of the road for the both of them. Or maybe just her, depending on how he played it.

"Hurry," he whispered urgently, with his heart trapped in his stomach. "Come on!"

Cameron pulled her hand free from Daniel's grasp and stopped running. "Wait," she said. "Oh God wait a minute, please!"

Before Daniel had a chance to protest she put both of her hands on her knees, opened her throat, and her mouth, and vomited. Legs wobbled and hands quivered. Some of the discharge splashed onto her shoes and pants. Some of it made its way into her hair.

Daniel watched the sickness happen. It wasn't pretty, but it was better then the other event, which he looked at next:

The creature was eating Roger's remains, which wasn't much: two legs, a groin and part of a ribcage. It wasn't an act of violence; Roger was a meal. Whether that was better or worse, Daniel did not know.

Watching Cameron be sick was less disturbing.

And what about Patrick? He wondered. *Am I just going to leave him here? Is that the plan?*

The first beads of sweat appeared on Daniel's temple and a wave of helplessness engulfed him. This was bad, so very, very bad. Pat was about to be eaten alive. He was about to die.

Daniel shook his head, snapping the daze.

He had to be optimistic, not pessimistic. That was the key to everything. Optimism. Confidence. Intelligence. There was still a hope if he demanded it, which is what he would have to do. Demand it.

All is not lost. I can escape this. I can survive.

Yes, but what about Patrick? And what about Cam? Will they survive? Or is it time to look out for number one?

The ladder was close, less than fifteen feet from where he stood.

Cameron was sick again. Behind her, the beast snatched another bite. A leg fell to the ground, splashing in blood.

Daniel could see Patrick. He was alive, trapped beneath the beast.

He couldn't wait any longer. Waiting, Dan firmly believed, was suicide. And he waited long enough already, perhaps too long.

He grabbed Cameron by the hair and pulled her towards the ladder. He wasn't nice about it. His fingers closed into a fist and he pulled her as hard as he could manage. In a different situation he would have earned a punch in the mouth and a trip to court.

"COME ON!" he screamed. And it *was* a scream. He sounded like a siren, or like a scream queen in a movie. He had never sounded like *that* before. "GODDAMN IT! WE'VE GOT TO MOVE OR WE'RE GOING TO DIE!"

He pulled her again.

Now Cameron screamed.

She screamed in pain, but getting her hair pulled was the least of her worries. This pain was nothing compared to what was coming. She needed to get her ass in gear. Daniel knew it and she knew it too. She stumbled another foot or two, falling to one knee while she slapped his hand away. She felt her stomach churn; it continued working against her. She was going to be sick again.

Daniel looked at the monster, then Pat, and then he stepped away.

Enough, he thought.

Something inside him changed.

"I have to go, Cameron," he said, panting, with a voice that seemed distant. "I'm sorry." His bottom lip trembled. A drop of sweat rolled along his cheekbone. He wasn't screaming. Not now. That time had passed; his voice was practically a whisper.

He was leaving her.

She was going to die.

Daniel didn't want Cameron or Pat to be ripped into pieces by that thing—whatever it was—but it was going to happen. He didn't have time for this, for her, for them. Cameron was going to get them both killed if he let things continue this way; he understood that now.

There was no saving this girl.

This stranger, he reminded himself. *I can't get myself killed over somebody I met an hour ago. It's not fair to me, or my wife.*

Maybe Cameron didn't want to be saved. It was a possibility. Or maybe she did. Live another day; die another day. It didn't matter now. She was going to give up the ghost right here in the basement— or cellar, or bomb shelter, if that's what it was. He couldn't change her fate. He couldn't change anything.

Daniel turned away from Cameron.

"Wait," she begged. She picked herself up and stumbled towards him, coughing and spitting. She reached out with unsteady fingers.

"We've got to go, Cameron," he said. And with that, he made for the ladder. And somewhere behind him, the creature shifted its weight and shuffled its legs.

And Patrick screamed.

19

William and Beth entered the basement just as Daniel began to climb. They didn't hear the screams. They didn't hear anything.

But Hellboy did.

Hellboy heard everything, sensed everything. He didn't want to leave the main floor of the house and wander down those thirteen steps. He didn't like the smell that was coming from the basement. Smelled like blood, some type of predator, possibly a wolf. The scent made him nervous, made him scared, made him growl.

Beneath his breath, Hellboy released a pair of protest barks. He snapped his teeth. Not once, but twice. Then he paced back and forth at the top of the staircase. Eventually, he made his way down a few stairs, followed by a few more. He sniffed the railing and lowered his tail, holding it tight against his legs.

Beth stood in the center of the empty room with a shit-eating grin creeping across her face. She said, "Wow. What wonderful friends you have here, Will. These people are amazing."

William issued Beth a lengthy light-hearted scowl. "Very funny."

"Thank you." Beth gave a little curtsy and kicked a chunk of dry-wall. She hadn't noticed the hole in the floor. It was easy to miss with the entire basement in shambles. "Looks like they've been doing some renovating," she said more seriously.

"Yes, it looks that way. Maybe they went into the backyard for a smoke. Wanna go check?"

"Yeah, I guess. There's no point in being down here."

Just then, as Beth was speaking, Hellboy came down the last few stairs. He made his way across the basement and stood at the edge of the hole, clearly upset, looking down, growling louder now than before. Very uncharacteristically, he began barking and flaunting his teeth.

"What is that thing?" Beth asked with a nod, referring to the hole in the floor.

"Not sure. Looks like a hole. Maybe there's a sub-floor?" William couldn't help thinking that something strange was happening here. Was there a rodent near by, or a fox? If so, that would explain a lot. Hellboy hated wild animals. Always had.

Will made his way to the opening and stood beside his dog, looking down with one hand curled in a fist. "Oh my," he said. Surprise washed his face clean. "What in the world is going on?"

20

Daniel heard something: a dog perhaps, a dog barking. He didn't know for sure what he heard; he didn't own a dog. Had one when he was a kid but that was a long while ago. The dog, Sputnik was her name, had been hit by a car back when Christmas meant toys, girls were yucky, and parents knew everything in the whole wide world. (*A truck, he reminded himself. Damn thing got smucked by a truck, not a car. You were there, remember? Sputnik was squished on a hot summer day by a full-sized transport truck. The streak of blood stretched thirty feet.*)

Dan didn't want to think about it.

He climbed, with arms and legs moving at a rate that would have made his father proud, God rest his soul. His heart raced inside his chest. His fingers throbbed, still sore from renovating. He didn't notice the pain in his fingers, not yet. Not while he was climbing. His mind was elsewhere: on Patrick and Cameron, on survival, on moving up the ladder as fast as he could and escaping the monster below.

He made his way past the work light, which hung by the extension cables like some ridiculous science experiment designed by children. He heard the sound again, the sound of the dog. A dog was barking, he was sure of it.

Slowing his pace, he looked up.

People were looking down at him, two of them. And there *was* a dog. Good, good. He wasn't going crazy, not yet anyhow. And that was a very promising sign, all things considered.

The ladder shook in his hands.

Oh *shit*, he thought. *I'm a dead man now. That goddamn thing is climbing the ladder, coming to get me, coming to chew me into paste.*

He slowed his pace another notch and looked down.

The glare from the work light made his eyes squint. The monster wasn't shaking the ladder. It was Cameron. Thank heaven. He was glad it wasn't the monster, and glad to see that Cam was all right. He was worried, figured she was a goner too—like Roger, like Patrick.

No, he thought. *That's not fair. I don't know if Pat is a goner. That thing trapped him, yes, that's a fact. But I didn't see him getting killed. He could still be alive. He could still be okay.*

Daniel kept climbing. The ladder kept shaking.

He could feel the sweat on his skin, his shirt clinging to his chest. The air was getting warmer now, and with the energy he was expelling he found it hard to breathe. This level of exercise was unexpected after working all day and sinking several beers. But like it or not, he was getting a workout, a big one.

At the halfway point he stopped climbing and he looked over his shoulder. The creature was nowhere to be seen. Cameron was alone and climbing, but moving very slowly. Her lack of speed made him want to strangle her. The fact that she was okay made him want to kiss her.

He thought about Patrick again.

Pat needed help.

Daniel took a deep breath and tried to yell down; the words became snagged in his throat. He put a hand on his chest and tried again: "HURRY UP CAMERON!"

Overhead the dog kept barking.

He could hear people talking, telling the dog to shut-up.

Six more steps, followed by a four more. He wondered what the monster was doing now. Perhaps it was killing Pat, or maybe it had returned to its home, its nest. Was that possible? Was that likely? He didn't know. He was halfway up the ladder and his sense of urgency was fading. He felt safer now. In fact, he almost felt *safe.* And he didn't know what the monster was doing. All he could do was guess. Part of him wished he'd never know.

After eight more steps he looked down again.

Cameron was climbing up the ladder, but things had changed.

The monster was beneath her now, scaling the wall with slow methodical steps. Three legs gripped the concrete as two more found the ladder. There was a system to those legs; they moved with logical discipline. And yet each leg seemed ready to fight, ready for war.

Mouths opened and closed. Chewing.

The beast is still eating Roger, Dan thought. *Or maybe that's Pat. Oh man, it's gnawing on bones. Oh shit, oh shit. What is that thing? This can't be happening. This can't be—*

Cameron shrieked, cutting his thoughts in half. She must have looked down, seen the beast and realized it was coming after her.

"HURRY," Dan shouted.

Then the creature screeched loudly:

SQUUUUUUEEEE*EEEEEEEEEEE.*

The sound made Cameron's shoulders lift and her face turn pale, morphing into a mask of grave terror. Eyes, flooded with dread, bulged from their sockets, ready to pop from her head.

The monster's legs found new positions. Claws snapped shut, clamped together.

The ladder shook more now than before.

And Cameron screamed again, sounding like a terrified child. Once she was done screaming her limbs jumped into high gear; her arms and legs scrambled up the ladder like a cockroach scurrying across a cupboard door.

She wasn't the only one.

Daniel also climbed madly. The feeling of relative safety he briefly enjoyed had been instantly swept away. He was in danger now; they both were. This was their moment of truth, the moment both lives could end.

Up and up they traveled. Each rung looked the same as the next: rusty and solid. Only the shadows changed. Climbing the ladder was hard work, and even with the work-lights blasting, the shaft was *still* dark, and more than a little bit disturbing.

Daniel moved with grace and speed, and everything seemed to be okay until he slammed his knuckles on a rung. And lost his footing.

He was falling.

Oh God, he thought. *Oh please Lord no.*

Falling.

Falling was the worst feeling in the world, the absolute worst. Thankfully, it only lasted a moment. He slid down four rungs, grappling everything he could until he grabbed hold. His chin slammed against iron and his teeth clunked together, chipping a nugget from a tooth. Pain shot through his mouth and into his brain, causing him to release a squeal. There was a ringing in his ears, but at least he had stopped falling. It was something to be grateful for.

SQUUUUUUEEEE*EEEEEEEEEEEE.*

After the monster's shriek he heard something very faintly. It sounded like Pat yelling, "I'm still down here!"

He's still alive.

Dan pinched his eyes together and imagined Pat being devoured by the creature, one limb at a time. The pain of those teeth ripping through muscle and bone would be colossal. It would be death. But pain or no pain, Cameron or no Cameron, Patrick or no Patrick, Daniel had to keep moving. He just had to.

Life depended on it.

Daniel scrambled past the top rung and crawled free of the pit. He flipped onto his back, expelling huge mouthfuls of air. He put one hand on his chest and one hand to his face. He fingered his broken tooth. Needle-like pain riffled his gums.

William looked down at him, lost in his thinking. "What in God's name is going on, Daniel? Where's my brother?"

Daniel didn't answer.

Beth looked down at him, resembling a construction worker standing over a manhole. She rubbed her hands together.

William had said to her: *You might know Daniel. He's a summer guy. Good looking, friendly, has that city vibe.* She realized, looking into his face, that—*yes*, she *did* know Daniel. Not very well but that didn't matter. They had shared a drink or two at the Waterfront Café, and she wouldn't hesitate to say hello if she saw him on the street.

Beth's eyes shifted away from Daniel. She looked down the hole. She put a hand to her mouth. Color drained from her face with such velocity it looked like a special effect. Her brow wrinkled and her nose widened. She seemed to be turning into an old woman, right then and there.

She said, "What is that thing?"

William eyed Beth like she had lost her mind. "What thing?"

"That thing!" Beth bounced up and down and her big arms began waving. She shouted, "OH SHIT, GIRL, RUN! RUN!"

William grunted. He walked towards the hole, curious and confused.

At first he didn't see it—the thing, the monster, the giant creature with twenty-six legs, twelve mouths and countless eyes, the animal that was squeezing its body through the shaft, the brute that was less than twenty feet from making a grand entrance in Daniel's basement, the beast that had killed Roger. Eaten him, it fact. Eaten him alive within a matter of seconds. No, he didn't see *that*. And the reason was simple: he was focused on Cameron, the girl he had know all his life. She was only a few feet away and moving like greased lightning. He was looking at her, at the horror in her eyes, the terror clutching her face. He couldn't help but wonder what had happened.

His eyes shifted. And that's when he saw it: the thing behind her. He figured it was a grizzly bear.

Then he started to scream.

21

Cameron wasn't looking down. She didn't have time. The beast was right there. She could smell it. She could feel it. And even though the monster looked far bigger than the area it was crawling in, it was right behind her somehow, squeezing itself into the least possible places. It filled the entire shaft. She could see the beast without looking down; that was the truth of it. She could see it without taking her eyes from the ladder. And that was the important thing now: the ladder. Climbing the ladder. It was all she had to do, just climb the ladder and do it quickly. She didn't have time for anything else. She didn't have time to think. And, sure as shit, she didn't have time to ponder her relationship with Paul LaFalce, that lying, stinking, two-timing stack of ape-dung that worked at Hoppers Gas over on the 9th line. No, she *definitely* didn't have time to think about *him*. She had to get out of the pit and away from the danger. Get outside. Keep moving and not look down. For the love of her mother's eternal soul, and everything else she cared about, she needed to climb the ladder and *not look down.*

At one point it almost had her.

The creature leapt. One long stalk shot forward, slamming the wall beside her. The stalk was thick, so, so, thick. She couldn't believe it. The damn thing looked like a wooly black elephant leg with a claw on the end of it. She kept climbing; she didn't slow her pace. As startled as she was by the abomination, she didn't slow. She *couldn't* slow. Slowing would be dying. Slowing would be the end, the final curtain, the last dance. Just like it was for Roger.

Poor Roger. Poor dead Roger.

Poor dead Patrick.

She looked up, surprised to find that she was near the top of the ladder.

She pushed on. People were yelling and screaming; a dog was barking. Daniel was no longer climbing; he was gone. He had climbed his way to safety and survived. She wondered if William's dog was doing all that barking: Hellboy. She loved Hellboy; he was the cutest dog in the world, but it didn't matter. All that mattered was climbing.

She kept going.

She had nine more rungs.

Eight.

Seven. Six. And Hellboy kept barking. And yes, it *was* Hellboy! It was! She could tell by the sound of the bark.

Thank God! Hellboy had come to her rescue!

He had come to save her—which meant that William was nearby too. And William was a good man, a great man. He was amazing. He had strong arms and strong legs. He had a kind heart and a generous soul. And he'd know what to do about the situation, this awful nightmare that reared its ugly head. Yes sir. He'd know all right, and he'd get the job done lickety-split. And when he found out what happened to Roger, look out! He'd kill the creature with his bare hands; like a knight battling a dragon, he'd slay the beast!

Five. The monster opened a half dozen mouths; it began to scream. The voices sounded like a gang of sirens.

SQUUUUUUEEEE*EEEEEEEEEEEEE*.

Four. Three. Cameron's left foot clipped a rung, throwing her off balance, making her gasp, changing her momentum and slowing her down. Making her hesitate. Making her scared. But that was okay. It would *have* to be okay. If it wasn't she was done-for. Kaput. Defunct. Dead meat. Tag the toe and close the drawer, people—if she didn't get a move-on there would be nothing to see but a corpse, or what was left of it.

Two.

The creature made a move. It raised a limb, suspended the appendage near Cameron's feet and stabbed it into her. The poisonous stinger hit a leg, ripping a giant hole in her calf muscle, piercing her bone. It was in and out like a flash of lightning, leaving a gap the size of a doorknob.

Cameron crushed her eyelids together and stumbled. Biting back a scream, she ground her teeth and made a face that suggested she'd eaten something sour.

One.

Another flash. The stinger hit Cameron in the lower back, inches from her spine. The pain was enormous, historic.

Her mouth popped open. Now—from somewhere deep inside her lungs—she was screaming. Blood squirted from both wounds. White bubbles that looked like puss and milk mixed together streamed down her skin. Screaming. She was screaming and screaming. Her heart was racing, pounding in her chest.

Daniel's gutted basement appeared in front of her eyes. It was like she had changed channels. One channel was the ladder; the other channel was the basement.

She dragged herself halfway from the hole with her eyes watering, her body convulsing and her fingers digging marks into the floor. Her stomach was on fire, her back seemed broken, and her wounded leg was already turning numb.

Blood, mixed with something that tasted like battery acid, or maybe bleach, filled her mouth. She wanted to let go, fall, end it, but figured the creature would feast on her body the same way it feasted on Roger, swallowing her down in shark-sized bites.

She didn't want *that*.

Beneath her, the monster squeezed into a new position. It was good in tight spaces. Its body seemed to be built for it.

More sirens: SQUUUUUUEEEE*EEEEEEEEEEEE.*

She could see a dog.

It *was* Hellboy. Yes, the dog had come to save her.

It kept barking; someone stuck a hand in front of her face and she found herself grabbing it. Someone squeezed her fingers very hard before they let her go. She was grinding her teeth. White-bubbled puss ran from her mouth. Her heart felt like it was going to explode. Her stomach felt like it was boiling beneath her skin.

The beast was so close.

It would find its way inside Daniel's home any moment now. Then she would die, be eaten. They would *all* be eaten, even Hellboy. Hellboy wouldn't save her, the poor dog—poor unfortunate dog. It couldn't save the day. Nobody could. This was the end.

She caught a glimpse of William. His hands were beneath her armpits; his fingers were digging into her skin. She was being dragged away from the trapdoor, dragged across screws and drywall, nails and tools. He was saving her. She wouldn't fall to her death. Somehow she would be okay.

Her heart raced faster now, pounding her insides like it was trying to escape. *Let me out you stupid bitch*, her heart screamed. *Let me out!*

Everything began changing color; things were turning brown. Things were turning yellow, or were they green? She didn't know.

Her heart felt like it was being squeezed by vice grips.

She saw Daniel lying beside her, exhausted and panting, looking at her with a troubled smirk. His face reminded her of a scarecrow. He was saying something; with his eyes wide and his lips trembling he was saying something. But she couldn't make out the words. She didn't care. Not now. Her chest hurt too much for caring. She was in too much pain.

An oversized crab leg came through the hole in the floor. The leg had a stinger that looked like a half moon. There was blood on it—Cameron's blood, Roger's blood.

The creature had arrived.

She wanted to taste the blood from the stinger. It was a strange thought, but it was true. She loved blood. She wanted to lick it, wanted to suck it. She wanted to tear off her shirt and rub her tits up against it.

She saw a woman she barely recognized. The woman looked like Beth, but she looked like a bitch too, like a dyke—like a dry-cunt wench that needed to get shot. Cameron wanted to wrap her fingers around the woman's throat and strangle her until her eyes bugled out of her sockets. She wanted to bite off her nose and piss in her face.

The woman slammed the trapdoor.

With a BANG the monster's leg disappeared beneath the wood.

Was the woman was trying to save her?

Maybe, the rotten bitch. When she slammed the door on the beast, the door sounded like it locked. Why the hell did the woman do that? Who made her boss of the world?

The dog barked and barked. The sound was making her crazy. If she didn't know better she'd think the stupid thing was barking at her. *At her!* She eyed the dog for a moment only to find that it *was* looking at her. It was growling, with teeth exposed and saliva hanging from its jaw.

What's wrong boy? she wondered.

Then her heart stopped hurting and her stomach settled. Just like that, she felt better.

She felt better!

Everything was going to turn out just great!

She turned away from Hellboy, the senseless animal. Animals were so stupid, so fucking dense. They all were. She hated animals. She always hated animals. She wanted all the animals in the world to die in an enormous mammal holocaust.

She caught a glimpse of a crowbar lying on the floor beside her.

It was the future.

The future seemed very bleak.

The room swayed. She looked at her pants and her shoes. Her shoes had blood on them. The floor had blood on it too. William was trying to calm the dog down. Daniel was lying beside her. That stupid cunt was kneeling on the trapdoor. And the crowbar, oh boy, the *crowbar*. It was sitting next to her, calling her name. *Come get me*, it was saying. *I'm all yours!*

She snatched the crowbar off the floor, grinning. It felt heavy and cold. It felt good. Someone was screaming. The dog was barking. People were asking questions. *What are you doing?* they were saying, like it was any of their business. Might have been Daniel. Might have been the dog.

Daniel was an asshole. He left her down there by herself… with that thing! How could he? Who did he think he was? Didn't he know better? Didn't his momma raise 'em right?

She looked at Daniel lying on the floor next to her.

He looked scared now, so scared—like a boy that had seen a ghost. Or had come home from school to find his father swinging from a noose and his mother's head torn from her body.

Daniel looked cool in his jeans and his faded Black Sabbath t-shirt. She wanted to fuck him and suck him, but she hated his guts now. She wanted to stick her fingers into his eyes and make him scream until his brain bled. She wanted to cut off his head and shit down his throat.

He was a bitch. All men were bitches.

But she wanted to fuck him.

She thought about Paul LaFalce. If she ever got her hands on that son of a whore it would be game over for sure. She'd cut him into a million pieces and throw him in a fire. She'd scoop out his eyes and swallow them whole.

Things turned bad. The acid in her mouth seemed to be poison. The dog was snapping at her again and again; it looked insane. Its teeth were wet and glistening and huge. The crowbar: it was right there in her hand. It was the future, and it felt so fucking good, so fucking *right*.

She squeezed the iron tight.

Daniel looked like a little boy, like a brainless child.

Afraid of the big bad wolf, she thought. What an asshole.

But it wasn't the wolf that frightened Daniel; she understood that now. Oh yes, everything was crystal clear.

Daniel was afraid of her. Of her! She could tell.

The fucker was so stupid she wanted kill him. She wanted to rip off his balls and stuff them into his ears.

She tried to spit in his face and failed miserably. Blood and puss ran from her mouth, down her chest and onto the floor, creating a puddle. She didn't think it was getting pumped out. It rolled out of her, it seemed, like the liquid had nowhere else to go.

The trapdoor bounced up and down.

The fucking dyke-cunt screamed.

Cameron wanted the dog to stop barking. She wanted to take Daniel's fears away. She wanted to open the trapdoor and feed the dyke to the beast.

The crowbar felt good in her hand. It felt like the future.

It felt right.

∞∞∞ ⊖ ∞∞∞

At the top of the staircase Nicolas Nehalem stoked his shotgun. He was listening to the turmoil in the basement, wondering what the fuss was about.

He considered his options: it seemed like a good time to strike. A damn good time, perhaps this was the moment he'd been waiting for.

"Cameron," he whispered. "Cameron, my child."

He smiled then, and a runner of drool rolled over his lip and down his chin. He thought about her fingers: they would be healthy and fresh, juicy and sweet.

They would be delicious.

CHAPTER THREE:
JUNE 1ST, MONDAY NIGHT

1

Lying on his back with a hand on his chest, Daniel caught his breath. Cameron was beside him. Chunks of drywall sat near his feet; baseboards were at his sides. Various tools and piles of dust were scattered throughout the room.

Daniel turned his head to one side, trying to discount the chaos.

Cameron came into view.

She looked hurt; that much was obvious. But there was more. Cameron looked mad. Not furious mad, but *screwy* mad, maybe even insane.

Dan wondered how that was possible. *People don't just go insane*, he thought justly. He was right. This wasn't insanity; it was something altogether different. Cam's eyes had turned dark; her skin had become pale. Loss of blood, Daniel assumed. But there was something else, something more. She looked rabid. Yes, that's what it was: something akin to rabies had entered her bloodstream, making her crazy and unpredictable, making her shady. She seemed nothing like the girl he met in the restaurant.

Dan said, "Cameron, you okay? Hold it together." His voice was weak; his words seemed futile.

He looked away, watching the trapdoor bounce up and down as Beth knelt on top. Her thick arms and sturdy legs made her look like a football player crouched into position, ready for the play, ready to score, ready to give one hundred and ten percent while shouting *Go*

Team Go! Her eyes, however, carried a different expression. They weren't playing a game. Beth was scared shitless.

Hellboy didn't help the situation.

The dog barked loudly, adding to the tension, galloping across the room on his snowshoe feet like a disgruntled horse. The dog didn't like Cameron now; it didn't like anything. It ran to Beth barking and sniffing the floor. It raced to William snarling. Then it barked twice more and returned to Cameron, ready to strike.

Dan looked at Cameron.

Her face had changed, but not in a manner he could have predicted. Anguish was gone, replaced with anger and rage. If Daniel didn't know better he'd swear she was about to tear the hair from her head in bunches.

Daniel whispered, "Cameron?"

Without warning, Cameron grabbed the crowbar off the floor and held it in a way that could only mean trouble.

Worried she'd do something terrible, Dan sat up. He felt pain in his legs, hands, and stomach—the long climb up the ladder had come with a price. He said, "Cameron! What are you thinking?"

Hellboy barked wildly, holding a position near Cameron's feet. Its muzzle was pulled up in a vicious sneer. Long teeth were exposed.

Why now? Dan wondered. *Couldn't the dog pick a better time to go mad?*

"Stop that!" William said. He advanced on the dog, making it flinch.

At the same moment Cameron swung the crowbar. The iron hook connected with Hellboy's head and the dog went down, folding upon itself like a lawn chair. Blood sprayed the air, hitting Dan in the face and chest. The dog's legs twitched and the barking stopped. Blood poured from Hellboy's skull—lots of blood, enough to create a puddle.

Daniel gasped.

William screamed.

The room became slightly less chaotic.

Beth didn't seem to notice. She was busy dealing with the thing inside the shaft, the creature that had eaten Roger alive.

The floor rattled and shook. Hinges strained as the beast pounded the trapdoor with its thick, meaty limbs.

Beth, on her knees, rode the trap door as it bounced up and down. Her eyes were hockey pucks; her mouth was a basketball hoop. Her expression seemed to be asking the question: would it door hold, or would it fling open and toss her across the room like a rag-doll?

She said, "I need help, guys! This thing wants in! What are we going to do?"

Cameron slammed the iron down again.

This time, the heavy hook demolished Hellboy's face. The dog's nose exploded and blood shot across the floor. Its eyes bulged from its skull. The dog's legs flinched twice more as William and Daniel screamed in unison.

William didn't move. He couldn't. Shock had cemented his feet to the floor.

But Daniel *could* move, and he did. He pounced on Cameron like a wrestler, slamming her shoulders to the ground. Cameron lifted the crowbar and Daniel knocked it away. Kicking her feet and swinging her arms, Cam tried to knock him off. Dan pulled back, grabbing Cameron's hands one at a time.

William dropped to his knees beside Hellboy—his companion, his family, his friend. His eyes were watery; his face was a wrinkled display of assorted emotions. It was clear that he wanted to help the dog, but how? He leaned in, moved closer. Somehow he got blood on his hands and he looked at it. The blood glistened on his fingers.

The dog was dead, bleeding a pool of gore that was expanding by the second. The fur around its nose was bunched together in clumps. The snout was crushed. Hellboy's skull was cracked.

Cameron had killed it.

He looked toward her with anger and hate stamped across his eyes. He lifted the crowbar off the ground and stood up. Blood dripped. Drywall dust fell from his pants. Not surprisingly, he seemed to be unsure of what to do next. His knees were shaking and his teeth were clenched.

As Daniel fought with Cameron he caught a glimpse of William's face. Revenge seemed to be written beneath his features. Dan wondered if William was thinking about hitting Cameron with the heavy iron stick, making her pay for her outrage. Maybe he wanted her to scream in pain and feel what Hellboy must have felt when she killed him. But that didn't seem right. Cameron wasn't a stranger, or some escaped psychopath from a nearby penitentiary. She was William's family and friend. She was a good person that had lost her way, and William always said that violence was a tool of the weak minded, and was only to be used as a last resort.

William raised the crowbar up, holding it in both hands.

Perhaps his beliefs had changed.

Cameron snapped her teeth like an animal. Her eyes were large and her nose was crumpled into a sneer. Daniel couldn't believe it. She was acting like a werewolf. He tried to talk her down but it was no use, she was out of control.

Cameron twisted a hand free and clawed Daniel's face.

Daniel pulled back, cringing in pain. His weight shifted and Cameron took advantage. She pulled her other hand free and pushed him off balance.

Trying to recapture his poise, Daniel fell.

Fingers clawed his face. A mad scuffle occurred and suddenly she was on top of him, in control, attacking him with her fingers.

With a sinister grin, Cameron laughed. She clawed him twice more, once with each hand. Daniel grabbed one of her wrists. In response, Cameron grabbed his neck and squeezed it, compressing his neck muscles and trapping the air in his throat. For a moment he was afraid he'd never breathe again. Mercifully, it didn't last. He knocked her arm away with a fist and lifted a knee, pushing her to one side.

Another loud bang came as the trapdoor lifted and fell.

Beth didn't seem to care. She was too busy watching the battle between Cameron and Daniel in a state of disbelief.

Referring to Cameron, Beth said, "What's she doing? What's happening?"

Confused and distraught, William turned away from the scuffle and looked at Beth. Fear and confusion was in her eyes. The trapdoor bounced beneath her again. How long could she hold the creature off by kneeling on the door—a minute, maybe two? Something needed to be done.

All four of them needed to get out of the basement before things went from bad to worse.

Sadly, Daniel knew what had to be done.

Will adjusted the crowbar in his hand, eying Cameron. He seemed to know what needed to be done too. Or did he think that smashing

Cameron with the iron was too dangerous?

Dan's eyes shifted from Cameron, to Beth, to the dog.

The dog kept bleeding. The poor thing was lying in a red lake.

Cameron fought like a rattlesnake backed in a corner. Her eyes were sunken. Her neck muscles bulged beneath her skin like tightly wound cables. Blood and puss hung from her mouth as her fingernails dug into Daniel's shoulders.

"Don't just stand there, Will!" Dan shouted, struggling to keep Cameron from ripping his head off. "DO SOMETHING!"

The trapdoor bounced up and down.

William threw the crowbar in the corner. It banged off the wall and hit the floor with a clang, leaving a skid mark in the dust. He took two quick steps forward and kicked Cameron in the face just as hard as he pleased. Red and white dots puffed the air as her lips split open. Sounded like a kicker punting a football.

Cameron tumbled back in a daze with both hands in the air.

If Will could see into her head, he'd know that a million tiny shimmers of light sparkled before her eyes.

2

"WILLIAM!" Beth screamed, shocked by the unexpected violence. "STOP IT!"

William ignored her, which was okay with Daniel.

Beth clearly didn't understand the situation and neither of the men had time to explain. Truth was, William wasn't trying to hurt Cameron. He was only trying to stop the insanity. Dan knew it; Beth needed to know it too.

It seemed to Dan that William's anger had subsided, his outrage had settled (as much as it could in such a short amount of time, anyhow), and with a moderately clear mind he made an assessment and came to a conclusion that was both simple and straightforward: he needed to change the current situation, and knocking Cameron out would accomplish that. Dan couldn't have agreed more.

Yes, he felt bad for Cameron. She was obviously hurting and leaving a wake of blood everywhere that she went. Worst than that, she was out of her friggin mind. However, Cameron was dangerous and impulsive, a threat to herself and those around her. She needed help. She needed medication. She needed treatments and supervision—even if that meant putting the boots to her.

Cameron sat up like Dracula in his coffin, arms across her chest, snapping her teeth like an angry wolf. Irate. Her eyes had turned black, completely black. Her skin looked bloodless, like fair paper.

Daniel couldn't believe what he was seeing. He said, "Oh my—"

Then Will stepped past him, hoisted a leg and blasted Cameron in the face a second time. Cameron's head snapped back, smashing against a large piece of broken drywall. Her feet lifted into the air.

The trapdoor rattled beneath Beth. She screamed.

The creature, less than six inches from where she stood, clearly wanted in.

Beth said, "I need help!"

Cameron sat up again.

William tried to kick her in the face a third time but it didn't work. Cameron grabbed Will's foot, squeezed it, and twisted.

William huffed, lost his balance, and fell on Daniel.

Daniel threw up his hands. Then, with William sprawled out on top of him, he looked Cameron in the face and felt his assessment of the situation change. Cameron's eyes were cold and emotionless, like an insect, like she had no soul. For a moment he wondered if she was possessed by the devil but quickly dismissed the thought. Possession was out of the question.

The situation was obviously fantastic, Daniel accepted, but it was also uncomplicated. They had encountered a species that was either previously unidentified and unknown to today's scientific community, *or*, known, but not publicized. If he were a gambling man he'd put a thousand bucks on unidentified. In today's media savvy world, things didn't stay unpublicized for long. But even if he was wrong on this account, the point was this: the creature—mammal, he assumed—had poisonous stingers, like a wasp, and Cameron had been stung. Nothing more. Shame the poison was giving her a violent reaction.

Dan heard himself say: "Get the crowbar!"

"What?"

"You heard me! Get it! Get it now! You've got to take her down before this gets worse! She's not right!"

"She's my cousin!"

"She'll kill us all!"

William, slightly shocked by Daniel's suggestion, seemed to acknowledge the fact that they needed to end this pointless battle before the trap door blasted apart and the *real* danger showed itself. Because Cameron wasn't the *real* danger—the *real* danger was below Beth, trying to get in and eat them alive.

He crawled off Daniel and made his way across the floor.

He reached for the crowbar.

Beth felt the door shake. A clumpy string of hair fell in front of her eyes. A bead of sweat dropped from her chin.

With an unsteady voice, she said, "Don't you dare hit Cameron! You leave the iron on the floor!" Murder—was that really happening here? It couldn't be. Things were happening too fast.

Cameron fell forwards. She was on all fours, eyes wide, mouth agape, puss and blood dribbling from her lips, crawling towards Daniel like a creature at war.

Daniel, still sitting on the floor, tried to move away from her. He pushed away with his arms, sliding back a few inches. He didn't get far before Cameron grabbed his leg, yanked the pant leg up, and bit into his shin. He didn't have a chance to stop her. She was too quick and he was too overwhelmed by her actions. As the skin tore open, he screamed. His eyes watered and a pain he had never known made him yank his leg away. The skin tore apart more, spilling a splash of blood across the floor.

William stood up with the crowbar in his hand. He approached Cameron, pursed his lips, raised the iron above his shoulder, and did what he had to do: he brought the weapon down hard and fast, hitting Cameron in back of the head, closing his eyes as the connection was made.

Cameron went down, arms wide, face against the floor. Bleeding now, not just from her leg and back, but from her skull too. And this time, the assault came from someone that loved her.

3

The room fell silent.

Seconds passed.

"Did you have to do that?" Beth's voice was composed and calm, given the circumstances. She thought Cameron was dead. "Was there no other way?"

"No," William said, panting and shaken. "There was no other way. I had to do it. She'd gone mad."

Beth looked at Daniel for confirmation.

Daniel nodded. He was holding his wounded leg with both hands. Blood ran through his fingers; he'd need stitches for sure. Almost apologetically, he said, "Cameron was trying to kill me. I know it's crazy but it's true."

"But why?" Beth asked, on the verge of crying.

Daniel looked at the trapdoor before answering. There were no noises now, just the sound of the room. Everything was eerily quiet; he wondered how long they had until the next attack. "I'm not entirely sure, but I'm guessing that *thing* in the basement poisoned her. She needs a doctor."

William crouched beside Cameron and quietly placed the crowbar on the floor. He took her by the hand, feeling for her pulse. He wasn't sure if blood pulsed through her veins or not but she looked alive and that made him sigh with relief.

Gently, oh so gently, he put a hand to the back of her head.

There was a goose egg, a big one that would likely grow bigger as the evening wore on. Blood ran through her hair, making the strains clump together. There was a chance that Cam's skull had been fractured. With this in mind, William started to weep. He'd never forgive himself if he literally cracked her head open.

"She seems okay," he whispered between sobs. "What about you Dan? Your face is bleeding too, you alright?"

"Yeah," Dan said, touching the marks on his cheek. "I'm fine.

What about Cameron, she all right? That thing stabbed her, you know. Poisoned her too. She needs the hospital."

William's face seemed to sag. He didn't know she'd been stabbed, poisoned, *and* throttled with the crowbar. He knew she was bleeding and acting crazy but he hadn't put it all together.

He decided to have a look at Cameron's wounds. He pulled Cameron's shirt up a few inches, exposing her back. Her destroyed muscles looked like chopped liver. On a positive note her bleeding had all but stopped. It was almost like the gash had been cauterized.

Daniel wanted to call 911.

He said, "Do you have a cell phone? I left mine at home."

"I don't," William said, eying Cameron's suspicious looking wounds.

"No," Beth responded. "The reception in Cloven Rock sucks so I don't own a cell, probably never will." She looked at her feet and the door beneath it. Referring to the trapdoor, she said, "I want off this thing."

"That's understandable," Dan said. "Let's take Cam to the hospital. Get off the door, but do it slowly and quietly. The last thing we need is that thing in here with us."

Beth did just that. She pulled one foot off at a time, trying to be noiseless. At one point the door sounded like a rusty door hinge squeaking. Thankfully, the beast never stirred, never pushed its way into their sanctuary.

"Where's Roger?" William asked, looking like he had aged twenty years in the last ten minutes. "Was he here?"

A shiver crawled down Dan's spine as the memories of Roger being devoured came rushing in. *He was eaten like a cookie*, he thought. *Like a fucking cookie!*

"Daniel?"

"He went to the store." Dan lied, looking at the floor, avoiding William's eyes, ashamed of himself for evading the truth. But he didn't want *that* conversation. Not yet. Not so soon.

William sighed with relief. "Thank heaven," he said. "I figured he was in that well with you guys."

Desperate to change the subject, Dan grabbed Cameron's feet. "It's not a well, it's a bomb shelter. Now take her other end, will ya? Let's get Cameron upstairs. And for God's sake, do it quietly."

"A bomb shelter," Beth said, surprised. "Really?"

"Upstairs," Dan repeated. "Let's go. Now. We need to talk."

Beth said, "Are you sure we should move her?"

"I'm positive we shouldn't leave her here. Enough talk. Let's walk."

William lifted Cameron, holding her beneath the arms. It was a struggle to move her but they managed. She made it upstairs without too much trouble. Once they were in the living room they placed her on the couch carefully. Daniel slid a pillow beneath her head. Beth closed the basement door.

"There's no lock on this door," she said. "Should we board it up?"

"I don't know," Dan replied, thinking about Roger. "Most of my tools are lying near the trapdoor, and I don't want to go down there to get them. Making lots of noise with a hammer might be the wrong move anyhow. Leave the door for now. We'll deal with it later."

William looked across the room. "Dan, where's your phone?"

Dan drew a deep breath. "The phone is in the kitchen, but it isn't turned on. We disconnect the service every winter, what with us not being here. And this summer we were thinking about living without the home-line. We own cell phones, Sandra and I. The home phone seems like a waste of money these days."

"Oh," Beth approached the men. "That's too bad."

"Yeah."

"Okay then. No phone. So what's the plan?" William sat on the coffee table with his elbows on his knees and his chin resting in his hands. "Are we going to take her to the hospital? What do you think?"

Daniel considered the situation: Pat was in the pit somewhere. Maybe he was alive. Maybe he was dead. It was hard to say.

We went down a quartet and came up a twosome, Dan thought. *And Roger is gone for good.*

But Patrick, that was the sticky wicket, no doubt. What to do about Patrick Love?

William said, "Daniel? Hello? You with us?"

"Yeah," Dan said. "I'm here. Let's load Cameron into a car and take her to the hospital."

4

Pat was alive. He had been knocked to the floor by the beast, and by the time he knew what was happening he had a giant claw crushing his chest. The enormous pressure was not anticipated and as a result he couldn't breathe or sit up. All he could do was wave his hands and kick his feet, mouth gaping like a fish, but what was that doing for him? Nothing. Not a goddamn thing.

He needed air and he needed it pronto.

Something began raining in charitable portions. Not a trickle, not a sprinkle, not a drizzle or drop. Buckets. Buckets and buckets fell generously all around, splashing everywhere, making him wet. But what was it, blood? Was it blood?

Yes! It *was* blood!

Oh God.

Pat didn't know *whose* blood was falling. But it *was* blood.

Someone was dying.

The blood didn't belong to Cameron; Pat knew that much. Cameron had walked away from hidden room. That only left Dan and Roger unaccounted for. But who was being butchered? Was it Roger or Dan?

The animal shifted its weight and lifted its claw.

Air rushed into Pat's lungs. He coughed several times, stopping only when he saw a human leg fall.

"Holy shit," he said, feeling his jaw slink away from his face like it had a mind to crawl into a corner and hide. With his heart rate accelerating, his eyes widening, and his stomach muscles clenching, he whispered, "What the hell is that?"

But he knew. Oh God, it was a leg. A human leg, severed high upon the limb. It was white, nearly hairless and pathetically thin. There was a scrap of denim bundled near the shoe.

Eyes shifted. He saw the creature's head dip towards the floor, sniffing like a dog. He could see tiny holes surrounding each mouth, opening and closing in unison. They looked like miniature moon craters, crusted with a thin line of gray. Bugs crawled in the creature's fur. Flies circled; some went insides the mouths never to be seen again.

Pat watched in awe as three mouths were chewing at once, and the moon craters were sniffing, blowing, expanding and contracting. In many ways they were remarkable.

Then he realized something:

Very surprisingly, the beast hadn't noticed him. Yet.

This was a strange and nearly impossible certainty, which lifted Pat's spirits once he believed it. But luck could change quickly, so he tried to improve his situation by holding his breath and bringing his arms to his sides. He pulled his legs together and sucked his stomach in, making himself smaller, if only in his mind.

The beast shuffled its limbs.

He figured one of two things would happen. Either A) The creature would notice him and that would be the end of his story, or B) the creature would return to its home, giving him a chance to escape. Seeing things this way, he gave himself a fifty/fifty survival probability.

But then something happened, something he hadn't anticipated: the creature chased his friends. The scenario may have seemed obvious to the others, but for Pat, the notion had eluded him. Perspective is everything.

The stampede of legs moved in waves. Two clawed limbs trampled Pat's left arm, causing him to release a sharp scream. He was lucky. If either limb had been armed with a stinger the outcome would have been worse. Like Cameron, he would have been poisoned. His judgment would twist into hatred and his compassion would become violence. Fortunately for him, this wasn't the case. His arm wasn't pierced, nor was it broken. It wasn't even sore.

The stampede of limbs was terrifying, nothing more.

The threat was gone, for now.

Lying in Roger's remains, Pat lifted his head. He rested on his elbows on the floor and watched the beast scurry up the ladder in a centipede-like motion. The creature was incredible, a true wonder of the animal kingdom.

He sat up, shocked and stunned but not truly frightened. His hands trembled slightly, although he didn't notice. He looked at the shadows on the ceiling, the unpainted concrete walls, and the flies buzzing in the air. He looked at the florescent lights that hung from thin, sturdy wires, and at the ductwork that seemed more complicated than efficient. He looked at the floor and at the distance that separated him from the small hallway on the far side of the room. And finally, he looked at Roger's blood on his hands. Only then did he realize he didn't know what to do.

5

William lifted Cameron by the legs and Daniel took her beneath the arms. Beth cleared a path, and held the front door ajar as they brought her outside, leaving a trail of blood in their wake. They placed her inside Daniel's car, stretching her across the back seat with one arm lying across her chest and the other hanging to the floor. Knees were folded together, almost prayer like. Her face had turned white, making her look more frightful than ever.

Dan said, "You guys should drive Cam to the hospital. I'll stay here."

"Why?" Beth asked. "It's your car."

"Someone should wait here for the police. It's my place. And the car is full."

"My ride is right there, man," William said, pointing at his car. "I drove here with Beth, remember? We can all go."

"True, but I want to wait here. I'd like a few minutes to myself, a few minutes to patch my leg up and think things over before the cops get here asking a million questions, you know? Plus Pat's still down there somewhere. I don't want to leave him."

Beth eyed Dan suspiciously. "You sure?"

Daniel handed William his car keys. "I'm totally sure. Now go. It's a twenty-five minute drive to the hospital so get going before Cameron dies on you."

"Okay." William said with a reluctant nod. "We'll send the police ASAP."

"Yes, please do. And send an ambulance too. Patrick may need it."

William and Beth jumped into Daniel's car. They backed out of the stone gravel driveway quickly. William waved through the open window, frazzled.

Once the car was gone Daniel looked towards the lake.

Oaks, birches, and a few scattered elms, framed his view, blocking a small portion of the sky's only cloud. The cloud was small and feathery and fractured near the middle. An old picnic table sat on the beach with its legs embedded in the sand. Circular rocks surrounded a fire pit that was getting slightly bigger each passing year. Beneath the full and bloated moon, light shimmered in the peaceful water. There was a raft, anchored in place for eight summers now. It sat fifty odd feet from shore in water that was ten feet deep and clear enough to see through when the sun was shinning. He could hear crickets, frogs, loons, and the hum of a hundred million bugs. The air was fresh, warm but not muggy, neither dry nor damp. On the far side of the drink, a pair of fires burned brilliantly and the voices of those enjoying the flames echoed in spills of laughter.

He loved evenings like this.

In a different set of circumstances he would sit at the edge of the dock for hours, soaking in the nature, fishing rod in hand. The air was just right. The weather was perfect. On a typical day, he could sit on the dock for sure.

Daniel went inside the house and closed the door tight. He made his way upstairs and entered the bathroom. He cleaned the wound on his leg and wrapped it in gauze before entering the master bedroom. There was a cushy recliner in the far corner of the room sitting next to a reading lamp and a door that led to a bathroom. The king-size bed was just the way he left it: unmade, with silk sheets crumpled on the floor. There was an empty beer bottle on one of the night tables, sitting next to an iPod and the newest edition of Playboy. Everything looked the same, but he had a strange feeling that somebody had been inside the room, unannounced and uninvited. He didn't know why he felt that way but he did. Nothing seemed different; nothing seemed out of place. But still, he couldn't shake the feeling that something had changed.

Dan opened the closet door, pushed a duffel bag aside and pulled a stack of paperbacks from the top shelf. One book fell to the floor: Clive Barker, Cabal. He kicked it aside, grabbed an old shoebox and sat on the bed with it. He opened the box. It had a black metal gun inside, sitting next to a small case with four, seven-bullet clips. The gun was an unloaded Charter Arms .32 automatic. It had a charcoal colored grip and smelled like oil. He ran his finger along the trigger guard before he lifted the weapon from the box and loaded one of the clips. Then he held the weapon to his forehead, took a deep breath, and closed his eyes.

"Lord," he whispered, squeezing the cool metal with his fingers. "I don't ask for much, you know I don't. But if you exist... if you're really, really, out there somewhere... please help me now. Help me in my time of need. Give me the guidance, the courage, and strength I require. If not for me, do it for the boy. Do it for Patrick."

He opened his eyes and stood up, gun dangling in his hand. After slipping the three remaining clips into his front pocket, he unlatched the weapon's safety with his thumb.

He was ready.

It was time to enter the basement.

6

Pat stood in Roger's blood with his hands dripping red. His face was speckled and the front of his shirt was drenched. Intestines sat on the ground near his feet, steaming in the cold air. Roger's insides smelled strong and unsettling, like copper mixed with something unfamiliar.

He stepped away from the gore and walked towards the ladder, slowly, cautiously, knowing the creature was above him somewhere. He didn't know how far away the beast might be, or if it would return some time soon. Maybe he'd come face to face with the animal. Maybe he'd be eaten alive. With so many uncertain factors to consider he knew he was risking his neck for sure. But still, he wanted to look up the shaft. Needed to, in fact. He didn't know what else to do.

Once he was beneath the opening he stared up, into the passage, trying to be as quiet as possible, praying he wouldn't come face to face with terrible destiny.

He could see the 500-watt light tied to the extension cables, swaying back and forth like a body at the gallows pole. The light was still on; the area around it was bright. Everything else was dark. If the monster was hiding in the shadows it did not show itself. If it was creeping toward him it was doing so gently.

Was the trap door closed? It seemed that way.

Some friends, Pat thought despairingly. If the door was closed he was trapped. If the door was open the beast was blocking his path and the result was the same. Did it really matter one way or the other? He supposed it didn't.

He walked away from the opening with a fingernail between his teeth. This was bad. Very bad. He still didn't know what to do or what options he had.

Think Patrick... think.

Halfway across the room he remembered his cell phone. He pulled it from his pocket and dialed 911.

No reception.

He returned the phone to its place, cursing beneath his breath.

So much for that idea, he thought.

The phone wasn't going to work and he was too deep in the earth to expect anything different. So now what? He needed assistance but there was nobody to talk with. He was thirsty and without water. He was hungry and without food. He was worried with good reason. He needed to hide but there was no place to go.

Except—

He looked at the door the creature had come from, wondering what was on the other side. Perhaps there was another exit waiting to be discovered.

Or another one of those *things*.

He walked across the room and put his hand on the wood. Looking down, he saw Roger's arm lying next to a pile of intestines.

His eyes squeezed shut.

Slowly, cautiously, he pushed on the door and opened his eyes.

The room was dark. For a moment he considered announcing his presence and saying hello, but saying hello was a *terrible* idea, a *dreadful* idea. So he stepped inside the room with his neck extended and his hands curled into fists. The door stayed open, being that the bottom edge was wedged against the floor, and something else. Might have been a chunk of Roger.

The smell, he noticed, was appalling. It reminded him of spoiled fruit, dead animals, and compost.

He put a hand on the wall and came up lucky, finding a light switch. Flicking it on, he came up lucky again: florescent lights sprang to life.

Now he could see.

The room was approximately half the size of the first room, with the ceiling being at the same height. It had a hallway at the far end. Stacked against each wall were hundreds of metal cases and wooden crates. Each case was marked with a simple government label. Some of the cases were small, the size of a lunch box. Others were about the size of a small car. There were a few old bones on the floor, scattered and broken. Pat didn't notice the bones. He didn't notice the boxes either, not really, not at first.

His eyes were focused elsewhere.

Hanging from the ceiling in the back corner of the room was a large cocoon. It was twenty feet wide and eight feet tall. Beneath the webbing, more cocoons were attached to the crates and walls. Two dozen of them. But these silk houses were smaller, each being roughly the size of a washing machine. They were white, mixed with a dusty black tinge that looked like coal dust.

While Pat eyed the cocoons he saw something that made his legs feel weak: some of the cocoons were shifting, moving, shaking. The things that lived inside were ready to hatch. And the pair of cocoons he didn't see—the two on the ceiling, hanging directly above him—weren't ready to hatch. They already had.

7

Stones crunched beneath the wheels and a tree branch grazed the roof as William pulled Daniel's car onto the road.

"Do you think she'll be alright?" Beth asked.

"You want the truth or do you want me to make you feel better? I can lie if you'd like me to."

"That bad, huh?"

"I think so."

Beth turned towards the backseat and studied Cameron's face in the varying shadows. Touching her cheek, she said, "Cam might be dead already, you know. She looks dead."

"I can't believe she killed Hellboy. What was she thinking?"

A small bird swooped in front of the vehicle's headlights as they drove past Nicolas Nehalem's car.

Beth said, "I don't know. You hit her pretty hard with the crowbar."

William flinched like he'd been slapped. "What was I supposed to do? She was trying to kill Daniel! She was trying to strangle him to death, right in front of me! She would have killed us all if she'd been given the chance! Don't you know that?"

"Don't get so upset."

"But I *am* upset! *I am!*" William slammed a hand on the steering wheel, swallowing back half his frustration. "How can I not be upset? And what the hell was that thing in the shaft? Can you answer me that? It looked like something from a science fiction movie!"

"I don't know what it was, but it was strong. I thought it was going to smash apart the trapdoor."

"Damn right it was strong! Did you see how big it was? I've never seen anything like it!"

"You know," Beth said, speaking with a curiously calm tone, a voice designed to relieve some of William's tension. She looked down at her big hands and coupled her fingers together. "Scientists discover new species everyday. It happens so often its not even newsworthy. They're finding an average of two new species a week in South America. Did you know that? It's true. And I'm not just talking about bugs and stuff. I'm talking about all kinds of things. Bats and snakes and rodents that don't look like anything at all."

Beth was quite good in traumatic situations. She was a social worker in Maplebrook, a neighboring town. As a supervisor in a group-home for troubled teenagers she had a staff of nine working day and night, caring for six girls and four boys. The job fit her personality perfectly. She was big enough to deal with the physical confrontations, she liked having authority, and she enjoyed helping people in need. More importantly, the job made her feel like she was making a difference in the world. She couldn't imagine doing anything less.

William wasn't having it.

He shook his head. "Is that supposed to make me feel better? Scientists don't come across things like *that* everyday, now do they? That fucking thing is newsworthy!" He pulled a hand off the steering wheel and waved his index finger in the air like he was trying to accentuate a point. "You bet your ass that thing is newsworthy! It looked like a big hairy fur-ball with a whole bunch of mouths stuck to it! Have you *ever* seen anything with more than one mouth? I haven't!"

"Spiders have eight eyes."

"Spiders can go to hell!" Will's line of vision slipped from the road and locked onto nothing in particular. He looked ready to crack. "I can crush a spider with my thumb, Beth! With my thumb! Do you think I'd have any luck crushing that thing beneath my thumb? Christ! It was like a dinosaur or something. How the hell did the scientific community miss that little darling, huh? Tell me that!"

"Keep your eyes on the road. You're driving like a maniac."

William refocused.

Beth said, "A Goliath Tarantula is almost thirty centimeters across, you know? Thirty centimeters is bigger than a dinner plate. And I found an interesting article about a fossil. Apparently they discovered a spider-like creature that was a half-meter long."

Will gasped. "This thing was *giant!* Didn't you see it? Was I the only one there? It was the size of a water buffalo!"

"You're upset."

"Damn right I'm upset!"

"Well stop taking it out on me! I'm just trying to help."

William crushed his teeth together and closed his eyes. When he opened them he slowed the car down and apologized, saying, "I'm sorry. I'm just upset—"

Beth interrupted. "It's okay. Don't worry about it."

William turned a corner. He went from one dirt road to another. A few seconds later he stopped at an intersection, a four way stop. There were no cars approaching from any direction. Looking left he could see thousands of trees. It was the beginning of a forest that went on for acres. Stalks of corn inhabited the fields on his right. Beyond the corn, if you looked past an open pasture, there were two-dozen horses standing near a farmhouse. Maybe more.

In the backseat, Cameron stirred. Her eyes opened. A smile without happiness crept across her face and a giggle escaped her lips.

Neither Beth nor William noticed.

"Listen," Beth said, running her fingers through her hair. "Don't get all freaky on me here, just listen. When I was a kid my father ordered subscriptions from Time-Life books. He had books about history and war, animals, the sea, science, space... you name it; he bought it. Every couple weeks he'd acquire a new book and nobody was allowed to touch it. But I was a kid and I was curious, and whenever he wasn't around, which was fairly often, I'd sneak into his den and look through his books whether he liked it or not. I was always careful. I never looked at the newest one. I knew if I ever smudged dirt on a new one my ass would be redder than the sun." Beth paused, searching her memory bank.

William drove through an intersection and did what Beth had instructed: he kept his eyes on the road.

"He had this one series called 'The Mysteries of the Unknown'. They were beautiful hardcovers, filled with interesting facts and amazing photography. They were my favorite, tackling stories about UFOs, dinosaurs, and all the other things that made kids like me have a hard time sleeping. Well... there was this one volume called 'Unidentified Creatures'—something like that. It had those washed out photographs of the Lock Ness Monster and Sasquatch. You know the ones. They've been shown on television a million times."

Will nodded. He knew the ones.

"But inside this book they had these *other* photographs too, ones that don't get much publicity. And this was the stuff that just made me dizzy with excitement. I don't know why exactly. But the point is, in 1976 they found an unknown species of shark that had the expression of a man. Damn thing looked like a giant, squished boot with a face on it. In 1936 they found a fish off the Comoro Islands that had been extinct for seventy million years—or so they thought. In 1977 Japanese trawlers caught a four thousand pound carcass, snapped a photograph, and threw the creature overboard. The scientific community still has no idea what the damn thing was, but they know what it looked like: it looked like a dinosaur, like something that wasn't supposed to be here."

"You have dates and everything."

Beth said, "Yeah I have dates." The fact that she was guessing them didn't seem important. "When I was growing up my parents didn't believe in television. So yeah, I've got dates. I've got the library memorized."

"No TV? Really?"

"Oh, we had one. But I was never allowed to watch it. Plus we didn't have cable and my parents kept the only TV set in their bedroom… another room that was off limits, I might add."

"Sounds like your parents were tough on you when you were younger."

Beth could hear the change in William's tone. She was draining the anger from him successfully and forcing him to think about other things. She decided to give him a little *something* to think about, although she didn't enjoy bringing it up. "They were militant, that's for sure. They used their fists to communicate and they put me in the hospital more than once."

William's eyes widened. "No kidding. You were abused? But your parents seem so nice."

"They changed with the times, I guess. Everybody does."

"Yeah, I suppose. Was it your dad? Was he the—"

Beth interrupted. "Both of them had mean streaks and ruled the house by force. That's probably why I'm a social worker now."

"I had no idea."

"Do me a favor, don't tell anyone. That was a long time ago.

They're different people now."

"Yeah, sure Beth. I won't say anything. No problem."

Beth tapped her fingers against her leg and returned to her story. "Anyway... back in 1920 an expedition of travelers explored the jungles of Colombia and Venezuela. They were in the jungle a week or so before they were attacked. *Like us*, Will. *Just like us*. They were in the wrong place at the wrong time, I suppose, attacked by things unknown and undocumented."

William looked into his rear view mirror.

There was someone behind him, following closely. He didn't recognize the car.

Beth continued: "The explorers got lucky. They killed one of three beasts. The other two ran off. So the explorers, knowing they had something special, propped the dead body up on a fuel crate. They put a long stick beneath the creature's jaw to hold it in place and then they snapped a photograph. The photograph isn't blurry or taken from far away. It's perfect. To this day scientists have no idea what the animal is."

Beth took a deep breath.

"That photograph really freaked me out. I must have looked at it every evening for a year. It looked like Bigfoot or something, like an ape. It had human features and intelligent eyes. Its arms were almost the entire length of its body. Its feet and hands looked exactly the same, if you can imagine. All four of them seemed to be placed on the wrong limb somehow. It was like this thing was born with its left hand on its right arm and its right hand on its left arm. Its leathery fingers were the size of bananas. It was the craziest, weirdest animal I ever saw."

William tried to imagine what that would look like—to have your hands on the wrong arms. He couldn't do it.

They drove in silence for a moment.

"I dreamt about it for years. I figured one day I'd be making my way to school, or playing in the yard, and out it would come. The real Bigfoot, that's what it was to me: the real Bigfoot. That blurry photograph that gets pimped around is a joke, I tell you. It's a joke. This thing in the Time-Life book looked like it could tear your head from your neck in seconds. It was the real deal. And at night I'd keep my eyes glued to the window... waiting... watching... thinking it would come.

"I never told my parents about my sleepless nights. I couldn't. I wasn't supposed to see those books and I knew it, so I laid in bed scared of what was out there, scared Bigfoot was coming to get me."

"Why are you telling me this?" William looked in his rearview mirror again. The car was still there, driving so close that William wondered if the guy behind the wheel had an attitude problem. He touched the break pedal, trying to encourage the driver to back off a little.

Get off my ass, he thought. *You're way too close.*

Beth placed a hand on William's shoulder, saying, "Because Will... I know you, and I can see how upset you are. There are a lot of strange things in this world and not all of them get talked about television or gawked at in a zoo. Some of these unknown beasts don't *like* getting looked at. Some of them get angry. Some of them feel threatened, and sometimes they fight back. This might be only place in the world those creatures exist. Ever think of that? We may have discovered a new species."

"No," William said. "I hadn't thought of it that way."

Beth nodded.

She felt smart, but was wrong in her assessment.

Such creatures *had* been discovered before. Twice. The first nest was uncovered behind a wooden church in the northern regions of Hungary in 1276. Soon after, the church, and the village closest to it, was burned to the ground. One hundred and forty-nine years later three more nests were discovered high upon the slopes of the Transylvanian Alps.

The year was 1425.

Those nests were never destroyed.

And in a seemingly unrelated topic, the madman known as Vlad Draçulas Tepes was born five years later, eight miles away.

8

Daniel tried to be brave but his plan was only half realized. The details of Patrick Love's heroic rescue were beyond him. He wanted to save his friend, and he was willing to put himself in danger to do so. But what could he do, and how could he do it? Questions, it seemed, were easier to find than answers.

He pulled his t-shirt off and tossed it to the floor. An off-white dress shirt was lying across the arm of a chair. He needed something clean, and the shirt was right there, so Dan threw it on and buttoned it. It would have to do.

Now Dan was standing near the basement door with his ear to the wood. He couldn't hear anything. Not a peep. He put his hand on the doorknob and applied some pressure. He turned the knob. The latch gave and Dan wondered if his nerves would give with it.

He looked at the gun. Was he ready to use it? Maybe.

This was the moment of truth.

After clearing his throat, he swung the basement door open. His heart rate increased and his fingers trembled. Stepping back, he pointed the weapon nervously. He was ready, willing, and able to fire a shot.

The stairwell was empty.

"Still in the shaft," he whispered, exhaling a great and dramatic breath. Somehow it seemed like a mixed blessing.

He walked down the stairs trusting that the creature wasn't hiding around a corner. He was right. The room was the same as before. The trapdoor was closed; the floor was littered with hammers and saws, drills and screwdrivers, crowbars and wrenches. Rolls of carpet sat next to the rotting pickets on the warped staircase. Hellboy's doggy-corpse was in the heart of the room, lying inside a puddle of coagulating blood.

The poor, unfortunate thing.

Hellboy's face looked like it had been caught in the gears of heavy machinery. Its eyes were open, staring into space. Teeth had been smashed free.

Dan sighed. The dog's mangled snout was upsetting. It made him feel angry, sad, and confused, all at the same time. He ran his dirty fingers through his sweaty hair, wondering why Cameron turned so mean, so evil. It was almost like she had been possessed. He had never seen anything like it.

His eyes shifted.

The trapdoor wasn't bouncing up and down or straining against its hinges, which he supposed was a good thing. Things had turned quiet. Hopefully that meant that Pat was safe and not dead. He considered his options, finding the reasonable ones to be conflicting.

On one hand, he should wait for the police to arrive. More manpower and weaponry could only help. On the other hand, Pat needed assistance now. Not in five or ten minutes. Not in an hour. He needed it now. And waiting often led to more waiting, and authoritative assistance usually lead to red-taped bureaucracy.

Waiting was the easiest road to travel, but was it the right choice? Would it lead Pat to safety, or guarantee his death? These were the questions that ran through Dan's mind with inconsistent translations. These were the choices that made his heart ache.

Dan made his way to the trapdoor and got down on both knees. His wounded leg throbbed as he did so. After placing the gun on the floor he put his ear to the wood and listened. He couldn't hear anything at first. But then he could hear something. Didn't know what it was, but the image of a seashell came to mind. That's what he heard, the sounds of the sea, the winds and the waves, the water splashing against the rocks on the shore.

It was an illusion, of course. Not an optical illusion but an audible one. He couldn't hear anything. The beast wasn't there, or if it was, it was being very quiet.

He lifted the gun.

Assuming I don't want to wait for help to arrive, Daniel thought, *what now?*

Opening the trapdoor was an option easier said than done. He was afraid of this option. It might end his life.

Dan considered the alternatives.

He could blast a few bullets into the shaft, but what would that achieve? Would he kill the beast, make it angry, or shoot a hole into his friend? Blind shooting was risky, very risky. He needed more choices.

He could fire up the chainsaw and carve a hole in the door to see what he was getting himself into. He liked this idea more than opening the door blindly, which seemed like suicide. But what were the pros and cons of using a chainsaw?

Pro: Patrick would hear the saw running and know someone was coming.

Con: so would the creature.

Daniel put the barrel of the gun against the wood. Still kneeing, his legs were beginning to ache more than he could tolerate.

"Patrick," he shouted; his voice cracked. "You there?" He waited three or four seconds, cleared his throat, and tried his luck again. "Patrick? If you can't answer me that's fine, but I want you to know we haven't forgotten you! *I* haven't forgotten you! I'm coming down but first I'm going to fire a couple bullets into the shaft. If you're in the shaft stay close to the ladder. Do you hear me? I'm going to fire some bullets into the shaft!"

Daniel squeezed the trigger the smallest amount. Doing so made him more nervous than before. This was a dangerous plan. What if he pissed the animal off and it smashed through the door looking for revenge?

"Do you hear me? Do you? Here it comes, Pat! Stay close to the ladder! On the count of three! One! Two! Three!"

Daniel pulled the trigger twice. *BLAM. BLAM.* The noise was loud and the weapon shook violently in his hand. The smell of the gunpowder and oil mixed together made his nose irritated.

He listened but he didn't hear anything. He put his ear to the door.

Nothing.

"Pat! Are you okay? Patrick?" He began to suspect that his friend was already dead. It was more than possible; it was probably to be expected. But he didn't want to think that way. Not yet. Not until he was sure.

"Screw this," he whispered, pulling himself to his feet.

It was time to get the chainsaw.

9

Cameron sat up quickly. The wind blew in her face through the open window causing her dark hair to dance wildly in the air. Her makeup was smudged. Her skin was more pale than usual; her blood loss was apparent. One hand sped through the air and grabbed the side of William's face before he had a chance to look in the rearview mirror to look at her. As she bunched William's skin into her palm, Cameron's other hand latched onto Beth's hair and yanked on it fiercely, like she was trying to pull Beth's head from her body.

William screamed, more shocked than hurt. He shifted away from her, moving his head towards the open window, while fighting off the attack with his right hand. The car swerved. His foot pressed hard on the gas pedal and the vehicle sprang forward, heading into the wrong lane.

Cameron was thrown back, but continued to grip Beth's hair.

Beth squawked like a seagull. Her head snapped back and her throat stretched awkwardly. Pain stunned her body. She thought her neck would break. Positioning herself defensively, she grabbed Cameron's right arm with both of her hands and pinched her fingernails into her skin, shouting, "Stop it!"

Cameron's face contorted into a vile and repugnant sneer. She clawed at William again with her left hand, scratching a line of blood in his cheek.

As William tried to knock her hand away his foot to slipped from the pedal. He turned the wheel right, trying to recapture his lane. Overcompensating, the car veered off the gravel. Tires smashed through a patch of long grass. The car hit a street sign that said: HIDDEN INTERSECTION. The old wooden pole snapped into three separate pieces and cracked the windshield as it went flying over the hood. Wood bounced across the road like a drunken break-dancer. The car went into a ditch. The front grill mashed into the earth and the vehicle made an abrupt halt.

Everyone lurched forward. The steering wheel smashed William in the chin and a sprinkle of light danced before his eyes. Beth's seatbelt made a CLICK sound as it locked around her body, asphyxiating her momentarily. Cameron flipped into the front seat. Her head banged off the radio as she landed between William and Beth. The car's back tires lifted a foot from the ground and then bounced down hard. As the car landed dust puffed into the air.

Cameron flexed her muscles, opened her mouth and chomped William's leg as hard as she was able. As the pain shot through his body she scrambled towards the open window with her elbows flailing and her feet thrashing.

Beth covered her face with her hands. Dirty shoes pummeled her: Doc Martins, size seven. The kicks came fast and often. One snuck through her finger-blockade and smacked her in the mouth. Her lip cracked, leaving a metallic taste on her tongue. Now there was heel crunching her nose. Now there were toes kicking her breasts. Now there was a foot jammed into the side of her thick neck, ramming her towards the open window. It was too much. It was all happening too fast. It seemed as though someone had released a ravenous hyena inside the car.

"Get off," Beth coughed out, as rubber slammed into her eye. She tried to push the foot away but was unable. Cameron was too aggressive.

Arms and legs thrashed.

And as Cameron pulled her body through the open window on the driver's side of the car, her legs dragged across William's face and her feet kicked the roof. She knocked the rearview mirror from the newly cracked windshield and the mirror fell onto Beth's lap.

William shouted, "Stop it!"

Gravity pulled Cameron towards the earth, helping her escape. And with another shift of weight it was over. She was outside.

Beth held a shaky hand to her mouth. Blood dripped through her fingers. Her teeth hurt and her neck muscles throbbed. She said, "What's that girl doing?"

William looked out the window.

With a hand on his chest, he said, "Cameron!?" He wasn't sure if he was mad at her, worried about her, or scared to death of her. Might have been a mix of all three.

Cameron was on the ground with her shirt ripped open and her face in the dirt. The wound on her back was covered in blood and puss.

Hesitantly, William reached for the door handle, wondering if he should open the door or roll up the window. The little voice inside his head—the one that didn't enjoy getting brutally attacked—wanted the window up and the door locked.

But it's Cameron, he thought. *She's family.*

And dangerous, the little voice was quick to point out. *Very dangerous. She's not to be trusted, not even for a moment.*

William felt his heart ache.

Suddenly Cameron sprang to her feet and hissed like a rattlesnake. Her eyes were dark and vacant. Her teeth were covered in dirt and blood. And there was something attached to her, something colorless and threadlike, clinging to the skin around her neck. The fragile network resembled the fiber of a spider's web.

William gasped at the sight of her.

Cameron hissed again. The cords in her neck pulsed.

Convulsing and trembling, she stumbled in front of the car and slammed a fist on the hood. Using both hands, she grabbed her shirt and ripped it from her body. She might have looked funny, like a sad imitation of the Hulk, if not for the grave expression on her sick face. The black cloth fell to the gravel. Her *SEX PISTOLS* button rolled into the grass. She unlatched her bra and let it fall, exposing her breasts to them both.

"My God," Beth said.

William whispered, "What's she doing?"

He couldn't believe what he was seeing, and felt ashamed for looking. But he *was* looking; he was staring right at her. He couldn't help it. He couldn't pull his eyes away from her chest, and what he saw made him tremble.

Cameron's breasts were covered in silky mesh. Her dark and rigid nipples were almost crusted with webbing. And worse than that, tiny bugs were crawling across her skin. They looked like crabs.

Running and staggering, Cameron made her way up the far side of the ditch and over thirty feet of meadow. She pulled off her shoes and her socks, unlatched her belt, and unzipped her pants. Her pants came off. Her underwear came off next.

She hissed at the car one final time and ran into the woods naked. And once she was completely surrounded by the dark shadows of the forest she crawled up a tree and wrapped both hands around a branch.

This is where she stayed.

She was changing, and needed to be alone.

10

Daniel didn't walk and he didn't run. He stomped his way out of the basement, through the house, and out the front door. His eyes had a mean attentive glint, his teeth were clamped together, and his lips were pursed into a chiseled sneer. He looked ready to pick a fight, which in effect, was exactly what he was doing.

Standing inside the garage, he slid his gun in-between his belt and his jeans. He pulled his chainsaw off the top shelf, checked the gas gauge, and stormed back into the house.

Approaching the trapdoor, he pulled the cord on the saw. The chain-blade began spinning. He wasn't a thinking-man now. The time for good judgment and clear logic had ended. He was at war, ready to do battle. He wasn't afraid or nervous; he was excited, energized. It was a time for combat. He was ready to show the beast who was paying the electric bill around here, because this was *his* place, dammit. He bought it, paid for it, cleaned it, and loved it. The house belonged to him and he wouldn't share it with a killing machine. That concept was not an option.

The chainsaw was loud and powerful, with teeth that could bite.

Daniel smiled. His hair had become untamed and chaotic. His dress shirt seemed ironic, not elegant. His knuckles had turned white and his breathing was labored. His features expressed a growing hint of lunacy, the Joker without his make-up.

The spinning blade hit the trapdoor. Wood splintered. Sawdust clouded the area.

He hoped the beast was there, waiting on the other side. He wanted to take the monster on and get it over with.

He imagined the creature's legs being sawed off and the blood splashing the walls around him. He could almost see chunks of meat and bone flying over his shoulders in bunches. He could visualize the animal's retreat into a dark corner, wounded and bleeding, screeching for mercy.

It would receive none.

It would receive death.

Chunks of wood dropped into the pit, the saw kept spinning, Daniel began laughing, and the hole grew larger than he intended. He wanted a hole to see through, roughly three inches squared. What he generated was a two feet by two feet opening, big enough to crawl through. Or fall through.

Realizing this, his confidence faltered.

He wondered if the creature would attack through the opening, or squeeze through the hole somehow.

"Screw it," Dan whispered. He didn't care. Not anymore.

If the creature rammed a leg through the opening he'd saw it off. If the creature broke the door he'd kill it. He was planning on slaying it anyhow. Nothing had changed. Nothing had altered. He was on the warpath; nothing would stand in his way.

He pulled the chainsaw away from the trapdoor and looked down the hole. He couldn't see anything. Then, as the dust in the air dissipated, he knew the creature was no longer there. He could see the floor, way down at the other end of the shaft. Chunks of wood and the broken light sat together in a pile. With the lights in the big room on, the bottom of the shaft was easy to see. And it was *way* down there.

He opened the mangled trapdoor and dropped the chainsaw on the floor.

It was time to enter the pit.

11

Pat stood in the doorway, which divided the two large rooms, eying the cocoon-like nests that were attached to the wall.

And that's what they are too, he thought. *Oversized nests.*

From somewhere high above, Daniel's gun went off.

Pat's head snapped towards the hall that separated the ladder and the big room, wondering what happened, what *was* happening, and what would happen next. The muffled noise from the weapon echoed a moment before vanishing. Then came trampling noises, lots of them. They sounded worse than gunshots and scary as hell. The work light fell, smashing into pieces on the floor. And still, Patrick stood there. Not wondering what to do as much as wondering what *not* to do.

One gigantic leg dropped from the shaft, followed by another, and another, and another.

The thing that had eaten Roger had returned.

Putting a hand over his mouth, he watched the beast longer than he should have. Then he ran towards the hallway at the far side of the room. But where was he going? Was he actually running *into* the hallway? Was that the game plan, or his only choice? The hallway was dark, intimidating, and most of all—*he didn't want to go in there*. But did it really matter what he wanted? No, probably not. He had to do something, and hiding out in the hallway seemed to be it.

Boxes were stacked to his left and right. Some were metal; some iron, some were wooden crates. Most had a thin layer of webbing and a thick layer of dust. The spaces between boxes varied. There were a few gaps that he might be able to squeeze into; he wondered if should hide in there. Climbing on top of the crates was another possibility, but it would take time and probably wasn't worth the risk. So what did that leave?

The hallway was twenty feet away and the obvious choice.

That's what bothered him. It was *so* obvious that it begged the question: where did the hallway go? Would it lead him to safety or to a dead end room with no chance for escape? He wanted more choices, different choices. He wanted choices that made him feel like he was going to survive another hour.

Pat turned around, hunting more options.

He saw something the size of a raccoon crawl across a crate, leaving a trail of wet slime, a thin insipid web and a small wake of dust. It looked like two sea-crabs that had been designed by H. R. Giger and sewn together by Doctor Frankenstein. It had long legs and lots of teeth. Pat stared at creature in awe, and when he turned away he then saw another one crawling up a wall. But this one was had bulging globular eyes that hung off its body like feelers, and more limbs, and bigger teeth.

He looked towards the ceiling just in time to see a cocoon split open and six or seven more of these oddly formed crab-creatures plop out of it. Some of them were white. Some were black. All of them were wet and slimy and equipped with too many limbs and more than one set of jaws.

He spun around with his shoulders raised, his eyes wide and his hands opened in from of him. What was he going to do? How was he going to do it? He needed to escape, to get away, and live to tell the tale.

A crab-critter dropped from the ceiling and landed on its back, six feet in front of him. It flipped over and scurried away, favoring one limb.

Then he heard it:

SQUUUUUUEEEE*EEEEEEEEEEEE*.

Pat turned towards the sound with his mouth wide open. He saw the big boy, the multi-legged predator that killed Roger. It was scrambling towards him, moving fast, attacking.

Pat screamed but his feet never moved. And when he was done screaming he screamed again—then he moved. He ran into the dark hallway wondering if it was the wrong thing to do. With a little luck he spotted a light switch and clicked it on.

Nothing happened.

"COME ON!" he shouted, flicking the switch on and off unsuccessfully. "PLEASE!"

A heavy looking door with a small glass window was on his right. He threw his fingers around the knob and turned it. Dust fell from the knob to the floor. The door was locked.

The beast galloped faster.

SQUUUUUUEEEE*EEEEEEEEEEEE.*

Pat moved ahead five feet. There was a door on his left. He slapped a hand on the cold doorknob: locked again. He moved ahead another ten feet, dragging his fingers along the walls. The corridor was dark now; it was getting hard to see. There was a door on each side of him. He tried both, one after another. They were locked. And now there was a sinking feeling deep in his gut. He placed himself in a terrible position.

The beast moved closer.

The end of the hallway was less than twenty feet away now. There were two doors on his left hand side. He slammed a hand on the closest doorknob and cursed when it wouldn't turn. He tried the other door and wasn't surprised at the result.

This was bad—so very, very bad.

The beast approached the corridor entrance and screeched again. The noise was terrible, sounded like an air horn.

SQUUUUUUEEEE*EEEEEEEEEEEE.*

With his hands on his ears, Pat made his way to the end of the hallway. Three doors remained: one left, one right, and one in front.

He tried the one on his right.

Locked.

He tried the one on his left.

Locked.

The only door that remained looked just like the others. It was thick and heavy and it had a glass window the size of a tissue box. But this one *had* to be different, Pat told himself. It just *had to be*. Because it needed to open, otherwise he'd be sunk for sure.

He took the dusty doorknob in his hand, closed his eyes, and inhaled a deep breath. "Please," he whispered; his brow furrowed. "Please, please, please…"

His wrist turned.

It was locked.

"SHIT!" He was angry now, angry at his predicament and well beyond terrified. What the hell was he going to do? How was he going to escape?

The beast that killed Roger squeezed into the hallway, one leg at a time. It moved slowly, but it was coming. Oh God it was coming. There was no doubt about it. He could see the beast and smell the beast and soon he'd be able to touch it.

The creature moved closer, blocking the hallway's only source of light. Now it was dark, completely dark.

Pat's spirit was crushed; his shoulders were slumped and his head began to lower. Frightened and defeated, he tried the knob a second time, thinking it might turn if he simply tried his luck again.

Didn't work; the door was locked tight.

This was the end of the road. There would be no evading his fate. And when the creature arrived, as he knew it would, there would be no chance in hell he'd kill it with his bare hands.

He would be devoured.

Pat wasn't even twenty-two years old and he had kissed his last girl, drank his final beer, and laughed his biggest laugh. There'd be no more television, parties, paychecks, or purchases. He played his last game of poker, baseball, and soccer. This was the end, the absolute end. The fat lady was going to sing and he didn't want to hear it.

But he *couldn't* give up! He was in the prime of his life!

So where did that leave him?

I'll kick the door down, he thought, rubbing a hand on his chin. *I'll kick down the fucking door!*

He leaned his back against the door on the right side of the hallway, lifted his foot, and kicked the door on his left with the base of his shoe. BANG! The door shook in the darkness. He kicked it two more times, harder now that he had a feel for it. BANG! BANG! The door shook twice more.

The creature shrieked:

SQUUUUUUEEEE*EEEEEEEEEEEEE.*

He squeezed his hands into fists and kicked the door three more times, giving it all he had. BANG. BANG. BANG.

The creature shrieked again.

How close is it? he wondered. *How much time do I have?*

He faced the high-pitched sound as the creature shifted its position. A beam of light entered the hallway giving Pat an unexpectedly glimpse of something he had previously missed. It was on the wall, or was it *in* the wall? Looked like a hole—a small puncture hole about a foot in diameter, too small to crawl into, but it was something. It was——

The creature extended a pair of legs and shifted into position again.

The light disappeared.

Pat dropped to his knees and reached out blindly. His fingers touched the broken drywall. Could he dig through it? Sure. Breaking drywall was easy, really easy. But there was a problem. The wall wasn't made of drywall. It was made of plaster. The building was old, made with old-fashioned know-how. This meant that behind the plaster he'd find wood strapping nailed directly into two-by-fours and God only knows what else. Did he have time to tear the plaster down, pull the strapping apart and fight his way through the two-by-fours? Could he reach the other side? Maybe. Maybe not. If the other side of the wall happened to be constructed the same as this side, he'd have to fight through even more strapping and plaster. And what if there was a big desk on the other side of the wall, or a cabinet, or more of those crates? What if he was about to dig his way into a bathroom only to find that he had some nice big tiles to deal with, or some plumbing, or a bathtub?

This isn't going to work, he thought. *This is suicide.*

He pulled on a piece of strapping, causing a chunk of plaster to fall from the wall and land on his knees.

"Dig," he whispered.

He didn't want to become bogged down in negative scenarios; he wanted to create opportunities. So with that in mind his hands became shovels and he ripped the wall apart like a savage—growling, groaning, sweating, and swearing.

Patience and luck were needed if he were to succeed in the darkness. And although he bled, he did not slow.

Time did not allow it.

12

The car had its nose in the ditch and a back tire spinning. The motor was off. One headlight was wedged into the earth while the other brightened a small region of grass and clay. There was a crack in the windshield and when Beth and William looked through it they could see the hood had been crumpled like a pair of dirty jeans. They weren't looking at the hood though. They were looking through the passenger window, trying to catch a glimpse of Cameron in the forest, not that they had any intention of chasing her.

She was gone.

Beth tried to open the passenger door but it wouldn't open.

William just sat there, dismayed to the point of distress. What Cameron had done was beyond him. It made no sense.

Beth wondered if Cameron was on drugs. But what you'd snort, smoke, or inject, to act like that, she did not know.

William spoke first: "You okay?"

Beth flinched at the sound of his voice; her nerves were shot. "Yeah. I'm okay," she said, putting a hand on her neck. It was sore; later she might find it bruised. "How about you? Are you okay?"

Quite unexpectedly, there was a knock on the back windshield.

Beth and William turned towards the sound in unison.

Nicolas Nehalem was there. The rodent's intestine had fallen from his hair but his chin whiskers remained caked in dried blood. Fortunately for him it was dark outside and his features were hard to analyze. He stepped towards the driver's door. "You guys alright?"

William nodded. "Yeah, I guess so."

"You need help?"

"Maybe."

Nicolas placed a foot into the ditch and opened the door. As the car's interior light came on, he lifted his shotgun and pointed it at William's face.

"I don't give a shit if you need help. You're going to do what I say. Got me? Sir, you need to step out of the car. One fictitious move and I'll blow your head off, and I'm willing to bet that you don't want that. Fuck around and I'll make your brains explode across your lady friend. I can do that, don't mind at all."

William couldn't believe what he was hearing. He said, "You've got to be kidding me."

"I assure you I am not." Nicolas said as he waved his gun up and down, eyes slithering from person to person. When he was done his nose flared. And when he spoke again he bunched his words together, leaving small, dramatic pauses between each sentence. "You have answers. I have questions. How about that? I'd like to introduce those two items, if you catch my drift. But first, I'd like you step out of the car. Please. Don't make me say it a whole bunch of times. I don't like repeating myself. It seems *wrong*, like a waste of energy. So get out of the car. Now, before I kill you. I enjoy that sort of thing."

William turned towards Beth, mostly to shrug his shoulders in astonishment.

Nicolas didn't let it happen.

"DON'T YOU LOOK AT HER!" he shouted, causing William's head to snap around fast. "DON'T YOU *DARE* LOOK AT HER! *I'M* TALKING TO YOU; GET IT? LOOK AT ME, PRICK! *LOOK AT ME!*"

William's mouth and eyes popped open as if synchronized. If Nicolas failed to gain his full attention a moment ago he surely wasn't failing now. He had gained supreme control of William's interest very quickly. Nothing else seemed relevant, only the psycho with the gun mattered. Cameron was on her own. So was Daniel. He didn't want to admit it, but Beth was on her own too. William had his priorities reorganized in a hurry. It was the psycho's time to shine. No two ways about it.

"GET OUT OF THE CAR!"

"No problem. I'll do what ever you say!"

William pulled himself from the wreckage and stumbled up the slope of the ditch.

"Now lay down," Nicolas barked. "Face in the dirt! Oh, I want to SHOOT YOU! I want to do it so bad! You're not my friend. You're not my friend at all. You're nothing., you hear me? You're *nothing!*"

William placed himself on the road with his face in the dirt. Half mumbling, half whining, he said, "What do you want? I didn't do anything to you. I don't even *know* you!"

"SHUT THE FUCK UP A MINUTE, WILL YA?"

Nicolas turned towards Beth, aiming the gun barrels at her oversized chest. His neck muscles were bulging. His eyeballs seemed to glow. "GET OUT."

"Okay," Beth said. She kept her voice calm. She didn't want to do anything or say anything to upset the man. "I going to get out of the car just like you asked. I'm not going to try anything funny. I'll do whatever you say. But this door beside me won't open. It's stuck in the grass. You can look if you want, or I can try to open for you so you can see for yourself... I can do that for you. No problem. But the only way I can get out of the car is by getting out on the driver's side. If I do it really slowly, without any fast movements, is that alright with you?"

"Yeah," Nicolas said. "That's okay with me."

Beth nodded. This was good. Well... not *good* exactly, but it was better. Nicolas had stopped yelling and that was a start.

"Okay great. Look at my hands. See? They're empty. I'm not going to try anything here. I'm going to get out of the car, just like you asked." She crawled across the seat on her hands and knees. When she arrived at the door she crawled onto the slope until her feet were out the door. "Do you want me to stand up or do you want me to lie down? I'll do whatever you want."

"Lay on the ground."

Beth did what she was told.

Nicolas approached his car. His driver's door was open and the trunk was shut. He unlocked the trunk and opened it. Several flies buzzed around Pauline's corpse. Larva squirmed in her eye sockets. He smiled at the body before he moved away from it, leaned into his car, slid his engine key into the ignition slot, and made his way back to his hostages with his shotgun held tight.

He said, "Okay girl, what's your name?"

"Beth."

"Beth. I like that. Big Beth. Yeah, okay. Listen here, Big Beth. I was watching you guys. I saw the fight inside the car. I saw the accident and I saw Cameron run off naked."

William said, "How do you know Cam—"

The shotgun sprang to life like a threatened coyote. "SHUT UP, FUCK-NUT! OH SHIT! I WANT TO SHOOT YOU! I WANT TO SHOOT YOU SO BAD! SO FUCKING BAD! SAY SOMETHING ELSE AND MAKE ME DO IT! *MAKE! ME! DO! IT!*"

Beth took a risk and jumped into the conversation. She still had her eyes in the dirt, and she wasn't sure if it was the right thing to do, but something had to be done before William pissed the guy off again.

With her voice loud, yet composed, and calm, she said, "Talk to me! Talk to me! It's okay. Everything is all right. We're not going to hurt you! We're going to do whatever you want. There's no problem here. Really. There's no problem here whatsoever. Everything is okay. Everything is great so just talk to me... talk to me. Please. We're sorry. We didn't mean to upset you. Please sir, go on. We're listening."

Beth could feel the dirt clouding beneath her face as she spoke. It was getting into her eyes and mouth, making her lips dirty and her throat dry.

Nicolas lowered the shotgun, adjusted his glasses, and spat. "Okay then. Like I was *SAYING*, before I was so *RUDELY* interrupted."

Once he stopped talking he kicked gravel at them. Little rocks and chunks of dirt binged off their heads. He was mad, really mad. He kicked dirt at them twice more to let them know it.

While this happened Beth cringed, William assumed he'd be shot and Nicolas pressed his teeth together, looking towards the sky.

The night was implausibly dark, yet the stars were shinning and as a result the sky was gorgeous. The air was warm and the wind was calm. Everything was perfect. And nights like this—perfectly warm nights laced in beautiful stars—always had a way of easing the careless demons that set fires of rage inside Nicolas' mind, as if the darkness came across the land holding hands with an unknown force of infinite influence that turned an unseen switch, making him calm, in control, a different person.

"Like I was saying," Nicolas said. His voice was composed now, still crusted with an insane tinge, but there was no getting rid of it that trait. It had been with him for years. "I watched your car crash and I watched Cameron run away and I have lots of questions. Oh yes I do.

But my questions and your answers are going to have to wait since I can't get into this stuff now. Not out here in the open. Not where people can see. We've got to get moving before someone comes along and makes things confusing, because if someone comes along… "

He walked in a circle, kicking more dirt. He wasn't kicking the dirt in anger now, just kicking it in front of him. Suddenly his nose became wrinkled, like he was an animal that smelled something awful.

He said, "What's your name again?"

"Who, me?" Beth heard herself say. The words had slipped out, which was bad. She was trying to be a good little social worker and say all the right things. Her life depended on it.

"Yes you. I didn't ask the asshole what his name is. I don't care about him. I don't *like* him. He's not my friend. He's going to die. Why would I want to know the name of a dead man? It's a trick question. I don't want to know his name. When I figure out his name I'll give it to him. I want to know *your* name. *Your name*, not his… yours."

"It's Beth."

"Oh yes, of course. Beth. Big Beth, isn't that right? Big Beth, Big Beth. Okay there, Big Beth. If I remember correctly you said you'd do anything I want, isn't that right? Hmm? Speak up now, I can't hear you."

"Of course, I'll do anything you want. I'm not going to be a problem, not at all."

"Well that's good."

"Do you mind if I ask a question?"

"Which question? Are you going to ask something stupid? I hope not. I hate stupid questions. They make me… " Nicolas slapped the palm of his hand against his temple hard enough to hurt. "Know what I mean?"

Beth didn't know how to respond.

With her face still planted in the dirt, she said, "I'm wondering about your name. I don't know what your name is. Do you mind telling me? If you mind, that's okay. You don't have to tell me."

Nicolas grinned. "Awe, you're pretty cute for a big girl. You're very giving, very charitable and considerate. That's nice. I like that." He moved back and forth where he stood, like he couldn't stand still. Like he was thinking. He licked his lips and blinked his eyes a few times quickly. "I'll tell you what, Big Beth. You can call me daddy.

Yeah. Daddy. For now… and if that works out, well then… we'll just see. How does that sound, hmm?"

"Daddy?"

"Yes."

Beth tried to keep her spirits up but she didn't like where this was going. Calling the man 'daddy' was not what she had in mind. "Okay. I'll call you daddy."

"That's great. Say it for me, will ya?"

Beth hesitated. "Uh… daddy."

"Beautiful. That's just great. Now… Big Beth, I'm going to need you to do something for me and I don't think you're going to like it. But you said you'd do whatever I want, right?"

"Yes."

"Yes, what?"

Beth's closed her eyes. She didn't like this at all. She needed to find a way out her dilemma as soon as possible. She wondered if William was going to jump up and attack the man. She was starting to think it might be the best option available.

With a defeated voice, she said, "Yes, daddy."

"Oh, that is so good, Big Beth. That is *so* good. I think you and I could be best friends, don't you?"

"I suppose."

"You suppose, what?"

Again she hesitated. "I suppose so, daddy."

"That's just great. Stand up for me, will you? Let me get a better look."

Beth stood up and dusted herself off, looking him in the eye. The man reminded her of a snake. It was in the way he moved, the way he spoke, like his words were poisonous weapons and he was striking out with them.

"See, I'm liking you more and more already. You're not so bad, not so bad. Are ya? Naw, you're all right. So, I want you to do something, Big Beth. Are you ready?"

"Yes."

"Yes, what?"

A sigh. "Yes, daddy."

"Great. I want you to crawl into the trunk of my car."

13

Pat was on his hands and knees, digging at the plaster, making the hole in the wall bigger. His objective was to make the opening big enough to crawl through, but the hallway was dark and he had no idea if he was achieving his goal. He also didn't know what was on the other side of the wall, could have been anything, anything at all.

There was a pile of plaster between him and the aperture, and although he lost precious time doing it, he stopped his frantic digging and pushed the debris away with hands that were bleeding and hurt like hell. They weren't just bleeding a little either; they were bleeding a lot. Rusty staples and pins were sticking out of the strapping and it seemed like every two or three seconds he was impaling himself with at least half of them. He ripped a fingernail from his right hand at one point, possibly from the pins, possibly from the wood. He wasn't sure what happened exactly, but when his fingernail tore away from his skin a hot wave of pain came to him so fast, fierce, and unexpected, he felt dizzy, lightheaded, and ready to surrender all hope. Of course, he couldn't give up so easily. The average person can endure more than a sore finger before they hang up their skates and call it a night. Pat wasn't ready for that course of action, not yet anyhow.

After the nail ripped free from his dusty hand Pat rammed his blood-drenched finger between his lips. Blood squirted against the roof of his mouth and down his throat. It ran through his teeth and onto his chin. He thought he might pass out.

The feeling passed.

The creature moved closer.

Pat still couldn't see it, but he could feel the beast and smell the beast and it was only a matter of time before he would be able to touch the beast too.

And worse than that, it would be able to touch him.

Pat pulled his finger from his mouth, found a piece of strapping, grabbed it with both hands, and yanked. The strapping came out easily, which helped his depleted spirits immensely. He grabbed another piece of wood and tried his luck again. It also came free. He popped more planks from the wall, creating a good-sized hole, at least on the one side, but what about the other side? That was the question.

He stuck his hand through the opening and found that the wall in the other room was missing. It must have been an unfinished room. His spirits lifted higher than before and he began to work faster. His fingers continued screaming at him. Each digit was begging him to take a break, stop the madness, and create a new game plan. He disregarded the voice of his fingers completely. Digging continued. The pain continued. Sometimes the wood came from the wall effortlessly and sometimes the wood wouldn't break free no matter how hard he tried. In moments such as these he found that punching the problem areas seemed to be the best ticket. It hurt like hell to do it. Punching pins and staples always hurt, but with time being so valuable his first concern was escape. *Pain endured* rated a very distant second.

Dust entered his lungs. This caused a bout of coughing that slowed him down some, but not much. He removed another board, wondering if he'd be able to fit through the hole. If he could, that'd be great. But what if he couldn't? What if he tried to squeeze through and got stuck? Would he have time to abort the getaway attempt and remove another board or would the time wasted cost him dearly?

Something soft touched the back of his neck—the warm, boneless limb of the creature.

His body lunged forward and he almost screamed. *Almost.* He didn't. Screaming would do nothing but waste time and energy and he needed both. But now that the creature was within striking distance, it was time to scramble through the hole.

Or die trying.

The boneless limb tried to wrap around him and he pulled away from it, dropped onto his stomach, and stuck both arms inside the opening. He gripped the cold floor in the unexplored room and crawled like a lizard. Broken chunks of wood scraped against his body. There was a nail sticking out of the wall, digging a line into his right shoulder. It hurt lots but he pushed on bravely, clenching his teeth together. His shirt ripped and the skin beneath it began bleeding. His knees banged off the strapping and another nail stabbed his skin. He turned onto his back and pulled his legs through the opening.

Pressure on his shin; the beast was touching him again.

Pat pulled away from the probing limb and stood up. He did it. He was through. So what the hell was he supposed to do now? He needed to block the hole but the problem was, he couldn't see anything.

Question: What's the best way to find something in the dark?

Answer: Turn on a light.

Question: Where are most light switches located?

Pat felt himself panicking. It was strange that it was happing now and not three minutes ago. The entire time he was ripping the wall apart his thoughts were organized and under control, but now that he made it to another area things had changed. He was standing in a dark room, in the unknown, and his fears were ready to consume him. A few seconds ago he had a clear agenda; now he none. But he was *still* under pressure…

He stumbled towards the door he couldn't open from the hallway. He raised both hands towards the unfinished wall, searching. The back of his hand touched a thick cable of wiring. He felt—

A light switch!

He clicked it on and before he had a chance to wonder if it would work a florescent light hummed and flickered and came to life, causing him to stick his bleeding hands in front of his eyes. The light seemed very bright now. That was okay. It would pass, and when it did he'd know exactly what to do.

14

Daniel started down the ladder for the fourth time in the past few hours; he had his gun tucked into his belt and kept his eyes on the rungs. Sometimes he stopped moving and looked towards the ground because he didn't want to be ambushed. It was the smart thing to do.

The air was cold and with every rung he descended the air felt colder still. Somehow he had forgotten.

Climbing, climbing, climbing—with his limbs turning numb and his teeth pressed together. Inevitably he reached the bottom rung; that's when the fear claimed him. Not before, and arguably not after. But on the last rung fear strangled him without mercy. He felt exposed then—exposed, vulnerable, and in-between tasks. This caused his stomach to clench and goosebumps to form constellations on his arms. If someone drew his caricature the illustration would have his hair standing on end, his eyes shaped like eggs, and his mouth opened in the shape of an O. Next to the O shaped mouth there'd be a bubble and inside the bubble *OH MY GOD! I'M SO SCARED!!* would be written in terror shaped letters that dripped blood.

He had to get it together, didn't mind tell himself as much. *Get it together or die*, he thought. And what kind of choice was that?

The answer: none. It was no choice at all.

Daniel pulled the gun from his waist, unlocked the safety, and walked into the giant room, listening to his footsteps echo off the walls. The room, he soon discovered, was empty. He wasn't sure if this was good news or bad news but as he approached the place Roger had been killed, he moved cautiously, like the room might not stay empty for long. He looked at the floor. Roger's arm was gone and the area around it was wet, sticky, and peppered with bits of bone, entrails, and God knows what else. He looked at the mess for five seconds or more before kicking a chunk with his shoe. Was it a piece of flesh? He didn't kick it hard, or far. Just touched it really, making sure it was there, making sure it was real. He wasn't imagining things. The tissue was real but it wasn't flesh. It was half a finger.

Daniel stepped through the doorway.

He saw the cocoons and the crates and surprised himself by thinking about money. The crates belonged to him now; maybe he'd discover a treasure after all. And become rich. Or maybe he'd say 'screw it' and set the place on fire. It was definitely one way to go, but was it the right way?

After I find Patrick, I'll decide.

He heard something that sounded like fingernails clicking against glass.

He followed the sound with his eyes and saw a hatched cocoon with several dozen of those strange, multi-legged creatures crawling out of it. More monstrosities were creeping across the top of a wooden crate, each about the size of a human head. Some were faced towards him; some were faced away.

15

"Can you do that for daddy?" Nicolas said. "Be a good girl and crawl into the trunk of my car? Or should I cut off your lips with a straight razor?"

Beth felt something die inside of her. This was bad. Terrible. She said, "I'd rather sit in the front seat with you, uh… daddy. Do you mind if I sit in the front with you? I enjoy riding in the *front*."

Nicolas' face became an exaggerated frown. "Oh, I'm sorry Big Beth. The front is reserved for the dead man." He turned towards William, who was still lying face down in the dirt. "Did you hear that, asshole? I've got a new name for you. It's *'Dead Man Walking.'* Do you like that, huh tough guy? *Dead Man Walking.*"

William didn't respond. What could he say?

"Like I said, Big Beth. Dead Man Walking is going to sit in the front with your daddy and you'll be in the trunk. You'll do whatever I want, right? You're not a liar, are you? If you are, I'm going to punish you. Do I have to punish you?"

Beth chose her words wisely. "I'm not a liar, daddy. But I don't want to be in the trunk. Can I be in the back seat?"

"No."

"Oh." In the moment that slipped past next, Beth opened her mouth but found that she had nothing to say.

Nicolas did. He said, "Something else you need to be aware of, Big Beth. There's already someone in the trunk. So, you know… it might be crowded back there."

Beth looked at his car. The trunk was open but she couldn't see inside from where she was standing.

"Don't worry," Nicolas whispered. "The girl in the trunk has been dead for weeks."

Beth's thoughts drifted. She wondered if she was taking part in some elaborate joke but feared that she wasn't. So what was she supposed to do? Was she really going to crawl into the trunk of a mad-man's car and lie next to a corpse? If she said 'no'—a word she was trained to avoid using—what would happen next? Would the out-come be a pleasant one? Probably not.

It was a tough spot.

Getting into the trunk was the wrong move, possibly the *worst* move. But saying 'no' was also the wrong move. So what was left?

William needed to attack the man. Simple. She could almost see it happening too; see him leaping up like a comic book superhero with his muscles bulging and his eyes stern. And oh, wouldn't that be per-fect? But Will was in no position to fight, nor was he a stern-eyed muscleman. He had fat arms, a potbelly, and he was working on chin number three. Not to mention the fact that he was lying facedown in the dirt and was afraid to move—with good reason. The man with the gun wanted to shoot him. Might even do it.

William couldn't help; Beth was the one standing. Not Will. So was it was time for her to swing her fists into action? Was that her best option? Or was it the only option that didn't have her locked inside the trunk of a car—

She looked at the shotgun.

The gun was held low, pointed just below her chest.

"Don't look there, Big Beth." Nicolas said. "Don't look at the gun. I see what you're doing. I know what you're thinking. Yes I do. I know what you're thinking and I don't like it. You're wondering what to do because you don't want to get in the trunk. I get that, I really do. I understand. It's cramped back there, I know. And Pauline Stupid-Head is a tad slimy right now. She isn't the most pleasant girl in the neighborhood, if you catch my drift. She's stinky. She has flies on her. She has worms crawling out of her belly, cooties in her eyes, and mold on her skin. She hasn't brushed her teeth in years. She hasn't show-ered. She's been pissing on herself forever. I understand. I've seen her and you haven't—so trust me, I know how rough she is. I'm not sure I'd want to crawl back there and I like that sort of thing. But here's the situation… " Nicolas clamped his bottom lip between his teeth. His eyes narrowed. "Get on the ground, NOW!"

Beth dropped to her knees and put her face into her hands.

If he shoots me in the head my hands will blow apart too, she thought morbidly. *Oh Gawd, don't shoot me in the head. Don't kill me.*

"Hey! Dead Man Walking! Stand up. Let me get a look at you."

William pushed himself to his feet.

Once he was standing, Nicolas moved away from him. He didn't trust this man. He didn't trust him or like him. The easiest thing might be to shoot the asshole, right here and now. It was something to consider.

"Come with me," Nicolas said.

He backed away from William, moving towards his car. The gun was angled appropriately. Once he had William standing next to his car, he said, "Would you like to get in the trunk? It's nice back there, nice and disgusting. Naw... just kidding. You can lie on the road again. Do it. Do it *now.*"

William felt his chin tremble and his eyes water. There was nothing he could do to change things. He was beat, and at this point he didn't want to hesitate. If the psychotic man happened to be a '*three strikes, you're out*' type of guy, then Will's next error would be his last. He said, "Yes sir." He squatted, got onto his hands and knees and dropped onto the road.

"Open your arms and legs wide."

William did.

Nicolas made his way to Beth. "Okay Big Beth. It's time to get up again."

She got up slowly, trying to drag the moment out, hoping that something good would happen. She needed leverage here, because right now she felt like she didn't have any leverage at all.

Down the road, a blue minivan pulled from a driveway. After a slight pause it began driving towards them.

William—still lying on the road—tilted his head slightly, sneaking a dangerous glimpse.

Beth shifted her eyes.

This was the moment she'd been waiting for. But what was she going to do with it? How could she exploit the moment? One false move might push Nicolas over the edge, so where did that leave her?

Nicolas grinned. He didn't turn towards the vehicle or hide what he was doing. He didn't step forward or back or do anything at all. His eyes were locked on Beth. *Big* Beth. He was forging a new plan and feeling good about it.

"You ready, Big Beth?" He said, holding the shotgun low. "You ready to see something exciting, something you'll never forget? After therapy and nightmares and drinking yourself to death you're going to remember this one. Are you ready to see a gun go off? Ready to watch people die?"

The minivan approached with headlights gleaming. It slowed, presumably to see what was happening.

"No," Beth said.

"No what?"

The van was almost beside them now. The passenger window was lowering and the wheels were coming to a stop.

"No daddy," Beth said.

She wondered why the van was stopping. Couldn't the people inside the damn thing see they were in the presence of a maniac? Couldn't they see the shotgun, or William lying facedown on the road like a hostage?

William's heart raced and his mouth became drier than sand. If there was ever a time to run, or hide, or fight, or scream—the time was now. Right now. He had to do something. His hands began to shake.

Get up, he thought. *Get up. Get up. Get up!*

Still standing at the side of the road, Beth began to cry. She couldn't help it. She wanted to fight the man but she was afraid and she didn't know what do.

"No daddy" she said again, hating the fact that she sounded like a child now. And she did. Oh God, it was impossible to sound like an adult while calling someone 'daddy' as the snot built up inside your nose. "I'm not ready for this. Please don't do anything unpleasant. Just leave everybody alone. *Please!*"

She was unraveling. She knew it and Nicolas knew it too.

The van stopped.

A window rolled down.

"It's too bad you feel that way, Big Beth," Nicolas said. "You're in the wrong place at the wrong time, my love. Do you know that? Of course you do. Watch this."

Nicolas turned quickly, marched towards the vehicle, and rammed the shotgun barrel through the open window.

There was a man and a woman in the front and a baby girl in the back. The man's name was Brett Adkins. His wife's name was Tara.

The baby girl was Michelle Rose Adkins. She wore a pink jumper and was fast asleep.

The shotgun barrel smacked Tara in the nose and her face became instantly pale. Brett's eyes popped open and his jaw dropped. Tara raised a hand from her lap and—

Nicolas pulled the trigger. A gigantic outburst erupted within his hands and Tara's head exploded. A fountain of blood shot from her neck. Skull fragments, meat, brain, hair, and skin, tumbled off her shoulders.

Nicolas pumped a new shell into the chamber.

Brett, covered in gore, wore an expression that said: *Tara's head didn't really get wiped off the face of the earth, did it? This can't possibly be real! This must be a dream!*

He managed to say, "Wait!" then Nicolas pulled the trigger again and *his* head burst into a sea of brains, bones, and blood—splashing against the windows and doors, the seats, the dash, floor, ceiling, and everything else in the car.

Beth, standing at the side of the road, watched in horror, pulling at her hair with both hands. Her mouth opened and closed pointlessly. She was trying to say something that would stop the madness but had no idea what that something might be.

Baby Michelle woke to the sound of her mother and father being murdered. She began wailing and kicking her feet in the air; little bubbles of saliva grew from the corner of her mouth. Tiny fingers stretched apart, desperate to latch on to something warm and consoling.

Nicolas had a furious grin carved upon his face. His gaze was cold like frost; his eyeballs glistened like diamonds. He pumped the chamber, pointed the muzzle into the baby seat and pulled the trigger again. A third blast came, somehow louder than the previous two. And with that, the crying ended. The family had been extinguished.

Beth was screaming.

William put his hands into the gravel. This lunacy had gone on long enough—too long, in fact. *Too long.* It was time to get up, time to show the psychotic fucker a thing or two about being human.

16

Dan pulled a fresh clip from his pocket. He didn't need it yet but he wanted it in his hand. If he remembered correctly he already pulled the trigger twice, which meant his Charter Arms .32 automatic was now holding five bullets.

Five bullets, he thought. *I've got to remember this. The amount of bullets I have is important. I need to keep track 'cause if I don't I might soon regret it. And I don't want to regret it. Regretting means trouble.*

He walked towards the crates eying the cocoons on top of them.

Creatures scrambled with mouths wide. They looked absolutely horrifying, not completely unlike a batch of mutant spiders that had grown to enormous magnitudes.

Daniel slowed his pace, ensuring that his feet touched the floor quietly. His fingers were stinging as he gripped the clip. He was nervous, but not overly scared. He figured he could kill all the creatures, no problem. Three seven-bullet clips, plus the five bullets in the gun––quick math said three times seven was twenty-one, and twenty-one plus five was twenty-six. Twenty-six bullets could slaughter a couple dozen crab-critters if his aim was true. And his aim *would* be true. He'd make sure of it.

Crab-critters, he thought. *Killer-crabs.*

They didn't look like any crabs he'd seen before, but somehow *killer-crabs* fit the bill almost perfectly.

Dan stopped walking, fifteen feet away from his nearest enemy, give or take a few inches. He raised the gun up and took three more steps, gently and watchfully. The crab he was creeping towards didn't notice him. Or maybe it didn't care. Either way, in today's little shootout this fella was first in line.

As the creature moved across a crate, Dan almost felt mesmerized by its black bubble eyes and the way its legs danced, the way its mouths opened and closed. The creature was so distinctive, so unique.

He watched the crab-critter lift itself high upon its legs and prance around in a semi-circle. Living art: that's what it was. Standing before him was the planet's most exceptional species, brilliant and extraordinary—an utterly rare breed in every way. Mouths opened and closed in harmony; he had never seen anything like it.

Oh well, he thought. *Bye, little fella.*

Dan pulled the trigger and the sound blasted, disrupting the silence.

The slug hit the creature square. Thick white puss and dark sticky blood splashed the critters behind it as the wounded critter tumbled backwards with legs twitching.

This is going to be easy, he thought. But then he changed his mind.

Legs clicked together. Mouths opened and closed faster then before, screeching a thin hollow screech. Crabs he hadn't seen crept out from behind boxes and crates in singles and in bunches; some moved towards him, some away. A few rushed from an open cocoon. Suddenly, they seemed to be everywhere. Quick math said twenty-six bullets would be cutting it close now. Or might not be enough. And Dan had already fired once so quick math said that he had twenty-five bullets left, not twenty-six.

He swung the weapon to the right, picked out another victim, and pulled the trigger again. A slab of meat went flying. The creature spun around in a circle before it flipped onto its back. Something green poured out of it. Next to the green liquid, blood pooled in the shape of a valentine heart. Long black legs came together like a jellyfish swimming against the current. A different crab scurried through the fresh pool of blood, put a leg upon the fallen creature and stood high upon its claws. It had a thin white stripe running an arched line between its mouths. Dan took aim and pulled the trigger again. Another hit. The creature tumbled off one crate and landed on another, making a SQUAWK sound as it landed.

Dan's focus wavered.

Crabs seemed to be all over the place now. Most were black but some were brown, white, and insipid. And with every passing moment there appeared to be more, lots more. They were running quickly, running in all directions too.

One of the bigger crabs caught Dan's eye. He followed it with his gun and pulled the trigger earlier then he intended. The creature slammed against wall with a severed limb and a hunk of meat missing from body, but it didn't die. Dan only winged it.

"Take it easy," Dan whispered, knowing he had almost missed the crab-critter completely. "I don't have bullets to spare."

Hearing himself speak was soothing. It made the situation more manageable, if only in his mind. He recognized this oddity and embraced it. He said, "Go for the ones that are just standing there. Don't be shy."

Daniel picked out a crab that seemed to be sleeping and yanked on the trigger again, scoring another bull's-eye.

Two crab-critters crawled off a crate and scrambled towards him, one in front of the other.

Daniel held his breath, steadied his hand and aimed for the nearest one. He pulled the trigger.

The bullet hit dead center and the critter's legs became instantly limp. It flopped onto its belly like a string-puppet after the show. Critter number two never slowed or changed direction. It crawled over the dead body like it had a job to do. Nothing, it seemed, would stand in its way.

Daniel lined the crab-critter up, smiling uncomfortably. He pulled the trigger again, confident of landing another hit.

CLICK: the gun was empty.

The crab was less than eight feet away now.

Three more scurried off of the crates and ran in his direction. Another crawled from a cocoon. This one wasn't black, nor was it brown. It was nearly transparent with a single red spot in the middle; looked like it had been born early.

Dan stepped back, pulled the empty clip from the gun and dropped it. The clip bounced off his shoe and onto the floor. He slid the next clip into place, clicked the safety, angled the weapon and pulled the trigger.

The shot went wide, way wide.

I'm not aiming, he thought. *Oh shit, oh shit... I'm panicking.*

He had a terrible flashback: the big creature devouring Roger's head, blood spraying like a fountain, arms and legs kicking, giant teeth chewing.

He didn't want to panic, *couldn't* panic. Panicking would be the death of him and he damn well knew it. Somehow—even as he was telling himself to keep it together—this information didn't stick.

Another thought went astray: he wondered what it would feel like to have a dozen of the little guys chomping him into pieces, laying eggs in his skin. Without question, it couldn't feel good. It couldn't *possibly* feel good.

Stop it, he told himself. *Just stop it! Stay focused on the job at hand!*

He eyed a single crab, the closest crab, the one that was less than five feet away now. He took a deep, calming breath and aimed. It seemed like weeks slipped past in that moment, and when the moment was over and the time had come to pull the trigger, he yanked on it twice very quickly. His aim was true both times and he hit his intended victim, spot-on. Twice.

It was dead. Thank heaven it was dead.

He was glad to have killed it but he felt like crying. He didn't need to shoot it twice. Only once. He was wasting bullets now. Oh merciful God above save us all, he was wasting bullets! How could he be so thoughtless, so careless? How could he throw away ammunition at a time like this? Wasting bullets was almost a sin. And not only that— he was freaking *right the fuck out*—that's what he was doing. He was FREAKING OUT, losing his poise, and forfeiting his edge in the battle. He had a hot case of the cold sweats and was turning into an unbalanced bundle of emotional nerve-endings.

Squandering my composure, he thought. *And that's not good.*

Mumbling, he aimed his gun at a pair of crabs and pulled the trigger twice more: a hit and a miss.

A translucent crab fell from a cocoon, a small one. It rolled into a ball, then got onto its feet and ran in a circle.

For no real reason, Daniel aimed at this crab. He pulled the trigger and shot it dead. It was a good shot, maybe even a great shot— but why-oh-why on God's green earth was he aiming at *that* one? It was at least twenty-five feet away. Why not focus on the two that were getting ready to crawl up his leg and gnaw on his belly?

I'm freaking out!

Four more creatures jumped from a cocoon, together in a loose bunch. Three of them were brown. One was black with little green dots on its back.

Three translucent crabs scurried up a wall.

Dan aimed at the nearest troublemaker. It was big and black and its long stalks moved very quickly. Teeth were snapping. Bulbous eyes were bouncing up and down.

He pulled the trigger twice and the gun fired once. It was a hit, but he was out of bullets. Again. He needed to replace the clip.

Two clips left.

While backing away from the nearest crab-critter he reloaded, dropping the empty clip indifferently.

A couple of black crabs crawled across the ceiling, capturing Dan's attention. He looked up, then away, trying not to think about them. He needed to stay focused on the nearest critter, which was three feet away. Two feet. One foot. He aimed and fired; half of its little body exploded. Strange round balls rolled from the wound. Most were soft and white; a few were black. All of them were coated in puss, mucus and blood.

And the crabs were on the ceiling now? How the hell did that happen?!

This was bad news, very bad news. He had to be realistic. He had crabs on the walls, the ceiling, the floor, the crates—crabs were everywhere! And here he was, wasting bullets with thirteen left. Or was it fourteen? No—he just pulled the trigger. It was thirteen, *thirteen*. He'd have to remember that. He had six bullets inside the gun and one clip left.

New questions came: *Did I count the crab-critters wrong? How many bullets do I have?*

He pulled the trigger again, killing another crab.

Pink mush splashed into the air.

Count wrong? He thought. *I didn't count the crab-critters at all! I made a quick estimate and started shooting, didn't I? Oh God, what kind of plan is that? And how many of those things are around me? What the hell am I going to do once I run out of bullets? They're still crawling out of the cocoons! Is that what is happening here? Oh man, I've made a terrible mistake! I've got to get out of here!*

He noticed something from the corner of his eye. Turning his head left, he saw four more crabs scrambling towards him. One began flapping a large set of wings. A moment later it was airborne, flying erratically.

"Where did you come from?" he barked loud enough for the whole world to hear. His voice wasn't soothing now. It sounded high and nasally, dreadfully troubled and plagued in fear. Things were turning bad fast; it was time for a new plan.

He squeezed the trigger three more times and all three shots went wide.

He wasn't aiming now, just shooting, which was absolutely the worst thing he could do. How many bullets did he still have—three in the gun and seven in the clip? Was that right—ten bullets... maybe nine, maybe eight?

What happened to counting?

He fired at the new batch of predators and scored himself a hit. A winged critter zipped past him, making a humming noise. He turned away and—

Oh dear lord. Big mamma had returned. It was pulling its body from the hallway one leg at a time. He had forgotten its size. The thing was massive, bigger than a truck.

One crab pounced onto his shoe and tried to spear him with a stinger.

Daniel kicked it away and the thing went tumbling. He fired recklessly into a cocoon. Something large and white and covered in hair fell from the ceiling and opened up like a flower, releasing thousands of tiny red spiders-crabs and a stench so bad the air seemed poisonous. The smell was a bit like a dog in need of a bath, but that wasn't completely accurate. Somehow it smelled like walnuts too.

I'm getting out of here, Dan thought, but when he looked through the open door, towards the exit, he wondered if he could.

The ladder was in bad shape. There were crab-critters all around it, at least twenty of them. Some were flying. Some were the size of a wolf; others were small like rats. Where they came from, he did not know.

Like it or not, crawling up the ladder wasn't an option. It was suicide.

And once again his gun was empty.

Shame he didn't realize it.

17

Nicolas spun around, screaming, "LAY DOWN!"

William, still all fours and in no position to argue, did what he was told. He cursed himself for being too slow, knowing he should have jumped up quicker. He was bigger than the trigger-happy psycho, probably faster too. So why did he wait? Why did he hesitate? Was he that much of a chicken-shit? Is that what it boiled down to… was he was afraid of this asshole?

The asshole has a shotgun, he reminded himself. *And the asshole likes to use it.*

Nicolas spun his gun towards Beth.

Beth was standing still, a zombie. The smooth-talking lady that rolled her words like butter across toast had packed her bags and gone the way of the dinosaur. Like the family in the car, the social worker was gone-baby-gone. All that was left was a frightened girl in a woman's body.

Nicolas said, "MOVE."

Beth walked towards Nicolas' car with tears in her eyes. She looked inside the trunk and felt sick. Pauline's corpse might have been dead but the things living in it, on it, and around it, were not. They were very much alive.

Nicolas looked at Pauline's corpse.

And pressed his teeth together. Hard.

He remembered standing at Pauline's cage, standing—*with a bottle of formula in one hand and a bag of chocolate-chip cookies, of all things, in the other. The cookies were for her, a gift. Each of his babies were getting an entire bag of cookies—not the cheap kind, the expensive kind, with chocolaty chunks—so they'd know how much he cared for them, how much he loved them, how much he needed them. And Pauline, that ungrateful bitch, that selfish cunt, that evil* witch—*she looked up from her cage, crying like a child. She said, "This is hell. I'm living in hell and you're the reason. I hate you."*

Ten minutes later she was dead.

"Pauline deserved it," Nicolas whispered. "She deserved what she got."

Beth didn't hear his words. She said, "I can't get in there," speaking honestly, looking in the trunk. She wasn't being difficult, only truthful. "I can't lie next to that *thing*."

"You can and you will." Nicolas stepped away from Beth and pointed the gun at William's neck. "And that's not a thing. It's Pauline Stupid-head. Now listen up a minute, 'cause I'm going make things very easy for you. Are you listening? You still with me? Yes? Good. Now pay attention, Big Beth. This is important. If you don't crawl into that fucking trunk I'm going to blow Dead Man's head clean off his body. I'm not going to shoot him *in* the head. Oh no. Do you see where I'm pointing the barrels? Do you? Look at me, you fat fucking swine. LOOK! Can you guess where the shells are going to end up? Can you? Just in case your sense of projection is a bit rough around the edges, let me enlighten you. The shells are going to come out of the gun barrel at a speed of about eight hundred feet per second; expanding as they move, getting wider than the barrels they travel through. Did you know that they do that? They do. And they're going to enter the back of his neck, see? And let me tell you… they're going to make GREAT BIG HOLES on the way in. They're going to make *really* big fucking holes. And then they're going to come out on the other side of his neck, see? They're going to come out even bigger. That's where his throat is, by the way… lest you didn't know. Follow me? They're going to go in BIG and come out BIGGER! His throat, keep in mind, is really important. Without a throat breathing gets tougher than shit."

"Okay," Beth said.

"Oh no, it's not okay. You just listen to me, Big Beth, because it's *not* okay. Don't say things are okay if you don't really believe it. And you don't, I can tell. But listen a minute: his head is going to pop off his body, see? It's going to pop off and roll across the street. It'll be like when you get together with your friends on New Years Eve, you know? Somebody has a problem and somebody doesn't. Somebody kisses somebody and somebody cries. Somebody lost twenty pounds and looks great, while somebody else gained twenty and looks like a sack of donkey shit. Somebody sneaks into a bathroom room and gets a hand-job from a drunken slut that's high on coke and wearing too much make-up, and somebody pulls out the champagne, sticks a thumbs beneath the cork, and pops it off. And the cork is a little too small for the bottle. Did you ever notice that? Huh? Did you? It's kind of like gunpowder being a little too explosive for the shells, and the shells being too volatile for the shotgun. Right? Am I right? Of *course* I'm right. It's the same thing, Beth. That's what I'm trying to say, you fucking cow. It's the same fucking thing. This asshole's head is going to pop off of his body and it's going to roll across the road like a cork from a bottle on New Years Eve. You see that van there, the one with the lights on and the carcasses inside it? That's where the head is going. It'll probably get stuck beneath the door or something."

Beth said, "I'll get in."

"You'll get in?"

"Yes. Just don't pull the trigger again. Please, don't shoot William."

"There is no *William* here, Big Beth. Just *Dead Man*... Dead Man Walking. So get in the fucking trunk and get comfortable and have a nice time and I won't make Dead Man's head pop off his body and roll across the road like a champagne cork. Deal?"

"Yeah. Okay. Whatever you want."

"Well... get in then. Go on. Pauline is waiting. I haven't got all day. What do I look like, an idiot? Get in the fucking trunk."

Beth crawled into the trunk and forced herself into a laying position, facing away from Pauline's black and green withered skin. She was about to say something about there not being enough room for two bodies when Nicolas slammed the trunk down, smashing it off her head and shoulder.

She was right. There wasn't enough room and the lock didn't catch. So Nicolas slammed the trunk twice more before he put all his weight into it. Finally the latch clicked and the trunk locked.

Beth was squished. She couldn't move much of anything, just her hands and feet, and those appendages weren't moving far. Worse than that, the smell was enough to make her stomach churn.

"All right, Dead Man Walking," Nicolas said. "Get up."

William stood.

Nicolas put his index finger to his lips, making the universally recognized sign for 'shut up.' He whispered, "Be quiet, okay?"

William nodded.

Suddenly Nicolas shouted: "I'M GOING TO KILL YOU! HERE I GO! ONE, TWO, THREE!" He pumped the chamber, fired into the trees and pumped the chamber again. He had a grin from ear to ear.

William flinched at the sound.

From inside the trunk, Beth screamed, "NOOOOOO!"

"That's so funny," Nicolas said, smiling comically. "Honestly. She probably thinks I shot you. Damn. She is going to be *so* surprised. But she'll be surprised in a good way, don't you think? In a good way."

William couldn't believe his ears. This guy was Loony-toons.

After shaking his head in disbelief, he swallowed back his anger and tried to make the most of the moment incorporating Beth's strategy. He didn't like being called 'Dead Man Walking,' and was hoping to change that.

He said, "I'm really sorry we got off on the wrong foot, sir. No hard feelings."

Nicolas looked him in the eye. "Really?"

"Yes sir. Really."

"Well that's great. Just great. Maybe you and I can be drinking buddies, is that it? Maybe we can go to picnics and barbeques and strip joints together. Eat some burgers and lick some pussy; sound good? Let me think about it, because I've got to be honest with you. We've had a rough beginning. I think people call that *getting off on the wrong foot*. Oh wait, that's what you said, of course. But you know, here's something… maybe you can gnaw on this one while I mind-hump your intelligence. I don't *like* getting off on the wrong foot. I enjoy getting off on the *right* foot, you hear me? Are you feeling me brother? Are you? The *right* foot. You see—I'd like you to do me a favor. Can ya do that, you fucking asshole? Can you do me a solid, brother?"

William nodded. "Yes sir. I can do whatever you'd like me to do."

"Now that's more like it. Look at you. You aren't so bad. You're coming around. You might have a future yet."

Nicolas smiled a very odd smile and held it on his face far too long. The shotgun never wavered, never moved.

If William didn't know better he'd think an alien laid eggs in Nicolas' brain. He considered saying something but didn't want to chance it; the guy was crazy.

Finally Nicolas dropped the smile and raised the tone of his voice up a notch. "Can you drive me home? It would mean a lot to me. I live right around the corner and I don't feel like driving. Do you ever get like that? I do. There's a road called Stone Crescent. It's nice. Its got lots of trees and a couple of cabins and there's this one little spot where somebody puts firewood next to a sign that says FREE FIREWOOD and I was wondering if you'd be kind enough to drive me home."

William nodded. "Sure. I can do that for you."

"Okay then. Get in the car."

William walked to the car, opened the driver's door and said, "You want me to sit here, right?"

"Yes. Of course I do. That's the place the driver sits. You're the driver. Get in. Sit down. Put your feet up. Make yourself comfortable."

William got in, sat down and… there was a squirrel torso on the dash.

Seeing it made Will's stomach turn and his body break out in a new layer of sweat. Instinctively he turned away from the animal. Now he was looking at the minivan. The engine was still running. The headlights were lighting up the gravel. He could see the mess inside the vehicle a little, but thankfully, the interior lights weren't on so he couldn't see the explicit details.

From inside the trunk, Beth released a long scream.

This was bad, very, very bad. William needed to do something, but what?

Nicolas opened the passenger door and sat down. He had the loaded shotgun pointed at William's head. He lowered it to body level, and said, "Lift your arms."

William lifted both elbows, grabbing the steering wheel as he did so.

Nicolas pushed the double barrel against his ribcage.

"You might think you're fast," Nicolas said. "But you're not *that* fast. I'm pulling the trigger right now, you know. It's about eighty percent pulled. If you do anything at all the other twenty percent will pull itself. And I'm not sure if you noticed this but the barrels are actually behind you some. You won't be able to push the gun forward is what

165

I'm trying to say. Only push it back, towards the seat. In which case the double barrel will bounce off the fabric and I'll pull the trigger and most of your spine will blast right out that fucking door. You might want to think about that. I know I would."

"I will."

"I'm glad to hear it. Don't try any funny stuff. The keys are hanging from the ignition. This car's an automatic so driving ought to be nice and easy for you. Start the car and turn this puppy around."

William did what he was told: he got the car moving and within three minutes they were pulling off Stone Path Road and onto Stone Crescent. One minute later they were pulling up a long narrow driveway that weaved its way to a cabin. The cabin wasn't perfect but it wasn't Castle Frankenstein either. It was just a cabin, nothing special about it. A white van sat deep in the driveway; it looked about fifteen years old. There were a few tires leaning against the house, rusted cans stacked in a pile and a wooden shed with a lock on the door.

"Home sweet home," Nicolas said, easing the shotgun from William's ribcage the slightest amount.

William tried to smile but found he couldn't do it. He was worried about Cameron, Beth, and himself. He wondered if he'd ever see his brother again, or home again.

The answer, unfortunately, was no.

His brother was dead. Soon he'd be dead too.

18

After Pat flicked the light switch on he put an arm over his eyes to keep the light from blinding him. The blinding sensation passed quickly, and when he moved his arm he instinctively looked towards the hole he had crawled through.

There was blood on the floor—his blood, he presumed. There was also a big meaty leg poking its way inside.

He stepped back.

Thoughts, questions and schemes came erratically.

I need to block the hole. Is that my blood? Of course it's my blood. Who else would be bleeding? Am I alone? Is the creature going to break through the hole? How messed-up are my hands? They hurt so much. My shoulder hurts too. Maybe the creature is bleeding; it got shot, didn't it? How long will this light stay on? Why is there power down here? What the hell is that thing, a giant spider? If I find a sharp stick, maybe I can stab it. But what'll happen if I do that? Will it try to get in here? I guess it doesn't matter. It already wants in here. I can't believe I dug my way through the wall! I can't believe I tore my fingernail off. Is it going to grow back? Are my hands gross looking?

Pat looked at his hands.

Yes. Beneath the plaster and dirt his hands were gross looking. There were no broken bones, thank God, but his hands had never looked so bad. In several places his muscles were bunched up like discarded towels in a locker room, the area around his knuckles had bulged into oddly shaped knots, and the skin around his fingertips had become mangled to a point of vulgarity. There were also dozens of deep pricks that were swollen and bleeding non-stop. Only one finger was missing a nail, but with every finger covered in blood and coated with plaster it didn't look different then the others.

While he studied his hands, the creature moved its leg towards him.

He didn't look at the leg, not yet. He was too enthralled with his wounds. He wondered if his hands would be permanently damaged or just temporarily injured. Assuming his injuries were fleeting, how long until his body healed? As a child he always recovered quickly; his mother often commented on it. But he was older now, not much older, but older.

Three weeks, he thought. *Maybe less?*

From the corner of his eye he saw the limb sliding across the floor. Gunshots blasted and the leg zipped out of the hole, grazing the strapping. In spite of his pain, Pat smiled a big goofy smile. He knew what was happening: someone was firing a weapon, trying to save him. Best of all, it seemed to be working. The creature was leaving with a new objective, one that didn't include him.

I'll get through this yet, he thought, turning away from the hole. *Oh yes I will.*

More shots were fired.

He noticed a door that looked like all the rest. He walked towards it, put a hand upon the knob and opened the door.

19

Nicolas said, "Get out of the car, do it slowly and don't make any sudden moves."

William felt like crying. He needed something to happen, something good. Hopefully he hadn't missed his chance to turn the situation around. It would be a shame it he had.

He said, "Should I leave the keys in the ignition?"

"No. Turn the car off and take the keychain with you. Once you're outside you should approach the front door. Don't bother running away, I'll only shoot you down."

Will removed the keys, opened the door and stepped out of the car. He slammed the door shut harder than he intended, glimpsed at the squirrel torso and made his way to the cabin, following a cobblestone path that was rather nice.

Nicolas tagged along at a safe distance. He said, "Check the door, will you? It might be open. Sometimes I forget to lock it."

William checked. The door wouldn't open. "Locked," he said.

"That's alright. We can get through this, no problem. By the way, you might want to remember that Big Beth is still in the trunk. So if you're going to play hero—and fail—I'll punish her for your actions. That's the way I do business. I'll chop her into a thousand pieces and fertilize my lawn with her. When I'm done I'll blame you."

"I understand."

"The key for the front door is in your hand. It has a blue casing. Find the key. Open the door."

William found the appropriate key and opened the door.

He expected the place to look like a scene from *The Texas Chainsaw Massacre*. He figured there'd be bones in the corners and chickens carcasses strung up on hooks. He expected blood splashed on every wall, an upside cross hanging above a pentagram, and a goat skull with flames shooting from its nostrils. He expected Satan to step through the gates of hell with a huge, red cape blowing wildly against his pitch-fork, singing 'Hell Ain't a Bad Place to Be' by AC/DC while blood poured from his eyes.

He was wrong.

The place was nice, clean. The furniture was old but well maintained. The walls may have benefited from a fresh coat of paint and new baseboards but the same could be said for his place. The fireplace looked like it could use a scrubbing but whose didn't? Bottom line, the cabin looked normal.

"Sometimes I make messes," Nicolas said, as if reading Will's mind. "But mostly I clean messes. I like cleaning. A woman's work is never done and all that gopher-shit. Got to admit though, downstairs is a different story. I've got rats and mice, flies and cockroaches. I've got seventy-five loads of laundry that needs to be washed and babies that need feeding. The house has a foundation problem I don't know how to fix, and I've got leaky pipes that get so cold in the wintertime, icicles hang from them like little fingers. Step inside and I'll show you around. Put the keys on the table. If you try anything funny I'll blast your arms off, scoop out your eyes and bury you in the yard."

A table sat below a mirror in the front hall. William placed the keys on it and kept walking. He needed to do something. He needed to fight back somehow, but every time he considered fighting the psychopath painted a picture of violence. He didn't want his arms blown off and his eyes scooped out. He wanted to go home, eat ice cream and watch television. He wanted to find a wife and start a family. He wanted to be free of this nightmare and think happy thoughts.

He decided to open the lines of communication. He said, "Hey, do you think—"

Nicolas interrupted. "Shut up Dead Man. Next to the kitchen, there's a staircase. See it? It leads to the basement. Go there. I'd like to show you the basement, if you don't mind."

Will stopped walking; his shoulders slumped. "What do you want from me?"

It was the wrong thing to say, of course. Nicolas knew it; William knew it too. But going into the basement wasn't a good move and if William could stall awhile he might come up with a plan.

Nicolas said, "We were getting along so well, remember? You told me you'd do anything I wanted, right? Yes or no: did you say that?"

"I suppose I did."

"You *suppose*? You *suppooooose*? What do you mean you suppose? You either did or you didn't. And you did, you did. I heard you. Don't start lying to me Dead Man. Don't you dare. If that's the relationship you wanna develop you can forget it. I'll terminate our affiliation immediately."

William turned around and Nicolas allowed it.

"You're getting brave now, I see. Is that what *you* want, hmmm? Do you want me to conclude our coalition? Do you?"

Will's eyes closed. "No sir. I'm sorry."

"That's better. Get your ass in gear and go downstairs. There's something I want you to see."

William did what he was told.

When he entered the room loaded with clothing, Nicolas said, "Stop. Turn around."

William did.

"Take off your clothes."

"What?"

"You heard me. Take off your clothing or I'll shoot you dead. You can leave your underpants on if you want. I don't want my babies seeing something they shouldn't be seeing. They're too young and innocent. Now go on… do it. Do it now. And throw your clothing in the pile."

Reluctantly, William removed his clothing and threw them on the floor. He didn't toss them far; he was hoping he'd need them before long.

Nicolas said, "Now keep walking. We're going into the cellar."

"You have children down there?"

"I sure do."

William walked down the rickety staircase and into the cellar with nothing on but his underwear. He created a mental image of a baby in a crib needing a change of diapers. He knew better, of course. The psychopath couldn't be doing an okay job taking care of a baby. It wasn't possible. Knowing this, he braced himself for what he was about to see. He expected it to be bad. Not just bad, in fact, but horrific. He imagined underfed, unloved babies needing a doctor and a real home. He imagined a *dead* baby, a murdered baby. He even forced himself to imagine a baby that had been burned to a crisp and nailed to the wall, because he knew it would be bad. It had to be bad. *Of course* it would be bad.

He thought he was ready but he wasn't. He never imagined adults. The shock of seeing two women locked inside separate cages twisted a screw inside his mind he never knew existed.

He looked at Cathy first, then Olive, then at the empty cage.

Cathy. Olive. Empty cage.

Empty cage.

His mouth slinked open and his eyes dawned like the morning sun. His shoulders raised and his knees began to shake.

Why was there an empty cage? Oh shit... why?

He turned around quickly, shocked and disgusted and scared half to death. He thought the empty cage had his name written all over it. He held out his hands as if to say, *this isn't really happening, is it? Not to me—not to good old William McMaster! I've got a business to run and a house to maintain! I've got a new television and a handful of DVD's that need watching! I've got some good years ahead of me and this isn't the way I want to spend 'em! And why would I? I don't want to be locked inside a cage! I'd rather die!*

The forecast for the days ahead came with such vivid force that Will almost coughed up his lunch and released his bladder at the same time—him living inside a cage for years and years, tortured on a daily basis. Was this his future?! Dear God, really? But it had to be! It just had to be! Why else would the psychopath lead him to an empty cage?

Olive screamed.

Cathy closed her eyes.

Nicolas squeezed the trigger.

William saw it happening but he didn't understand. Things couldn't change gears so quickly, could they? What about the cage? Was that not his future? Was that not the place he'd spend the weeks and months ahead? Maybe it wouldn't be so bad. Maybe he'd learn to enjoy it. If not enjoy it, he could surely teach himself to endure life inside the cage, couldn't he? Was it not possible for a man to live—

The shotgun blasted and William's kneecaps exploded beneath him.

There are no words to describe what he felt at that moment, for physical pain is an experience with boundaries and limitations. Physical pain has a kill switch that transforms all levels of suffering into a whole new entity, one that clouds the things you see and hear, one that deletes your thoughts and fears while erasing your dreams and emotions. Pain on such a scale is not a white-hot poker in the pit of your stomach. It is not fire melting your pores together. It is more. It is your universe being crushed by a God that punishes you with hatred and vengeance.

William crumbled forward with his eyes round and fit to burst. His face became as white as a face could be. He hit the floor hard, knocking two front teeth from his mouth while breaking his nose. His arms twitched, his body convulsed and his nose bled. His mouth opened and closed like an upstream trout. Both legs were destroyed. Even if he had been rushed to the hospital that very minute, nothing would have saved them. The bone above the knee, the bone below the knee, and the knees themselves—all had been annihilated. Veins hung from garbled meat like wet crabgrass. The neighboring flesh was charcoal black.

Body convulsing, William flipped onto his back.

"I'll be back in a minute guys," Nicolas said to no one in particular. He pumped the chamber and moved close to William. "Don't go anywhere, okay buddy? And keep an eye on the girls. See you real soon."

He squeezed the trigger a second time, shooting William one more time in the legs. A limb became severed. The concrete floor blasted apart. Blood sprayed the walls, the floor, the cages and the ceiling. Bits of meat exploded into the air before raining down like hail.

Olive screamed with her mangled hands held in front of her open eyes. Cathy broke down in tears, looking directly at the floor. William twitched several times and passed out. And Nicolas Nehalem left the basement with his shotgun at his side, happy with the day's events, whistling tunelessly and wondering if there was anything good to eat waiting for him inside the fridge.

20

Beth's hands were at her face and her knees were pulled towards her stomach. With a tire-iron sticking in her ribcage and the trunk's roof squishing her body, she found it hard to breathe and nearly impossible to move. Pauline's foul-smelling corpse didn't help the situation. It was pressed tight against her back; many flies and maggots were now crawling across her skin, finding a new home. The putrid odor was one of decay, rotting flesh and germinating mold. The foul stench wasn't just inside Beth's nose either. It had also found its way into her mouth and lungs, it reached into her stomach, it seemed to be consuming her. She was surprised she hadn't been sick. But she was a tough woman, and being a tough woman she was able to hold it in. Just like she was able to suspend her screaming lunacy. Mostly.

But at first she nearly lost her mind.

Before they started driving Beth heard the shotgun blast and knew what happened: Nicolas killed William. Obvious.

She screamed after the blast and when she was done she screamed some more, feeling it was only a matter of time before she'd suffer the same fate as her friend. She may have blacked out; she did not know.

Then the car started rolling and her screaming ended.

She cried and shivered and prayed to the Lord above for the first time since she was a child. And when the car stopped moving and the engine turned off, her eyes were stinging and her throat felt like it had been rubbed with sandpaper and coated with a thin layer of rot. All at once she decided to get it together, be brave, be strong. She decided never to scream again. Would she be able to do it? Time would tell. But the fact she was thinking this way caused her tears to dry up, and the little girl she regressed into seemed to dry up as well.

She would not allow Nicolas to steal her life from her. She would not deteriorate. She would not become her inner child and allow her emotions to run free. Not any more, not at a time like this. Beth would get through this tragedy; she just needed to stay strong.

A door slammed shut. She heard someone talking. She listened, but couldn't make out the words. Another door closed. It wasn't a full slam but that hardly mattered.

Two doors closed. Not one. Two.

What did it mean?

Perhaps William hadn't been killed after all. Perhaps it only a warning shot. It was something to wish for, something to hold on to.

She would be strong regardless, an adult worthy of respect. Falling apart was not an option.

She listened. Nothing.

Her social worker mentality returned, threatening to take control of the situation. She thought about talking to the man, reasoning with him. She wondered if she could figure out why he did the things he did and help him. After all, he was still a human being. He had a mother and a father. He had feelings. He could be rehabilitated.

"He's *not* a man," she whispered. "He's a creep."

That's what he was: a creep. Nothing more and nothing less. Screw the fact that years ago, he was just a kid, probably being raised in less than ideal conditions. Screw the fact that he needed professional help by someone that cared, like a social worker, like her.

Beth pushed the social worker far, far away. She already tried the psychological approach with this man (*Creep*, she reminded herself. *He's a fucking creep...*) and it didn't work. She wasn't about to try again. The stakes were too high. She needed to find a different Beth Dallier, figure out what she could do and what she was capable of. It was time to be honest. Her life depended on it.

Strengths and weaknesses: what were they?

She always considered her mental ability to be her greatest strength. But that wasn't her only asset. She was physically strong too.

At two hundred and thirty-five pounds, Beth moved slowly. There was no point in pretending she didn't. But if she changed her game plan, changed the way she approached her situation... Or to put it another way, if she punched the psycho in the face, what would happen then? She was strong. Damn right she was strong, but could she outmuscle him? Could she drop him to the ground with a quick left hook before he considered the possibility that she'd try such a thing?

Maybe she could.

Maybe...

It was decided. She could fight, and she would.

But could she snag the shotgun from Nicolas' hand and take control of the situation? That question wasn't so easily answered. And there was another issue, possibly the most important issue of all: if she fought him and won, and took the gun from his hand, would she be brave enough to use it? Could she pull the trigger? Did she have the stones to kill a man?

A bug crawled across her nose and Beth flicked it away with her finger.

He wasn't a man. He was a cold-blooded killer, a creep. She needed to remember that.

He was a creep.

Killing him wouldn't be easy but she could justify it simple enough. After all, he murdered the family in the minivan. He probably *wanted* to murder Cameron and from the look of things, he was planning on killing her too, but what about William? Did he shoot William? It seemed that way. But then why did two separate doors slam? Why not just one?

He was messing with her. Had to be. He slammed the door himself, and then... then... what? Started talking to himself?

Beth considered these things and more. Adding them together painted a series of question marks, but it also painted the image of a terrible man, or at very least a seriously disturbed one.

So here was the question, the *real* question: was killing a man with mental issues wrong?

If she had to be honest, then—yes, it certainly was wrong. But was killing a sick and twisted murderer immoral?

She thought her answer would be complex enough for different interpretations. It wasn't. For Beth, the answer was as clear as the sky above: killing was morally wrong. Always.

I can justify it, she thought. And she was probably right. Finding validation for questionable actions was always waiting for those who looked. But if she killed him, could she live with her justifications? Would she sleep sound, or would the justification make her crazy? And on a different tip: if the creep lived long enough to kill more people, could she live with herself then? These were big questions, for which she had no answers.

Wondering why the creep hadn't opened the trunk yet, Beth closed her eyes. "I'll kill him if I must," she whispered.

There was no anger in her voice, only the subtle tone of deliberation. It had been decided. She would fight. If she killed the man, so be it. She was in a tough spot, which needed a tough solution.

Seconds passed.

She heard the shotgun go off again. Twice. It sounded like it came from far away, or maybe from inside a house.

She pushed her body against the corpse, giving her arms more room to move. Lots of flies sprang to life. Bugs scurried inside her shirt, along the folds of her skin and into her hair. She wedged her fingers beneath her ribcage and wrapped her fingers around the tire-iron. She pulled it free, releasing a squeal as she did so. She was more comfortable now. Not only that, she was armed with the tire-iron.

Immoral or not, when the trunk opened she'd come out swinging. And let the chips fall where they may.

21

The big creature, the mamma he presumed, came charging towards Daniel with its legs slamming the ground like a five-horse stampede. Mouths opened and closed, not together, but slightly askew, creating a hypnotic wave-type effect. Black bubble eyes glistened in the florescent light and stingers punctured holes in the floor three inches deep.

Daniel stumbled back and tripped, feeling his stomach clench. Another six or seven crab-critters were crawling from a hole in the wall, scuttling towards him. He landed hard on his ass, raised the gun and pulled the trigger. With his upper lip curled into a sneer and half his teeth showing, he said, "Take this!" He may have looked brave, but there was no bravery in his voice, no composure or tranquility in his tone, either. The words displayed some level of misguided confidence, but they were only words—lies perhaps, as flat and meaningless as a map to a world that doesn't exist.

CLICK.

His eyes widened and his face became cloaked in fear.

"It's empty," he whispered, trembling. And now the words that fell from his lips came out just right. He wasn't lying this time. Oh no. His voice sounded terrified and his face wore an expression that fit the tone perfectly. He couldn't believe his gun didn't fire. Surely there must have been at least *one* bullet left. He couldn't have fired all *seven* times. It wasn't possible, was it? Was the clip half-empty when he loaded it? He thought he'd been counting. Was it possible that he counted his discharges incorrectly?

As giant stalks pounded against the floor, causing tiny explosions in the dirt, mouths opened and closed, teeth clicked, jaws snapped, and Dan pulled the trigger twice more, just to make sure the gun was truly empty. It was.

"Oh shit."

Dan looked at the gun like it betrayed him while fighting back the

178

urge to throw the damn thing across the room. He pulled the empty clip from the weapon and tossed it aside. Slamming his hand into his pocket, fingers circled the final clip. He had it, and not a moment too soon. Pulling the clip from his pocket couldn't happen fast enough; he was running out of time, running out of ammo, running out of luck. The beast was almost on top of him now, and very soon it would be. The thought of being devoured made him feel like crying.

With eyes glued to the big boy he started to scream. His knees shook and his chin quivered.

Two killer crabs scrambled across his legs and onto his lap. One was translucent; the other was brown. They were trying to pierce him with their stingers and nip little bites from his chest, but they didn't quite know how.

With the clip in one hand and the gun in the other, Daniel swatted both creatures off his body. The little brown monster rolled twice and landed on its claws, six feet away. The other clung to his arm before doing a loop-de-loop in the air. Once it landed on the ground it crawled in a different direction before opening its wings and flying off.

Long dark stalks pounded the floor harder now than before.

The creature stopped running; it was above him. Time had run out.

Dan slid the clip into the weapon and clicked the safety. The brown crab came at him again; this time it had company. Two more crabs were right behind it, a black one and another brown one.

Daniel pointed the gun at big momma and pulled the trigger twice.

BLAM. BLAM.

Big mamma lifted several legs in front of its face and stumbled back. The black crab-critter jumped and Daniel pointed the gun right at it. BLAM. The crab went tumbling through the air. He pointed the gun at the other two and picked them off one at a time. BLAM. BLAM. His aim was true.

The giant creature lifted its body high into the air. It looked down at Daniel with countless eyes.

SQUUUUUUEEEE*EEEEEEEEEEEEE.*

Daniel pointed the gun into an open mouth. And this time, he knew how many bullets he had left: he had two.

22

Pat looked into the darkness, hearing gunfire blast in the other room. On the floor he could see an odd-shaped rectangle of light and his silhouette standing within it, not much else. So he stepped inside the dark new space, surprised that the door had been unlocked. He placed an open hand on the wall. Only then did he realize that his hand was rebelling against all contact, even the slightest amount. Touching things with his swollen and battered fingers hurt like hell no matter how careful and delicate he tried to be, but what could he do? His hands were a mess but he needed to use them.

Deal with it, he thought. *Such is life.*

Ignoring his throbbing wounds, he slid his bruised, bloody, and swollen fingertips along the wall until he found a light switch. He flipped it on. Nothing happened—then slowly, almost painfully, a florescent light flickered, faltered, and came to life. His silhouette, and the rectangle residing in it, vanished.

The space was not big, not big at all. But it seemed *huge* because the wall on the far side of the room was home to a giant hole.

Looking at the aperture, Patrick's expression revealed a surprised kind of bewilderment. It seemed safe to say—at least in his eyes—that the giant creature had chewed its way through the wall. When he looked beyond the opening he could see another hole in the far wall of that room too. The creature, he assumed, had been busy.

There was a door on his left. He walked past without looking at it, eager to see the next room. He stepped through the hole in the wall. The room, like the one before it, was mostly empty. There were a few boxes stacked in a corner and debris at his feet, but that was about all.

More gunshots blasted.

Why the empty rooms? he wondered, approaching the next hole.

Then he noticed a hole in the ceiling, every bit as big as the first

two. He thought about the creature, about the crates in the big room—
—the *unopened* crates.

"They were just moving in," he whispered. And with that Pat
closed his eyes, creating a full-blown scenario inside his mind:

*A strange and wealthy apocalypse-fearing eccentric built the shelter and
loaded it with army supplies. After the supplies were delivered, the movers found
themselves face to face with a giant bug and left the shelter in a hurry. The eccentric, perhaps named Rockefeller, complained because the shelter had not yet been
organized the way he wanted it. The movers didn't care. They were not going
back down and that was final. Neither threats of law suites nor increased wages
could convince the men otherwise. Finally Mr. Rockefeller reached into his pocket
deeper than he thought he should. He said that he'd pay fifty thousand to any
man willing to finish the job. It was a lot of money, and the men found themselves weighing the pros and the cons. Some said money means nothing if you are
not alive to use it. Others discovered that fifty thousand was a number worth
risking your neck over. After the deal had been negotiated and money exchanged
hands, eight men returned to finish the job. Several crates were opened. Several
items were placed in different rooms. Then things turned bad. The beast returned
and it wasn't alone. The men found themselves surrounded. One man escaped
while the others died. Rockefeller learned his lesson and built a house on top of the
shelter, concealing the fact that it existed. The one remaining man——*

Patrick opened his eyes and put a hand to his mouth. "The men
were surrounded?"

There's more than one of them, he thought. *There has to be.*

He didn't know if his scenario was the least bit accurate but he
knew one thing for sure: animals procreate; it takes two to tango.

He looked down.

There was a giant hole in the floor, lost in shadow but there. It
was seven feet in diameter and looked like something a four thousand
pound groundhog would have dug if it could chew through concrete.

Pat stepped away from the hole with a new scenario brewing.

*Rockefeller stumbled upon something resembling a gigantic anthill beneath
the earth but he didn't know it. He built the bomb shelter and one of those creatures dug its way inside. But it wasn't alone. Oh no. It was never alone. There
are hundreds of those creatures, maybe thousands of them. And, and——*

Thinking changed gears, becoming a mental question and answer
debate inside his mind: *Why had the creatures not surfaced until now?* Man
invaded their space, and keep *this* in mind Einstein—they *didn't* surface; we came to them. *But why had the species not been discovered before?*

181

Simple. Most animals have a native land, and many animals are on the brink of extinction. This might be the only place on the planet that this species exists.

Pat stepped forward and looked down. He couldn't see much, but he had the feeling that his little anthill scenario was right on the money.

An anthill, he thought, *an anthill for giant, mutant ants. Damn.*

Five gunshots blasted within a matter of seconds.

He turned his head left; there was a door. He hadn't noticed it before but he noticed it now, and he had a pretty good idea where the door would lead him. He approached it and put a hand on the knob. Doing so caused enough pain that his eyes squinted and his nose wrinkled. He turned the knob as much as he could.

It was locked.

Of course it was locked. It was locked a few minutes ago and it was locked now, but things were different now, because now he could *unlock* it.

Pat turned a latch and unlocked the door. He opened the door and was right where he knew he'd be: in the hallway. On his left was the hole he created in the wall. On his right was the big room with the cocoons. He could see the creature there, facing the opposite direction. It had several legs raised high in the air. He assumed the beast was being shot at.

This is my best time for escape, he decided.

He ran towards the beast, screaming, "Here I come! Don't shoot me, whoever you are! I'm alive and I'm coming out of the hallway! Don't shoot! Don't shoot!"

And that's when he heard Daniel shouting…

23

"Patrick? Is that you?"

Pat came running out from behind the creature with his hands in the air and his eyes wide with fright. He said, "Yes! It's me! It's me! Don't shoot!"

The creature turned.

Daniel fired another shot.

Pat figured he'd be hit. When he realized the gun wasn't pointed in his direction a moment of serenity washed him like sunshine.

The feeling didn't last.

Crabs were everywhere. Some were scuttling towards him; some were sprinting away. He had no idea the cocoons would hatch so quickly, but they did. He looked towards the ceiling and saw something Daniel hadn't: a big cocoon with crab-critters pouring out of it.

As Pat made his way towards Daniel, who was still sitting on the ground, he punted a crab like a football. The crab split into several pieces. White and red pussy goo splashed up his leg and a chunk of meat soared through the air as something resembling spray cheese squirted against the floor.

"Are you alone?"

"Yeah."

"Then let's get out of here!" Pat said, offering Daniel a hand.

Daniel grabbed the outstretched hand. He squeezed it tight and hauled himself off the ground.

Pat screamed; he had forgotten how mangled his hands were. They hurt so much. He couldn't be doing things like that; he had to be more careful.

"What's wrong?"

With both arms held out in front of him, and blood dripping from his fingertips, Pat said, "My hands."

Daniel snatched a quick glimpse and pointed his gun at the big creature. It was backing away, giving them room. Two crab-critters flew past. A damp smell followed. "We can't get up the ladder, and I'm almost out of bullets."

"Why?"

"'Cause I've been using them."

Pat raised his knee to his waist and stomped another enemy. Guts splashed up his leg. "No, you idiot. I mean why can't we use the ladder?"

"Oh. Those things are all over it."

Pat crushed another crab and kicked a different one a second later.

Daniel saw what Patrick was doing and liked what he saw. He lifted a leg high and stomped on one too. White puss and red gore squeezed out of the creature's side like toothpaste. A second later he squished another, surprised to have it pop like a balloon.

Killing them was a sick form of fun, he realized; the crabs had no bones. They were like insects that way, and when you stomped on them they turned into twitching, bloodstained, mush. He wished he had of known earlier; he could have saved his bullets and used them on the big guy.

"Listen," Pat said, backing away from the big mama. He stomped on another critter with his eyes growing wide and intense. "We can't stay here, we have to get out. These little guys might grow up to be big and strong, but right now we can handle them. And look up there!"

He pointed towards the ceiling. Blood dripped from his finger.

Another winged critter flew past.

Daniel took his eyes off big momma and looked at Pat's damaged hands. After making a mental note of how bad they were, he looked up. There were a least seventy-five crabs crawling around on the ceiling.

"Holy shit," he said.

"Holy shit is right. This place isn't getting better; it's getting worse. And I found great big hole in the ground. I truly believe there's more than one of these big guys. I think there's a whole bunch of them."

"Really?"

Pat killed another small creature; innards squirted onto his sock.

"Do you think these little ones are done growing… yes or no?"

Dan, moving away from big mama, felt his shoulders slump. "Jesus."

"I'll take that as a 'no.'"

Dan didn't want to be negative about everything; he wanted to be positive. Pat was being positive and his hands looked like they had been caught in a blender. He said, "Crawling up the ladder is going to be tough, so be ready."

Without missing a beat, Pat said, "I know it'll be tough, but we have no choice."

Big momma bolted towards them and Daniel shot it again. The beast stopped on a dime and backed away; it didn't like getting shot and was smart enough to know it.

"That was it," Dan said.

"What?"

"My last bullet."

A sigh. "Then let's get the hell out of here," Pat said. "Before it's too late."

Stomping another crab, Daniel agreed.

24

Nicolas Nehalem placed the shotgun into his gun rack next to two riffles and another shotgun. Then he put the kettle on, washed a few dishes, wiped the counter down, swept the kitchen floor, and turned his boiling water into a fresh cup of lemon tea. Between sips he ate a banana, dissected the peeling into four pieces, and flushed them down the toilet, one piece at a time. After the water in the toilet bowl had settled he flushed the toilet again—just to make sure—and he took his tea to the back porch. There he released an embellished sounding sigh.

Nicolas enjoyed gazing across his little piece of Cloven Lake with a tea in his hand; it made him feel nice. It reminded him of his mother and the happy days he had spent with her before she disappeared, before his father had been convicted of killing her.

The area in front of Nicolas' place was marshland for the most part, and not the type of place people visited for long periods of time. Some nights the bugs were so bad that you'd get bitten every few seconds and after ten minutes you'd look like you had a case of the measles. The marsh was the reason he had no neighbors, the only reason. That wasn't a bad thing, just a truthful one.

Having no neighbors was fine with Nicolas. In fact, he quite liked it.

In his humble, questionable, and often psychotic option, the marsh was doing right by him. It was a good place to put things that needed to be put away.

Crickets sang and frogs croaked. A squawking crow flew overhead and Nicolas looked up wondering where it was going and what it was doing and how long it would take to get there. It was too dark for him to see the bird but he ignored the obvious and looked up anyways.

Darkness and stars blanketed the sky in a 1000:1 ratio.

Once his cup of tea was nearly empty he considered going for a late night swim in the marsh. He did that from time to time when things were bothering him. He had to be careful though; there were snapping turtles in there. There were snakes and leaches too. Tonight he considered risking it. He had a whole cluster of items grinding his mind into a sharpened point; his thoughts were making him antsy.

A swim might be nice.

He killed people and left them on the road.

It was a bad move, one he had never done before.

So now what? Should he go back and deal with the mess or pretend nothing happened and enjoy a nice brisk swim?

He considered marching over to the police station and telling the authorities that he's was just a regular Joe—a normal guy with no interest in killing innocent people or turning his neighbors into his own personal possessions. But would they buy it? That was the question in the forefront of his mind, as noticeable as an alligator in a daycare. *Would the authorities buy it?*

The police would come knocking before long, he knew. There was no use in denying it; they would come knocking for sure. Probably check every house in town, too. So what should he do?

He considered running. That was an option. That was *always* an option. He had done it once before, but should he do it again?

No, he thought. *I don't want to run away. This is my town. Mine.*

And what about Cameron, where was she? Where'd she go?

Nicolas slapped a fly from his arm and went back inside. He finished his tea and washed out the cup. After returning the cup to the cupboard he went into his bedroom and opened a drawer. Inside the drawer were a handful of bullets and a loaded Colt Python .357 Magnum revolver. It had a four-inch barrel, a royal blue finish, smooth trigger pull, and a tight cylinder lock up. It was one of the finest guns Colt ever created and the only handgun Nicolas owned.

Nicolas put some bullets into his front pocket and tossed the gun in a backpack. He wore the bag like a schoolboy and put a baseball hat onto his head to complete the look. The hat was black and it said: *New York Yankees.* He nabbed it from a kid he pushed in front of a subway train years earlier. It was a tad small for his head, but that was okay. He liked the way it looked.

Nicolas entered a bedroom. It was filled with all kinds of stuff.

Tools, mostly. He grabbed a cordless drill from inside a toolbox and put a nice fat drill-bit in it. He licked his teeth and smacked his lips together.

Stepping outside, he started to chuckle.

This was going to be good.

25

"Hey," he said, with a tough sounding voice. "Hey... you in there!" He pounded an open hand against the trunk of the car. "You still with me?"

He heard the fat woman say, "Yeah."

Nicolas didn't know Beth was curled up into the best striking pose she could manage. Or that she had a tire iron in her hands and she planned on smashing him in the face with it as soon as he opened the trunk. If he had known her intentions he might have done things differently. Then again, he might not have. He was unpredictable that way. His thoughts changed direction like the wind.

"I want to talk to you about your friend Cameron," he said. "And I've got something for you."

Beth gripped the tire iron even tighter. "Okay. I'm ready to come out now."

"You ready for what I've got?"

"Yep."

"You sure?"

Just open the trunk, you asshole, Beth thought. *Yeah, I'm ready all right. I'm ready to knock your block off as soon as this trunk opens.* ·

"Alright then," Nicolas said, after a moment. "Here it is!"

He pulled on the drill's trigger and started drilling into the trunk.

Beth screamed. She didn't mean to scream, or want to scream, but she had been burdened with a momentary loss of bodily control. The sound of the drill chewing its way into the car caught her by surprise causing a scream to sneak from her body like a burp after a large swig of Coke.

Laughing, Nicolas pushed hard on the drill. Sparks flew and shavings appeared around the spinning bit, growing into something that resembled a metal anthill.

Beneath the drill, Beth regained her wits. She had a pretty good idea where the bit would come through; she could feel the weight upon her shoulder. She had to move. That seemed to be a fact. If she didn't move into a different position that sharp, twirling cylinder was going to zip its way into her arm, and what that would feel like she didn't want to know.

She dropped the tire iron, placed her open hands in front of her body and pushed as hard as she was able, into the corpse. Muscles bulged and her face curled up like a fist. Flies started buzzing and maggots crawled actively. Until that moment Beth didn't think she had any room to move. Turned out she had lots of it if she was willing to squeeze into Pauline's rotting shell and ignore the fact that doing such a thing made her want to be sick.

Beth kept pushing.

The drill bit pierced the metal and came into the trunk like a bullet, slamming into her extended arm. A light mist of blood sprayed her face and chest. She yanked her arm out of the way and the drill bit carved a groove into her muscle.

She was screaming again, screaming and in serious pain.

She heard someone say, "I'LL KILL YOU, YOU ROTTEN MOTHER-FUCKING PRICK! I'LL KILL YOU!" The voice turned out to be her own.

Nicolas slammed the drill up and down and few times. He was laughing and smiling and having a great time. He didn't know if he was hitting Beth or missing her completely; didn't care either. This was the best, the absolute best. Like a linebacker tackling a quarterback and loving it, this was a sport to him. He never thought of it that way, but he felt it. After he pulled the drill from the car he laughed until tears rolled down his face.

"Oh that's priceless!" he said, allowing the drill to die in his hand. "That's completely priceless! *I'll kill you; I'll kill you...* ha-ha! Lady, you're *too much!*"

Nicolas stepped away from the car and put the drill on the front porch, still laughing and grinning. Eyes, wet with tears of joy, were wiped clean as he walked down the driveway and along Stone Crescent. He was having quite a day. It was a strange one, and he may have put himself into a big heap of trouble, but was quite a day nonetheless. It seemed obvious to him that the best type of fun was the dangerous kind. Living on the edge. How much fun would it be to turn things up a notch?

"Let the good times roll," he shouted, kicking wildflowers as he strolled along the edge of the road with his backpack strapped on tight.

Inside the trunk, spooned by a corpse, Beth cried. She tried to be strong but cried anyhow. This guy was going to be the death of her. Of this she had no doubt.

26

Officer Joel Kirkwood was sitting inside a police cruiser at Hopper's Gas when the call came in. It was a 911 call, which meant a regional call center dispatched the information to the office before it was transferred to the car.

It had been three months since he had gotten a 911-dispatched call. The last one occurred when Mrs. Tally had a heart attack; her ten-year-old grandson phoned it in. As always, the police arrived before the ambulance. Cloven Rock had a modest Police Station but nothing that resembled a Hospital or a Fire Hall. Mrs. Tally survived, but her grandson cried long and hard before the ambulance arrived to take the woman away. The experience put Kirkwood in a bad mood for days. If there was one thing Joel Kirkwood didn't like about 911 calls in Cloven Rock, arriving at the scene first was surely it.

Tony Costantino, the officer on duty with Joel, was standing across from Jay Hopper inside Hopper's gas station. They were talking about football and how *this* team was better than *that* team and who would make it to the Super Bowl and all kinds of other stuff that had nothing to do with being a cop. He held a bag of ketchup-flavored chips in his hand and waved them in the air when he was making a point.

Jay was all ears; he could talk football for hours. His team was the Cowboys, mostly because he liked the Cowgirls that cheered them on. Sometimes he admitted this nugget of information with a smile that made the wrinkles in his face seem twice as long and three times as deep.

The siren came on.

Tony and Jay looked through a stack of peanuts and chips and out the dirty window. Joel gave Tony a wave, letting him know that shit shootin' time was over.

"Got to go," Tony said. His face changed from *happy-go-lucky sports fan* to *officer of the law* inside a blink. "Have a good night."

"Hope everything's okay," Jay replied, scratching behind his ear like a dog.

"Me too," Tony said.

Once outside, Tony got into the car, stuffed himself behind the wheel, and slammed the car door shut. He was a big man, an eighteen-year veteran of the force. He looked so textbook Italian he should have been running a mafia pizzeria. With slow, deep-sounding words, he said, "What do we got?"

If Tony Costantino had an opposite, Joel was it. He had a thin face, pale skin, and the small blue eyes of a university bookworm. Every time he spoke the words shot from his mouth like bullets spiked with a mild dose of helium. "Down by the waterfront. Stone Road, west side, away from everything."

"How far west?"

"Ten minutes west of King."

"Shit." Tony dropped the chips onto his lap and pulled out of the parking lot like Rambo at war. He threw on the emergency lights and kept the siren off. "It'll take us fifteen minutes to get there from here."

"I know. But if we're lucky we'll be there in twelve."

"What's the situation?"

"A car accident. But there might be... get this... shotgun wounds."

"Shotgun wounds?"

"Apparently Holbrook phoned it in."

"Peter?"

"The one and only. Two cars were in some type of accident. One is in the ditch and the other is on the road. Three people are in need of medical attention but may be D. O. A. The wounds may or may not be the result of the accident they were in."

The two men exchanged an awkward glance.

Tony said, "Was Holbrook in the accident?"

"I don't think so." Kirkwood said, "Do you want me to call 'em back, dig around for more information?"

"Do they ever give us more information?"

"Nope. Those call center bitches only give us a hard time."

"That's what I was thinking."

"Me too. We'll be there soon enough. We'll straighten it out then."

"With any luck the ambulance will be there first."

Kirkwood considered the statement, dismissing it only because he was a realist. Knowing the truth, he added, "Or a fire truck."

Tony nodded. "It's a shame it's not going to happen. It'll be twenty minutes before those guys to show up. It always is." He was a realist too.

"We'll be there first."

"Absolutely."

After thirty seconds of high-speed driving Tony turned the siren on and passed a slow moving car that looked ready for retirement. Once the car was behind him he turned the siren off and kept his foot on the accelerator. He said, "I hope it's not too messy."

Kirkwood agreed. "I hope it's not someone I know."

Tony didn't respond. Problem was, they knew everybody in town.

After eight minutes Tony turned the siren on again, sighing as he checked his features in the mirror, wondering what they were getting themselves into.

27

Nicolas Nehalem walked along the dark road alone, and it *was* dark. In towns like Cloven Rock most of the roads had no streetlamps. Oh, there were the exceptions. The area where the Yacht Club, Tabby's Goodies, the Waterfront Café, Starbucks, and McDonald's were all nestled together like a big happy family was lit up like New York City, day and night, and the two streets people jokingly called *the downtown core* had its fair share of light as well. This consisted of King Street, running north and south, and Queen Street, running east and west. Of course, downtown wasn't much more than a couple of restaurants (the newest one being a Subway), a 7-11, a hardware store, Miller's Gas Station, and a post office. So how much light did it really have? Not much, or to be more accurate, three streetlamps worth. Five if you counted the pair of posts a quarter mile south on King Street between Spooky's Antique Palace and Cloven Rock Secondary. To be fair, the Rock's eleven blocks of residential housing—sitting between downtown and the waterfront—had lampposts too. But along the back roads, where the buildings were sparse and cottages sat vacant most of the year, light was hard to come by. And that's where Nicolas lived, in the area where light was a rarity. Stone Path Road and Stone Crescent had no streetlamps, not even to elucidate the intersections.

Nicolas' eyes adjusted to the darkness. He turned off Stone Crescent and onto Stone Path Road. He didn't hurry; he didn't slow. He walked at a comfortable pace with his shoes scuffing the earth and his knees knocking together every few steps. He wasn't worried but he was thoughtful. The way he played out these next few minutes would shape the days and weeks to come, of this he had no doubt.

Over the roll of a hill he could see a white haze that looked like a miniature sunset. There were no flashing lights, which he decided was a good thing. But there did seem to be a glow coming over the horizon larger than he expected, and with each step the forged sunset shone brighter still. As Nicolas moved beyond the arc of land the situation came into view.

There were four vehicles now, two more than he wanted to see.

Dan's car was the way he expected: facedown in the ditch with its backlights shining up at the stars like a pair of red eyes. The minivan was still sitting in the center of the road with its motor running, home to the bloody mess inside. And there were two new vehicles. One was a Dodge Charger and the other was a Corvette. The Corvette was new. The Charger had its driver's door open, causing the interior light to shine.

Looking into this light, Nicolas could see a twelve-year-old girl with dark hair tied up in pigtails. Two men stood next to the car, five feet from the girl. One was tall and lanky. He had a bald head and a thin face. Looked like an alien. The other was forty-something and quite handsome. His hair was cut short and his white t-shirt was tucked into his jeans. Nicolas recognized this man as Peter Holbrook.

Peter owned and operated the Waterfront Café, a Cloven Rock favorite. His house, which sat next to the café, was luxurious, beautiful, and on a very large lot. Mr. Holbrook owned many acres of lakefront property and everyone in town knew it. He was the wealthiest man around; many considered him to be the only reason Cloven Rock didn't expand too quickly and for this the town was grateful.

Holbrook noticed Nicolas walking towards them; he nudged the man Nicolas didn't recognize, the man that looked like an alien.

The alien lifted his head.

Nicolas sensed that both men were on edge; he could see it in their eyes and the way their bodies were poised. Maybe they figured that *he* was the shotgun killer. Maybe anyone and everyone within a fifty-mile radius was a suspect.

Nicolas raised a hand and walked towards them with a curious look forged upon his face. His features morphed into a goofy smile. He was trying to get into the mind-frame of a character he knew nothing about. "Hi there!"

Peter Holbrook raised a hand in return.

The alien put a hand to his brow and looked at the ground, fighting back a river of tears.

Nicolas said, "What seems to be the... oh my! What happened? What in tar-nation is this?" He ran to the van with his mouth open and his eyes full of wonder. He considered throwing his hands against the vehicle and screaming in mock-terror but decided against it. He wanted to be dramatic but he didn't want to leave any prints.

"Careful," Peter said. "Don't touch anything. Mr. Burton arrived first and touched a few things but I haven't. You shouldn't either."

"This isn't a car accident," Nicolas said, acting surprised.

"Nope," Peter shook his head solemnly. "It's a triple murder."

"Triple?"

"There's a baby in the back seat."

"Or what's left of her," Burton mumbled; turned out aliens could talk.

Nicolas stared into the backseat gore and placed a hand against his face, concealing his smile.

He loved this. Oh Silverman shit-dogs, these idiots had no idea. How wonderfully dreadful for them.

After a moment passed he looked Holbrook in the eye.

Holbrook was a stupid, ass-licking halfwit. He hated the man, truly hated him. Holbrook thought he was so goddamn good, so goddamn *smart*. He figured he was better than everyone else and he rubbed it in people's faces. The way he lived, the way he acted. Oh corn-dog crapper—he was a bad seed, all right. He was the worst of the worst. He deserved death. He deserved to have his head crushed in a vice.

Nicolas pulled his backpack off, sat it on the ground, and crouched beside it. "Did anyone call the police?"

"Yeah," Burton moaned. "I called 911."

"911, huh? How long ago?"

"Dunno, maybe five minutes ago."

Jesus, Nicolas thought. *Five minutes? That's bad. I better make this quick!*

28

As Nicolas unzipped his backpack his mind drifted. He was thinking about shooting them—all of them, even the girl. But he was also cooking up an extra little something for Holbrook. He wondered if killing them was smart. It probably wasn't but he didn't care, so he stuffed his hand into his bag, yanked his gun free and took control of the situation.

"Don't move, any of you." Nicolas' words were for everyone but the revolver was for Holbrook. It never wavered; the business end of the weapon was locked on the man's face.

Burton lifted his head slightly. Then he pressed his body against his car, as if doing so would protect the girl inside.

Holbrook opened his mouth and lifted a hand.

"No, no," Nicolas said, cutting into whatever debate may have been coming. "Don't get excited gentlemen. Don't yell and whatever you do, don't start asking stupid questions. Get on your knees, both of you."

He looked past the men, into the eyes of the girl with the pigtails. Her face carried an expression of confusion mixed with trauma.

"You too, toots… get out of the car and plunk your ass on the ground. No. Better yet, get out of the car and come to me."

Returning his attention to Holbrook and Burton, he said, "What? Are you knuckleheads deaf or something? Hands behind your heads and drop to your knees—let's go people. I haven't got all day."

Holbrook dropped to his knees first. Burton reluctantly followed. They put their hands behind their heads slowly and in unison.

As the girl climbed from one bucket seat to the next, Nicolas saw her for what she was: barely old enough to fart and scared half to death. She was wearing a pink dress with red flowers on it. Her shoes were shiny and white. Her teeth were nearly perfect.

"What's your name?"

The girl flinched at the sound of Nicolas' voice and responded nervously. "Mandy."

"Oh yeah? What's that short for?"

"Miranda."

"That's nice."

"Please don't hurt her." It was Burton that said it; his voice sounded troubled and anxious.

Nicolas' head snapped towards the voice.

Still inside the car, Mandy froze.

"There it is, I was wondering which one of you fuck-wads was the daddy... now I know. Perfect, just perfect."

"Don't—"

"I won't hurt her if you do what I say, how I say, when I say. Can you do that?"

With his hands behind his head, Burton's elbows began shaking. "Yes."

"Yes what?"

"Yes, I can do that."

"But will you? That's what I'm wondering." Nicolas looked at Holbrook. "How about you, tough guy? Do you know how to build dynamite? I do. Three parts nitroglycerin, one part diatomaceous earth, and a small admixture of sodium carbonate. That makes me the boss. Will you do what I say, or will you be the reason I shoot Mandy in the head?"

"I'll do whatever you want," Peter Holbrook said. "I'm not being a tough guy, just don't hurt the girl."

"Oh, but you *are* being a tough guy, you are. Everyday of your life you act like Mister Big Shot... Mister *'I know everything and that's why I'm rich.'* Driving around in a goddamn *Corvette*. Just looking at the two cars I know who owns what. Do you think people *like you*? Do you? Do you think anyone in this two-bit town doesn't want to see you *hang*? You're a *fool* it you think people like you or respect you, Mr. Holbrook. If I cut off your balls and stuff 'em down your throat this town will throw a goddamn parade."

"That's not true," Burton said.

Nicolas' eyes slid from Holbrook to Burton like they were greased. "Do you want to stick up for this chunk of shit or keep your daughter in one piece?" Nicolas' head slinked towards Mandy. "And what about you? What did I say? Get out of the car! Now! I'll bury you in the swamp if you don't get moving."

Mandy pulled herself from the car with tears rolling down her face. She wasn't crying full on, not yet. But she was close. She walked past the two kneeling men, past her father. She inched towards Nicolas.

Burton wanted to reach out and touch her, tell her everything was all right. He wanted to tell her not to worry but he didn't chance it, because things weren't all right. And there was reason to worry. The situation was getting worse all the time.

Nicolas grabbed Mandy by a pigtail and pulled her close, making her shriek, making her cry.

With one hand around her neck and the gun pointed at her temple, he said, "Okay assholes, ready to play a game? Yes or no? Say the wrong thing and I'll put a bullet in the girl's head."

Burton said, "But the police are coming!" And as soon as the words escaped him, he knew—

It was the wrong thing to say.

29

They ran towards the ladder with dozens of crab-critters moving towards them. Some seemed to dance while others limped.

Dan stomped two.

Pat kicked one against the wall. It exploded like a watermelon in a microwave, splattering his face. He turned away, saying, "You first."

"No, you first."

"No Dan, look at my hands! I'm going to be moving slower than cold shit and I don't want you behind me. I want you in front. I mean it. I might need help near the top too, so get going."

"But—"

"But nothing. You first. Go, and stop fucking around! We're out of bullets, remember? This is no time to argue!" He stomped another crab, but eight more were moving in and getting close, *too* close.

Dan didn't like it but Patrick was right, no point having them both climb slowly. "Okay," he said, shaking his head as he mounted his first tread. A few rungs later he noticed that his shoes were gooey with critter guts, limiting his traction.

Pat followed; after two steps he stopped climbing and reassessed the situation. The pain in his hands was an issue, but not the main issue. With something as simple as pain he could have accepted the circumstances, climbed the ladder, and endured the discomfort. Yes, it would hurt but it wouldn't last forever. Pain wasn't the *big* problem. The *big* problem was the fact that his fingers were so bruised and swollen they couldn't grip the rungs.

Dan was fifteen feet up when the first crab-critter climbed its long-stock body onto him, making its way up his left arm. It touched his neck with a claw. Wasting no time, Dan flicked it off.

He looked down, watching as the crab-critter tumbled through the air end-over-end. It landed on its back with a *WHAPP*. Spiny legs twitched wildly. Beside the critter, Pat stood practically motionless, staring at his hand in a state of unease. Critters were all around him, scuttling and scampering, a moment away from attacking. Some had thirty legs or more. Some had eyes the size of apples, clustered together in a bunch.

Dan shouted, "Hurry!"

"Keep climbing. I'm trying to figure this out!" Pat wrapped his arms around the back of the ladder. Using his forearms to keep balance, he climbed. It was a better approach, one that didn't hurt his hands because he wasn't using them.

A crab scooted across the wall.

Dan knocked it away before it got too close. He looked down, saw Pat climbing and continued his journey. But he moved slower now, allowing his friend time to catch up, figuring they should stay together. He wanted to keep Patrick's path clear.

For the first while everything was great; the crabs kept their distance. But everything changed near the sixtieth rung. Three crabs scurried quickly, attacking Dan at the same time. One was small and translucent. Dan knocked it away easy enough, but he allowed a big, black crab to crawl between him and the ladder. It had yellow eyes and tentacles hanging from its abdomen. He swatted it a couple times before using his fist. A brown crab with purple eyes and thin wings flew through the air and landed on his back.

Disregarding the winged critter, he slammed the black crab against the wall. Gray foam squirted from its side. He pulled away from the ladder and the critter fell, legs scrambling, mouths opening and closing, stupid eyes turning dim.

It landed right on Patrick.

Pat had no idea it was coming, and when it plopped onto his head it grabbed on tight and stabbed him with two stingers. Patrick made an *AWOOOO* sound and the creature climbed down his face and onto his chest, wedging itself between him and the ladder. He didn't see the irony in this, didn't know the same crab had set camp in Daniel's lap a moment ago. Trying to gain his wits and deal with the situation appropriately he knocked the creature a few times with his right hand, accidentally sliding his mangled index finger inside one of the open mouths.

The creature bit down hard. Bone crunched and blood squirted onto the wall.

The finger was severed.

Pain came roaring in, and with it came the screaming.

Hearing Pat shriek, Dan knew something bad had happened but he couldn't do anything about it; he had problems of his own. The crab clinging to his back was taking little bites out of his shoulder.

Patrick—with his face white and terror stricken—thought for sure he would fall from the ladder. It seemed logical. *Don't fall*, he thought as the crab tried to snatch another nip from his ruined hand. *Whatever you do, don't fall.*

Dan reached behind his back, grabbed the winged critter by a leg and pulled it as hard as he was able. The leg tore from the creature's body and the creature squealed in pain. He reached behind his back, grabbed another leg—a thick hairy one—and pulled again. "Come on," he said. "Get off me!" Same result: the leg tore free. He tried to grab a third leg, hoping to rid himself of the pest once and for all. The crab tried to bite him on the knuckle twice. Then for reasons unknown, it released its grip and flew away.

Pat wasn't in the way of a falling critter this time. The flying monster skimmed his shoulder and zipped past, membranous wings flapping quickly.

Dan climbed.

Pat climbed too.

And the black crab-critter that had eaten Patrick's finger was still there—wedged between him and the ladder with tentacles wiggling, yellow eyes watching, gray foam running from its wound.

Pat didn't care. He needed his feet to rest upon solid ground again; he didn't have the time or the energy to fight.

Thinking he'd faint, he climbed.

The crab took a nip from his knee. He stepped on it and the creature fell. Ten rungs later he was attacked by a villain with little white tuffs of fur under its belly. It grabbed hold of Pat's shoe and crawled up his leg.

Pat didn't fight it; he kept on going.

Dan looked down and assumed things were all right. But he was nervous now; his battle with the crabs left him on edge. The little guys could knock him off the ladder quick enough if there were more than one of them, and with that in mind he started to pull away from Pat, just a little.

The crab with the white tuffs climbed onto Patrick's ass, nipped him a few times, and got a claw caught in his front pocket. His belt unbuckled and his pants—a pair of dirty blue jeans—began sliding down his legs. Pat figured he'd lose them before he reached the top of the ladder and he *did* see the humor in that. Escaping without pants would be embarrassing; he wasn't wearing underwear.

Dan climbed. He was almost at the top now.

Pat felt dizzy. He thought about letting go, falling. He wasn't sure if he could make it to the top and the crab clinging to his waist was adding another eight pounds, easy. Then something happened. Given the situation it was good news: a pocket tore open, the belt pulled free of a loop, pants ripped and the crab dropped to its death. Unfortunately Pat's cell phone, wallet and keys fell with it.

Dan stopped climbing, exhausted. With only a few more rungs to go he looked down. "You okay?"

A crab scurried overhead.

Pat stopped climbing, took a deep breath and nodded his head. His pants were hanging off; he wanted to pull them up but he couldn't. Looking down he saw more crabs climbing towards him.

Better keep moving, he thought.

He climbed two more steps.

He was going to faint. He couldn't help it. The world was spinning, blood was pouring out of his finger, and the crab's poison was in his bloodstream. It was going to happen; there was nothing he could do.

Daniel made his way to the top rung, pulled himself onto the basement floor, and breathed a heavy sigh of relief. There were three crabs inside the basement. When he saw one scrambling towards him he knew his battle wasn't over. Not yet. He raised himself to his feet, struck with a morbid thought: *Wouldn't it be funny if the crab knocked me off balance and I fell down the shaft?*

No, he thought. *It certainly would* not *be funny.*

He stomped the approaching crab and kicked the second one against the wall.

It slammed against a two-by-four with legs broken; then it danced around in a crippled-man's jig. Dan stomped it twice more, bringing an end to the activity. Meanwhile, the third crab ran up the staircase and escaped into the house.

A bottle of beer sat on the floor, half full. Daniel didn't know who opened it or how warm it was, and he didn't care. He lifted the bottle and finished what was inside. The beer was room temperature but that was okay. He was thirsty and warm beer was better than no beer.

Looking into the hole he saw Pat.

"Oh no," he said, wiping a dirty hand across his wet mouth. "Oh dear God, tell me it isn't so."

30

Nicolas rammed the gun against Mandy's temple.

Holbrook closed his eyes; he didn't want to see the girl die.

Burton wondered why he gambled his daughter's life away. Was he really that careless? Was he really that stupid? Apparently he was.

Mandy, who was young and upset, didn't grasp the fact that a line had been crossed. She was afraid, terrified in fact. But she didn't know things had gotten worse, specifically for her.

Nicolas was momentary stunned. He was bluffing, that was the truth of it. He had a plan brewing and splashing the girl's brains across the Milky Way wasn't a part of it.

Yet.

He tightened his grip on the girl's neck. "That was your one and only screw up, fuck-nub. Next time you say something stupid the girl's dead meat. From here on in you'll do what I say, how I say, when I say. You got me?"

"Yes," Burton said.

"And how about you, tough-guy? You got me?"

"Yes. I do." Holbrook said, conquered.

"You sure?"

"Yes."

"You're going to do what I say then, knowing that if you hesitate I'll pop this girl?"

Mandy squirmed.

Holbrook nodded. "I understand completely."

"Good. I have a closet you know. I have this little closet in my hallway and I keep it empty. It has a heavy wooden door and a yellow knob and sometimes when I close the door it gets stuck in the casing. It's nearly impossible to open the door at times, unless I put a foot against the wall and yank it as hard as I can. There aren't any shoes in the closet; there aren't any coats, there isn't even a shelf to put things.

It's empty, just empty... and do you know why? Do you know why I keep it empty? Because sometimes I like to go inside the closet and close the door tight, lock myself in. And when I'm in there I scream and I scream and I scream. Sometimes I scratch myself. Sometimes I shit on the floor. Sometimes I bite my fingers but mostly I just scream. Stand up or I'll fucking kill you."

Holbrook couldn't believe what he was hearing. He wanted to pretend that he didn't understand but he understood everything perfectly. The guy was psycho. He stood up quickly because not doing so was the stupidest thing in the world.

Nicolas walked backwards, dragging the girl uncaringly. He said, "Step in front of the car."

With his heart pumping fast and his hands clenched into fists, Holbrook followed the instructions and stood in front of the Dodge Charger.

Nicolas grinned. "Now lay down."

Holbrook hesitated; he opened his mouth to object. Something cold swelled inside his heart, and for a moment he thought about funerals. Or more specifically—pine boxes. He looked at Mandy and decided to keep his mouth shut. He didn't like where this affair was leading, and felt compelled to say so. But he kept quiet all the same.

Holbrook dropped to his knees for the second time in two minutes.

Nicolas pushed the gun against Mandy's head harder than before, squeezing her neck forcefully. And as her face pinched into an expression of pain, Holbrook placed himself belly down on the road.

"Nicely done," Nicolas said. He wrapped his hand around Mandy's throat. "I was going to put a bullet into this girl because of you. But you were smart. You kept your mouth shut and did what I said. I wonder if you'll be smart enough to follow instructions again." Nicolas chuckled. "I've got to be honest with you, Holbrook. I wanted you to disobey me, I really did. I wanted to put a bullet into this girl's head, see? Want to know why? Because the very next thing I'd do is shoot you two assholes. I wouldn't kill you though. I wouldn't kill either one of you fudge-packers. I'd make sure you lived, in pain... with your kneecaps and your elbows destroyed. Might put a bullet in your back, too. Not sure yet. Still trying to figure it out."

Nicolas tightened his grip on the girl's throat and shook her around a bit, shook her like a dog with a squeeze toy.

Burton said, "Oh please. Please don't! Please don't hurt my girl!"

"Look who's talking? Did I say you could talk?"

Nicolas squeezed the girl's neck tighter and shook her more violently. Her hands slapped at him; her feet began kicking. The barrel of the gun was digging into her skin now, and a small line of blood ran along her check. Mandy couldn't cry, not with her throat being squeezed shut. But she wanted to start howling and as soon as she was able she'd do just that.

"Please," Burton said, still kneeling. "Please stop shaking her! Stop choking her!"

"Did I say you could speak?"

"Please!"

"Did I? Answer me!"

"No, but you're her hurting her! Stop hurting my baby!"

"Holbrook," Nicolas said, with his eyes focused on Burton. "You ready to do what I say?"

Holbrook made an expression that was hard to read. It seemed like he was trying to say 'yes' and 'no' at the same time, like he was trying to wake himself from a terrible dream.

"I can't hear you."

"Yes, yes," Holbrook said, almost moaning. He wanted Nicolas to stop shaking the girl, stop strangling her. Her face was turning white, her hands were getting weak and her eyes were glossed over. Soon they would be rolling into the back of her head. He knew it. He could tell. "I'll do what you say! Just stop it! For crying out loud, stop it!"

"Good! Put your head in front of the wheel."

"What?"

"You heard me! Put your face against the rubber, right up against the treads."

"You can't be serious!"

Nicolas pulled the gun away from Mandy and pointed it in Holbrook's direction.

Holbrook's eyes widened.

Burton felt his entire body quiver. He wanted to jump up and save his daughter. But could he do it? Could he get off his knees and run across eight feet of road before the man with the gun pulled the trigger?

The answer was no.

Just as Nicolas was about to fire a bullet, Holbrook crawled across three feet of gravel and rammed his face between the tire and the road. He was under the car now; the smell of oil and rubber was strong.

"Now you," Nicolas said. He eased his grip on Mandy and put the barrel beneath her temple. "Get in the car, driver's seat. Now."

Burton got off of his knees and plunked himself inside the car.

Nicolas pushed Mandy ahead a few feet. Quietly, he said, "Where are the car keys?"

"In the ignition."

"Good. Start the car and drive forward."

Burton eyes widened.

"I said drive forward."

"You can't mean this. You don't want this."

Nicolas heard a siren buzzing in the distance. Ignoring it, he whispered, "Oh yes I do. I'm going to give you to the count of three, fuck-nut; then your daughter is going to take a pair of bullets in the teeth. I promise you. I've done it before and I'll gladly do it again. Ready? 'Cause I'm about to start counting. One. Two. Three."

Nicolas threw Mandy to the ground.

Mandy landed on her back and elbows. She gasped for air as her eyes rolled in their sockets. She wondered what happened, and was surprised to find that her simple little life had turned tragic and un-pleasant.

Burton's eyes popped open and his hand grabbed the car keys. His wrist turned; the car started. He couldn't believe the situation he was in, or what was expected of him, or what he was currently doing. But he was doing it; oh Lord above have mercy on his soul, he was doing it.

Nicolas pointed the gun at Mandy's face.

Holbrook, with his nose crammed against the wheel's treads, flinched at the sound of the car starting. Not wanting to be run down, he pulled his head away from the tire just as Burton threw the car into gear.

The car leapt forward.

The tire clipped Holbrook's forehead and wedged it into the

earth.

Mandy screamed, "Daddy! Don't let him—"

Nicolas pulled the trigger twice. Both bullets entered the Mandy's skull, just beneath her left eye, causing the back of her head to vomit onto the road and her body to convulse like a fish out of water.

Burton slammed on the brake.

The tire crushed Holbrook's head, making a POP sound. Bone, blood and brains splattered in every direction. A moment later, one of Holbrook's hands became a fist that pounded on the tire twice, even though his head had been flattened. Then the fist dropped to the earth, opened and trembled.

Burton screamed and jumped out of the car, which was parked on Holbrook's head.

Nicolas turned the gun towards Burton and pulled the trigger twice more. The bullets caught Burton in the heart. Burton didn't feel pain but he couldn't breath and his legs were no longer responding to his mind's commands. He staggered, thinking his last thoughts, thinking about his baby, about the man that shot his little girl, about killing for revenge. Dark blood bubbled through the hole in his shirt as he crumpled against the car. If he'd been granted one final wish he'd scoop Nicolas' eyes out with a fork.

In the distance, the sound of the siren grew louder and louder.

Nicolas Nehalem, knowing that time had grown short, grabbed Mandy by a pigtail and lifted her head. Hair, matted with dirt and blood, clung to the gravel road valiantly. Thick liquid ran from her skull to the ground in a rope. He slid both hands into the girl's wound until his fingers were red and wet. He put his hands to his face and smeared the blood across his cheekbones like war paint.

It wasn't enough.

He took off his glasses and sat them on the road. With a grunt he turned the girl over; then he got onto his hands and knees, pushed his face into the opening in her skull, and snorted her juices like a barnyard pig. After his face and hands were soaked he rubbed her blood into his hair, and onto his shirt, and onto his pants. When he was finished washing himself he dragged her towards Daniel's car, lifted her up, and stuffed her into the backseat. Blood drizzled from his chin like rain.

Mandy's head rolled from one shoulder to the next, like her neck had been broken. Her mouth hung wide. A chunk of brain hung from her skull. Her face was pale, except around her eyes. The area around her eyes was swollen black and purple.

With blood dripping from the scruff of his chin, Nicolas put his glasses back on, lifted Burton up, and plunked him into the driver's seat of the Charger.

"You pissed me off, fella," he said. "You know that? Did ya?"

The siren grew louder.

He walked to the far side of the car and opened the passenger door. He sat inside, closed his eyes and concealed his smile, pretending to be dead.

31

Tony Costantino killed the siren and parked behind Holbrook's Corvette. "Four cars," he said. "Four, not two."

"Let's take a look." Joel Kirkwood stepped onto the road. He waited near the hood of the car for his partner to join him. The night seemed terribly quiet. And dark.

Tony walked past.

The men removed flashlights from their utility belts and turned them on. Beams of light scored the air in long funnel-shaped tubes. Joel allowed Tony to gain some distance; then he walked to the far side of the street, towards the car in the ditch.

"Hello," Tony said. He listened. There was no reply. Pointing his flashlight inside the Corvette he found nothing.

Now it was Joel's turn to speak: "Is anybody here?"

"Look," Tony said, approaching Burton's charger. "There are two dead bodies in here, nope, wait... three dead. Someone's in the backseat."

"And here," Joel said, pointing his flashlight into the minivan. "Oh God. Come look."

Officer Tony Costantino stepped towards the minivan. He didn't know what he expected to find, but two people with their heads blown off wasn't it. And when he looked in the backseat, and he saw the splattered remains of the newborn, he turned away horrified.

"Oh man," he said, putting a hand to his mouth. "This is terrible."

Pointing his flashlight towards the big lump of meat beneath the Charger, his eyes widened, his face flushed white and his stomach turned against him. His hands began shaking. The world became blurry and he realized he was stumbling. Didn't fall though. Somehow he managed to stay on his feet.

"There's another one," Kirkwood said. He walked around the

minivan and took a good long look at the corpse beneath the wheel. "This guy's head is beneath the wheel. What's going on here?"

Costantino mumbled, "I don't know."

Kirkwood saw that his partner was hurting. He hurried across the road and put a hand on his shoulder. "You alright?"

The two men exchanged a strange, authority-shifting glace.

Costantino was the veteran, not Kirkwood. He was forty-eight years old; Kirkwood was only twenty-seven. Yet it was Kirkwood handling himself like a chief. Costantino was almost ashamed. On top of that, he was on the verge of being physically ill.

Kirkwood said, "Let's go back to the car, Tony. It's okay. Let's just sit and collect ourselves a bit, shall we? We're can't help these people now. Whatever happened, happened. These people are dead."

Costantino may have been overwhelmed, but he knew what needed to be done. He said, "We need to check pulses, make sure they *are* dead. We need to call it in, and search the area and look for survivors. We need to check license plates, block off the road and notify the F. B. I. We need, we need…"

His voice escaped him. It was replaced with a quivering lip and tears in his eyes. He always considered himself a tough guy, a guy that could take anything. Now he wasn't so sure.

"And we will, Tony. We will. But right now we need to breathe again, okay? Do you know these people? Do you recognize 'em?"

"Have you looked inside the van, Joel… or beneath the car? How do you recognize that, huh? How do recognize someone with a head beneath a tire? I've been on the force twenty-three years, Joel. *Twenty-three!* I've *never* seen anything like this."

"Tony, you need to relax. Come to the cruiser with me, okay? Will you do that please?"

"I'm okay, I'm okay."

"You sure?"

"Yeah. Just give me a minute and I'll be fine. I'm just… God, I don't even know what to say."

Kirkwood nodded. "'Kay then. How's this? You take a minute; do what you have to do. When you're ready, verify the license plates and call 'em in. I'm going to check pulses and see if we have any survivors."

"Be careful."

"What?"

"I said be careful. Whoever did this might still be around."

"Okay," Kirkwood said, looking over his shoulder. He felt a strong sense of nervousness that simply didn't exist before Costantino stated the obvious. And it *was* obvious, that was the funny thing. Joel Kirkwood had been viewing the scene like it was an accident. Then when circumstances suggested otherwise, he assumed they were standing in the aftermath of the event. But he didn't know whether this was the aftermath or not. He had no reason to assume the bad times had finished. No reason at all. It was a terrible thing to consider, but what if this *wasn't* the aftermath? What if it was a break in the conflict? And somebody was watching? It seemed possible.

Kirkwood drew his weapon, slowly and nervously, like a first time gunslinger. He stepped away from Costantino.

"Don't go crazy there, Joel," Tony said with a bead of drool on his lower lip. His nerves began to stabilize. He could see his partner's fear now, and somehow that helped. "I'm just saying be smart. We don't know what happened here."

Joel heard the words but he didn't acknowledge them. The area had changed somehow. This was no longer a street he had been up and down a million times. This was a horror movie, a setting straight from the pages of *Creepy Magazine*. And it *was* creepy. Nighttime in these parts was creepy as hell, when viewed in a certain way. It really was. And exactly, how was he viewing things now that Costantino stated the obvious?

The bugs were buzzing, the moon was full; the trees were rustling. Animals and reptiles *(and who knows what else)* were just beyond his ears perception. The road was littered with the butchered dead. And worse than that, this wasn't an accident. Oh no. This was a killing spree, a multiple murder, a massacre. Someone decided it was time for bloodshed. And maybe it wasn't a *someone*. Maybe there were *two* of them, or *three* of them. Or a whole fucking *gang* of them.

Joel unlatched his safety, whispering, "Is anyone here? Is anyone alive?"

He walked towards Burton's car and eyed the corpse beneath. Then it clicked. Just like that: *click*.

He turned towards Costantino.

"That's Holbrook's car," he said, pointing his finger. "Right there, the Corvette. Nobody else in town has one and I think Peter Holbrook is the man with his head stuffed under the wheel. Oh God, I think it's him for sure. My dad has been friends with Peter for twenty years!"

"What?" Costantino staggered towards Kirkwood. Then he began running, pulling his gun from his holster. He didn't look sick now. He looked like a man that realized he was sitting in a boat that was tumbling over the edge of the world. "That can't be Holbrook," he said. "He's the one that called this in, right? *Right?* Oh shit… how could it be Holbrook?"

As the puzzle started fitting together a bat swooped between the two men, making them both jump.

"Christ!" Costantino said. "That's all we need."

Kirkwood dismissed the pest while his partner complained. He could hear a siren in the distance, maybe two. He dismissed them as well.

Flipping through the pages in his mind, he said, "I figured there was an accident, you know? I figured the guy under the tire was on the road for some reason. And one car swerved to miss him and the other didn't. I was thinking the tragedy brought out the worst in these people and someone pulled out a gun or something, and… I don't know! If that's Holbrook under the car, what the hell is going on here? How did he make the phone call with his head stuffed under the goddamn wheel?"

The sirens grew louder.

"I don't—"

Kirkwood glanced inside Burton's car and let out a sharp, high-pitched scream, cutting Costantino's words short.

"What is it?" Costantino asked. But then he knew.

The corpse in the car was grinning.

32

Daniel looked down the shaft, and said, "Oh no."

Pat didn't hear him. He was dizzy, thinking about closing his eyes and letting go. He couldn't help it. His pants were hanging off and blood was pouring from his severed finger causing his vision to fade in and out. But he was moving. His feet pushed onward and upward and for that he was grateful. It wasn't an act of determination. It was just something he was doing. It was almost miraculous, really— considering the fact that he wasn't holding the rungs. With his arms wrapped around the ladder he was hugging them at best.

He heard a voice, or a least he thought he did.

The ladder shook; he wondered why. A moment later it shook again.

Voices.

Voices.

Looking down he couldn't see much, just the ladder, the walls, a few crab-critters and—*oh shit*. It was the big one, the mother. Damn. The big one was in the shaft, coming straight for him.

"Patrick!" Daniel yelled. "Hurry!"

The cloud that was fogging Pat's thoughts cleared like a bell. He realized where he was, what he was doing, and what the stakes were. He remembered the creature devouring Roger and his adrenaline doubled. He thought about getting eaten alive and his adrenaline doubled again: he was next in line and would die a painful and horrific death if he didn't get his ass in gear. He knew it, and knowing such a thing helped.

His feet moved faster.

Looking up, he could see the top of the ladder. It was right there.

Daniel looked down with teeth clenched; his face was dirty and his eyebrows were raised.

Something flew past.

Patrick lifted a mangled hand and Daniel grabbed it, causing Pat to scream.

Blood gushed along his arm. Again, he thought he might faint. In fact, it seemed like a certainty.

Daniel pulled.

Pat's chest scraped against the ladder. His feet kicked. The cold air turned warm and he was out. He was being dragged across the floor and it hurt like hell but he was out. Daniel said something but Pat didn't understand. He couldn't focus, couldn't decipher the message. His eyes closed, opened, and closed again.

Dan slapped Pat across the face hard, with resentment and concern bubbling from his emotions. He wasn't nice about it. He hit him like he was pissed off.

Pat's eyes blasted open. He heard the words and understood their meaning.

"That *thing* is climbing up the shaft, Patrick! It'll be here in a few seconds! GET UP! GET UP, YOU FUCKING DICK-HEAD! GET UP! WE'VE GOT TO GET OUT OF HERE!"

With the help of Daniel's strong grip, Pat sat up.

The room spun, tilting on one side.

Three crab-critters crawled through the opening in the floor: a black one, a brown one and a grey one. The black one scurried up the wall. The brown one backed into a corner and crouched into a ball. The grey one moved towards them.

Daniel kicked it into the shaft. He ignored the other two, yanked Pat to his feet and led him across the room. From there, they made their way past Hellboy's corpse and up the rickety staircase, holding on to each other like drunks after the bar stopped serving.

Something the size of a toaster flew overhead, banging into the ceiling. It had two long tentacles hanging from its belly.

"What's happening?" Pat mumbled, pulling his pants up with his thumbs. His face was pale and his eyes were hollow. He needed medical attention and rest. He needed water, a doctor. "Where are we going?"

"I'm taking you out of here, buddy. Don't worry; the police are coming. Help is on its way. We made it Pat; we made it. Everything is going to be all right."

The big creature crawled into the room, one giant leg at a time.

SQUUUUUUEEEE*EEEEEEEEEEEE.*

Daniel snatched one last glance of the monster and slammed the basement door. He helped Pat walk down the hallway, and led him outside.

The outside air was nice and warm. It tasted good in his lungs.

"Where's my car?" he whispered; then he remembered. William and Beth took it.

A crab-critter scurried past him and Daniel wondered how it got outside. Was a window broken? Was a door open?

Didn't matter.

With a great amount of effort he led his friend across the yards, opened the door to Pat's cottage, and brought him inside. He dragged him into the nearest bedroom and laid him on a bed. The cuts in his fingers and hands, which he earned while renovating, throbbed from the strain. But Pat's hands were worse; they were awful.

Daniel wondered how long until help arrived. He hoped it wouldn't be too much longer.

"Hold on buddy," he said.

Pat's eyes closed.

Inside a bathroom Dan found a first aid kit, antiseptic cleaner, and painkillers. He wet a couple facecloths, washed his hands, and popped a couple pills. He returned to the bedroom with a bunch of supplies, forced painkillers into Patrick's mouth, and convinced him to drink some water. Once that was taken care of, he cleaned Pat's face and hands and wrapped some gauze around his wounds.

Then he entered the living room.

On the couch, his head fell against a cushion and he found his energy draining. The day was catching up with him. He was tired and ready to fade into dreamland.

What a day, he thought.

Then he imagined being at home with his wife, and drifted into slumber. It would be his last, filled with no dreams. Only nightmares.

33

Nicolas watched the pig-mobile stop and two pigs step outside. One was an Italian pig with a fat gut and fingers like sausages and the other looked like an accountant. They oinked at each other awhile and approached the carnage cautiously.

Nicolas smiled when the flashlights turned on and he smiled again when the bodies were found. A giggle snuck free when sausage-fingers stumbled across the road like he wanted to cough up his lunch. A full-on laugh snuck out when the accountant came running. Goddamn he looked funny; watching the pig unload a mouthful of Captain Crunch would have been the best thing he'd ever seen.

Tears appeared in sausages-fingers' eyes. The accountant said something consoling. Oh sweet herpes, hand-jobs, and hand-grenades, those two fuck-knobs looked like they were going to kiss. They were putting on quite a show. Oh yes they were. Then the most amazing thing happened: a pig looked Nicolas right in the face. What a rush. It was hard for Nicolas to act dead when his grin was crawling past his eyeballs in an attempt to circle his head.

"You got me boys," Nicolas said, smiling like a lunatic. He pointed his gun it at sausage-fingers; wasn't fast about it either. He just did it.

And pulled the trigger.

The booming sound shocked the silence of the land. The bullet entered Sausage-fingers' eye. Blood sprayed. A chunk of white skull ripped from the back end of his head and bounced against the mini-van.

Sausage-fingers fell.

The accountant stepped back with his mouth hanging open. As he lifted his weapon Nicolas shot him too. The bullet went into his open mouth, destroying a bunch of teeth and a whole lot more. This was good, but not good enough. So Nicolas shot him again. The second bullet erased his nose and everything buried behind it.

Blood sprayed out of the accountant's face; his gun fell from his hand and he tumbled to the ground like he was putting on a comedy routine.

Nicolas pulled himself from the car, ran a hand through his hair, and sat down on the road.

The sirens grew louder. Soon more pigs would arrive.

Nicolas untied his laces and took off his shoes. Then he took off his shirt and his pants and he placed them in a pile. Once he was down to his socks and underwear he yanked the jacket off the accountant pig. Blood ran from the pig's head; some went on the jacket but most went on the road. Nicolas took off his shirt next, followed by his pants. The pig's pants proved to be tough. The belt was new, heavy, and hard to manipulate.

Nicolas considered the plight of the approaching authorities. What if they arrived while he was standing around in his underwear, fondling a pig, surrounded by dead people? They would think he was crazy!

He needed to hurry.

Nicolas dressed himself in the pig's attire. The clothing was small but it didn't matter. Again, the belt was hard to work with.

Pig belts are a pain in the ass, he thought, struggling to fasten it. *Why do those dick-wads put up with such bullshit?*

Flashing lights appeared in the distance.

He hooked the belt, put on his shoes, and dusted himself off. Then he picked the pig's gun off the ground, checked the safety, and slid it into the empty holster.

"All right, I'm ready," he said to nobody. Followed by, "Oh shit! No I'm not!"

Nicolas grabbed the naked pig by the hair, dragged him to the side of the road, and tossed him in the ditch. Then he grabbed his stack of clothing and tossed it in the ditch too, but what about sausage-fingers? What was he supposed to do with that waste of meat?

The flashing lights grew brighter.

Nicolas cursed under his breath, stuck his fingers into sausage-fingers' mouth and dragged him as far as he was able. The man was *heavy*, very heavy. After a few feet Nicolas' grip slipped from the gaping maw, ripping lips apart.

"Fuck!"

Nicolas grabbed the man's jacket and pulled. It was easier, but not much. Nicolas gave up after dragging him a few feet. But he didn't want to leave the pig lying on the road, so he walked away from the corpse, hesitated, and went back for one last attempt. He took hold of the pig's boot, spun him around, and dragged him to the ditch. If the authorities saw what he was doing, so be it. At this point, he didn't care.

A fire truck rolled over the nearest hill. It parked behind the police car and the siren turned off. Firemen started pouring out of the truck.

Nicolas counted four of them—no wait, *five* of them.

One man jumped to the ground and began opening the large cabinet door on the side of the truck. Nicolas didn't know this, but the man's name was Mark Croft. He was new. He'd been a volunteer fireman for less than three months.

Nicolas ran towards him and said, "Quick man! Give me an ax!"

34

Once the cabinet door was open, Mark turned towards Nicolas. He said, "What?"

"You heard me! The ax! The ax! Oh God man, hurry up! I need the ax! It's an emergency!"

Mark hesitated; something wasn't right. But the policeman seemed to be panicking and he wanted to do the smartest thing so he reached into his rack of tools and grabbed a large fireman's ax. And as he handed it to Nicolas, he asked, "What's the situation, officer? You have blood all over your face!"

Snatching the ax from Mark's hand, Nicolas shuffled back a foot, giving himself some room to move. He said, "I do? Goddamn, I forgot all about that! Watch this, fucko!"

Nicolas raised the ax up and brought it down. Hard.

Mark Croft, who turned twenty-nine the week before, saw what was happening but his response was inadequate.

Hands raised, eyes squeezing closed, he said, "Don't!"

The ax soared between Mark's open hands and smashed into his helmet. The helmet, which saved his life, split apart but stayed in one piece as Mark dropped to the ground with legs like balsa wood, suddenly thinking about his mother.

He had told her—no, *promised* her—that he'd visit tomorrow. He said he'd stay for dinner, maybe even spend the night. He hadn't seen his mother or his father in nearly six months and for Mark and his parents, six months was an outrageous amount of time. He had never been away from them for such an extended period. He had a great family; he loved them so very, very much. And it was his parents—Colin and Janine—that he thought about as the blade hit home.

WHAM!

Mark dropped to the ground and Nicolas spun around, gripping the ax with both hands.

A fireman stood a few feet away, holding his hat near his chest. His eyes were wide and his mouth was agape. He had a grey beard and gigantic eyebrows. This was Gary Sharpe, father of three—soon to be the *late* Gary Sharpe. Father no more.

"Perfect," Nicolas muttered, with his lips pinching together.

He raised the ax up and brought it down again.

Gary's response was even less effective than Mark's. He looked up, his stomach flipped, and his chin quivered. He squeezed his fingers into fists and his throat made a noise that sounded like a groan. Then he took the blade right in the face. This caused his neck to snap, his skull to split open, and an eye to pop from his head. As his skull cracked apart and the grey matter from his brain exploded, blood gushed through his giant eyebrows, down his beard, and onto his chest.

The ax blade came free.

Nicolas turned towards Mark once again.

Mark was on the ground, a hand in his lap. Fingers were opening and closing as blood ran from his chin.

Nicolas kicked the hat off, spun the ax around, and smashed him with the blunt end, which wasn't very blunt. It was shaped like an icepick.

All four inches of the pick went into the center of Mark's skull, making a slapping clapperboard *POP!* as it went in.

His neck crunched; his vertebrae shattered.

Nicolas tried to pull the pick free but found it was stuck. He wiggled the tool back and forth, widening the hole he had created.

Mark's body seemed boneless now; blood ran from his eyes and nose. The blood was so dark and thick it looked like molasses.

A voice: "What the hell are you doing?"

Nicolas abandoned the ax and spun around. He pulled the gun from the holster and pulled the trigger three times.

Barry Doreen, a veteran on the force, was born with one blue eye and one brown eye. As a result, he spent his entire life being called 'Wolf.' And when all three bullets caught Wolf in the chest, it caused him to release a noise that wasn't completely unlike a howl. He was dead before he hit the ground.

Two firemen left: Douglas Waterier and Kyle Van Ryan. Neither knew they were under attack but both heard the gunfire. For Douglas, the sound of firing came a second too late. He stepped from behind the truck just as Wolf exhaled his last, copper-flavored breath, and Nicolas shot him down.

With Barry on the ground, it was official: the area looked like a battlefield.

Tara and Brett Adkins sat in the minivan with their heads blown off.

Baby Michelle, strapped in her baby seat, looked like a sack of wet entrails—the word *horror* doesn't begin to describe her remains.

Twelve-year-old Mandy Burton was stuffed into the backseat of the Dodge Charger with a pair of bullet holes in her innocent looking face and parts of her brain smudged against her thin shoulder.

Her dad, slumped over in the front seat with blood still streaming from his chest, had turned bleach white.

Beneath the car, Peter Holbrook's skull was crushed, flattened beneath the car's front tire.

Officer Joel Kirkwood had been stripped to his socks and his underwear and dumped in a ditch. In the moonlight, his face seemed to be locked in a scream.

A few feet from Joel's corpse, Tony Costantino had been shot to death.

Fireman Gary Sharpe had been bludgeoned with an ax and had a hole in his face three inches long.

Mark Croft had the ice-pick end of an ax buried in his skull.

Barry 'Wolf' Doreen and Douglas Waterier had been gunned down at point blank range and were lying on the road, less than five feet from the vehicle that had driven them to their fate.

And—

Almost miraculously, one man was left unharmed: Kyle Van Ryan.

Kyle, standing on the far side of the fire truck, wasn't moving. Once he heard gunfire his instincts told him to stay put. Now he could hear someone talking. It wasn't Barry or Douglas; it wasn't Mark or Gary. So who was it?

"This isn't going the way I planned," Nicolas was saying. "What am I supposed to do now?" He did a quick headcount of the slain firemen.

One. Two. Three. Four.

There were four. But five had gotten off the truck. One missing.

Nicolas said, "I know you're there. I don't want to hurt you, I just want the keys to the truck."

Kyle didn't exactly believe the man but decided to take a chance. "The keys are in the ignition."

Nicolas heard the voice; now he knew where the man was hiding. He was on the other side of the vehicle, not far away. It would be easy to pinpoint the exact spot, but for reasons beyond him, he didn't want to hurt the man. Not that one; not him.

He said, "You the driver?"

A pause. "No."

"Then how do you know where the keys are?"

A longer pause; then Kyle answered with the truth. "We're trained to leave the keys inside the ignition in case the driver is injured. Sometimes we need to move the truck."

Nicolas shrugged his shoulders. "That sounds about right. Well, I can safely say your driver is injured. Sorry about that. I'm going to borrow the truck." He climbed onboard and sat in the driver's chair. Sure enough, the keys were there, free for the taking.

Nicolas started the motor, threw the truck in gear, and drove.

"Thanks buddy," he said through the open window. "Have a nice fucking night."

The truck pulled away and Kyle watched it go. Then he looked at his butchered friends and wondered what the hell just happened.

35

The ax was embedded in Mark Croft's skull. The wooden handle sat on the road like a fallen tree. Gary Sharpe's corpse was less than six feet away; his face had been split in half. These men were like brothers to Kyle Van Ryan. He had lived with them, trained with them, and played a million games of cards with them. He had gone to weddings and funerals together. And although he enjoyed Mark's company more than Gary's, he cared for both equally. These men were family. They were part of the brotherhood.

On the road beside Gary was an eyeball. It was wet and bloody and it had dirt on it. Kyle was staring at it when he heard the voice.

"Help—"

Kyle turned towards the sound. It was Douglas Waterier; he had been shot but he was still alive.

"Dougie," Kyle said.

Douglas had been transferred from a fire hall in Chicago a few months back. It was his decision. He was fifty-two years old and tired of the big city. He wanted to live in a place where the living was easy. Now he was lying on a road with a broken spine and a punctured lung and a pool of blood beneath his shoulders deep enough to drown in. His eyes had turned dark and his skin had gone pale. The man was dying; soon he'd be dead.

Kyle got down on his knees. "Oh Dougie, what happened here?"

"I got shot," Douglas coughed out. "Somebody shot me."

"Let me see."

"No." Doug begged, before Kyle had a chance to touch him. "Just, no. Don't move me. Please."

Kyle nodded. Doug's life was draining away and he didn't want to spend his last moments getting examined.

"I understand," Kyle said.

"Stay with me."

"I will, brother. I will. And don't worry; the ambulance will be here soon." Kyle said it because it meant it but he was wrong; the ambulance would never arrive.

∞∞∞Θ∞∞∞

Nicolas turned a corner a headed for town. He was smiling and singing, wondering if he could get a fire-hose working so he could have some *real* fun. Before long, he saw an ambulance racing towards him with sirens blaring and lights flashing. When the vehicle got nice and close Nicolas pulled the fire truck into the wrong lane and laid on the horn, playing a friendly game of high-speed chicken. He hoped that the two vehicles would collide because he liked his odds of survival.

The ambulance swerved. The driver lost control and the vehicle rolled four times. When it stopped rolling it was upside down on the far side of the ditch with its windshield shattered and its hood crumpled.

Nicolas, still singing and smiling, parked the fire truck at the side of the road and stepped out. He walked over a small hill and past several trees. He shot three medical workers at point blank range, even though two of them were clearly dead.

He was tired, decided to call it a day.

He got in the truck and turned it around. It was not an easy feat but he managed, somehow he managed. And on his way home he drove past Kyle Van Ryan and saw that the man was holding onto a corpse like he had fallen in love. Nicolas waved and smiled and drove on by.

Kyle watched him go.

When Nicolas arrived home he parked in his driveway, thinking about how exciting the day had been, thinking about the bitch in the trunk, and the guy in the basement with his legs blown off. He'd deal with them in the morning. In fact, he'd deal with the entire town in the morning.

The time to wage war had arrived.

36

Lying in the trunk next to Pauline Anderson's corpse, Beth cried many times. The psycho's trick with the drill had done its damage, both mentally and physically. This fact could not be disputed or denied. Her physical injuries were painful but her mental wounds kept the tears rolling long after her physical abrasions became manageable.

Beth thought she'd go crazy.

She wondered if she'd suffocate. Or bleed to death. Constructing the psycho's features in her mind gave her shivers. But more disturbing, *much* more disturbing, was thinking she'd never see him again. If that happened, she'd be locked in the trunk forever. How would she survive, by eating what was available? She *knew* what was available: Pauline's corpse, the things living within it, and not much else.

Time crawled. Flies buzzed. Maggots scurried across her skin and she pretended not to notice. Outside, a raccoon walked next to the car and Beth figured Nicolas had returned with another brilliantly sick joke. The next forty-five minutes were spent waiting for the punch line. And when she heard the fire truck pull into the driveway, she wasn't sure what to think.

If someone other than psycho-boy was in the driveway, she needed to yell—draw attention to herself. But it *was* psycho-boy; it *was. Of course it was.* Who else could it be, the garbage man?

She waited, quite literally holding her breath.

Nicolas walked past the car, slammed an open hand on the hood and shouted, "How're you doing in there?"

Beth didn't answer; instead she picked the tire iron up and held it near her chest.

"Not talking huh? Why is that? Is it because I got you with the drill? Is that it? You mad at me? You dead?"

Still no answer.

"Won't talk." Nicolas scratched his head. "I can make you talk, you know. Oh yes I can. Do you think the drill is all I can do? Is that it? How would you like me to stick a water hose into that drill hole for the next few days? Would you like that? Huh? Would you? I can do it; I don't mind. You and the corpse can go swimming together, yes? Do you know what else I can do? I can make a little bonfire beneath the car."

Nicolas listened.

Nothing.

"I've got a jar filled with hornets, too. I ever tell you that? I do. I found a nest near the swamp and I put it inside this big mayonnaise jar that I've had since, gosh, I don't even know when. I poked a bunch of holes in the lid. Every now and then I give 'em a little water. Sometimes I give them honey. I'm not sure what hornets eat but I know one thing for sure: they're ready to get out of that jar. Oh yes they are! If I shake the jar, open it, and place it upside down on the trunk... do you think the hornets will crawl through the drill hole? I think they will. Yeah, I'm pretty sure of it. You do you know what else I think? I think they'd be pissed off and ready to wage war. I also think you're a fucking twat."

Nicolas listened.

"Maybe you *are* dead. Is that what you'll have me believe? *Oh no. That brainless bitch is dead. Whatever will I do?* I'll tell you what I'll do, ya stupid whore... I'll drive the fuckin' car into the lake. How about that? How do you like them apples?"

Finally, Beth said, "What do you want?" feeling defeated. Again. "Why are you doing this to me?"

"Oh! There you are! Well, well... what do we have here? You *are* alive! Isn't that incredible?"

"Yes. I'm alive. Are you going to let me out now?"

"I don't know. I guess it depends."

"On what?"

"On what answers you give me."

"Just ask them! I want to get out of here!"

"You don't have to get all snippy. I just want to ask a few simple questions, *God.* By the way you've been talking you'd think I've mistreated you."

Nicolas went suddenly quiet. He didn't ask his questions. He just stood there looking at the trunk, smiling. He was tired and ready for bed, but he was also smiling. This was a big day, a very big day. Everything would be different tomorrow, absolutely everything.

"Well?" Beth unleashed. She was starting to hate the psycho on all kinds of uncharacteristic levels.

"I want to know about Cameron," Nicolas said flatly. "I want to know where she is and why she took off her clothing. That was the strangest thing I ever saw."

"She's sick."

"Sick? What kind of sick?"

"I don't know; she has some type of infection. She's not thinking clearly."

Nicolas shrugged. "So... you don't know where she is?"

"I have no idea."

"Well okay then. Wasn't that easy?"

"Are you going to let me out now?"

Nicolas thought the question was ludicrous. Why would she want out? He was going to kill her, or stick her in the cage, so what's with the hurry? He said, "I'll let you out in the morning."

"No!"

"Yeah. I'm tired. I'm going to bed, you dumb twit. Don't forget to keep your mouth closed. Otherwise the bugs will get in, and there are some big fucking bugs in there. Trust me, I've seen 'em. Well, I guess that's it. Good night." Nicolas slapped his hand on the hood twice more; then he went inside.

Once he was in, he locked the front door and approached the closet—the *empty* closet, the one in the hallway. He put his hand on the doorknob and gave it a good yank. It was hard to open but he managed.

Once inside, he closed the door.

And screamed awhile.

Beth did too.

She tried not to think about the spot she was in or the things she had witnessed. She tried to forget the fact that the warm air tasted like death. Thinking about her future was out of the question. She didn't feel good about anything. In time she closed her eyes and fell asleep, keeping her mouth closed.

37

The tree was old and dead, branches were knuckled and knotted like witch fingers, half-inch trenches separated thick chunks of bark, which were infested with worms and termites. A wasp's nest was attached to a branch. It was the very branch that a very large cocoon clung to, and although the insects had stung the body inside the webbing, the body did not register pain. The cold blood beneath the changing skin remained impervious.

Cameron opened her eyes, covered in a silky mesh.

Below the crude, off-white thread, her exposed skin became darker. Her breasts bloated and elongated and turned completely black. Not a healthy and attractive African black, but the color of tar, the color of something burning in a chemical fire. All of her skin turned this way, even the tips of her fingers and the balls of her feet. The black skin was oily and greasy, covering muscles that had grown large and swollen.

As time forged ahead she looked like a strangely mutated corpse, except for her eyes and teeth. Her teeth had fangs now, fangs like needles, like daggers. Her eyes bulged and the whites had turned dark. Each eye had a red dot in the center. To look there, into the place surrounded by gloom, was to look into the heart of a demon, a succubus—the devil's chilling and exotic whore. To look into those eyes could only bring madness.

Cameron crawled from the tree and sat at its base. She wrapped her arms around her swollen knees. And in time, she picked the silk away, freeing herself of its sheath. She was in no hurry; she was still changing, transforming, post-embryonic.

Leaning forward, she listened. She could hear so much now; she could hear everything for miles and miles. Yesterday she was deaf in comparison. Now she could hear footfalls in the heart of the town, people laughing at the waterfront cafe, boats slapping against the docks at the Yacht Club. She could hear lovers crawl into bed; fish swim in Cloven Lake, deer rustle in the forest. She could hear radio frequencies in the air, crickets in Nicolas Nehalem's marsh, the beast from Daniel's basement.

And she could hear more—much, much more.

Cameron could hear George Gramme talking lovingly about motorcycles, even though a Harley had amputated his fingers two summers ago. She could hear Jay Hopper ring in his final sale of the night, all the way out on the 9th line. She could hear Stephen Pebbles brooding inside his two-bedroom apartment. He lived there now—now that a fire had destroyed his farm and everything he owned. She could hear odd-job Martin West limping across the kitchen like a ninety year old man, knowing he wouldn't *have* to limp if he hadn't been shingling his neighbor's roof—something he was dangerously unqualified to do. She could hear Lizzy Backstrom roll her wheelchair across the hardwood towards the window; for the window was the place she kept watch. Lizzy didn't trust Cloven Rock, not anymore. Not after seeing the great multi-legged beast creep across the street on that long and terrible night, the night that changed her life forever.

Cameron could hear Stanley Rosenstein, who had been a foreman at the docks and an all-around good guy before his wife left him and his sanity was questioned: he thought there were monsters in Cloven Rock. Stan pulled his shades down and triple bolted his door. He did that every night, and often times, checked to make sure they were locked.

She could hear Father Mort Galloway, sitting in his house by the church, secretly and shamefully watching his X-rated movies and thinking about Leanne Wakefield. Ever since Leanne's husband Simon had drowned in the backyard pool she had been attending church religiously—so to speak. And every Sunday morning at nine, she arrived at mass wearing a shirt that was tight enough to make the Pope take notice. Galloway wasn't sure if Leanne felt remorse for talking on the phone while Simon died, or if she was trying to land a new husband. Maybe it was both.

She could hear Nicolas asking questions, and Beth—locked inside the trunk—giving answers. In fact, she could hear Nicolas thinking. And when she put her mind to it, she could hear Beth thinking too. Listening to the thoughts of the entire town seemed almost within reach. She just needed a little more time.

And—

She could hear Daniel.

Oh yes, she could hear Daniel McGee quite well.

She could hear him breathing while he slept.

She liked listening to Daniel; he was a good man, a nice man, the right man for her. He was handsome and smart, funny and kind. He was someone she could be with and love—not in conventional ways, of course, not now. But that hardly mattered. She wanted him. She wanted to be with him forever.

There were others she could hear. Others she needed to see.

She had a list of them.

Paul LaFalce was on that list. Paul LaFalce, the lying cheating, cunt-hungry prick that fucked every open-leg slut in town. Oh yes, oh yes. He was on that list for sure. He wasn't alone, there were more. Like Lizzy Backstrom's ex-best friend Julie Stapleton, who didn't know how to keep a secret but knew how to sleep with Paul and act like nothing happened. But Paul was first. Oh yes. She couldn't wait to see Paul LaFalce. She couldn't wait to see the 'the Gasman.' She wanted to give him a little piece of her mind. And take a piece of his.

Her dark and bloated skin was fading now, fading, fading—color returning to normal. And beyond. Becoming wilted and pale, insipid and palled, almost toneless. Her organs and bones looked gloomy beneath her skin, which seemed as transparent as the webs she picked from her body.

With a grin she lifted herself to her feet. She was almost ready.

Her transformation was nearly complete.

CHAPTER FOUR:
THE KYLE THREAD

1

Kyle Van Ryan squeezed Douglas Waterier's hand.

Douglas coughed twice, spraying blood into the air. He exhaled one final time and shivered. His fingers opened, his eyes locked on nothing and the tension seeped from his body.

He was dead.

Kyle was holding hands with a dead man.

He looked away from the corpse with grief-stricken eyes, seeing the carnage on the road instead. With the headlights cutting the darkness into various shapes and shadows, the area looked like something from a horror movie. He felt like crying, like turning off his mind and shutting down the world. The dead man's hand slipped from his own, making a soft thump against the ground. And although he didn't see it, a moth landed on the unmoving hand after it dropped, fluttering its wings like it found a new home. In time, the insect stood very still, as if waiting for the future.

Kyle felt terrible, but not for long. Soon enough the feeling was replaced with something unrelated to grief, anguish, misery, and sorrow. This was a new emotion—a vile sentiment, and quite possibly a dangerous one.

He was being watched.

Deep down where his instincts dwelled, Kyle Van Ryan knew he wasn't alone. There was something in close proximity he couldn't put his finger on. Might have been an animal, might have been something else.

Something worse.

He glanced at Barry 'Wolf' Doreen's haunted features, his blue

234

eye and his brown. He sized up the minivan and the bodies within. He looked at the car in the ditch, the ax embedded in Mark Croft's head, the blood on the road, the tread marks in the gravel. If he could teleport himself into another time and place he would. Of course, he couldn't. All he could do was gaze across the dark and evocative road to a place he didn't want to see. And it was there, near Daniel's car—a white shape against a black background, watching him, studying him, like a ghost. Was it hiding near the forest or was it just too dark to see? He didn't know; didn't want to know. He wanted it to be gone, just gone—nothing more and nothing less.

Go away, he thought. *Jeepers bum-fuck, just go away.*

He felt his nerves unraveling and the muscles in his neck stiffen. He felt a cold chill along his spine. His arms grew goosebumps and face felt flush. There was a knot in his stomach tightening like a noose.

Standing at the side of the road, waiting, lurking, looming. What was it?

No—not it. *Her.* It was a girl.

The woman at the side of the road seemed to be a phantom, but not transparent. Real. With pale skin and the eyes of a demon she moved towards him, naked and seductive, dominant and strong. Her feet, colorless and exposed, dragged against the gravel until she was close enough for Kyle to smell her rotting decay. Or maybe it wasn't decay; maybe it was something different than decay, something tainted and sour that had no name.

He wanted to run but couldn't. His defenses were weak and his will to escape was drifting. She was beautiful, stunning—more breathtaking than his wife on their wedding night, more spectacular than a perfect morning sunrise. But she was hideous too. Creepy and foul; like something that crept from a tomb in a gothic tale from a time long since past. She mixed the two extremes in an equal concoction. He wanted to kiss her passionately and run screaming at the same time. He was excited and terrified. His eyes were wide, his mouth agape, his muscles clenched tighter than ever before.

"No," he whispered. But like the moth on the corpse, he stood motionless, waiting for the future.

Another stride. Two.

She was less than ten feet away now, getting closer. She almost appeared to be gliding towards him, lighter than the air she breathed, if she breathed.

He looked at her wilted breasts, her desiccated skin, her strange black eyes—eyes with bright red dots that seemed to dance in circles while not moving at all. The sound of her feet crunching against the pavement was louder now, her stench grew worse, and yet he remained in place, helplessly obeying her unspoken commands.

Her jaws opened terribly wide, something unnatural. And inside that tragic and cavernous maw, that gaping hole, he could see long, sharp spikes that had no business being inside a human mouth. But she was not human. Couldn't be. Not now. The teeth belonged to a wolf or a shark, not a woman, not a girl. They were awful and horrific, incisive and dangerous.

He felt himself growing hard.

He wanted her. And he wanted to give himself to her, wanted her to bite him; needed it, in fact. He longed for it pensively.

"Hurry," he said, sounding desperate and vulnerable. But, *oh God,* why was he saying *that?* The voice wasn't his. It *couldn't* be his, could it? It was. That was the worst part; his words were betraying him. He needed to shut up, stop talking, escape his own will. But his will was no longer *his* to escape. It belonged to her now. He would do what she wanted, what *it* wanted. He had no choice. He would become her concubine, if nothing more.

Deep inside, in the little place that still belonged to Kyle, he considered pulling the ax from Mark Croft's skull and chopping the abomination down. This was no woman; it was a monster, a thing. It looked like a girl but it was not. It was an evil succubus, a vampire, a fiend—or quite possibly a combination of all three.

She limped now, limped towards him. A living scarecrow wrapped in a corpse's skin.

A question mark flashed inside his mind: was the girl the walking dead, a zombie, a living corpse? She couldn't be, could she?

He looked at her chest again, and could see the heart beating beneath her skin, beneath her bones. That meant she was alive, didn't it?

But oh God, he thought. *Why can I see that? Why can I see her heart beating right through her skin and her bones? What's wrong with this picture? And what's wrong with her teeth? What's wrong with her enormous razor-like teeth?*

James Roy Daley

The answer was simple. She was a vampire.

Instinctively, he knew it to be true.

He tilted his head to the side, allowing it to happen, begging for it to happen.

There was a voice screaming inside his mind now, screaming and screaming, pleading for him to stop what he was doing, demanding that he run away. But the voice had no control. It was powerless.

She bit his neck. Not in a romantic way. She didn't leave two flawlessly round incisions in his milky, unblemished skin, like an amorous character from *The Vampire Lestat*. She didn't have a red and black satin cape fluttering in the wind. She didn't step from a wooden carriage along the mountainous slopes of the Transylvanian Alps, taste his sweet nectar, turn into a bat, and fly into the night before the backdrop of a full moon.

Drooling, she tore the meat from his neck and he cried out, releasing a scream of agony he never knew existed. She devoured him and the pain was overwhelming. A hot spray of blood spewed into the air, splashing his chin and cheek. It squirted across her face too, then it ran over her lips and down her chest—and he knew, right then and there, that she was killing him. He was about to die in a sea of anguish.

And as she chewed a second helping from his body his arms quivered, he knees became weak and his heart slowed. Then it did the thing that *all* hearts do in moments of extreme physical trauma. It stopped.

Everything stopped.

His eyes rolled back and his life was over; it had been extinguished. She murdered him and he was dead.

Then the impossible happened. His heart started up again, beating faster now, pumping his blood in reverse, causing an internal torture he had never imagined. His organs labored through the unpredictably faulty design and he screamed with a voice that was different, more animal than man, more beast than being.

He felt what she felt: hunger, hatred. Rage.

He was a monster now, but not like her. He was no vampire. He was a zombie, a ghoul, a slave to the Master—a slave to Cameron. His intellect was falling while Cameron's skills grew greater and greater. And as Cameron devoured him his hunger mounted; his eyes shifted

237

to the bodies on the road. If she allowed him to feed he would. He would rip meat from the bones and drink blood until the human shells had none left to give.

And she *would* allow him to feed. She would.

After—

After he did his duty.

The time had come for Cameron to rule the town; the populace had to know who was in charge. This was her time.

Tonight, it began.

2

Time passed. Kyle Van Ryan was on the road, alone. His fireman's jacket was off. His neck and shoulder had been chewed apart. He looked pale and shriveled, a fireman that had been withered rather than burned, with meat ravished from his body. Each eye had turned dark, with a red glowing dot in place of an iris. His body cooled. Muscles contracted. His cheekbones looked like large knuckles in his face. His fingers were twigs. Knees and elbows like doorknobs. Stranger than this, Kyle's teeth had begun to elongate. A second row of teeth was forming.

He lifted himself to his feet and grunted.

He was not like Cameron, not a true vampire. He was a zombie, but not like the ones he had seen on TV. He was a zombie with a mouthful of daggers, a hybrid zombie-vampire whose blood flowed in reverse, a zombie that needed to avoid sunlight. And although his thoughts slumped along in a thick and dull jumble of disorder, he was a zombie on a mission. He had a job to do. He had a Master.

Kyle put a foot on Mark Croft's shoulder and yanked the ax from his head. He entered the forest with blood dripping from the blade. He chopped and gathered long, sturdy pieces of wood. There was no need for Kyle to travel far; the woodland was thick and abundant with all that he desired.

But it wasn't *his* desires he looked to fulfill.

He was following orders, being a good little henchman, a fiend that knew his place.

He gathered six long sticks, straight as he could find, two inches thick and twelve feet long. He brought them to the side of the road and removed the branches and leaves, making the sticks relatively smooth. After sharpening the ends into spears, he returned to the forest and found six more. He sharpened and cleaned them. Laid them in a pile.

The road was hard but the grassy land next to it was soft. The bottom of the ditch was softer still, but he didn't want that—*she* didn't want that. He needed the spears to be in a place high enough for all to see.

He lifted a single spear from the pile. With straining muscles, he forced the spear into the soft earth at the side of the road. Just hours ago he would have been lucky to bury the stick an inch, but Kyle was different now. Stronger. Some might say he had the strength of ten men.

He returned to the pile, lifted another stick and repeated the procedure. He did this again and again—and again and again and again. When he was finished his task, four spears pierced the earth on the left side of the road, four more pierced the earth on the right. Another four stabbed the road itself. These last four were the not easily managed, but he handled it.

The spears were separated evenly; not perfectly, but close enough. Each stick was fifteen to twenty feet from the one next to it, enclosing Nicolas Nehalem's war zone in an oval ring.

Kyle lifted the ax from the ground, returned to the forest, and chopped apart an overturned tree. Once he was done he dropped the ax and returned to the road with a thick log cradled in both arms. He returned to the forest and grabbed another log, and another.

Placing the logs beneath the nearest spear, he created a makeshift stepladder. Then he eyed the bodies of the dead.

For no reason at all he started with Gary Sharpe.

Gary was the fireman with the grey beard and the gigantic black eyebrows. He was the father of three that had taken ax blade square in the face.

Kyle stripped Gary to his underwear, gripped his hands and dragged the man's heavy frame across the road. Gary's broken neck allowed his head to flop back and forth without resistance. Blood drained onto the ground. Kyle lifted the man up and threw him over his shoulder like a large bag of grain. Then he walked up his log stepladder, stood on the top, balanced himself carefully and hoisted Gary onto the spear.

The spear perforated both skin and muscle, traveling two inches into the dead man's belly before it became stuck. Kyle grabbed Gary by the hair and the beard and stepped off the log, pulling the corpse to the earth. The spear traveled through Gary's intestines and spleen quickly; it came through his back with a POP.

At that point, Kyle decided to get a couple extra spears.

He returned to the forest a retrieved the ax. Ten minutes later he had four more spears.

Officer Tony Costantino was next.

He removed his uniform and split him in half with the ax. He put his groin and his legs on one spear and his torso and head on another. It was easier that way. Smaller pieces were easier to work with.

He found little Mandy in the backseat of Mr. Burton's car.

He stripped her naked, chopped off her head, and placed it on a spear. He slid her twelve-year-old body onto a different spear, upside down. The stake entered the stump of her neck, traveled through her lungs and intestines and exited the place she was saving for her wedding day. Her arms hung straight down. Her legs were opened in a 'Y'.

He did the baby's next, impaling her mouth first. After he was done with the baby he impaled the child's mother on the same spike.

An hour and fifty minutes later he was done. He had twelve bodies skewered across fifteen sticks. The sixteenth stick was in his hand.

Covered in dirt and blood, he walked.

He walked away from the dead bodies, the abandoned vehicles, the bloodstained road. He walked away from the spikes and the clothing, which he left lying carelessly on the ground. He walked—not towards Nicolas Nehalem, Daniel McGee, and Patrick Love, not towards the pit in Daniel's basement. He walked towards town.

For the first twenty minutes he saw nothing but the moon in the sky, its glare upon the road, the fields at his sides. He listened to the earth crunching beneath his feet and the insects in the grass. He didn't know what the sounds were, or what they meant, or where they came from. They just were.

A row of houses came into view on the left side of the road. A row of houses came into view on the right. He walked past them, towards St. Peter's cemetery. He saw the church that sat next to it. And like all small-town churches, it looked abandoned in the darkness. He couldn't see the windmill or the wooden bridge that sat behind the graveyard; the night was too dark for that. But he could see the fence that surrounded the necropolis, an outline of the forest in the distance, and the one thing that his eyes were focused on—

Light.

The light was glowing dimly, not from any of the houses that were lined up in a neat little row, and not from inside the church. The light was coming from the humble residence that sat beside the church: Father Galloway's place.

Kyle stumbled towards the light with his body cooling. One hand was raised and one hand hung limp. He looked at the cross sitting high upon the tall steeple, the sea of tombstones, the scattered trees. His thin, dry lips pressed together. A crow flew overhead. Looking at it, he tightened his grip on the spear.

His mind was consumed with hunger and rage.

3

Father Mort Galloway opened his eyes, staggered out of bed and lifted his housecoat from an antique hook. The housecoat was white. The hook was made of wood.

He put the housecoat on and yawned.

On his way to the bathroom he flicked several light switches. After a squirt and a flush he wandered into the kitchen. He poured a drink of water, swallowed it down, and wiped his mouth with his hand.

On the wall was a crucifix. He looked at it and looked away.

With his dehydration somewhat relieved, he opened the cupboard beneath the sink, removed a half-empty bottle of gin, unscrewed the cap, and poured himself a shot. Not a big shot; just a small one, a mouthful. He only wanted to wet his whistle, nothing more.

He drank the gin straight, squinting his eyes as it went down his throat. His chest burned. He looked at the crucifix again, took a deep breath, and poured another shot, lying to himself about quitting his nasty habit: *I can quit. It won't be hard.*

He swallowed the shot and poured a third.

Then he heard a dull THUUMP, THUUMP on the door.

He sat the glass on the counter, next to several candles and a vase full of flowers. He wiped his lips with his hand and walked towards the sound, not wanting to open the door. After all, he *had* been drinking—not much, but some. And that was no way for a Catholic priest to present himself. He was a man of God, not a sales rep from Budweiser. In a town like Cloven Rock these things mattered.

But then, doesn't a man of God help a brother in need?

A hymn:

> *When I was hungry you gave to eat,*
> *When I was thirsty you gave me to drink,*

Now enter into the home of my father...

Damn, he thought. *I need to open that door.*

He certainly didn't want to open it, didn't want to do anything but swallow another shot or two of *London Dry,* crawl under the covers and wait for morning. Besides, it was late. *Real* late. Who comes knocking at this hour?

Someone in need, he thought. *Now enter into the home of my father.*

THUUMP.

"Okay, okay," he said. "I'm coming."

He scooted into his bedroom and threw on a pair of pants and a shirt. Then he returned to the door, unlocked it and opened it up.

"Hellooooo—"

Father Galloway's eyes widened and color drained from his face.

Kyle Van Ryan was there, dead but not dead, blood pumping in reverse. His shoulders and neck was gnarled; the blood on his shirt was soaking. His eyes shimmered and glowed like a cat caught in the headlights while his nose sniffed the air like a dog.

He grinned; he growled.

He dropped the spear and attacked.

Father Mort Galloway stepped back and Kyle was on him, grabbing his shoulders with his hands. They crashed against the floor. A statuette of the Virgin Mary fell from a shelf and snapped into three pieces. Kyle slammed a palm beneath the priest's chin, causing his teeth to smash together. A little section of Galloway's tongue was chomped off and pain shot through his body. His eyes bulged. His nostrils flared.

Kyle chewed a chunk from Galloway's neck while clawing at his face.

Galloway tried to push the attacker away and dispute the situation. "Son," he begged, "Son!" Blood ran into his throat. "Stop it! Stop this!"

Kyle lifted a clawed hand, straightened and flexed his index finger, and rammed the finger into Galloway's bugling eye.

"Son!"

The conversation ended with a scream. Galloway swung his arms madly while kicking his heels against the dark hardwood floor. He thrashed his head left and right. Little spots of red speckled the freshly painted walls around him. A painting of St. Christopher slipped from the wall and smashed against the floor.

Kyle's finger slid free from the man's eye socket. A long, glimmering stringer clung to his nail. He raised his hand up, flexed his muscles and stabbed the same finger into the same eye again. It went in easy; the cherry had already been popped.

Galloway convulsed. Blood drained from his nose. Legs shook and hands slapped at nothing.

Kyle wedged a second finger inside Galloway's skull, scratching a hole in his brain. It almost seemed like he was trying to dig a path to the other side. He scooped a scrap from inside Galloway's head and a piece of meat rolled free. He pulled his hand away and licked his finger's ravenously.

Galloway twitched twice more. Blood poured from his eye socket, his nose, and from one of his ears.

Kyle bit into the priest's neck again, feeding.
Feeding.

4

Father Galloway sat up. There was a blank spot in his memory. He remembered getting up from bed and having a glass of water. He remembered pouring a shot of gin and hearing a knock at the door. He remembered being attacked and then, and then—

He wasn't sure.

The blank spot was big enough to park a bus in.

Galloway looked at his hands; blood poured from his skull to his palms. He licked what was left of his lips and grunted. He tasted blood and forced himself to his feet. Chunks of his brain and mush from his eye rolled down his face. He didn't notice, nor did he care. All that had happened was in the past, and the past seemed pointless now. Previous thoughts and beliefs didn't matter. Religion didn't matter. His church didn't matter. His dwindling congregation and the community it represented mattered even less.

All that mattered was feeding.

But no, he quickly realized. That wasn't true.

What mattered wasn't feeding, but following the command of the Master. He was no longer the shepherd; he was among the flock. He knew the Master's needs even if he didn't understand the Master's plan. He knew the Master's order even though the Master remained a mystery. It was the town that mattered. Old Testament judgment was being forged in Cloven Rock. The people were to be divided. Some would be executed while others would be given a seat at the Master's table. Some would feed; others would be fed.

Eternal life: he preached about it but never understood the meaning. Now he knew; now he understood. Eternal life also meant eternal death. He would live inside his corpse, blood flowing in reverse, following the will of the Master, a servant of the damned.

Galloway stepped outside with half his face hanging from his skull and bite marks in his neck. He sniffed the air like a wolf.

There was a row of seven houses to his right, a cemetery to his left. He walked away from his home, along the great wall of St. Peter's church, across the parking lot and onto the lawn. He made for the houses.

The houses were dark, except one. In one the lights were on.

He heard a family screaming and a young girl crying. He heard a glass shatter and something heavy hit the floor. A bright light appeared behind one of the windows. Something might have been on fire. And as Galloway walked past the house he saw Kyle Van Ryan inside, strangling a child.

Dragging his feet against the road, he walked to Leanne Wakefield's house. He entered her backyard and stood by the pool.

He thought about Leanne a lot before the blank spot, which was growing bigger and deeper and somehow more relevant. He thought about her while he watched X-rated movies and drank himself sick with gin. The tight little shirts she wore to mass always looked so good. With her nipples peeking through the fabric and her lips painted red, she was the girl of his dreams. He wanted to eat her up.

He licked his lips.

Of course, him thinking this way didn't matter.

The Master's desire mattered now.

Galloway lifted a large stone from Leanne's garden and hurled it towards a bedroom window. The Master's desire shall be done.

CRAAAA—

5

—AAASSSSH

Leanne Wakefield flinched; her eyes opened.

"I'm up Simon," she said, slurring her words and licking the dryness from her lips. "I'm up."

But Simon wasn't there; he was dead and gone.

Simon drowned in the backyard pool two summers ago; Leanne had been sleeping alone ever since. She mumbled her late husband's name one last time, extended an arm and clicked the nightlight beside her bed. The light came on; it was bright, so very bright. Didn't matter. Even in her weary and lethargic state she knew something happened. So she sat up, put her feet on the floor and sighed. She had to deal with it... whatever *it* was.

"Is someone here?" she said, lifting her eyebrows rather than her eyes.

Being more awake, she realized the bedroom window was broken. There was glass on the floor, in the drapes, on a plant and inside several pairs of shoes.

Someone broke the Goddamn window, she thought angrily, rubbing a knuckle into her eye. But maybe it wasn't a 'somebody'. Might have been a bird, right?

She exhaled a deep breath.

No. It was a *somebody*. Not a bird. No bird could have done such damage, and if it did, where was it? Why wasn't it flying around or wounded on the floor?

She looked into the heart of the mess. No bird. But a rock peeked out from beneath her bed.

She stood up, naked except for her tiny underwear. She didn't care. She wasn't an exhibitionist but it had been so long since anyone had seen her body she felt like it was going to waste. And she had nice curves; she was lean and attractive and worth taking a look at. She knew this, even if she was the only one that did.

Leanne put an arm across her chest, walked to the window and looked into her yard. A slight breeze gave her a shiver and made her nipples erect.

A man stood by the pool. His head was down and his shoulders were slumped.

She didn't know who the man was; it was too dark to see.

Stepping away from the window, she lifted a blouse off the dresser and slipped it on. Then she returned to the window and let her emotions shine.

"Hey!" she said, with a cracking voice. She looked older when she was angry; the lines in her forehead changed her from thirty-seven to fifty in a heartbeat. "Whatcha doing in my backyard? Get away from here! Did you break my window? What the hell is wrong with you?"

Father Galloway snapped his tattered head towards her and growled. His single eye grew wide and blood dribbled from the remains of his chin. He lifted his hands, extended his arms, and shuffled towards the broken window. Chucks of his scalp hung loosely over one ear, flopping up and down as he moved.

Leanne, shocked, stepped away from the window.

A long sliver of glass dug into her heel. She let out a squeal and fell onto her bed. The pain was excruciating but her mind was elsewhere.

She recognized that man: it was Galloway.

What the fuck was going on?

Suddenly the priest was at the window, screaming like a lunatic. He slammed his forehead into the broken glass. Blood splashed. He raised his arms over his head and thrashed about like Kermit the Frog introducing a guest. Rage. He seemed to be filled with it. He smashed the window with his left hand. His smashed the window with his right. A chunk of glass fell to the floor. A layer of skin fell from his face and slid down his chest.

Leanne Wakefield hadn't released a good-sized scream yet but she could feel one crawling around her throat, ready to be set free. She had to get away from this man, this *thing*—if she didn't get away she *would* scream, and once she did she might not ever stop.

She tried to stand.

The shard of glass dug into her body deeper now than before.

She sat back down. Another squeal escaped, this one, louder than her first.

Don't scream, she thought, biting back her fears. *Don't scream, or it'll be over for sure!*

Still sitting on the bed, she looked at her foot and the growing puddle of blood beneath it. She eyed her wound and did a quick examination.

The bad news: she had a big hunk of glass hanging from her heel.

The good news: it would be easy to pull out.

Galloway tried to crawl through the opening but he couldn't do it; the broken glass was none too kind. It ripped his body apart. His arms were shredded now. His throat was cut. Three fingers were broken and blood poured from him generously.

Leanne grabbed the chunk of glass between her thumb and her index finger, closed her eyes and yanked it free. She let out a quick yelp and stood up, conscious of the mess on the floor.

The priest became more excited. He smashed his broken fingers against his mangled face. He smashed his mangled face against the side of the house. Then in his seemingly *exaggerated* aggravation—he bit a *HUGE* piece of meat from his own arm. A mouthful.

Now Leanne did scream. She did. She couldn't help it.

And when she figured things couldn't get worse, Kyle Van Ryan showed up at the window, next to Galloway, looking like death, eyes glowing red, with someone else's brains smeared across his face, smoldering fire in his hair, snapping his teeth like a caged hyena at feeding time, smashing his fists against the windowpane.

Galloway turned towards the gruesome fireman and hissed. He pounded Kyle with an open hand and ripped a chunk of smoking hair from his head.

With a snort and a growl Kyle grabbed the loose flap of scalp that hung from Galloway's head. He tore it off and stuffed it in his mouth like cake.

Galloway shrieked and spat and pounded Kyle in the face with a broken-finger fist. He growled like he had forgotten how to speak.

Leanne closed her eyes.

Her shoulders were high, her muscles were tense and her fingers were balled into fists. Blood drained from her foot. Her teeth clamped her bottom lip; one eyebrow was raised higher than the other. On top of it all, her hair was a complete mess. In short, she looked like horrified shit.

"I have to get out of here," she said.

She turned away from the zombies, walked out of the bedroom, down the hall, and sat on a bench. Yes, she *walked*. She didn't run and she didn't jog. She was trying to keep her composure. But it was hard; her poise was clearly slipping.

Sitting on the bench in her front hall, she put her shoes on.

"Easy," she said. She took a very large breath and cleared her throat. "Just take it easy, Lee. Stay calm. Don't panic and everything will turn out just fine."

She stood up, opened the front door and stepped outside.

It was the biggest mistake of her life.

6

The house beside Leanne's place had its lights on. So did several other houses. She figured her neighbors heard screaming and called the cops. That was good. Cops were good. A little bit of law enforcement was exactly what the situation needed.

She hustled across her yard and onto her neighbor's porch. Only then did she realize she had no pants on. Thankfully she *did* have underwear. She considered going back home. Then she dismissed the idea, opened her neighbor's front door without knocking, and stepped inside.

The foyer was smoky; there was a fire somewhere in the house.

She said, "Hey Tabby? You here? Is anyone here?"

Then she heard a growl.

Her neighbor, Tabitha Smith—owner and operator of Tabby's Goodies—came running out of the haze; she was naked, with one arm ripped off, her skull cracked open, and teeth that resembled a bear-trap.

Leanne lifted her hands in front of her face, opened her mouth and screamed.

Then Tabitha knocked her down and landed on top of her; blood drained from her arm-stump. She grabbed a hold of Leanne's shirt and ripped it halfway off her body.

Leanne screamed again. Breasts exposed, she pushed Tabby's chest and tried to get away—but it was hard, impossible even. Tabitha was clinging to her like hungry on a crocodile.

She screamed, "Get away from me!" And it seemed to work.

Tabby scurried off, resembling a three-legged dog.

Leanne shifted her position. But before she had a chance to get off the floor she saw Father Galloway standing above her with gore hanging from the place his face had once been. She looked away, only to find Kyle Van Ryan standing there too.

Galloway grabbed her left hand.

Van Ryan grabbed her right.

Feet kicking, she screamed at the top of her lungs. She was getting dragged outside now, but why?

She knew both men. Galloway was her priest.

And Kyle—oh God, she knew Kyle from the Yacht Club. He was a nice guy, a gentleman. He was a Goddamn sweetheart for crying out loud and she often wondered what it would be like to date him. But that didn't matter! Not now. What the hell was happening here? This wasn't Kyle. This was some kind of monster!

The concrete steps pounded her body as she was dragged across them. The stone pebble driveway scrapped skin from her ass, back and legs.

Van Ryan released her right hand.

Galloway released her left.

Leanne flopped against the driveway. As she tried to get up, Tabby jumped on top of her, pinning her arms with her knees, clutching her neck with her only hand.

Leanne had been doing a good job of keeping her wits; she was trying, still trying. But she was beyond scared now; she was terrified. Her heart was racing, her blood was pumping; she was on the verge of wetting herself.

She said, "What are you doing? Stop this! Stop this all of you! Are you crazy? Have you all gone mad?"

But when she looked at Galloway's face, and Tabby's missing arm, and the void in Kyle's eyes, she knew they hadn't gone mad. This was something different, something utterly ludicrous.

Kyle stepped away; he returned a moment later with a spear in his hand. He greased the tip with the blood from his neck and knelt down beside her.

Leanne saw the stick and went wild. Her fear intensified fifty notches. Feet kicking, eyes bulging, she screamed, "WHAT ARE YOU DOING? WHAT? STOP! OH DEAR GOD, STOP! ARE YOU INSANE? LET ME GO!"

Galloway forced Leanne's legs apart and reached between them. He grabbed her underwear and yanked them to her knees.

Leanne couldn't believe it. She said, "NO! FATHER GALLOWAY—NOOOOOO!"

Kyle forced the tip of the spear into Leanne's anus and started pushing. And there was a moment—before her blood squirted onto the stone pebble driveway, her cervix was destroyed, and her sigmoid colon was sliced into sections—when her fear hit its all time high.

Fear of the unknown is great.

But the fear of evident torture and anguish is much, much worse.

Leanne's protest became agony. She screamed as loud as she was able; she screamed with all of her might. She screamed as the spear shredded her rectum and poked a hole in her uterus. She screamed until the spear crept into her intestines, up between her lungs, and into her throat. Then her screams turned to gags, and her gags turned into a sick, knowing horror. There is no combination of words to describe her emotional and physical amalgamation of suffering. Her pain was a description unto itself.

Galloway continued holding her legs and Tabby continued holding her neck but there was no need. Leanne didn't want to kick and thrash—it made things worse. When she tasted the wooden spike in her mouth—mixed with blood, acid, and shit—she began thinking, *Kill me. Kill me. Oh please... why won't I die?*

But she *wouldn't* die. Not yet.

The interesting thing about being impaled: the pain goes on and on. Sometimes it can last for hours. Sometimes it can last for days.

The spear scraped the roof of Leanne's mouth and she opened wide; there was nothing else she could do. A moment later she could see the wood sticking out of her face. It had entered one end and come out the other.

Kyle Van Ryan, Father Mort Galloway and Tabby Smith began hoisting her up.

She slid down the pole another few inches, getting splintered from the inside. She couldn't scream. She made no sounds that were louder than a moan.

They planted the spear in the ground, somewhere between Tabby's garden and the road, near a ceramic frog that stood on a painted flower, holding a sign that said: *RIBBIT - YOUR PAD OR MINE?*

She had a nice view of the neighborhood. Not that she enjoyed the view.

Tears rolled from her eyes.

She heard somebody scream. Several lights turned on and a fight erupted in a neighbor's driveway. She watched in horror as an eight-year-old child she didn't recognize was strung up like she had been. The poor kid had been impaled on a stick with his arms and legs clearly broken.

Tabitha Smith, Father Galloway, and Kyle Van Ryan weren't the only ones acting like savages. More spear-carrying, bloodthirsty zombies wandered the streets every passing minute.

She saw 'odd-job' Martin West drag Lizzy Backstrom out of her wheelchair and across the road by her hair. He then proceeded to stab her with a shovel and hoist her into the air. Leanne closed her eyes and cried. When she opened them again she found Lizzy impaled on a long stick in the garden next to her. She was coughing and gagging. The spear went in through her vagina and out through her neck.

As the night marched on, so did the insanity.

She watched Azul Bunta, the cook that worked for Roger and William over at the Big Four O, have his ribcage ripped open and his lungs torn out. She watched Stephen Pebbles, the man who lost his home in a fire a few years back, be eaten alive by old Jay Hopper and his half sister Emily.

Leanne closed her eyes again, not being able to turn away. She thought about her late husband Simon, remembering the day he died. She felt so bad for standing there like an idiot, doing nothing as he drowned in eight feet of water, a stone's throw from where she had been standing. She didn't think there was anything worse than drowning. Now she knew differently. Some things were worse. Some things made drowning seem wonderful.

Once she was done thinking about Simon, she wondered why her friends and neighbors had turned into bloodthirsty savages. She wondered if things were bad all over. She wondered when her suffering would end, and if the time she spent in St. Peter's Church was time well spent. She wondered for a very long time.

And in time, she wondered no more.

CHAPTER FIVE:
THE PAUL THREAD

1

Paul LaFalce sat behind the counter, drinking a Coke and reading a paperback novel someone had deserted the better part of a week ago. The book was old and battered; it had yellow pages and a broken spine. Paul wasn't much of a reader; he liked Batman comics and magazines loaded with female celebrities. Reading a book with no pictures wasn't really his style. Truth be told, it seemed like work. But he was bored, the night was long, the magazine rack needed an update and instead of tossing the book into the garbage he decided to give reading a whirl.

James Herbert's *The Spear* was a fictional tale about a man battling Neo-Nazi cultists that practiced a strange and evil religion. Paul tried and tried but wasn't enjoying the story. It was too descriptive and for the most part, over his head. Girly books and comics: that's what he liked. Only he didn't think of them as girly books and comics; he considered them men's magazines and graphic novels whether they deserved such labels or not.

Mid-sentence, Paul stopped reading and glanced at the clock on the wall. It was 3:26 am but time moved slowly; in ten thousand years he figured it would be 3:27 am.

He considered watching a movie.

There was a small television beneath the counter. It didn't have cable but it did have a DVD player, and Hopper's Gas rented movies. The selection wasn't great but there were a few titles that hadn't been watched yet. Of course, there was a reason. Romantic comedies, movies about animals playing sports, and stories where old people rediscovered their youth, were not considered essential viewing for a guy like Paul. Most nights he'd rather mop the floor and smoke cigarettes.

Headlights brightened the parking lot.

This was both good and bad. Patrons made the time roll faster but they were a pain in the ass too. Some hung around asking stupid questions and counting nickels. Others made a mess everywhere they went.

Hey lookie, chips! I want 'em! Naw, maybe I don't want 'em. I'll just put 'em over 'ere. Oh wow, chocolate bars! I'll take this one, this one and this one. Oh wait––I don't 'ave 'nough money fer three chocolate bars. I'll put two of 'em over 'ere, by da magazines. Maybe I'll get ma-self a drink insteada chocolate. Where'd I put ma chips? Don't matter... I'll getta 'nother bag from da rack.

Assholes. That's what they were. Complete fucking assholes. And guess who cleaned up the mess? You guess it: Paul LaFalce. Then there were the jackasses, halfwits and morons that tried to steal stuff when he wasn't looking. *Nobody will notice if I hide a bottle of Coke in my shirt!* He hated those scumbags. The only guys he despised more were the small town, hip-hop, wannabe thugs.

Can I get a yo, dawg? Werd.

Give me a break.

Paul didn't want to be working, that was the truth of it. He'd rather be bored than bothered. If it were up to him he'd lock the door, spark a joint, and fall asleep in the back room listening to Bob Marley. Good thing the decision-making wasn't up to him. The place would go under in a month.

The car in the parking lot was a cop car, he noticed. It was parked right next to his piece-of-shit Honda motorcycle.

Should have known.

Cops were always popping by, just as bored as he was. Most nights they weren't too annoying, he had to admit. At first he felt guilty, seeing them up close, talking to them like buddies. He felt like he had done something wrong just because they were around. Needless to say, he didn't like cops, but what could he do?

It occurred to him one afternoon, while watching *The Best of Jerry Springer* and eating ice cream straight from the tub, that if he were robbed—or heaven forbid, *shot*—the cops would be there quickly. Might save his life too.

Looking through the car's front windshield, he tried to see which cops he'd be dealing with. Couldn't tell. Not yet. Not until the car's interior light came on and he could see who was behind the wheel. Of course, it didn't matter who was out there. Cops were cops. They were all condescending, self-centered and egotistical.

The phone rang. It was sitting on a counter next to a stack of cough syrup and cold medicine. Paul turned towards it and lifted the receiver, which felt greasy in his hand. "Hopper's Gas."

"Hi Paul, it's me… Julie."

Paul smiled. He was currently juggling two girls and Julie Stapleton was the latest. "Oh, hey babe," he said. "What are you doing up? It's late."

"Woke up, couldn't get back to sleep. You know how it is. You busy?"

Paul glanced over his shoulder but didn't investigate what was happening outside. He didn't care what the cops were doing; sometimes they'd sit in their car for fifteen minutes or more, taking their sweet-ass time. He wondered if they did that to freak him out… probably not. They were likely just killing time. Didn't matter. The door had a buzzer; he'd know when it opened. Besides, with Julie's unexpected phone call he *wanted* the cops to sit in the parking lot. They could jerk each other off for all he cared.

He said, "I'm never busy at four in the morning. Sometimes two hours will go by without a single visitor."

Julie giggled, trying not to wake her family.

Outside, a car door opened.

∞∞∞⊖∞∞∞

Cameron crept from the driver's seat, naked and disgusting, smelling like something that crawled from the river. She moved slowly, not unlike a zombie from a Lucio Fulci flick. She had dried blood on her face, across her exposed chest and along her belly. Red-dot eyes were unblinking. Her feet were swollen and bruised. Greasy flakes of skin hung off her legs and back. Both hands were stained in gore.

She could hear Paul talking; she could hear Julie Stapleton talking too.

Julie will be next, she decided. *Julie has to be next. That girl thinks she's so smart, so clever. Steal Paul from me and get away with it? Think again, Julie. Think again bitch!*

She opened the front door; the store-buzzer rang.

∞∞⊖∞∞

Paul ignored the buzzer. He also ignored the sound of the door opening and closing and the footsteps inside the store. He was busy. Besides, cops were cops. They weren't going to rob him. They were just killing time.

He began telling Julie about the book reading in an attempt to sound smart. He was saying the story was okay but not really his thing. Then he noticed Cameron in the fish-eye mirror. Spinning towards her, his mouth snapped shut.

The vampire stood before him, mouth open, knife-like teeth exposed. Inside her right hand was a long wooden stick. One end was rounded; the other was jagged, broken. It looked like a snow-shovel without the scoop.

The phone slipped from Paul's fingers and banged against the counter. From the other end of the line, Julie said, "Paul? Paul? Are you all right? What's happening?"

Cameron made her way to the counter, pressed her belly against it and leaned towards her Paul. A bug scurried across her chest and fell into the 'take-a-penny/leave-a-penny' tray. A flake of skin dropped from her face and fluttered to the counter.

Paul backed away, thinking about the button he was supposed to push if he found himself in a jam. He needed to push it. Oh God, he really needed to push it.

This wasn't Cameron English. How could it be? This wasn't Cameron and even if it was, he didn't do anything bad to her. He never said he loved her. He never said she was the one. He was still finding himself for crying out loud. He was barely out of school and every time he saw a nice pair of tits he wanted to run home to the spank-bank in his hard drive and shoot a handful of knuckles-babies onto the screen—so what the hell did *she* want? What was she thinking? Did she want to get married and raise a family together, 'cause that was just crazy! They had only been dating for three months! What type of irrational bitch would want to start a family with a guy after dating him for three months? And what the hell was wrong with her?

How can anybody look the way she does? What's with her teeth? They look like walrus tusks! And where is her clothing? What the fuck is going on?

Get away from me, he thought flatly. *Get away!*

And that was his *last* rational thought, because after that he looked into her eyes—her cold and haunting red-dot eyes.

And it was over.

She whispered, "Hang up the phone."

With tears rimming his eyelids he reached out, lifted the receiver, and did what he was told.

She said, "Come to me."

And God above have mercy, he did that too. His left foot moved forward; his right foot followed. And all the while his eyes were the size of baseballs. Tears dripped from his face. And now, he realized, he was screaming. Long words without meaning were escaping his throat, rushing past his lips, polluting the air. But screaming wasn't enough. It would never be enough.

As her cold hands touched his skin he felt himself getting hard. He wanted it; that was the worse part somehow. He wanted her to bite him and rape him and rip the lungs from his chest. He wanted her to shred his muscles from his bones and stick her fingers into his eyes. He wanted her to snap his spine and yank hair from his scalp in large, bleeding chunks.

And Cameron knew this. Oh yes.

Paul felt this way because Cameron demanded it; she was different now. She knew things; she could see things, hear things. Make people think things. And she was willing to accomplish Paul's needs.

And in time, she would.

She'd fulfill his needs most adequately.

∞∞∞⊖∞∞∞

When Cameron was finished with Paul, she picked up the phone and enjoyed a nice conversation; then she enjoyed another. After that she continued her journey. She had places to go, things to do, people to see: like Julie Stapleton.

It was time to visit Julie.

2

Andrew Cowles and Dean Lee pulled into the Hopper's Gas parking lot. Andrew was driving. Dean was riding shotgun.

Andrew said, "I'll pay for the gas but you've got to pump it, dude."

Dean said, "Fair enough. How much do you want?"

"Put in twenty."

"Have you got twenty?"

Andrew lifted an eyebrow and smiled. He had twenty.

Dean got out of the car, unscrewed the gas cap, lifted the nozzle, and pumped twenty bucks worth of gas.

Andrew scratched his head and pulled his wallet from his pocket. The wallet was made of hemp and had a poorly drawn pot leaf on both sides. It said, *THIS BUD'S FOR YOU!* beneath each leaf. He pulled four five-dollar bills from the wallet and handed Dean the money through the open window. Each bill looked like it had gone through the wash several times.

Dean entered the store with his oversized Nike sneakers grazing the tile floor, thinking about buying smokes and munchies, only to find Paul LaFalce lying on the ground by the counter. Seeing the man was startling, causing Dean to stop dead in his tracks. Seconds passed. He slid the bills into his back pocket and forgot all about them. Then slowly, somewhat carefully, he walked towards Paul. He couldn't believe what he was seeing. This was serious, very serious. But he wasn't scared, not yet, just curious. And excited. Yes, a little part of him was excited too.

He often wondered why nothing thrilling happened to him, why his life was drifting past without something worth remembering dropping in for a visit.

But this—

This was *something* worth remembering. It wasn't a good something, but it was something he'd talk about, something he'd be asked about: Paul, lying on the floor in a large pool of blood, arms broken, eyes closed, stomach obliterated, intestines sitting beside him in a lump, neck chewed, nose and lips missing, pants and underwear pulled to his ankles, a wooden pole stuffed so far up his ass that it shot through the side of his neck. The kid had been impaled with a broom handle, which in Dean's mind meant one thing: *this will be front-page news in the Rock for sure!*

Dean stood next to the body. Looking at the place Paul's lips and nose had been, the blood and the gore, he was amazed. *How could such a thing happen?* he wondered. Then it hit him: this was no accident; it was a murder. He was standing at the scene of a crime.

Dean released a crooked smiled.

The police would want to interview him, newspapers too. He'd probably get his face on television and be the talk of the town for the next few weeks. He would probably get famous. Suddenly he felt special, like he mattered, a celebrity.

People are going to ask me what I did when I saw the body, he thought. *And what am I going to tell them? The guy was dead so I robbed the place. Got three hundred bucks and bought a used couch off my step-dad.*

Dean shook his head.

"No," he whispered. "I'm not going to rob the place a buy an 'effing couch... that's a stupid idea."

Dean decided to check the kid out, make sure he was dead. He looked like a corpse, no question there. And surely he *was* a corpse, but making a thorough investigation seemed like the right thing to do. Plus it was something he could tell people about later. It was a better idea than robbing the place.

He knelt down, put an ear to Paul's lipless mouth and listened for signs of life. He was careful not to touch it anything. This *was* a crime scene after all, and everybody knows that you need to be careful at a crime scene.

There were no signs of life.

Of course, he thought. *The kid's intestines are on the floor. Do I expect the dude to jump to his feet, dance the wango-tango, sing a little song, and ask me about my love life?*

Dean sat up, noticing Paul's teeth for the first time. They looked strange, hiding behind the mangled and bloody remains of his face.

They looked like they belonged in a shark. They were uncanny and bizarre, like something from a bad dream. But as weird as they seemed, Dean shrugged the teeth off and placed his fingers on Paul's chest. Because Paul was dead, right? He couldn't do anything. Teeth or no teeth, his intestines were sitting floor like an overturned bowl of spaghetti. So what could he do?

Nothing, that's what: nothing.

Dean felt movement beneath his fingers.

But how was that possible? Was this guy alive?

He put his ear close to Paul's mouth a second time.

Listening.

He thought about the teeth again. Oh God, those 'effing teeth. They were big and sharp, looked like could bite a carburetor in half, like they could—

Paul's corpse moved again; the eyes opened.

And suddenly Dean was scared. Really scared. Fear swirled inside his belly, chest and throat. His blood felt like it was getting thicker by the moment. His right leg quivered and the fingers in both hands squeezed together. His eyes opened a little wider then they were before, and then—

And then—

Paul growled, opened his mouth as wide as he was able and wrapped his broken arms around Dean's body. The shattered limbs wiggled and flopped as they circled his back, but somehow managed a slight grip.

Dean screamed. And Paul bit into him with his outlandishly massive fangs, ripping Dean's ear from his head.

Blood sprayed.

And as Dean put a hand on Paul's face and pushed himself away, a little piece of his mind was thinking, *I knew it! I knew it! I knew those teeth were dangerous! Why don't I listen to my instincts?* But a bigger piece was thinking, *AHHH DUDE! What the hell is this?! What just happened?!*

A warm stream of blood squirted from the place Dean's ear should have been, and *had* been his entire life. And as the red liquid sprayed, Dean's fingers slipped into Paul's mouth and Paul did the same thing the crab-critter did to Patrick Love hours before. It was almost funny, when looked at from a certain angle—almost, but not quite. And Dean would see no humor in the fact that Paul LaFalce was chomping down hard, severing two of his fingers at the knuckle. He would see no humor at all. But it happened, and now blood poured from Dean's hand and his head. The world spun. Vision diminished.

Paul chewed.

Dean fell onto his back and lifted his gnarled hand in front of his face. Gore ran from his digits like a faucet—hitting him in the eyes, nose, neck and chin. It was on his lips and in his mouth; it was in his hair; it was on his chest. It splashed the floor around him. It was everywhere, reaching comical proportions, and every moment that passed more leaked free.

"Oh shit-dogs," he said, voice trembling. "I'm not a witness, I'm part of the story!"

He rolled across the floor, leaving a thick red trail on the tiles. Hot and cold flashes came in waves. A thin line of liquid shot from his knuckle and made it all the way to the ceiling.

The Paul LaFalce zombie-monster tried to stand up, but with his arms broken and the wooden stick impaling his body, it was impossible. He grunted, slinking across the tiles, still chewing Dean's fingers like a ravenous dog.

Dean hauled himself to his feet, ready to pass out—ear gone, two fingers gone; blood rolling out of him in a stream. It was definitely time to get going. Standing, he lost his balance and stumbled into a display of snacks.

Potato chips tumbled. The rack fell over.

The monster kept coming: Paul crawling, looking like an insect on a fishhook, grabbed Dean's ankle and pulled his feet from under him.

Dean fell, smashed his head off an industrial-sized ice-cream freezer. He saw a cartoon drawing of a kid licking his lips. *Yummy*, the kid seemed to be saying. *Yummy, yummy... good for the tummy!* Then everything went black, quiet, calm—and slowly, too slowly, senses returned. He could hear again, smell again; think again. His eyes opened.

Paul was on top of him, chewing his throat.

Dean tried to scream but only managed to squeal. He pushed Paul away with his ruined hand, discounting the pain in his fingers. The pain raged in a new place anyhow. The pain was in his neck, burning him like fire.

Paul flopped in the opposite direction; he tried to bite the floor. He howled and hissed and slammed his broken arms together pathetically.

Dean lifted himself to his knees, then to his feet. Blood poured from his neck in quantities he didn't want to think about. His witty '*MY OTHER SHIRT HAS A SKULL ON IT*' t-shirt was covered. His ripped jeans were covered. His shoes were covered and when he stumbled towards the door, through chips and chocolate, dizzy and disorientated, the color drained from his face like a magic trick.

Moaning, Dean pushed the door open with his shoulder and made his way across the parking lot, leaving a trail of bright red splotches that were big enough to see from thirty feet away.

3

Andrew had greasy hair, dirty fingernails and food stuck in his teeth. He sat in the car, in the driver's seat, wearing a *Misfits* t-shirt that said *Die, Die My Darling*, and a pair of work boots that had the laces untied. He was completely oblivious. Not just now, but always. He was the type of guy that would wear the same pair of underwear eight days in a row and then try to pick up girls. He had big bushy hair and nicotine stained fingers. He had a habit of going on welfare because he didn't like to work, and a girlfriend that was five months pregnant. He had three cats he didn't bother naming and a litter-box so loaded with turds that more often than not the cats shit on the floor. He had a dusty black flag with METALLICA – KILL 'EM ALL printed on it, hanging in front of his bedroom window like a curtain. And he had a best friend: Dean Lee, who was running towards him, covered in blood, lost in terror.

Andrew was looking for something good on the radio but having no such luck. He turned the power off in disgust and was about to pick his nose when Dean slammed a bloody hand against the passenger window and said: "Open the *dooooor*! Open it dude, quick!"

Andrew froze.

Dean screamed, "OPEN IT!"

Andrew leaned across the car and opened the passenger door with his eyes wide and his mouth wider. "What the hell happened?"

With blood splashing everywhere, Dean plunked himself inside the car, gurgling: "Just drive man! Drive!"

Andrew didn't. Instead, he looked at his friend in awe. Then he looked towards the store and saw nothing out of the ordinary. He scratched his head and considered the getting out of the car. He figured he should go inside the store and buy some bandages, because bandages would come in handy now that his good buddy was—

Dean screamed, "GET THE 'EFFING HELL *OUT OF HERE!*"

"Okay dude," Andrew said, startled. "Don't freak out... I'm only trying to help!"

Andrew threw the car in gear and drove, causing the passenger door to slam shut. Then he started shooting out statements and questions faster than anyone could respond. He paid little, if any, attention to driving.

He said, "Oh shit man! What the hell happened, Dean? Are you okay? Who's inside Hopper's? Who did this to you? Did you see 'em? Are you hurt? How bad are you hurt? Is it bad? Are you hurting really bad? It's bad, isn't it? Oh shit dude... it's bad! I know it's bad! Look at you, man! Look at you! You're bleeding all over my car! I don't care about the car, even though I just cleaned the 'effing thing, I care about you, but look at you, dude! Just look! You're going die man! Oh shit! Are you going to die? Please don't die on me man! Please don't die! I'll take you to the hospital; I'm taking you right now, see? That's where we're going... to the hospital; I'm taking you to the hospital so just hang in there Dean, just hang tight good buddy! Everything will okay if you just hang on and don't die on me! It's not so bad! It just *looks* bad. Oh shit man... it looks *really* bad, Dean! It looks REALLY 'EFFING BAD!"

Dean's eyes opened wide. A red bubble appeared on his lips. He took his hand off his neck; the blood was wet and glistening. He tried to point at the road ahead but his finger was gone. He said, "Loooook out!"

Andrew Cowles glanced at the road just in time to see a stop sign he didn't know existed, and the car they were about to sideswipe. The car was a blue Mustang with a lot of bodywork. He saw two people inside: a guy and a girl.

The driver turned towards him; looked about twenty. Her mouth dropped open.

Andrew cranked the wheel left and slammed the brake. Too late: he clipped the mustang's trunk.

Andrew's seatbelt locked.

Dean wasn't wearing one, and in his final moment of life he closed his eyes and hoped for the best. Then his face smashed into the windshield and his neck snapped; sounded like a campfire crackle.

Spinning.

The whole world was spinning.

And when it stopped spinning Andrew saw nothing but darkness. Then slowly, almost reluctantly, he opened his eyes. Everything was blurry. The steering wheel was in his hands. The windshield was fractured and speckled with cherry splotches. The hood was crumpled and a thin line of smoke was sneaking out from under the car. Looking through the smoke he could see the Mustang: the driver's door was open, the driver had a crushed head, but worse than that, his jaw had been pulled from his face.

Andrew turned away.

There was a girl lying on the road leaking generous amounts of blood from her mangled legs. Her legs were broken, so terribly broken. They looked like they had been smashed apart with a sack full of scrap metal. Beyond the girl, he could see a wooden stop sign post that had been snapped in half. It looked like a broken stalk of corn now, dry and forgotten at the end of a season. There was knapsack next to the sign, sitting up straight as if nothing had happened. Its contents were spilled across the intersection.

Andrew's eyes closed again. And when he opened them he looked at Dean and felt his heart break.

Dean's head was rammed into his chest. The passenger door was hanging open and there was blood everywhere.

Dean was dead, undeniable dead.

And a moment later, he wasn't.

4

Dean opened his eyes for what seemed like the first time. He smelled blood, dust, rotting food, gas, sweat, smoke, and dirt. He shifted his weight and his head rolled around his broken neck like a golf ball circling the hole. He looked at his friend and grinned.

Things became clear.

Dean had been given a seat at the Master's table. He was one of the chosen few, a disciple. Andrew, unfortunately, was not a disciple. He was to be made an example of: a warning sign for others. There was a new law, a new power.

All hail the new regime.

∞∞ ⊖ ∞∞

Andrew, still shaken from the accident, couldn't believe what he was seeing. His friend was alive; Dean was alive! He was hurt badly (*Oh so badly, how can anyone be alive when they're hurt so badly? It's not possible, is it? No! It can't be possible! It just can't be!*) but he was alive! Thank heaven! He said, "Thank 'effing Slayer dude; you're alive! I figured you were dead meat for sure!"

Dean growled, revealing the animal-like teeth growing inside his mouth. He reached out, grabbed Andrew by the hair and pulled.

Andrew, surprised and distressed, tried to say something half-funny. Something like: *Hey man, don't squeeze the merchandise.* Or: *You broke it you bought it!* But all that came from his mouth was ARRRAGHHHH!

Dean yanked hard, ignoring the fact that Andrew wore a seatbelt.

Andrew slapped at Dean's hands. He managed to say, "Don't asshole! That hurts!"

Dean let go. He opened his door, pulled himself from the wreckage and walked around the car, favoring one leg. Blood ran from his face, neck and hand. His head rolled around his shoulders in a slow moving circle; his neck was clearly broken.

Andrew watched in shock, thinking his friend's teeth were best suited for a saber-toothed tiger. Once he realized that he was in danger, he tried to roll up his window. Too late: Dean reached through the opening and grabbed Andrew by the hair. Then he pulled, *really* pulled.

Inundated with pain, Andrew waved his hands frantically and slapped at nothing, screaming: "The seatbelt's on! The seatbelt's on!"

Dean pulled harder.

Andrew tried to unlock the belt. He was willing to do anything to relieve the pressure in his head, which seemed to be getting torn from his body.

Dean yanked in sharp violent surges. Seatbelt or no seatbelt, Andrew was getting out of the car.

Andrew gained a new fear: he thought his neck would snap. It seemed more than possible; it seemed unpreventable. His fingers danced around the seatbelt switch. Every time he thought he had it, Dean jerked him and his thumb slid off the button.

He began crying, kicking his feet. Drool hung from his bottom lip. A long red crack appeared just below his hairline. The crack his skin crack widened; then widened again. Blood poured down Andrew's face and into his eyes. He tasted it in his mouth and realized that his forehead was being torn apart.

Dean yanked again and again.

Squiggly-cracks emerged like miniature earthquakes, cutting across Andrew's brow. Screaming, he slammed his thumb onto the seatbelt button and pushed it hard. This time it worked; the seatbelt released. The belt slithered across his waist.

Dean pulled on Andrew's scalp one final time, heard a *RRRRRIP* and stumbled back. He tripped and fell, holding a flap of hairy skin. Looked like a rug, or a flattened puppy. He dropped the pelt and stood up.

Andrew was bald now; he was scalped. His bony white skull glimmered beneath the car's interior light. There was hardly any blood on it, except around the fault line, the place the skin tore free.

Andrew saw himself in the rearview mirror. In a different set of circumstances he would've looked funny. His haircut was preposterous. It was clean-cut, right to the bone. He put a shaky hand on his head, knowing but not really knowing—not really *believing*. His eyes widened. His mouth crept open.

He whispered, "No."

It didn't hurt, not the way you might imagine it would. It was stinging and it was numb; it felt itchy, cold, and just plain wrong. But pain wasn't the right word. All of his nerve-endings were sitting in the dirt like road-kill, so no—there wasn't much pain at all. It felt terrible though. It felt worse than anything he had ever imagined.

Dean reached into the car, grabbed Andrew's shoulders and dragged him—squirming and begging—through the open window. He dragged him past the injured girl, the girl with the broken legs. He dragged him past the corpse inside the other car, whose skull had had been crushed, whose jaw had been torn from his face. He dragged him towards the broken stop sign, scalped head reflecting in the moonlight. Then he lifted Andrew up and fulfilled his Master's commands. He slammed Andrew's body on the broken STOP sign pole, growling insanely.

The wooden pole tore through Andrew's back, ripping apart his intestines as it shot through his belly.

Andrew screamed once, but only once; he couldn't do it again.

Dean stumbled across the road, still favoring one leg. He grabbed the girl by the face and dragged her—kicking her broken legs and screaming—towards the sign.

The girl's name was Amy Lopes. She was nineteen. She liked Johnny Depp, Orlando Bloom, and books by J. K. Rowling. And for some unknown reason she thought about J. K. Rowling, her wonderful storytelling ability, and the book she was currently reading: *Harry Potter and the Goblet of Fire*. Then Dean slammed her body on top of Andrew and she didn't think about anything else.

CHAPTER SIX:
THE JULIE THREAD

1

Julie Stapleton crawled out of bed wearing nothing more than a pair of underwear. She crossed the room and flicked on the overhead light. Thinking about her conversation with Paul LaFalce, she wondered what happened. Was he playing a trick on her, making a sick joke that wasn't funny? Somehow she doubted it. Paul liked comedic movies and smoking pot. Sick humor wasn't his style. So what did the phone call mean? Was he in trouble? Was he hurt? She thought about the way he was screaming and goosebumps cultivated her arms. She needed to do something, but what?

The obvious answer: dial 911.

But what if Paul was playing a practical joke on her? What then?

The fact of the matter was this: she didn't know Paul very well. He was three years older and they had been seeing each other less than three months. She wasn't even sure if they were a couple or not. She *hoped* they were, and some days it *seemed* like they were, but other days it was hard to tell. He kept secrets; that was the truth of it. He kept secrets and some days he acted strange, like he wanted to get rid of her as fast as possible. She had to wonder, what did *that* mean? For all she knew, Paul was seeing another girl. So how much could she trust him? And how much did she know about this guy? Unfortunately, not enough—so where did that leave her?

Truth or fiction, television taught Julie that calling 911 meant traced phone calls. And if the call were traced, her parents would be notified, even if she didn't offer up her name.

And if her parents were notified she'd get in trouble.

She didn't want that.

Her parents thought she was too young for a boyfriend. Of course, she disagreed. But if they knew she was dating someone three years older they wouldn't be impressed. Plus Paul had a motorcycle. She had to take *that* into consideration too. Guys with motorcycles were bad news, her parents often said. They were nothing but trouble and innocent girls should stay away from them.

She tapped her hands together.

Whatever she decided, she needed to do it quickly.

"Okay," she whispered, trying to push Paul's screaming voice from her mind. "Think."

If she called the police she'd get trouble. And if he were playing a malicious joke she'd be heartbroken. However, if Paul was in trouble and she did nothing, she'd never forgive herself. Not ever. Doing nothing while her boyfriend (if that's what he was) screamed would haunt her for the rest of her days.

She had to act. That's what it came down to; she had to do *something*—even if it meant getting in trouble.

She lifted the phone and hit redial.

No answer.

"Damn," she said.

Then she threw her pajamas on and opened the bedroom door.

∞∞∞ ⊖ ∞∞∞

Julie's parents were asleep. Gina Stapleton—Julie's mom—was on the far side of the bed, close to a window and a patio door that opened onto a newly renovated deck; Ron Stapleton was stretched out like a grizzly bear; his left foot hung from the mattress, showcasing toenails that needed to be trimmed.

Julie didn't knock; she opened the door and turned on the light. "Mom, Dad… we need to talk."

Ron put an arm over his face and grunted.

Gina squeezed her eyes shut. "Turn off the light," she mumbled. "Turn it… off. What are you doing? Go back to bed."

"No mom. I need your help."

"What?" Gina forced her eyes open a crack and rubbed a hand across her face. "What is it Julie? Are you sick?"

Ron pulled his foot beneath the covers, turned on his side and tried to ignore the exchange. He had to work in the morning; he needed sleep.

"No," Julie said. "I'm not sick but we need to talk."

"Now? We need to talk *now*?"

"Yes."

"It can't wait?"

"Mom, listen. And don't get mad; just listen. I couldn't sleep. Actually... I fell asleep and woke up. And I have this friend named Paul. He used to go to my school. He works over at Hopper's Gas. He works the night shift."

"What kind of friend?"

"A friend, mom. He's just a friend."

"Okay. Go on."

Julie sat on the edge of the bed next to her mother, lowering her voice to little more than a whisper. She said, "I phoned him. That'll probably make you mad and I'm sorry. But I was awake and bored. I knew he was sitting at work so I phoned him. The thing is, after I talked to him a few minutes he started screaming."

There was a break in the conversation.

Gina said, "What do you mean, *screaming?*"

"I mean he was screaming... like he was under attack. The truth is, I'm worried about him, mom. I'm worried."

Gina closed her eyes and ran her fingers through her hair. She was too tired for drama, and she wasn't completely sure she understood what Julie was telling her. She said, "Do you phone this boy in the middle of the night often? Is that why you've been dragging your butt around lately?"

"No Mom," Julie said, aggravated. This wasn't the discussion she wanted to have. Not while Paul needed help. "I think we should call the police."

"The police?" Gina sat up.

Ron, listening to the conversation but not wanting to hear it, said, "Take it to another room, please."

"This is important Dad."

"This is teenage nonsense and I've got work in the morning. Go to bed."

Gina cleared her throat. "The police? Really? Isn't possible the boy is trying to be funny?"

"He screamed and the line went dead. I called him back and there's no answer."

"Please," Ron pleaded. "Take it to another room."

Gina recognized the truth: this conversation was going to be bigger than she wanted it to be. Ron was right. It was time to change rooms.

"Get up," she said.

Julie made her way to the center of the room while her mother crawled from bed. They left the room together. Gina turned off the light and closed the door. Once they were in the kitchen Gina poured water into a glass and Julie sat at the kitchen table.

"Do you need a drink?"

"No. I'm okay."

Gina sat across from Julie, placed her glass in front of her. "What do you want me to do?"

"Call the police."

"And what if this boy is playing a practical joke? Did you think of that?"

"If that's the case, he can explain himself to the police. He'll be in trouble, not us. I think we should call, just to be on the safe side. What if he's hurt? What if he's dead?"

Gina didn't think someone would end up dead tonight, but the boy working at Hopper's might have been robbed. Might have been kicked around a bit too. Julie was right; better safe than sorry.

She said, "Let me call Hopper's first. If there's no answer, I'll call the police. Then we can go back to bed. Okay?"

"Okay Mom."

"Tomorrow we'll discuss the appropriate hours for making phone calls to strange boys."

Julie nodded. "Alright."

"Having that phone in your room might have been a bad idea."

"*Mom...* " Julie whined.

"Get me the phone number, would you?"

Julie went into her bedroom with her shoulders slumped. She grabbed a small white envelope off her dresser, which had the words *PAUL'S WORK* written in bubble letters on the back. She brought it to her mother who looked at the envelope and snickered before dialing the number that was scribbled beneath the name.

The phone rang.

Cameron answered. "Hello Mrs. Stapleton. How nice of you to call."

Gina made a puzzled face. "Who is this?"

"It's Cameron."

Gina was suddenly very confused. She thought a *boy* was working, not a girl. She asked, "Are you working tonight?"

"Who me?" Cameron laughed; there was no happiness in her voice. "No. Paul *was* working. Didn't your daughter tell you? It was Paul. She's been sleeping with him, you know. They've been having *sexual* relations. What do you think of that?"

Gina shot her daughter an evil eye that would have made Hitler nervous. She didn't think *much* of *that*. She said, "Oh, really?"

"Oh, yes."

Interrupting the conversation, Julie said, "What is it Mom? What's happening?"

Before her mother had a chance to respond, Cameron continued. "I can tell you what *I* thought of that Mrs. Stapleton. I can tell you what I thought when your slutty little girl spread her legs to my Paul. *I* didn't like it. In fact, *I* didn't like it... *at all*."

"What?"

"Do you know what I did Mrs. Stapleton? Do you? I bet you don't. I bet you don't have a fucking clue what I did. So let me tell you. Let me tell you *all about it*."

Gina shook her head, stunned. "What are you talking about?"

"I came to visit my Paul and guess what? I found him talking on the phone with that slut daughter of yours. They were talking about how much fun they were having, sucking each other off, yes? Oh, yes. That's what they were talking about. They were talking about their *sexual* relations. Paul looked so guilty when he saw me. He looked like a cat with two paws in the fishbowl. He said, *Oh, please don't get mad at me for fucking Mrs. Stapleton's daughter. Please don't get mad! I couldn't help myself. She's so slutty and willing. She loves fucking me, she loves it! So don't get mad!* But it was too late. I *was* mad. I was *very* mad. So do you know what I did, huh Mrs. Stapleton? Do ya?"

Gina didn't respond.

"Answer me Mrs. Stapleton or I'll make you wish you did."

Gina's mouth began to slink open. She was getting a sick feeling.

This didn't sound like a joke. It sounded like the real deal. Anger was being replaced with concern. Who was this Cameron girl? Was she dangerous? Was she insane?

She said, "I don't know what you want me to say."

"Ask me what I did to Paul."

"Okay. What did you do?"

Cameron laughed. "I thought you'd never ask! I kissed him, right on the lips. I kissed him and I bit down. Those were *my* lips, Mrs. Stapleton. They were *mine* and I took them, swallowed them like sushi. Do you like sushi? I did, but now I like other things. *Revenge*, Mrs. Stapleton... I like *revenge*. And *murder*. I asked Paul about your cunting daughter, you know that? I did. Weeks ago, maybe even months ago, I said, '*Are you sleeping with Julie Stapleton? Tell the truth now.*' And he said, '*No... of course not! What kind of person do you think I am?*' I wasn't sure what to think, if you can believe *that*. I was confused and I wanted to trust him. So I said, '*Are you sure?*' And he said, '*Oh yes. I'm sure, I'm sure! You're the only girl for me.*' And do you know what happened? I believed him! He looked me right in the eye and lied his head off and I believed every word of it!"

Gina Stapleton didn't like this conversation. Certain words were making a very big impact on her. *Revenge* was one of them. *Murder* was another. She said, "What do you want?"

"You called me, Mrs. Stapleton, remember? You called me."

"I suppose I did. Maybe I should let you go."

"After I ripped Paul's lips from his mouth with my teeth, I dug my fingers into his face and dragged him across the floor. Paul screamed so loud I figured he'd die. I didn't want him to die. I wanted him to know how upset he made me, and I was very upset, Mrs. Stapleton. Very upset. So I broke his arms. Well, actually I broke his fingers, wrists *and* his arms. Then I chewed on his belly and chest. I have very sharp teeth Mrs. Stapleton. *They're very sharp indeed!* His muscles tasted like raw hamburger and I swallowed them down, just like his lips. I swallowed and I drank. I rammed my—"

Gina hung up the phone. "Oh my God," she said. "I think we're in trouble."

"What happened Mom," Julie asked.

But before Gina had a chance to respond, the phone rang.

2

Gina didn't want to answer the call, but the phone in her bedroom would wake her husband if she didn't. She lifted the receiver. "Hello?"

"Don't like my story, huh? I can't blame you." Cameron laughed. "I broke his arms, I ripped his nose apart and I tore the muscles from his bones. I did a lot of other things too, but that's not the point, is it? No, it sure isn't. Let me make something clear, Mrs. Stapleton, mother of Julie. I'm coming over. I'm comin' to *getcha!*"

The line went dead.

"Oh my God," Gina said, hanging up.

"What is it Mom? Julie asked. She looked scared now. She looked ready to cry. "Tell me!"

"We need... " Her words trailed off. She didn't know what she needed. She was too busy making sense of it all. Was the threat was legitimate? *It was a threat, right? Had her family been threatened?* If so, it was time for... what? Time to wake Ron? Time to call the police? Time to lock the doors and windows and hope nothing bad happens? Yes, yes and yes. It was time for all those things; probably time to get a weapon too. But she didn't want to think that way. Getting a weapon meant *using* a weapon. And she didn't have any guns.

What do people use when they don't have guns?

A knife, she figured. *I could get a knife for me—one for Julie, one for Ron. And, oh yeah—we have those pointy things from the fireplace. I could—*

"Mom?"

Gina snapped free of her daze. She got up from her chair and ran to the bedroom, which suddenly seemed far away from the kitchen. She flicked on the overhead light, shouting, "Get up Ron! Get up!"

Ron rolled over and dragged the pillow in front of his face. His incoherent mumbles might have been, "Oh... what is it now?" Might have been something else.

"We're in trouble. I'm calling the police, so get up, get up! Your family needs you!"

"The police?" Ron said, slightly more articulate. He pulled the pillow from his face and rubbed his knuckles against his head. "Why in the world are you calling the police?"

"Ron, get up. Your family has been threatened."

"By who," he whined. "One of Julie's high-school sweethearts? You can't be serious. He was probably drunk; go back to bed."

"You don't understand!"

She lifted the phone that was sitting on the night table and dialed directory assistance.

Julie stood at her parent's bedroom door, more worried now than before.

Ron forced himself to sit up. "You're really calling?"

"Yes. I am."

The operator came on the line and Gina said, "Cloven Rock Police Department please. Can you put me through?"

"Hold the line."

"If this is such an emergency," Ron said, "why not call 911?"

Gina put a hand over the receiver. "I don't want to talk with 911 dispatch. I want to talk with Mary O'Neill. She's working the night-shift at Cloven Rock PD, as far as I know."

Ron grunted. He was waking up now, and although *he* wasn't worried, his wife and daughter were upset and that was enough to get his blood pumping.

The phone rang twice and Mary O'Neill answered. Her voice was all business. "Cloven Rock Police Department."

"Mary, is that you? This is Gina Stapleton."

"Oh, hi Gina. Is everything all right?"

"I don't know. I just had a strange phone call and I was threatened, my *family* was threatened."

"Who were you talking with, someone from town?"

"I don't know."

"Crank call?"

No, not exactly. My daughter had… " Gina's words dried up. She was trying to explain quickly but didn't know how to do it.

Mary O'Neill, being the professional, understood Gina's thinking immediately. "Do you want me to send a car over?"

"I think it would be for the best."

Mary said, "Gina, I'm going to put you on hold. Is that okay?"

"Yes, it's fine."

"You live on Hunters Road, right? What's the house number?"

"Hunters, yes. Number Three thirty-two."

"Three thirty-two." A slight pause. "Got it. Hold the line; I won't be long."

The line clicked off and Gina waited. After a moment she whispered, "I'm on hold."

Ron nodded.

Julie sat on the edge of the bed, worried.

When Mary O'Neill got back on the line she said, "You still there?"

"Yes."

"Okay, listen Gina. I don't need to tell you that Cloven Rock isn't the biggest place in the world… our police force fits the town, you know what I mean?"

"Yes."

"There was an accident. Joel Kirkwood and Tony Costantino are the officers on duty tonight. They went to investigate and right now they're not answering my call. They might get back to me in two minutes, but they might not get back to me for an hour. I can put this through to our 911 call-center and they'll dispatch someone from the nearest station. The nearest police station is in Maplebrook, and you know where that is. Fortunately there's another option. I have two officers on call and I can wake 'em up and send them over but again, this takes time. Are you in immediate danger?"

"No, but I think someone might be on their way to the house."

"A man or a woman?"

"A woman."

"Armed?"

"I don't know."

"Okay. This is what I'm going to do: I'm going to come over and sit with you guys, and in the meantime I want you to stay indoors. I'll try to get hold of Officer Kirkwood and Officer Costantino again. If I don't talk to them soon, I'll call Maplebrook and see if they can send some men my direction. Either way, hold tight and I'll be there shortly. You can fill me in with the details later."

"Thanks you, Mary."

"Make sure the doors and windows are locked. Don't opened them until you see my police car in the driveway."

"Okay, I'll do that."

"See you soon."

"Bye Mary, and thanks again." Gina hung up the phone thinking about the woman that threatened her, and the things that she had said.

I have very sharp teeth Mrs. Stapleton. They're very sharp indeed!

3

Gina left Ron and Julie in the master bedroom. She double-checked the doors and windows, and turned most of the lights on, thinking the dark corners might turn against them somehow.

Ron sat up with the blankets wrapped around his waist like a skirt. He looked through the patio door, but couldn't see much, just a bit of the deck, the sky and the outline of a few trees.

Julie exhaled a deep breath. "Will everything be okay Dad? I'm worried about Paul."

"I'm sure Paul is fine, baby." Ron said, but he wasn't sure about that. He wasn't sure about anything.

After several minutes Gina returned to the bedroom. "Everything's locked tight. I even checked the windows in the basement. I think we're safe."

Ron nodded, rubbing the stubble on his chin with a knuckle.

Julie faked a smile.

Another few minutes slipped past.

A car pulled into the driveway. Nobody heard the motor or saw the headlights; the master bedroom was at the back of the house.

Ron said, "How about I meet you guys in the kitchen? I want to get dressed."

Gina, knowing her husband was naked beneath the sheets, said, "Come with me Julie. Let's give your father some space."

"Okay."

Julie left the room and Gina followed. They sat at the kitchen table again, same seats as before. Gina considered the phone call, even though it made her feel anxious. The more she thought about it, the worse she felt.

There was a knock at the door.

Gina flinched and said, "Stay here." She entered the living room and looked out the bay window, thinking she'd see a crazy woman with teeth that were *Very sharp, very sharp indeed!*

A police cruiser sat in the driveway.

"Thank heaven," she whispered, touching a hand to her chest. Followed by: "Cop car. Nothing to worry about."

Julie, still sitting at the table, felt her muscles relax.

Gina turned away from the window, put her hand to her mouth like a megaphone and shouted, "Hey Ron, Mary O'Neill is here!"

Ron shouted back, "Okay, I'll be out in a minute!"

Cops are here, he thought. *Good. Let them sort this shit out. I need sleep, not that I'll be getting any now. I've got to be at the docks at six thirty. What time is it now, four? Jesus. Tomorrow is going to be a bitch. Tomorrow? What am I thinking? Today! Today is going to be a bitch!*

He opened a drawer and pulled out a pair of socks that were rolled up like a grenade. He dismantled the grenade and put a sock on each foot. He opened the closet door and took a moment deciding which shirt complemented his current mood.

Plain black t-shirt, snug fit. Great choice.

There was a bathroom attached to the master bedroom. He entered it, washed his hands and face, fixed his hair and turned off the bathroom light.

Then he froze.

Cameron was on the deck. She was naked, looking through the patio door with a grin that consumed her face. Her skin was pale, like the belly of a dead fish. She had dried blood on her face, chest, stomach and legs. It was in her hair and on her feet too.

She tapped a finger against the window.

"Let me in," she whispered, staring at Ron with her haunting red-dot eyes. "Come to the door."

The muscles in Ron's stomach scrunched together; pins and needles danced across his arms and legs. Something cold slithered down his spine; his mouth opened and his heart rate changed gears. He stepped back, towards the bathroom and away from her.

She tapped on the window again, leaving a red smudge on the glass. "Hurry up," she said. Drool formed around her mouth. "I've got something for you. Come to me Ron Stapleton. Come before they catch us and put a stop to it."

She pulled her finger from the glass and touched her nipple, making it hard.

Ron cringed.

Cameron was the opposite of sexy; he couldn't imagine enjoying anything she had to offer. He wanted her to go away; he wanted her to stop looking at him. But she kept looking and he returned the favor. He was gazing into those horrifically evocative red-dot eyes like he had never seen anything better. And the more he looked, the more power she had over him. He wanted her to feed on him now. So he moved towards her: one step, followed by another, he walked a straight line to the door. But only a fool opens the door for a vampire, right? He might as well put his neck on a plate and smear it in barbeque sauce. Still, he didn't care. He wanted her fangs digging into him, even if meant the end of everything he cared about.

She's not a vampire, some logical thought challenged. *Vampires don't exist. And if they* do *exist, that's not what they look like. They aren't naked, pale and covered in blood. They don't have eyes that look like fire. And I recognize that girl. She serves coffee at the Big Four O, so how can she be a vampire?*

He kept walking.

She hypnotizing me, he thought. *She's casting a spell with her eyes.*

Maybe she *was* a vampire. But no—that couldn't be right.

"Do it," Cameron said, unkindly.

Ron reached out, unlatching the lock with his finger. A small groan escaped his lips.

Cameron slid the door open. Although she didn't need an invite——only the vampires on television needed an invite—she said, "Invite me in."

"Come in," he responded, helpless and weak.

She stepped through the doorway, opened her mouth and revealed the true length of her fangs.

Ron whispered, "No."

She leaned in, placed a hand on each of his shoulders and bit into his neck like she hated him, making it hurt. Warm blood blasted into her throat. It ran down her chest and splashed across the bed.

Ron's eyes rolled back and his hands became fists. From the depths of his soul he released a small, harsh cry, not loud enough for the family to hear, only meant for the two of them. It was the last sound the *real* Ron Stapleton would ever make.

Cameron smiled with lips red, having drank until her victim's eyes locked in place, his shoulders slumped and his heart stopped beating.

And after that, when his eyes shifted again, she pushed him away and watched him stumble across the room, knowing he wanted to feed, glad he felt that way, eager for the moments that lie ahead to take their course.

4

Gina opened the front door.

Officer Mary O'Neill stood before her. She was big woman, a strong woman. She looked like she could handle herself in a physical confrontation. She had dark eyes, tanned skin, short hair and knuckles the size of walnuts.

"Hi Mary," Gina said.

"Hi Gina. Everything all right?"

"So far, yes. Everything is fine. Come in." Gina opened the door wider and stepped to the side, giving Mary room to enter.

Mary stepped into the front foyer. "Thanks. Let's hope it stays that way. I have a question… have you seen Officer Kirkwood or Officer Costantino? Have they dropped by?"

"No, I haven't seen them."

The two women stepped into the kitchen.

Julie was there, sitting at the kitchen table, looking sleepy and guilty and wondering how one phone call could have led to all of this. "Hi Officer Neill," she said.

"Hi Julie, how are you?"

"Okay, I guess. Did you send somebody to check on Paul?"

Gina sat down, putting both hands on the kitchen table. The lines on her forehead grew deep. "Paul?"

"Yes, Paul LaFalce. He's working at Hopper's Gas tonight. Don't you know?"

"Actually Julie, I came *here* just as quick as I was able. I wanted to make sure that *you guys* were all right. You haven't had any visitors in the last few minutes?"

Gina interjected. "No. It's been quiet here. I'm thinking of putting coffee on. Would you like a cup?"

"Sure."

Julie couldn't believe what was happening. Coffee? Was her

mother on crack? Paul was dying and she was making coffee? Trying to keep her emotions in check, she said, "Officer O'Neill, someone needs to check on Paul right now. You need to send somebody!"

Mary nodded. "Do I? Okay. I will. But listen a minute first, all right? Most nights in Cloven Rock nothing happens. There might be a fender bender or somebody that had one too many wiggly-pops down at the Yacht Club, but that's about it. Occasionally we have two minor disturbances at the same time, in which case we inform the Maple-brook Police Department that we *may* need assistance. Now this doesn't get everybody's juices flowing, it just means a couple things are hitting the fan concurrently. The officers in Maplebrook send a cruiser in our direction in case we need them, but they don't enter our jurisdiction unless we ask. And in situations like this, where the officer working the night shift at the Cloven Rock PD steps out of the office, we notify our two on-call officers. I've done both of these things. I've notified our on-call officers and I've talked with Maplebrook. Right now I have two men pulling themselves from bed and making their way to the station. Plus a car from Maplebrook is headed in our direc-tion."

Gina said, "What happened with the officers that are on duty to-night?"

"Officer Kirkwood and Costantino haven't reported back to me. I noticed their car parked down the road. That's why I asked if you've seen them."

"Oh, no. We haven't seen them at all. What do you think they're doing around here? That accident you mentioned earlier… was it on *this* street?"

"No," Mary said. "It wasn't."

"Who are you sending to Hopper's Gas?" Julie asked. She was angry now, clearly angry. It seemed very obvious that something needed to be done twenty minutes ago and nothing was getting done. She wondered if this was what people meant by *red tape*. "Are you sending the policemen from Maplebrook?"

Mary hesitated. "Sure, Julie. I can send the Maplebrook officer's to Hopper's. But this is the first I've heard there was trouble. Why should I send men there? Can you tell me, because frankly, I don't know."

Julie shot her mother an uncomplimentary glance, thinking, *Mom dropped the ball. I asked her for help and she did everything except what needed to be done. Paul LaFalce is probably lying at Hopper's in a pool of blood and nobody is checking in on him! It isn't right. It isn't fair. Do I have to steal a car and check on him myself? Is this what it has come down to? If he dies, I'll never forgive her for this!*

She said, "You don't even know what happened, do you?"

Officer O'Neill said, "No Julie. I don't. I got a call from Gina and she said you've been threatened. That's all. That's why I'm here… to keep you safe. And that's what I'm doing. I'm keeping you and your parents safe. Now if you'd like give me more information, I'd be happy to respond appropriately."

Julie felt like yelling, crying and kicking her feet. She hated when old people treated her like a stupid kid. Why were adults like that? Why couldn't they treat her like an equal? Did they think she just plunked out of the womb this morning? She wasn't five years old. She was sixteen… *sixteen!* Soon she'd be seventeen!

As calmly as she could manage, she said, "I phoned Paul at Hopper's tonight. While I talked with him he started screaming. It sounded like he was getting killed. I was worried about his safety so I told my mom. I wanted her to help out somehow. You know, drive me to Hopper's Gas or something; call the police. Do something to help Paul out, 'cause he was screaming like he needed help. Don't you get it? It sounded like he was dying! He needs help!"

Julie looked down at her hands, which were balled into fists.

Officer O'Neill said, "Go on."

Julie nodded, keeping her eyes on the table. She thought she might cry, and she didn't want that. She *really* didn't want that. "My mom called Hopper's to see what was going on. And she talked to somebody. I'm not sure who she was talking with because she wouldn't tell me."

"I don't know," Gina exclaimed, trying to remember the girl's name. Was it Cynthia? Cameron? She wasn't sure. "I have no idea who I was talking with!"

"Okay then, fine. My mom didn't *know.* Then she called you. She was supposed to tell you to check on Paul, because Paul needs help. He *really* needs help… not like us. You should be at Hopper's Gas checking on Paul, not sitting here with us!"

"Okay," Mary said. "I'll send somebody right now."

She stood up.

Then a howl came from the bedroom and all three women turned towards the sound. Something bad was happening. It seemed that Paul's assistance would have to wait.

5

Gina ran down the hall.

Mary followed.

Julie didn't move. She just sat there, eyes wide, hands on the table, lost in thought.

Gina reached a hand towards her bedroom door and was about to open it when Mary said, "No! Don't! Let me go first!"

Gina stepped out of the way.

Mary rushed past, brimming with courage and authority. She pushed the door open, looked across the bedroom and out the open patio door. Then her eyes fell to the floor, her hand trembled and her teeth pressed together.

Ron was on his hands and knees; his head hung low. Blood drained from his neck.

Mary wanted to pull her gun from her holster because she was afraid; she didn't. The gun stayed put. Ron needed help. That's what Officer Mary O'Neill figured when she first looked at him—there was no immediate danger and the man needed help. She was wrong of course, and knew it almost at once. 'No immediate danger' didn't mean 'no danger'; the man received his wounds *somehow*. He didn't rip apart his own throat, did he? No, of course not. That meant someone else was here. That meant danger.

She reached for her gun.

Ron looked up, revealing teeth that didn't fit his mouth. His red-dot eyes glowed within their sunken black pits.

Gina screamed. Seeing her husband this way was as shocking as it was terrifying. He looked like he swallowed a handful of boxing shears.

Mary stepped back. She was scared now, beyond scared.

This man doesn't need help, she thought. *He needs to be put down.*

Ron charged across the floor like an insect. He leapt, with teeth snapping madly in the air.

Mary tried to pull her gun free but her hands were trembling. She was unable to draw it quick enough. Pulling a gun from a holster like a professional hit man was a talent that eluded her. Some cops were gunslingers, but most of the cops in Cloven Rock were like her, all thumbs.

She tried—

Too late. The Ronald Stapleton zombie-monster was attacking and she was falling back. Her head smashed off a wall as she crashed against the floor. A photograph fell from its place, shattering into pieces at her side.

Ron crawled on top, slammed a hand on her face and squeezed it into a fist. When he pulled his hand away Mary O'Neill's nose and lips came with it. The pain Mary felt was unbearable. And when she cried out, Ron's wife Gina raised both of her hands in the air screaming: "What are you doing? Stop it, Ron! Stop it!"

But Ron wouldn't stop. He looked at his wife with anger and rage cattle-prodded across his features. Then he slammed his hand on his victim's face again.

Julie, still sitting at the kitchen table, got up from her seat. She walked into the hallway slowly. She was scared but she needed to see what was happening. One foot in front of the other, she walked; staring at the floor, lips pinched together.

Then she looked up.

What she saw made her gasp and flinch.

Her mother's fingers were clutching her jaw.

Her father was on top of Mary O'Neill. His eyes were different now, silver—no black, centered with a crimson dot. His hands were forged into talons, having just raked them across the officer's face.

And Mary O'Neill—poor, unfortunate Mary O'Neill—she was on the floor, half in the hallway and half in the bedroom. Her gun was still in its holster. Her neck was twisted strangely. Blood drained from her throat, eyes, nose and mouth. Half of her face was lying on the floor in a pile.

She coughed and gasped for air.

Gina shrieked.

Ron licked his lips and growled. He sounded like a wolf. He bit into Mary, ripping the remaining half of her nose off.

Gina screamed again.

Mary screamed again.

Now sixteen-year-old Julie was screaming. Screaming, with both hands at her ears, fingers digging her scalp, watching the chaos in absolute horror.

Ron bit a piece from Mary's throat. He rammed her head against the floor and snapped her neck.

Gina turned away from the violence, no longer looking like a mother with all of life's answers. She looked like a victim in shock. She said, "Run Julie, run!"

Julie nodded, mumbled and ran into the kitchen.

Gina followed.

Suddenly Julie slammed on the brakes.

Cameron was there, inside the house, blocking the exit. Ron's blood was on her face and chest, wet and glistening. Gleaming.

In her hand she held a very long stick.

"Hi Julie," she said, smiling like an angel that lost her way. She tapped the stick against the floor. "Hi Mrs. Stapleton. Remember me? We talked on the phone. I said I'd drop by and... here I am. Glad to see me? I hope so. I'm here to see your daughter, Mrs. Stapleton. I'm here for revenge. I'm here for *murder*."

"Get out of my house," Gina said, her voice anxious and terrified. "I mean it. Just turn around and go."

"And if I don't? What then? What if I decide to stay for a bite?" She smiled, purposely flaunting her teeth.

Gina gasped.

Then she heard Ron coming down the hallway. She didn't want to turn around and face him. After what she had witnessed, she never wanted to see him again. But she did turn. She did.

My husband looks like a rabid dog, she thought. *He looks insane.*

Then Ron leapt onto her, biting and scratching and out of his mind with rage.

Gina tumbled back, away from her husband, the man she had fallen in love with, the man that needed to work in the morning. She fell into Cameron's arms and screamed one final time and then it was over. The last thing she saw was Ron slamming his blood-soaked hands inside her mouth and ripping her face apart.

CHAPTER SEVEN:
TUESDAY MORNING

1

4:15 am. Sunrise.

4:44 am. Cameron entered Patrick's cottage, licking her lips through teeth that had grown a full inch during the night. They looked like they belonged inside the mouth of a rattlesnake now; they were sharp, thin and strong. Above the slender of her nose, dark and haunting red-dot eyes were locked on Daniel, fixed on him like a mother to a newborn child, watching his chest rise and fall as he lie helplessly asleep on the couch, lost within his private world. Time mattered. In eight short minutes the sun would rise, burning Cameron to a crisp, wiping her from existence. She understood this, but did not subside to the spoils of fear. She had enough time to bite Daniel and turn him into her slave while staying clear of the morning sun. Doing so only took a moment; a single bite and she'd be off. But there was a problem: she didn't want Daniel to be a slave; she wanted him to be more than that. She wanted an equal, someone to spend eternity with. She wanted Daniel to be her mate. Instinctively she understood that forging any man into her likeness took three nights, despite the fact that her transformation only took one. Why were the rules of becoming a vampire this way? Because. Because she was bitten by the source of the infection, and he, if things played out the way she wanted, would be bitten by her. And now she had to drain him in modest amounts and infect him progressively, augmenting his contagion over time. Then on the third night he would become like she was—an equal, a vampire, immortal. Only then could they be together. Otherwise he would be a ruined shell, an empty husk, no better than all the other senseless zombie hybrids that were obeying her every will and command. No, this was not the Hollywood way, but this was the way that it was—the truth behind the vampire legend. A single bite meant Zombie. A triple bite meant Vampire.

4:46 am. Six minutes remained. By now the town would be free of the zombies that had terrorized every home, every building. The zombies would have found shelter, in an attempt to hide from the sunlight. They would have crept into the basements and cellars, the closets and the attics. But Cameron, naked and filthy, had not. She still had a job to do. Dropping to her knees she pushed apart Daniel's legs. She crept between his thighs and tilted his head to the left. Leaning in, she put her mouth to his neck. Her cold tongue licked his warm flesh, tickling him, tasting him, enjoying the moment for as long as possible. Her fangs slid deep and his blood entered her mouth. Her nipples grew hard as her pussy turned hot and wet. She wanted to devour him, consume him; she wanted everything he had to give and more.

Daniel felt the bitter lips sucking the life from him, the acidic teeth inside his flesh. As his eyes opened his neck turned numb and his heart began racing. He didn't know what was happening but fear crashed upon him like an ocean wave to the shore, saturating him, overshadowing his will. He wanted to push her away—needed to, but his body wouldn't respond. He was powerless, becoming feeble and immobilized. Blood ran down his neck in a dark, thick channel, a liquid rope. The room seemed to spin on one corner. Stranger still, he felt himself growing hard. Part of him didn't want the moment to end, wanting instead to seize hold of more pain and fright, disorientation and confusion. Thoughts flipped end over end, falling apart before he could comprehend their value. What was happening here? What horrors sat before him, poisoning him, exterminating the very spirit of the man he was born to be?

Cameron sucked more blood from her victim's body. Running her fingers through his hair, she pulled away. Her fangs slipped from his skin, releasing him from her deadly hold. A string of blood dangled between them, shinning like silk, glimmering in the moonlight before its integrity was compromised.

"Sleep," she said. "Close your eyes."

Daniel did what he was told; his heart rate slowed immediately.

4:49 am. Cameron stood up, wiped a line of blood from her

mouth and licked Daniel's taste from her lips one final time. Her chin was covered. She had blood on her breasts, dripping from her nipples to the floor. His flavor was nothing short of ecstasy, bliss. She wanted to swallow another mouthful but wouldn't chance it. Drinking more could turn him into a zombie and spoil everything; it wasn't worth the risk.

4:50 am. She left Patrick's cottage and made her way to Daniel's place. As she stepped through his front door she saw a multi-legged creature with numerous eyes and an abundant amount of jaws. It crawled across the floor on stalks that were fourteen inches long, snapping its teeth at random. She walked past the beast calmly, blood glistening on her naked flesh, knowing she was safe, knowing the creature wouldn't attack, for she had become one with the critters, a queen among the hive.

4:51 am. She entered Daniel's basement.

4:52 am. Cameron made her way down the ladder. Once she was deep in the earth, in the place the others believed was a bomb shelter, she curled her body next to a large cocoon and closed her eyes. For this new version of Cameron, the first of many nights had ended. The time for sleep had come.

2

5:23am. Nicolas Nehalem woke, shifting into a different position as he held his pillow tight. His eyes opened, closed, and opened again.

The babies were crying.

He rubbed the sleep from his face, lifted his librarian-issue spectacles from the nightstand and slid them into place. He sat up, putting his feet on the floor one after another. CLUMP. CLUMP. For no real reason he looked over his shoulder, lifted his feet and dropped them down again.

CLUMP. CLUMP.

He put his hand into the empty space on the far side of the bed and gave the sheets a squeeze. They felt soft and nice.

He stood up, stumbled across the room and entered the bathroom. He relieved himself, washed his hands and face very thoroughly before pouring himself a glass of water. The glass had a cartoon dog on it. The dog was wailing its tail and smiling happily. He drank the water from the glass and emptied the remaining few drops on the floor. After returning to his room he lifted his brown-checkered housecoat from the shiny brass hook and pushed his furry blue slippers together on the floor with his foot. He put the housecoat on and tied the cotton belt in a cute little bow. He slid his feet inside the slippers and stumbled down the hall. With a yawn and a fart he entered the kitchen and opened the refrigerator door.

Last month's turkey sandwich was still there. So was the empty carton of orange juice. He lifted the empty carton, shook it and tossed it in the garbage.

There were no bottles of formula; if he wanted to feed the babies he'd have to make a new batch. Or—

He grabbed the sandwich from the bottom shelf and sat it on the counter. The green and black moon craters inside the plastic wrap were bigger now. The plastic felt squishy beneath his fingers.

The babies kept crying. Or was it just one?

Nicolas opened a cupboard door and grabbed a box of powered formula. He lifted a spoon from the sink and licked it. He opened the container of formula and rammed the spoon inside. From a different cupboard he found six baby bottles. He opened them, put a spoonful of formula in each and filled the bottles with water. He capped the lids and shook them all; then he put four in the fridge and two in the microwave. He turned the machine on for nine minutes. After five minutes he opened the microwave door. The formula was boiling. When the bottles were cool enough to handle he lifted two of them up and headed downstairs, formula in one hand, sandwich in the other.

5:31 am. At the base of the staircase he clicked on a light. Several large cockroaches made for the shadows. He walked across the room that was filled with shoes and coats, jeans and shirts, wallets and belts. He opened the cellar door and flicked another light switch.

Today the crying didn't stop. It became louder.

And yes—only one baby was crying. Still, he didn't like it. Didn't like it at all. It might be time to teach those babies a lesson; he wasn't sure.

Nicolas slid the bottles of formula and the sandwich into his housecoat pockets. He walked down three stairs and stopped. There was a cupboard on his left. It was deep and dirty and the perfect place to store paint cans, mason jars and all the other stuff people hold on to but rarely use.

He opened the door.

Somewhere inside, a mouse squeaked and ran for cover.

The cupboard was home to a wide assortment of things that made his babies quake with fear: a pair of pliers, a wrench, a long hunting knife, gasoline, razor blades, a nail gun, a chainsaw, hedge clippers, a blowtorch, a hammer, a sledgehammer, vice grips, a curling iron, a cattle prodder, a cork screw, an electric sander, rat traps, an ax... the list went on and on. Today he reached for one of his favorite items: a medical scalpel he bought off the Internet. It was neat and clean, fun to use and easy to work with. And boy, was it sharp! Sharp enough to slice through leather.

The crying continued.

He walked down the remaining six stairs, crouched down and entered the room with the low ceiling.

William was gone. In his place was a large puddle of hardened blood and a severed leg. Connected to the puddle of blood was a trail that led to Cathy Eldritch's cage. It was empty.

Cathy's cage was empty.

Nicolas couldn't believe it. That cage hadn't been empty in fourteen years. And Nicolas, completely surprised, looked at the cage for a long while before his eyes finally shifted to another trail of blood, which led to Olive Thrift's cage.

It too was empty!

Nicolas dropped the scalpel; he couldn't believe what he was seeing. And he could hear screaming now. Not crying but screaming. But why? Who was making that noise?

He turned his head towards the sound and found Cathy sitting in the corner, naked and wilted and covered in scars. She wasn't alone. William was beside her with eyes open, his mouth agape and his skin white like a sheet of paper. The man's legs were destroyed, his hands were drenched in blood, his fingers were opened and facing the ceiling like overturned spiders, like he was expecting something to be placed in them. Cathy didn't seem to notice. She was holding onto William, arms wrapping around the dead man like a blanket. And she was screaming—screaming and screaming; a woman that had finally lost her marbles.

Nicolas said, "Where's Pumpkin?"

But Cathy didn't answer. She couldn't answer, couldn't think. Being set free from the cage was the final straw that caused her sanity to crack apart in a way that could never be salvaged. She was lost; her mind was elsewhere, drifting, floating; reliving the horror…

3

Cathy watched Nicolas lead William inside the room. She knew what would happen next. Will wasn't the first man to be led into the basement over the years—led to the slaughter, as she often thought of it. He was the twelfth.

The unfortunate souls were always dealt with in a similar fashion: Nicolas would walk his victims down the stairs, force them to strip and allow them a nice view of the cages. Then after a brief reaction he'd pull the trigger. On two separate occasions Nicolas shot his victim in the head. Twice he shot his victim in the stomach. Three times he shot his victim in the back. Three times he shot arms and legs off, one at a time. And on one terrible occasion—an occasion that haunted Cathy's thoughts still—he shot his victim in the groin, and when the man went down screaming he shot him again in the neck, lopping the poor bastard's head clean off.

After his victims had fallen Nicolas would do the unthinkable: he would eat them, or cut them into pieces, or set them on fire, or suck out their eyes, or dismember them with an ax. Often times he made intestine soup and fed it to his babies. Other times he'd strip the victim naked and have sex with the corpse. One time he chopped a man apart with a hammer; one time he operated with a chainsaw. One time he covered a man in chocolate and licked him semi-spotless. But he had never—as far as Cathy had seen—never, shot a man in the legs and left it at that.

Until now.

Cathy wondered why.

Perhaps Nicolas was tired. Perhaps he was out of shotgun shells.

Cathy didn't know. She didn't *want* to know. Truth was, she didn't care any more. She hated thinking about Nicolas and all of his crazy bullshit. It was too much. *He* was too much.

After Nicolas shot William he went upstairs to scream in his closet or piss in the sink or do whatever it was that he was doing, and Cathy watched the wounded man screech and cry and pass out where he lay. She thought he was dead.

He wasn't.

Somehow William found the strength to open his eyes and drag his body across the floor, one leg dangling by a pair of tendons and a rope of meat, the other leg left behind, dribbling blood on the floor. Then, with his teeth clenched and his fingers quivering, he unlocked Cathy's cage.

She knew what William wanted. He wanted her to save him. He wanted her to crawl from her coop and hunt down the medical attention he needed—but how? Didn't he know how mistreated she was? Couldn't he see that she had been abused too?

Cathy was in no position to help. She was under enough strain without being asked to play hero. And besides, that part of her personality died years ago. She couldn't resurrect it now. Not for him. Not for anyone. She wasn't a hero; she was a psycho's plaything. Didn't he know that?

In the other cage, Olive cried and begged. She said, "Come this way! Come here! Open this cage! Set me free!"

William turned away from Cathy, squealing in pain, fading in and out of consciousness. He crawled across the floor leaving a trail of blood three feet wide. And in time, somehow, he unlocked Olive's cage.

Olive pushed the door open, crept from her cage and lifted her head high. She started to laugh. It was a terrible sound. There was no humor in that laugh, no happiness. She looked at her hands, her fingers, her bony little stubs... and the strangest thing occurred: she laughed louder than before.

She was almost free; she could hardly believe her luck!

Cathy, however, was not free. She remained in her cage, far away from the wide open door, afraid to step through, afraid of the future. The reason was easy to understand: she was institutionalized now, with her cage being her establishment. Leaving the pen meant leaving the safety of her home. Not to suggest that her home was a safe place to be. It wasn't. And she knew that—but home was home and the cage was it. Stepping outside meant God knows what, and she was simply not ready for it.

Did stepping from her cage mean a daring escape followed by a barrage of questions from policemen, doctors, news crews and talk shows? Did it mean being captured by Nicolas again, and a punishment so severe that all of her past penalties would seem pleasant in comparison? Or did it mean something worse? Like seeing her family again, for that was the one thing she wanted least of all. Looking into her mother's eyes now would be a torment she couldn't possible handle. The very sight of her family would break her heart into pieces. And her mother wouldn't cry. She would run away screaming in terror. She would run from the monster that Cathy had become, wishing her child had never been born. She was a living nightmare now, an unsightly ghoul. Cathy knew these things, and that's why her home inside the cage was good enough. She knew her place. Escaping the cage was opening a door to an entirely new brand of nightmare she wanted no part of.

4

Olive crawled past William and scurried towards the stairs. She was smiling. For the first time in five years, ten months and thirteen days, she was really smiling. This was the chance she had been waiting for, the chance she had dreamed about. Her fantasy.

William said, "Help me, please."

Olive didn't say anything to the man. She just looked at him and looked away. Then she climbed the stairs like a spider, pretending he wasn't there. Later she could help, or not help, or do whatever she needed to do. But right now she had to think about herself, she had to escape.

She entered the room filled with clothing and tried to stand up straight. She couldn't. After years in the cage it hurt too much to stand; plus her balance was wrong, thanks to Nicolas' little surgeries on her feet.

Didn't matter. At least, right now it didn't.

Olive didn't want to stretch; she wanted to see her mother again, her father again. She wanted to spend time with her younger brother Dale. She wanted to go back to school, play video games and be on the track-and-field team. She wanted to go to baseball games and complain that the seats were bad and the ref was blind. She wanted to read magazines and listen to music. She wanted to organize her dolls and put them in her dollhouse. She wanted to get away from Nicolas.

On the way up the stairs she heard someone yell. No—not someone. Him. He was screaming and yelling again, being insane.

Was this good news, or bad news?

She didn't know. It would definitely be better if he was asleep but he wasn't, and nothing was going to stop her from trying to get outside, because being outside, even for a minute, would be the best thing that happened in *years*.

She made her way to the top of the stairs and pushed open the door. It opened slowly; the hinges sounded like they belonged inside a haunted house: CREEEEEEEAAAAK–AK–AK. Once the hinges stopped squeaking she listened to the sounds of Nicolas grunting and cursing and pounding his fist against the wall. POUND. POUND. POUND. The noises were coming from inside the closet, which was beside her; the doorknob was next to her head.

Thinking about Nicolas made her cringe. She could just see him opening the closet door and saying, "Ah ha!" Then he'd drag her downstairs and cut off another finger and piss in her face and talk about setting her on fire. Or maybe he'd lop off an arm this time. After all, this was *bad*. Trying to escape was very, very *bad*. And if she found herself caught there'd be a serious punishment attached to her crime. *Extreme* punishment.

POUND. POUND.

"That's good," Olive whispered. "Be loud. Be really loud."

Suddenly the noise stopped.

Olive put a mangled hand to her mouth.

Did Nicolas hear her whispering? Did he know she was there? No. That was impossible, wasn't it? She was being quiet. Wasn't she?

Nicolas pounded on the wall again, crying as he did so. POUND. POUND. POUND. POUND. He followed the pounding with a good long scream.

Olive grinned a frightened grin and scuttled down the hall, towards the front door. She reached for the knob, knowing that freedom was just a few feet away.

But—

She only had three fingers now, two on her left hand and one on her right: two pinkies and a ring finger. Not much to work with, but she *would* work with them. Oh yes. She would do whatever she had to do because she was *getting out*. The time for escape was now. This was her chance, her *only* chance.

Nicolas kicked the door—not the wall but the door—and Olive nearly jumped out of her skin.

He could come out of the closet at any time, she thought. *Any time at all!*

Kneeling at the front door, she wrapped her fingers around the knob. She tried to turn it. Didn't work. She didn't have a good enough grip. She tried again. Same result. She put a palm on each side of the knob, pressed her hands together and tried her luck again. Now it worked; the knob was turning.

But it wouldn't open! She couldn't believe it!

The doorknob was turned all the way and she was pulling on the door and it wouldn't open! It wasn't fair!

It just wasn't—

"Oh," she whispered.

The door was locked.

Olive's eyes widened. Unlike the lock on her cage, this was a lock she could open. This was a lock she *would* open! Come hell or high water she was getting through that door.

She put a pinkie to the lock and gave it a push. The lock turned so easily she could hardly believe it. With a hand around the knob, she turned and pulled. The door creaked and cracked and made lots of strange sounds but it was opening.

Thank heaven; it was opening!

A cool summer breeze hit her in the face. She thought she might be dreaming and hoped that she wasn't. She wasn't. As abused and mentally fragile as she had become, she knew that her escape was really happening. Outside was right there, less than two feet away. Oh God, she felt like crying.

She crawled back a foot, giving the door some room to swing open. Then she did it: she moved through the doorway and onto the porch. She closed the door very quietly and made her way down the steps and along the driveway, hunched over, walking on her hands and feet like a primate.

Laughter came. It was a sick laugh, one that didn't sound connected to comedy in any way, but there it was. She was laughing, and tears rolled down her face.

Olive realized something: she hadn't stood up straight in years. She tried again but couldn't do it. Not yet. Not here. She had to keep moving and worry about her posture later. Slumped over, she lost her balance often. Walking was difficult with every toe amputated, but she would do it; oh yes she would.

She moved past the fire truck, which seemed large and completely out of place sitting in the driveway. Once she was past it she had a choice to make: follow the road left or follow the road right. She couldn't see much in either direction: the moon and the stars, the trees and the sky. That was about all. The moonlight wasn't much help. It was dark. Real dark.

She turned right and continued her journey. It wasn't a bad choice; it wasn't a good one.

Stone Crescent was like a lollipop: it went around in a circle. She needed to get off the circle if she wanted to get noticed by the people of Cloven Rock. She needed to get onto Stone Path Road and into town.

She followed the loop, hoping a car would pass. None did. The road swerved left and right, but mostly left. She didn't realize she was walking in a circle. And she didn't see Stone Path Road when she came to it. Not the first time, the second time, not the third time either. Stone Path Road looked the same as everything else, like darkness.

After two hours and forty-five minutes she became tired and slightly dizzy. Being in no condition for long distance hiking, she made a decision. She would lie down at the side of the road and sleep. A car would come by soon, she trusted. It had to. It just had to. She had no idea that Nicolas was still only a few hundred feet away. Had she known, she would have continued on.

5

5:34 am. "Where is Pumpkin?"

Cathy didn't answer. She kept screaming and crying and holding William's corpse close to her body.

Her high-pitched voice was annoying, and before long Nicolas decided enough was enough. He turned away from her, walked up six steps and looked into his cupboard. He put his hand on the hedge clippers, then he touched the blowtorch, and finally he decided on the sledgehammer. The sledgehammer was good. It was sturdy and heavy. Too bad there wasn't much room in the cellar to use it.

He lifted the tool and made his way down the stairs, approaching his plaything with evil on his mind. He grabbed her bony ankle and dragged her from the corner. His beady eyes were slightly askew behind his glasses, making him look crazier than ever.

Cathy screamed louder, holding William's corpse like her life depended on it. It didn't; the corpse couldn't help her. What she needed to do was beg for Nicolas' forgiveness, and even that wouldn't be enough.

Nicolas pulled her into the center of the room. The corpse slipped from her remaining fingers and a moment later Nicolas released her. As she flopped to the ground, writhing in mental agony, he positioned himself above her, holding the sledgehammer—not in a traditional way, but the way an executioner would hold his battle-ax while waiting for the condemned man to arrive—with the mallet at his feet, not over his head. And when he raised it up, he raised it to his waist, balancing it above Cathy's teeth.

Cathy was on the floor, squirming and laughing, screaming with her eyes opened very wide. Something changed inside her mind and she looked right at him, right into his face with knowing awareness. She howled like an animal, saying, "SHE GOT AWAY! OLIVE GOT AWAY! YOUR PUMPKIN IS *GONE*, NICOLAS! SHE'S GONE,

GONE, *GONE!*"

Nicolas continued holding the business end of the sledgehammer a foot and a half over her face. It swayed left and right like a pendulum. He said, "What did you say? What!? How dare you speak to me like that! She's not gone! She's not gone! She's mine, you hear me? Mine!"

"SHE'S GONE, SHE'S GONE, SHE'S G-O-N-E! OH, YOU STUPID MISERABLE PSYCHOTIC FUCKER, SHE'S GONE AND SHE'S NEVER COMING BACK! NOT NOW! NOT EVER! SHE ESCAPED YOU! YOUR *BABY* ESCAPED YOU!"

"Don't say that! Don't you *ever* say that—!"

"I'M SAYING IT YOU STUPID PRICK! OH LORD, I'M SAYING IT!"

"I'll kill you!"

"DO YOU THINK I CARE? I *WANT* YOU TO KILL ME! DON'T YOU KNOW THAT? I WISH YOU HAD DONE IT YEARS AGO! KILL ME! KILL ME, YOU PATHETIC PIECE OF SHIT! DO IT! DO IT NOW BEFORE I GET UP AND WALK OUT OF HERE THE WAY PUMPKIN DID!"

"You're not going anywhere!"

"KILL ME YOU BASTARD! I DARE YOU TO!"

Nicolas heard enough. His hands were shaking. His nostrils were flared. His knuckles were turning white from holding the wooden handle so tight.

Raising the sledgehammer another two inches, he screamed, "YOU WANT ME TO DO IT? YOU WANT ME TO KILL YOU? OKAY *BITCH*! I'LL DO IT! IF THAT'S WHAT YOU WANT I'll GIVE IT TO YOU! I'LL KILL YOU RIGHT HERE AND NOW! HERE IT IS, BITCH! HERE IT IS, RIGHT IN YOUR FUCKING FACE!"

∞∞∞Θ∞∞∞

5:37 am. Nicolas mashed the mallet into her eyes, crushing her skull like a beer can. He raised the weapon up and slammed it down again. Cathy's head cracked open. Blood, brains and bone rolled free. Legs trembled. Hands flinched. Her nightmare ended, and the next time Nicolas hit her she was already dead. But that wasn't enough to stop him from smashing his fury into her empty shell until her head looked like mush. Nothing would stop him. And when he finally grew tired of beating her with the hammer he kicked her four times and threw the weapon across the room.

Now he was done—now, and not a moment sooner.

And with that, it was decided: the town would pay for this outrage. Everyone would pay.

Every. Fucking. One.

6

5:40 am. Nicolas stormed his way upstairs. He was furious! He wanted to kill everyone, everywhere—right now! This was shit! Complete fucking donkey shit! How did Pumpkin escape? How did she get out of the house? It made him so MAD! He felt like sticking his hand into a blender and turning the knob to mince. Maybe *that* would ease his thinking. Maybe *that* would make things better.

After stomping through the house, he kicked his way into his laboratory and considered slamming together a mix of sulfuric acid and nitric acid right then and there, real fast like. But building nitro-glycerin wasn't something you 'slammed' together when you were pissed off at your babies. He was mad and crazy, but not mad enough and crazy enough to try something like that.

"FUCK!" He screamed. "FUCK! FUCK! FUCK!" He tore a handful of hair from his head and cracked his knuckles against his ears. "HOW DO YOU BUILD NITROGLYCERIN? ONE PART SULFURIC ACID AND ONE PART NITRIC ACID! HOW DO YOU MAKE DYNAMITE? THREE PARTS NITROGLYCERIN, ONE PART DIATOMACEOUS EARTH AND A SMALL FUCK-ING ADMIXTURE OF SODIUM CARBONATE! AND HOW DO YOU BLOW UP THE TOWN? YOU PUT DYNAMITE IN EVERY HOUSE AND SET THE WORLD ON FIRE!" Nicolas clomped out of the bedroom, balled his hand into a fist and punched a hole in the wall. "FUCK!"

He went into his bedroom, tore off his robe and kicked off his slippers. He threw on pants without underwear, shoes without socks, and a white golf shirt that had a snappy green alligator above the left breast. He combed his hair real nice and checked his teeth in the mirror. They were clean, but not clean enough. He entered the bathroom, brushed his teeth and clipped his fingernails, making sure they were rounded and spotless. After that he shaved and applied a generous amount of aftershave. Perfect. He looked like a lunatic.

Reaching into his pocket he found his keys sitting next to a stick of gum. He pulled the gum from his pocket and tossed it on the floor.

A new idea came: he hustled his ass to the basement, pulled the chainsaw from the cupboard and grabbed the sledgehammer from the corner of the room. He took both items upstairs and blasted his way outside.

∞∞⊖∞∞

5:45 am. The morning was beautiful in Cloven Rock. The sunshine was bright, the air moved with a gentle wind and no matter which way you looked, the day seemed absolutely gorgeous. But Nicolas wasn't looking at the beauty of the landscape; he was looking at his car and thinking about the bitch inside the trunk. With an ugly smirk he squeezed the sledgehammer in his left hand. Then his smirk became a sneer and with his right hand, he lifted the chainsaw high.

Chainsaw/Sledgehammer.

Chainsaw/Sledgehammer.

Chainsaw/Sledgehammer.

Chainsaw.

He dropped the sledgehammer, flicked the saw's safety switch and yanked on the cord. The machine came to life, easily and without delay.

"Big Beth!" His voice was barely heard over the roar of the spinning blade. "You in there? Are you? I got something for you! Here comes a big fat surprise!"

Nicolas didn't have time to fuck around. He didn't have time to make the most of the situation and enjoy the subtleties of the terror he was about to inflict. It was time to kill people, simple as that. He was about to rip the town a new asshole, starting with that rotten whore he had stashed away.

Holding the saw tight, he reached into his pocket and pulled out his keychain. He shuffled the keys through his fingers until he found the appropriate one. The key entered the lock. His wrist turned. He heard a CLICK and the trunk was unlocked.

Then came a big fat surprise all right: Beth kicked the trunk with her knees and the trunk flew open. Almost comically, it nearly bounced shut.

Beth squealed.

The *last* thing she needed was a surprise attack that started and finished with her getting locked in the trunk again. It was almost funny but holy hell, it wasn't. She stuck her knees up just in time and the trunk lid bounced into them.

"Look at you!" Nicolas screamed as Beth worked her body into a sitting position. "Look! Coming out swinging, are you? Do you know what you look like?"

Beth felt like she had spent six weeks living inside a used coffin. Her hair was wet, her face was dirty and her eyes were glossy and red. She had bugs crawling on her skin and maggots in her hair. Her lips were dry, turning white and starting to crack. She was dehydrated. Her arm was bloody and mangled, with a wound that was getting more infected by the minute. And she stank. Oh boy, did she ever. She smelled like Pauline Anderson's corpse, fresh urine and old sweat mixed together in a tub of compost. On top of everything else, she was scared; it was easy to see. Her eyes were wide, her teeth were clamped together and her muscles were as tight as a hangman's rope.

Do you know what you look like? he had asked. Truth was: yeah, she supposed she did. She looked like a woman that had tasted hell, a woman with nothing left to lose, a woman that had spent the night in the trunk of a madman's car, lying next to a dead body, wondering if she'd ever see her family again. She wasn't happy about it, not one little bit. And she wasn't going down easy; she wasn't going to give up living without a fight.

Beth lifted the crowbar as high as she was able. She said, "Back!"

Nicolas started shouting: "Oh, you want to play do you? Okay bitch! We can play! We can play all morning long! I haven't had breakfast yet... how about you? Did you get something to eat while you were in there? Did you break off a little piece of Pauline Stupid-Head for a late-night snack? Yum! Pauline tastes good, yes? She tastes good to me, you fat fucking cow. Her fingers taste like steakhouse ribs!"

Beth didn't hear much of what Nicolas was saying; the chainsaw was too loud and piercing. She understood the gist of it though: Nicolas was explaining that he was crazier than a hen-house fox and he was going to chop her into pieces. Simple.

She swung the crowbar wildly. "Stay back I say! Back!"

Nicolas moved a little closer and revved on the engine. "What's that? You want me to saw your face off? I can. Won't be a problem. I can saw off your arms and legs off too."

"Get the hell away from me!"

Nicolas' glasses sat low on his nose, threatening to fall from his face. He didn't seem to notice, or care. His focus was firmly directed on Big Beth, the ugly man-dyke with a neck like a tree trunk and a head like a bowling ball.

He smiled with good reason: he was happy. A moment ago he was furious but bingo-bango—things had changed. Just looking at that stupid tub of mule piss was a knee-slapper. She looked like an over-the-hill babysitter trying to extinguish a house fire with a glass of pudding. Where did her smart talk go? Where was her existentialism philosophy when she needed it? Apparently her Mother Teresa attributes evolved into a big brown loaf of underwear-munchies once she became bed-buddies with a corpse.

"Hey Einstein," Nicolas said, revving the motor louder. "Why don't you sweet talk the chainsaw?"

Beth felt a cold chill creep down her spine. She needed out of the trunk, otherwise she was a goner.

She put a hand on the trunk's casing and shuffled her legs around so she was kneeling. Now her head was touching the trunk door and her feet were pressed against Pauline's corpse. She didn't care about the corpse. Not now. The bugs, maggots, flies and rotting flesh meant nothing at this point. The girl was dead. It was bad but she was over it. And she was alive. Bugs and maggots could be washed away, memories could be suppressed, and without a doubt, she had bigger things to worry about than the creepy-crawlies nesting on her skin.

Beth's eyes shifted; she caught a glimpse of the white van. Then her eyebrows lifted and she looked up.

"Oh my—"

There was something on the roof—big, black and loaded with legs. It had a dozen mouths and was roughly half the size of riding lawnmower.

7

5:48 am. The crab-critter crawled down the wall and onto the porch. Its mouths opened and closed in unison.

Nicolas saw Beth's eyes shift towards the monster and he decided to make the most of the moment. He lifted the chainsaw high and came at her quickly.

For one terrible flash Beth thought her life was over. It wasn't. She lifted the crowbar up and the spinning blade crashed into it. Sparks shot into the air as he pressed the saw towards her, putting muscle into it. If she couldn't hold her ground he'd chop her into hamburger patties for sure.

And it was going to happen. Oh God, it was going to—

Nicolas stepped back and pulled the saw away. The sparks stopped flying.

He was laughing now. Laughing, but his face was pinched into an expression of pure hate. The two facades made him look like he might turn the saw against himself and like it.

Beth snuck another glimpse.

The creature from Daniel's basement was smaller than the one that tried to break through the trap door, but it was just as ugly. Its mouths opened slowly and snapping shut fast. Bulbous eyes were unmoving. Long pink tongues, not unlike the tongues of lizards, flicked the air. Long, limber stalks tickled the area around it.

The trap door must be broken, she thought. *That big mamma escaped and brought a few friends outside with it.*

Nicolas realized that Beth was *honestly* looking at something behind him. He was surprised; at first he thought she was bluffing, which seemed like a straightforward line of defense. What else could the bitch do aside from bluff her way free? He had a chainsaw and she was geared up to change a flat tire. Bluffing was her only move, wasn't it? He thought so. But when he saw the look in her face—in her eyes–

–he knew she wasn't pretending. There *was* someone behind him. He'd bet the farm on it. And who, he wondered, would that *someone* be?

The answer was so simple, so obvious.

Nicolas revved the saw, spun around and shouted, "Alright Pumpkin! You wanna mess with me? You want some of this? You want—"

Beth gripped the crowbar tighter.

The creepy-crab leapt off the porch. It came straight at Nicolas, lost two legs (courtesy of the chainsaw) and landed on Nicolas' face with teeth snapping.

Nicolas pulled the saw towards himself recklessly; he stumbled backwards.

Crab guts exploded everywhere.

Beth steadied the crowbar and swung it like a baseball bat. There was a loud, vibrating CLUNK as the iron banged off Nicolas' head.

Nicolas saw stars, waved the chainsaw hastily in front of his chest and fell forwards. As he dropped to his knees, a second crab leapt off the rooftop. This one was bigger than the first. It looked like it weighed a hundred pounds or more.

Nicolas didn't see it coming; it landed right on him—and the saw.

More guts splashed.

Beth crawled from the trunk. She turned away from Nicolas, and the crabs, and ran down the driveway. Something large and loaded with teeth flew past. Not surprisingly she dismissed it, and within seconds she was standing on Stone Crescent Road, wondering what to do. She looked left and right but she didn't trust the road *at all*, so she crossed it, jumped a ditch and a fence and hid in a field.

In the distance she heard Nicolas cursing and swearing. And a moment later she looked across the road. There was something there. She thought it was another crab-critter but it wasn't.

It was Olive.

∞∞ ⊖ ∞∞

When the crab jumped into the chainsaw and exploded, it pushed the spinning blade towards Nicolas. The blade clipped his head and he fell back—shocked, startled and alarmed. As the saw fell to the ground it came dangerously close to chewing his leg apart, probably in half. It missed his limb by less than an inch, coughed twice and died with its nose in the dirt.

The world suddenly seemed very quiet.

Nicolas released his weapon and sat up. He placed a trembling hand to his head as his vision blurred. The saw blade, he realized, got him pretty good. It bounced off his forehead and gnawed his skin to the bone. A generous amount of blood was running down his face now. It was in his eyes, dripping from his chin, onto his chest and draining between his legs. He pushed blood from his face with an open hand and squeezed his eyes tight. When he was able to see he looked at the area around him, surprised by what he found.

Crab guts and severed monster legs were everywhere: on the car, the driveway, the porch, the bush beside the porch; there were chunks on his lap, in the trunk, in the flower garden—you name it, it was there.

Nicolas reflected: he stuck a cat in the microwave once or twice, maybe three times, maybe four. Same result.

He pushed critter husk off his lap and looked to the roof.

A small crab, roughly the size of a housecat, was clinging to the eaves trough while spraying a web like a spider. Another danced around next to the chimney.

"What are those things?" Nicolas said flatly.

A small one scooted under the car. Then it ran in a circle, made a quick dash in his direction and jumped on his back.

Nicolas—still sitting on his ass with his legs shaped like a V— waved his arms and kicked his feet. He turned, crawled on his hands and knees and swung his head from side to side. "Get out of here," he said. "Get off me! What the fuck? Get the hell... ouch!"

The creature bit into his neck and chopped at him with its little pinchers.

In desperation, Nicolas threw himself onto his back and squished the crab against the driveway. It popped apart like an egg, legs twitching. Dead. He stood, wiped himself off and looked at the car.

Beth was gone, and seeing the empty space in the trunk made him furious. He had barely crawled from bed and already he had lost both of his babies and the bitch in the trunk. He couldn't believe it.

"Oh no you don't," he said. "Not on my watch."

He lifted the sledgehammer off the ground, slammed the trunk shut and headed down the driveway, keeping both eyes open. He didn't know what those little crab-things were, but they were a solid pain in the ass. He knew that much. He also knew that his back was covered in a runny gel, not unlike a moisturizing cream. His shirt was sticking to his skin in a way that wasn't the slightest bit pleasant.

Reaching Stone Crescent, Nicolas looked left and right.

On his right he saw nothing. No wait, that wasn't accurate. On his right he saw one of those things crawling across the road. It was far away, wasn't a threat.

He looked left and saw—

8

Lying on her side, Olive opened her eyes. The sound of a chainsaw roared in the near-distance. She hardly noticed. What she *did* notice was the sun and the way it was shining around her. It was so bright, so unbelievably bright. She couldn't remember anything being so intense, not ever. It felt *warm* against her skin, appeasing too. This was a good feeling, an amazing feeling. And the air was so clean! The cold stench of the basement had been a constant for so long she had forgotten the simple pleasures of a summer's day. The air tasted satisfying and sweet, a little slice of heaven.

She rolled onto her back and looked at the sky.

The brightness hurt her eyes, but it was beautiful. Words couldn't describe how wonderful the sky looked. After years in the basement, seeing an open space was the single most important thing she had ever witnessed. It was stunning, spectacular. It was fantastic and magnificent and glorious. Over the last few years her mind had erased the uncomplicated delights of a scenic landscape, and looking at it now was completely shocking in the most wonderfully miraculous way imaginable. The fact that she was naked, disfigured, and in serious need of medical attention didn't matter. The fact that she had been tortured half her life didn't matter either. Not here. Not now. The only thing that mattered was her freedom. And she had it. She finally had it. She wasn't dreaming. This was real.

The sound of the chainsaw sputtered to an end.

Now the world was perfect.

Everything was nice, warm, alive, blooming—and peaceful.

The word 'peaceful' had been lost in her vocabulary for so very long. Often times it had been quiet, but never peaceful, never *ever* peaceful. Peace isn't something a child in a cage feels. Peace is something that disappears quickly in a situation so cruel and unfair. Now it was back. She was outside on a gorgeous and peaceful day. Was there anything better? Was anything more amazing?

She sat up, noticing that her back hurt. She wasn't surprised. Her back always hurt. It was nothing new.

With effort, she stood. Once she was on her feet she forced herself to stand up straight. It hurt but she did it. Pain didn't matter. It was the standing that mattered. She hadn't stood up straight in a long, long time.

Olive looked around; she couldn't believe her eyes.

She was outside! She was free!

Inevitably her mind turned to Nicolas and her happiness became clouded with fear, apprehension and concern. She hated that man, hated him so much. He was mean, terribly mean. She had never known anyone who could treat people so poorly. He was cookoo in the head; that much was obvious. And once he realized that she had escaped he would come looking. She knew it, but didn't want to think about it. Not now. Not yet. She just woke up and besides... she was free! *FREE!* Couldn't she enjoy a moment of freedom without thinking about *him*? Didn't she deserve that much?

Olive didn't know the cage she spent so much time in was less than three hundred and fifty meters from the place she was standing. She had no idea that she had walked in a circle three separate times. She thought she was miles away from Nicolas. If she knew the truth she'd walk more and sightsee less. But she was only fourteen, and being outside was as thrilling at it was breathtaking.

She saw something a quarter mile up the road. It might have been a dog or a cat. Maybe—

Something big flew past. It had lots of legs, mouths and teeth.

Olive didn't notice because the sun was casting a glare that made her put a hand in front of her eyes. Sunglasses would be good.

Ah, sunglasses. She couldn't wait to get herself a pair.

Olive began walking. Her legs were sore but she didn't mind. She walked for two minutes, then for no reason at all she turned around and looked down the road.

There was a man, and for the first time since she escaped she thought about her nudity. Truth was, she had been naked so long that she didn't even care. Modesty and humility were not relevant. She needed help. She needed to be saved. That's what mattered here. The fact that she was naked meant nothing.

She raised a hand.

The man waved back.

"Oh no," she whispered.

It was no man; it was Nicolas. And now he was running towards her, holding a large hammer in both hands.

Olive turned away from him. She tried to run, stumbled and fell; she didn't have the energy or the skill to run. She didn't know how.

Suddenly the beautiful day wasn't important. The sunshine, clouds and the unbelievably fresh air all took a back seat to the dilemma at hand. Escaping her daddy. That was the important thing now.

Escaping.

But Nicolas wasn't her daddy, no how many times he said that he was. He was a psychopath, a killer, an abductor of children and the most sinister man she had ever known. He was the reason she was in such poor physical and mental condition. He had tortured her and abused her, punished her and condemned her. He had chewed off her fingers and chopped off her toes. He pissed in her face and forced her to eat human flesh. He set half of her cage on fire and splashed acid on her legs. He was the devil; that's what he was: the devil, pure and simple. And she needed to escape the devil if it was the last thing she did. And why? The answer: She didn't want to die. Not here, not now. She was too close to salvation, too close to freedom. She had survived the dungeon and she was going to find her way back home—to her *real* home. She was going to see her *real* daddy.

Olive ran, but running was impossible.

She felt a pain in her spine and she cringed. Her back was aching. Her legs were aching. She fell.

And after she fell she turned over, facing the sun.

The sun disappeared, replaced with the outline of a man: Nicolas. He stood above her, looking down and breathing hard. His eyes were wide and his teeth were pressed together. The cords in his neck were sticking out like jumper cables.

He said, "Running away, are you?" ARE YOU?"

"No daddy!" Olive screamed. She rammed her mangled hands onto the dirt road and pushed herself into a sitting position. She was scared; it was nothing new. She had felt this way so many times before, too many times too remember; it never got any easier. The fear was always the same: grounded in reality.

Nicolas raised the sledgehammer above his head, inhaled a deep breath and brought the tool down hard.

Olive's eyes widened.

In a feeble attempt to stop what was happening she lifted a hand, but she couldn't stop what came next. It was too late.

The heavy iron mallet smashed Olive in the left kneecap. Her leg exploded and before she had a chance to scream Nicolas raised the weapon up again; he brought it down again. This time he went for the other leg. Now her right kneecap exploded; blood and bone splashed into the air.

Olive put both of her degraded hands to her open mouth as her face turned white. She fell onto her back and squeezed her eyes together.

Nicolas changed his footing, raised the hammer above his head and brought it down a third time. He could feel the sweat beneath his fingers and smooth lacquer of the wooden handle. It felt good. It felt right. He smashed her in the ankle and the weight of the hammer nearly amputated her foot.

A large pool of blood began forming.

Olive's body convulsed as she tried to pull her right leg in. It didn't work. For some reason her leg wasn't responding. Neither leg was responding. And that was bad news for Olive because her legs needed to respond; they needed to respond right fucking now because the psychopath was raising the sledgehammer again.

Oh shit, he was raising it again—

The fourth time Nicolas slammed the weapon down he smashed her other ankle. Then he went for the shin. Then he went for the other shin.

The shins, he realized, were the best. They SNAPPED like brittle pieces of wood. Snapping them was fun. It was exciting. He wished that she had more shins so he could snap them too; she didn't. She only had two, so he circled her body and raised the heavy iron mallet above his head again. This time he smashed her in the elbow. It almost seemed like she wanted it. As the hammer was balanced above his head she laid her arm on the road. She might as well have put a sign on it that said: SLAM IRON HERE. It was perfect, and so was his aim. He got her right in the elbow and the blood splashed high enough to catch him in the chin.

Panting like a wild animal, he said, "HOW DO YOU LIKE THAT, HUH PUMPKIN? DO YOU LIKE IT? DO YA?"

Pumpkin wasn't responding, but her body was quivering and shaking like she was being electrocuted.

It was then—as Olive's body was deep in shock and blood was pouring from three of her four limbs—Nicolas realized that he wasn't putting her back in the cage. She was finished now. It was obvious.

He decided to end their relationship with a bang. And when he brought the mallet down its final time he didn't aim for a limb; he aimed for her face. And although she was alive when the iron slammed her in the nose and teeth, her mind was already in a different place.

Nicolas was right; she was finished.

And in the end, she didn't feel a thing.

9

6:02 am. Nicolas made his way back home. Twice the crab things attacked him and twice he smashed them with his mallet.

He unlocked his shed.

The shack's interior looked just like he knew it would: filled with homemade explosives. Technically the explosives were considered dynamite, although they didn't look like the dynamite you might see on television. The dynamite still contained diatomaceous earth and sawdust soaked in nitroglycerin, and each piece had a blasting cap attached to a wire. But the dynamite was wrapped in a shoebox-sized square box, rather than a tube shaped cylinder. He liked them better that way.

Nicolas pulled his van beside the shed and loaded the boxes into it. Once the van was full, Nicolas was behind the wheel. He drove past Olive's corpse and made for town. He dropped off his first box of explosives in the place he abducted Beth and William.

The bodies impaled upon the sticks were surprising, and he wondered if he had done it himself and forgotten about it. It was possible. Sometimes he forgot things, and last night was a big night for him. He killed people, and was still killing people. But still, impaling people on sticks seemed like the type of thing he would have remembered.

Nicolas shrugged.

He supposed that it didn't matter one way or another. He was going to burn the town to the ground and nothing was going to stop him.

6:26 am. He noticed Leanne Wakefield, impaled in front of her home. And she wasn't the only one. There were seventeen other men, women and children impaled in their yards, and Nicolas knew he wasn't responsible; he didn't have the time.

7:29 am. He placed explosives at St. Peter's Catholic church.

7:36 am. He entered the residential area, and began hiding explosives every few houses. The streets were empty, save the fact there were more bodies impaled in the yards. The neighborhood looked like it had gone through a war. Windows were smashed and doors were kicked in. Some of the impaled were still alive. One man begged to be saved. A woman asked him to end her suffering. He saw a pregnant woman impaled with a child that couldn't have been older than two. He saw a man impaled with his dog.

Nicolas smiled. He was living in one fucked up little town.

7:54 am. Nicolas entered the downtown core. Everything was quiet. Windows were smashed and blood was on the street. Several bodies and been tossed together in a pile. None of the stores were open and no cars were on the road, aside from one that had crashed into a telephone pole.

He placed packages at The Big Four O, the 7-11, Spooky's Antique Palace, Miller's Gas Station, Cloven Rock Secondary and the Post Office.

8:14 am. Nicolas entered the waterfront area. The carnage was everywhere, including the Police Station. He went there first, happy to see an officer impaled with an iron rod and left to die on the floor.

After he placed packages around the fallen officer, he visited the Yacht Club, the Waterfront Café, Tabby's Goodies, Starbucks and McDonald's.

8:29 am. Nicolas headed for home. He needed more explosives.

9:17 am. Once again, the van was filled with boxes. He sat behind the wheel and drove into town, wondering what the hell was going on.

CHAPTER EIGHT:
THE FOURTH BULLET

1

Daniel woke, still wearing yesterday's clothing. He rubbed his fingers through his hair not knowing where he was. He didn't recall the things that had happened. Not yet. Then, as the room came into focus, it came back to him. One by one, the memory of yesterday's events began creating an image—a bad one.

He was inside Patrick's cottage.

He remembered climbing the ladder. He remembered the giant room beneath his home. And Roger. Oh God, that thing ate Roger.

He took a deep breath and rubbed his hand along the back of his neck. His arms were sore. His neck was sore and bleeding. His legs were aching and he hadn't even tried to stand yet. Standing was going to hurt. He knew it just by thinking about it. By the time he was up and walking about he figured his entire body would be writhing in agony. He renovated, climbed up and down the ladder more times than he could remember, battled monsters—it was no dream. Yesterday was a full day and his muscles were completely unprepared.

"Where's Patrick," he mumbled to himself.

Then he remembered. Patrick was in bed. Good enough for now.

Daniel stood up and sure as shit, his body was stiff and his muscles were screaming at him.

He thought about checking in on Patrick but he didn't want to. Not yet. Not until he was awake. Patrick was doing all right, he told himself—but somehow he didn't really believe it. Patrick needed a doctor, maybe more.

And maybe, just maybe... he was dead.

There was a part of him—the nicest part, most likely—that

wanted to check in on Patrick as soon as he was able. He couldn't though. He was getting a bad feeling about Patrick. He remembered Cameron (*I had a dream about Cameron, didn't I? Yes, I'm sure I did...*) and the way she turned violent. What if Patrick turned violent? What then? Did he have the energy to fight? No, he most certainly did not have that type of energy. Not yet. Not now.

Daniel relieved himself in the bathroom. He washed his hands and face in the bathroom sink before stumbling into the kitchen. He looked in the cupboards and in the fridge for something worth eating, or drinking. He drank a glass of water, brewed a pot of coffee, and sat down, trying hard to keep his mind from reeling. Once the coffee was ready he poured himself a cup. Then he poured a second cup and made his way into Patrick's room with a drink in each hand.

The door was half-open, just the way he left it. So far, so good.

He entered the room, wondering if he should have a weapon. But why was he thinking that? There was no reason to think he was in danger, was there?

Sure there is, his mind suggested. *Remember Cameron? Remember what she did?*

As he stepped inside the room he looked at Patrick and his hands began to shake. Coffee spilled over both cup rims. He clomped the cups onto the dresser and stared at his friend with a hand over his mouth and his eyes wide open.

"This isn't right," he said, shaking his head in denial. "This is impossible."

But it wasn't impossible. It was unlikely but obviously not impossible. What he was seeing was as clear as day.

Patrick Love was inside a cocoon.

2

Daniel approached Patrick slowly, eyeing him like he came from another planet. A moment passed before he turned away. Mind racing. Spotting his coffee, he lifted it from the dresser and quickly left the room. He marched down the hall, into the living room, and sat on the couch. A splash of coffee spilled onto the floor as he sat down. He didn't notice. He wanted to phone someone but he didn't have a phone. He wanted to talk things over but there was nobody to talk with. Patrick Love was inside a cocoon. And what, exactly, was he supposed to do about that?

He drank from the cup.

His eyes were playing tricks on him. That had to be the answer, right? Because it wasn't Patrick inside the cocoon, it was one of those crab-things.

Yeah. Sure. That sounds good. It's one those crab-things.

No.

It *wasn't* one of those crab-things. It was Patrick. He could see Pat's young and handsome face through the silk, turning dark, turning black. So where did that leave him? Should he pull Patrick out of the cocoon, or leave him inside it?

Would Pat die inside the cocoon?

Would he die if he were yanked from the webbing?

Daniel didn't have the answers for such questions. He wasn't a doctor. He wasn't a scientist. He was a moneyman: insurance, mortgages, real estate—that was his game. Friends living inside a cocoon? Not his field.

He drank another sip, and another. After he finished his coffee he looked in on Patrick one more time.

Nothing had changed.

He needed to do something, anything—but what? He didn't have a car. So where did that leave him? Walking. Was that really the answer? Was it time to lace up his shoes and make his way into town? It seemed like there was nothing else he could do, so yeah, walking into town. That was the answer.

Right?

Maybe.

God, he thought. *What a mess.*

A sound was heard; Daniel snapped his head towards the window.

A crab-critter was walking across the glass. He could see little hooks, needles and suction circles on the bottom of the creature's feet. Its stalks were long and thin. Its mouths were opening and closing quickly, like they were hungry. The thing looked like an oversized inkblot on pelican legs. And seeing it forced Dan to re-evaluate his thinking.

Was stepping outside really the game plan?

His mind returned to Patrick inside the cocoon.

Sadly, he decided, it was. And on the heels of that thought he stood up, looked at the thing that was clinging to the window and decided to find a weapon. Locating a gun in Patrick's cottage would be impossible. Patrick's father was an anti-gun man; he believed all firearms should be outlawed.

So where did that leave Dan?

Ironically, the first weapon he thought about was the same one that Nicolas used to smash Olive's face: a sledgehammer. Of course, there wouldn't be anything like that inside the building—perhaps in the shed or under the deck, but not inside. And he didn't want to go outside to look, not while he was unarmed, so what now?

Daniel entered the kitchen. He didn't see anything worth grabbing. He opened a closet and discovered coats and jackets, sweaters and shoes. There was a broom, however, but the handle was very thin and brittle looking. There was also a small toolbox that he didn't bother opening. He didn't believe a hammer, a tape measure, or a screwdriver was going to cut it.

He returned to living room, looked at the fireplace, and found his answer attached to the wall beside it. The answer came in the form of a heavy, black iron poker. It had a nice handle on one end and a sharp hook on the other.

"Perfect," he whispered.

After checking on Patrick one last time he made his way outside. The sun was shining; the air was almost still. He glanced at the raft floating in the lake and the small waves that crashed against it.

A crab-creature ran across the yard, heading straight for him. Another leapt off the roof and landed at his feet.

Without much thought, he kicked the closest critter, spun around and stabbed the other one with the poker. The poker pierced the creature easily, but creature was still alive. He stepped on it and moved away from the house, nervous that another attack might come from above.

He walked away from Patrick's place cautiously, heading for his summer home.

William's 1979 firebird was sitting in the driveway. His cottage windows were smashed and his side door was wide open. He spotted three more crab-critters, but none were attacking.

How many of the creatures are running free? he thought. *And what harm have they caused? Have people been hurt? Have authorities been notified?*

His mind shifted gears. Now he was thinking about Cameron, William and Beth: *they must be at the hospital.*

Another crab-thing moved towards him and he stomped it, creating a ball of mush beneath his shoe. Then he walked away from his house and headed down the driveway.

His eyes were stinging; the sun seemed very bright.

3

After hiding in the woods for hours, Beth returned to the road and approached Olive with a hand at her mouth and tears rolling down her face.

That son of a bitch, she thought. *That fucking prick.*

She couldn't believe her eyes.

The word 'tragedy' didn't even begin to describe the naked girl's remains. She looked worse than anything Beth had ever seen or imagined. Olive had been abused for years, then pulverized. Her head looked like a smashed coconut covered in human gore.

And—

Lying beside the broken corpse was a Colt Python 357 magnum. It must have fallen from Nicolas' pocket.

Beth lifted the weapon, checked to see if it was loaded, and smiled. Given the chance she would shoot the man, of this she had no doubt. He deserved death. If anyone in the entire world deserved death, it was Nicolas. And although she never thought she would kill a man, not in this lifetime, for him she'd make an exception. She wasn't sure if she believed in God or not, but if there was a God, he would understand. He would forgive.

After wiping away her tears, she continued on.

A few crab-things scurried along the edge of the road, less than twenty feet away from her, but none of them attacked. But she kept an eye on them, and she kept the gun ready.

A few minutes later she was nearing Daniel's place. When she arrived she was surprised to find Daniel on the driveway, walking towards her. His eyes were busy checking nearby trees. He looked nervous and upset.

"Daniel!" Beth shouted.

Daniel looked up. "Beth?"

"Oh my God," she said. "Am I glad to see you!"

They met with a hug; then Daniel said, "What happened to you? Where's William? Where's Cameron?"

Beth's strong features became laced in heartbreak. Her eyes, which looked swollen and tired, glistened with tears. Her bottom lip quivered momentarily, and with a deep breath she put a hand to her mouth.

"Oh Daniel," she said. "I don't even know where to begin."

"Where's my car?"

Beth shrugged. "It's in a ditch."

"Where's William?"

"I don't know."

"Do you have his car keys? Because his car is still in my driveway, and if you have his keys with you—"

"No, I don't have them. William has them."

"Where do you think he is? Is he at the hospital? Is he—"

Beth interrupted. "Dan, we never made it to the hospital. I think William is dead."

"Dead?"

"I not positive, but… yeah. I'd be surprised if he survived the night."

"My God, what happened?"

Skirting the question, Beth looked over her shoulder to make sure there were no crab-critters around. "Where are you going right now?"

"Town," Dan said flatly. "And if you don't have the keys to William's car, I think we should start walking."

Beth nodded.

They started walking.

"Where in town are you thinking?" Beth asked.

"Honestly, I haven't been thinking. I just woke up and Patrick…" Daniel trailed off, trying to find the right combination of words. Somehow saying that 'Pat was inside a cocoon' sounded absolutely insane, and he didn't even want to admit the things that were happening. It was all too much.

Beth said, "Who's Patrick?"

"What, you didn't meet him?" A slight pause. "No, I suppose you didn't. Pat's just a kid, but he's also a good friend of mine. His parents have a cottage next door, and he was in that bomb shelter when Cameron and I escaped."

"Bomb shelter? Is that what that thing is?"

"I think so. It might be something else. I don't know what it is."

Beth noticed two crab-things crawling up a tree together. She nudged Daniel, and he saw them too.

"Some of them are aggressive," Beth said.

"Yeah. And some of them aren't. Killing the small ones is easy enough. I've stomped a whole bunch of them with my shoe."

"I've got this," Beth said. She showed him the gun.

"I noticed."

"I'm sure it'll do the trick."

"It will, but it's overkill."

Something was on the road behind them. Hearing it approach, they turned around.

A van was racing towards them—a *white* van.

"Oh thank God," Daniel said. He raised his arms, waving the vehicle down.

Beth's face became fortified with concern. The van was traveling too fast, and she couldn't help thinking that she had seen that van before.

She had. It was sitting in Nicolas Nehalem's driveway.

"Oh no," she whispered.

Dan looked at her confused. "What's wrong?"

The van was accelerating, heading straight for them.

Beth screamed, "DAN! LOOK OUT!"

She pushed Daniel towards the side of the road with her free hand and bolted in the opposite direction.

Dan stumbled, not realizing what was happening.

The van swerved towards him as he was stumbling. He didn't have his balance. And the van was close, too close; it was going to hit him. If he didn't do something quick he was going to get run down!

His mouth opened and his eyes widened.

He whispered something inaudible.

At the far side of the road Beth turned around. The van, she could easily see, was *not* going to hit her. It wasn't *trying* to hit her—it was aimed at Dan. And oh sweet, sweet, mercy, it looked like it was going to hit him dead on.

Dan raised an arm and opened his mouth wide.

Beth caught a glimpse of Nicolas behind the wheel. His face was contorted into an evil smile that seemed more reptile than man.

And that was it.

The van slammed into Daniel.

Dan fell back. His body was sucked beneath the front bumper. The back of his head slammed against the road and his left knee got caught on something beneath the vehicle. Perhaps it was the muffler. His body snapped in the middle and rolled into a ball. Arms and legs went spinning. A loud, terrible CRUNCH sound was heard. The van bounced up and down and when it was finally finished driving over its victim Dan appeared to have no head. It seemed to be missing, but it wasn't. His head was packed into his chest.

Beth screamed, "NOOOOOOOOOOOooooooooooo!"

It didn't matter; what was done was done. Daniel had been crushed into something that looked like 180 pounds of raw, pulverized, blood pudding. Broken bones stuck out from all angles. His fingers were twitching. A pool of red liquid was rapidly expanding across the road.

Beth looked away from Dan and clamped her teeth together.

The van was driving away.

"FUCK YOU!" she screamed, pointing the gun towards the van. Her voice sounded so upset her own mother wouldn't have recognized it. Her hands were trembling. "FUCK YOU! FUCK YOU! FUCK YOU!"

She pulled the trigger four times quickly.

The first three shots went wide.

The fourth one hit home, shattering the back window, puncturing one of the many boxes.

Nicolas turned his head.

The explosion was enormous.

∞∞∞ ⊖ ∞∞∞

And Cameron—buried deep in the earth—opened her eyes.

"No," she whispered. But there was nothing she could do; she was trapped in her tomb until darkness fell, and by then the town would be lost.

CHAPTER NINE:
EPILOGUE

June 3^{*rd*}

    Cloven Rock—

    A series of explosions in the little town of Cloven Rock has caused a massive fire, forcing thousands to evacuate while creating a growing concern across the country. Hundreds are feared dead, as over one thousand people remain unaccounted for. The cause of the explosions is yet to be determined and officials are now speculating that foul play may be at hand. City workers have been called in from four separate states, and while over two hundred firefighters and firefighter volunteers are working around the clock to contain the blaze, many believe that things are going to get worse before they get any better.

    Geoff Walter, a witness to what he believes was the first of over eighty-five explosions in the town best known for its annual country music summer fair, is quoted as saying, "I was in my car when that first one happened, and I couldn't believe the size of it. Damn thing was thirty stories if it was a foot. One minute everything was fine and the next, BOOM. I've never seen anything like it."

    Cloven Rock, with its population of 1,690, has been all but wiped off the map, and not since the fires of…

∞∞∞ ⊖ ∞∞∞

June 3^{*rd*}

    Cloven Rock—

    A grisly discovery has been made in a gas station on the outskirts of Cloven Rock. Paul LaFalce, 19, was found mutilated in his workplace. Other than saying that the young man is still alive, officials are giving little in the way of information on this one. They are quick to point out, however, that at this time there they have found nothing to suggest that there is a connection between Mr. LaFalce's condition and the massive fire that continues to rage only a few short miles away.

Schoolteacher James Monogyny, the first person to arrive at the scene, said that...

∞∞⊖∞∞

June 4ᵗʰ

    Cloven Rock——

Fires continue to spread as thousands are forced to evacuate their homes in what is quickly becoming one of the worst fires in North American history. Maplebrook was the first of nine towns to receive its evacuation notice. The town's police chief Fabian Levin was quoted as saying, "It's not surprising that the people in the neighboring towns are stepping away from the disaster. At this point, the cause of the explosions has yet to be determined, and although the fires will likely not spread much further, the amount of smoke that the fires are causing is nothing short of troublesome."

So far there have been thirty-four confirmed deaths in relation to the blaze, including local billionaire Peter Holbrook's wife Penny Holbrook, mother of two. Peter Holbrook is one of over six hundred people still considered missing. The number of deaths caused by this tragedy is expected to rise.

Rumors continue to mount, and questions remain unanswered in regards to what originally ignited the inferno. Chemist Morris Penniman, great grandson of Russell S. Penniman, who invented ammonium dynamite in 1885, has gone on record as saying, "Whether or not these explosion is an act of terrorism is yet to be determined, although it is now safe to say that nitrating glycerol has been used in at least some of the blasts."

∞∞⊖∞∞

June 6ᵗʰ

    Cloven Rock——

Five people have been reported as missing since the search for survivors began three days ago in the now infamous Cloven Rock. Tempers among the locals are rising, and speculation continues to mount, forcing government officials to re-evaluate their policies concerning...

∞∞⊖∞∞

July 14th

World news—

It's been six weeks since an abundance of explosions in the little town of *Cloven Rock caused an estimated 845 million dollars worth of damages, killing 834 residents, injuring 44 more, and leaving 407 people unaccounted for—and now the infamous Cloven Rock is in the news again. It seems that the remains of unknown species has been found among the wreckage. Scientists are calling this newly discovered mammal the Clade Thoracotremata Chelicerata; also labeled the Buccal Crab.*

The hard-shelled, multi-legged carcass, weighing in at seventeen pounds, three ounces, is being described as a cross between a giant spider and a crab. It has several extremely unique attributes, the most amazing feature, most scientists agree...

More great titles from
BOOKS OF THE DEAD

BEST NEW ZOMBIE TALES (Vol. 1)
BEST NEW ZOMBIE TALES (Vol. 2)
BEST NEW ZOMBIE TALES (Vol. 3)
JAMES ROY DALEY'S - INTO HELL
JAMES ROY DALEY'S - 13 DROPS OF BLOOD
MATT HULTS - ANYTHING CAN BE DANGEROUS
BEST NEW VAMPIRE TALES (Vol. 1)
MATT HULTS - HUSK
CLASSIC VAMPIRE TALES

BOOKS of the DEAD